MIDDLE OF THE NIGHT

ALSO BY RILEY SAGER

Final Girls

The Last Time I Lied

Lock Every Door

Home Before Dark

Survive the Night

The House Across the Lake

The Only One Left

MIDDLE OF THE NIGHT

A NOVEL

RILEY SAGER

DUTTON

DUTTON

An imprint of Penguin Random House LLC
penguinrandomhouse.com

Interior image: Spooky Forest © Stone36 / shutterstock.com

LIBRARY OF CONGRESS CATALOGING-IN-PUBLICATION DATA

Names: Sager, Riley, author.
Title: Middle of the night : a novel / Riley Sager.
Description: New York : Dutton, an imprint of Penguin Random House LLC, 2024.
Identifiers: LCCN 2023054931 | ISBN 9780593472378 (hardcover) |
ISBN 9780593472385 (e-book)
Subjects: LCGFT: Thrillers (Fiction) | Novels.
Classification: LCC PS3618.I79 M53 2024 | DDC 813/.6—dc23/20231204
LC record available at https://lccn.loc.gov/2023054931

International edition ISBN: 9780593850718

Printed in the United States of America
1   3   5   7   9   10   8   6   4   2

BOOK DESIGN BY GEORGE TOWNE

To Patricia Cole,
I think you would have loved this one.

MIDDLE OF THE NIGHT

Morning sunlight seeps into the tent like a water leak, dripping onto the boy in a muted glow. The trickle of light on his cheeks wakes him from a deep slumber. He opens his eyes, just a little, his vision hazy through a web of lashes still sticky with sleep. Peering up at light tinted orange by the tent's fabric, he tries to pinpoint the position of the sun, wondering what time it is and if his mother is already awake, sipping coffee in the kitchen, waiting for them to come in for breakfast.

It's stuffy inside the tent. The July heat never abated during the night and now fills the air, thick and heavy. He'd wanted to keep the tent flap open while they slept, but his father said mosquitoes could get in. So the flap remains zipped shut, trapping the heat, which mingles with the distinct smells of boys in summertime. Grass and sweat, bug spray and sunblock, morning breath and body odor.

He wrinkles his nose at the smell and feels a pop of sweat on his brow as he rolls over in his sleeping bag. It feels safe. Like a hug.

Although awake, he doesn't want to get up just yet. He prefers to stay exactly where he is, as he is. A boy on a lazy Saturday morning, smack-dab in the middle of a lazy summer.

His name is Ethan Marsh.

He is ten.

And this is the last carefree moment he'll have for the next thirty years.

Because just as he's about to close his eyes again, he notices another bit of light. A bright vertical slit glowing on the side of the tent.

Strange.

Strange enough to make him sit up, eyes now fully open, taking in the single slash in the fabric that runs from the top of the tent all the way to the ground. It's slightly puckered, like skin that's just been sliced. Through the gap, he sees a sliver of familiar yard. Freshly cut grass. Light blue sky. The glare of sun that's only just now clearing the distant trees.

Seeing it, Ethan is hit by a realization he's vaguely known since waking but is only now beginning to understand.

He is in a tent.

In his own backyard.

Completely alone.

But when he went to sleep the night before, there had been someone else with him.

Someone now gone.

ONE

*S*criiiiiiiiitch.

I wake with a start, unnerved by the sound zipping across the dark room. It echoes off the walls and snakes back to me in multiple waves. I lie in bed, completely still, eyes wide open, until the noise fades.

Not that it was ever there to begin with.

Decades of experience have taught me that it was just in my head. Dream, memory, and hallucination all at once. My first since coming back to this house. Honestly, I'm surprised it took so long, especially with the anniversary of what happened here fast approaching.

Sitting up, I look to the clock on the nightstand, hoping it reads closer to dawn than midnight. No such luck. It's only quarter after two. I've got a long night of no sleep ahead of me. With a sigh, I reach for the notebook and pen I keep next to the clock. After much squinting in the darkness, I find a fresh page and scribble four frustrating words.

Had The Dream again.

I toss the notebook back onto the nightstand, followed by the pen. It lands with a clack against the notebook's cover before rolling onto the carpet. I tell myself to leave the pen there until morning. That nothing will happen to it overnight. But the bad thoughts arrive quickly. What if the pen leaks, its midnight-black ink staining the cream-colored carpet? What if I'm attacked in the middle of the night and the only thing I can use to defend myself is an uncapped Bic, which now sits out of reach?

That second one, as alarming as it is improbable, pulls me out of bed. I grab the pen and set it on the notebook. There. *Much* better.

Anxiety soothed—for now—I'm about to crawl back under the covers when something outside catches my attention.

A light.

Not unusual for Hemlock Circle. Despite the lack of streetlights, it's never completely dark here. Light spills through bay windows onto immaculate front lawns and brightens second-floor bedrooms before the sun rises and long after it sets. The sconces flanking the Chens' front door burn from dusk to dawn, warding off both trespassers and the bats that occasionally try to roost in the eaves. All summer long, the Wallaces' backyard pool glows an alien blue. At Christmas, lights twinkle at five of the six homes in the neighborhood, including the Patels', who put theirs up at Diwali and don't take them down until a new year begins.

Then there are the garage lights.

Every house has them.

A pair of motion-activated security lights centered above the garage doors that glare like headlights when triggered. In the evenings, they flick on and off around the cul-de-sac with the frequency of fireflies as residents return from work in the waning light, go out to fetch the mail, haul recycling bins to the curb.

As it gets closer to midnight, a few will continue to spring to life. When deer skulk through the neighborhood on their way to the woods. Or when Fritz Van de Veer sneaks out for a cigarette after his wife, Alice, has gone to bed.

The light that's caught my attention is the one above the Patels' garage, two houses away. It illuminates a patch of their driveway, the glow turning the asphalt ice white. Curious, I go to one of the windows in a bedroom I still don't consider my own. Not technically. The room that once was mine, and in my mind still is, sits across the hall, now vacant. This is my parents' bedroom, where I rarely ventured as a child. Now, though, through a series of recent developments I'm still grappling with, it's become my own.

The windows in this new room offer a panorama of Hemlock Circle. From where I stand, I can see at least a piece of every house on the cul-de-sac. I glimpse a sliver of the old Barringer place on the left and a corner of the Chens' house to the right. Across from me, in full view from left to right, are the Van de Veers', the Wallaces', and the Patels', where the garage light still glows.

What I *don't* see is anything that could have set it off. Mitesh and Deepika Patel are presumably inside and fast asleep. No animals scurry from the light. No wind blows that could have caused a nearby branch to sway hard enough to trigger the motion sensor. All I can see is an empty driveway on a quiet cul-de-sac in the dead of night.

Soon I can't even see that, for the Patels' garage light suddenly goes out.

Ten seconds later, the one at the Wallaces' house clicks on. It's next door to the Patels', separated by the single road that leads into the cul-de-sac, which is currently free of cars, free of people, free of anything.

I draw close to the window, my nose almost touching the glass, straining to see something—any small thing—that could have triggered the light above the Wallaces' garage.

There's nothing.

Nothing visible, that is.

Still, I stay pressed to the window, watching, even after the Wallaces' garage light clicks off. The only thing I can think of that could have triggered it is a bat. They thrive here, as the Chens' porch lights can attest, feeding off the many insects that live in the woods circling the cul-de-sac. They're also notoriously difficult to see in the darkness.

But then the light above the Van de Veers' garage springs to life, and I know my theory is wrong. Bats flit willy-nilly, chasing prey. They don't methodically move from house to house.

No, this is different.

This is . . . worrisome.

Unease spreads through my chest as I think about thirty years ago. I can't help it. Not after what happened here.

When the Van de Veers' light turns off, I begin to count.

Five seconds.

Then ten.

Then a full minute.

Long enough for me to think that whatever is out there has moved on, likely into the woods, which means it was an animal. Something simply too small and quick for me to spot, but not small and quick enough to evade the hair-trigger garage lights of the houses on Hemlock Circle. The tightness in my chest eases, and I allow myself a sigh of relief.

Then the light above the Barringers' garage turns on.

The light itself is just out of view, but the glow it throws onto the lawn and sidewalk makes my pulse do a stutter step.

Whatever's out there isn't gone.

In fact, it's getting closer.

Several scenarios pop into my head, starting with the worst, because that's my default mode. Always going straight to the most alarming, the most dire. In this case, that would be that someone is circling the cul-de-sac.

Someone I can't see but who is definitely out there.

Moving from house to house, searching for another child to snatch.

Second in line, and just a shade less worrisome, is the idea that whoever is outside has come to case Hemlock Circle, testing the security lights to see how easy it would be to break into one of the houses here.

The third scenario is that it's just someone going for a late-night walk. Someone from one of the other cul-de-sacs located in this two square miles of suburban sprawl. Someone who, like me, is riddled with insomnia and decided to try to walk it off.

But if this is just an innocent stroll, why doesn't whoever is out there make themselves visible?

The paranoid-but-logical answer is that it's *not* an innocent stroll. It's something else. Something worse. And I, as likely the only person on Hemlock Circle currently awake, owe it to everyone else to try to put a stop to it.

When the light at the Barringer house next door flicks off, I make my move. Knowing that this house is next, I hope to catch whoever it is in the act. Or at least make it known that not everyone on the cul-de-sac is asleep.

I leave my parents' bedroom and hurry down the hall to the stairs. On the first floor, my bare feet slap against hardwood as I cross the foyer to the front door. I unlock it, fling it open, step into the warm mid-July night.

There's no one else out here.

I can tell that instantly. It's just me, breathing heavily, dressed in only a pair of boxer shorts and an LCD Soundsystem concert tee. I hear and see nothing as I cross in front of the house toward the driveway. When I round the corner, my movement triggers the security light above the garage doors, which flicks on with a faint *click*.

For a second, I think someone else has set it off and whirl around, panicked. By the time I realize it's just me, bugs have already started to swarm the garage light. I watch their incandescent spinning, feeling simultaneously foolish and on high alert.

An annoyed voice in my head that's plagued my thoughts for years now, suddenly pipes up. *Get a grip, Ethan. There's no one out here.*

Just to be certain, I stand completely still, scanning the cul-de-sac for signs of someone else. I remain there so long that the garage light eventually switches off, plunging the driveway—and me—back into darkness.

That's when I sense it. A presence, faint in the night air. It lingers in that way certain smells do. Cigar smoke. Perfume. Burnt toast. It's like someone had been here mere seconds ago. Perhaps they're still here, hidden among the trees that ring Hemlock Circle, watching me.

You're being paranoid, the voice in my head tells me.

But I'm not. I can *feel* it. The same way you can tell someone is in the next room, even though they're not making a sound.

What's more unnerving is how familiar the presence seems. I don't know why. It's not like I know who's out here—if it's anyone at all. Yet the hairs on my arms stand on end, and a chill slithers through me, defying the balmy air.

Only then do I realize whose presence I'm sensing.

One I'd never thought I'd feel again.

"Billy?" I say.

Although a mere whisper, the name seems to fill the night, echoing through the restless dark, lingering long after it's been spoken. By the time it fades, I know I'm mistaken.

Such a scenario is impossible.

It can't be Billy.

He's been gone for thirty years.

TWO

remain outside for another minute or so, waiting in the dark, desperately hoping to sense more of Billy's presence. But it's gone. Not a hint of him—or anyone else—remains.

Rather than go back to bed when I return inside, I roam the dark and silent house that both does and does not feel like home. I can't remember the last time I slept a full eight hours. For most of my life, sleep has come in fits and starts. I fall asleep quickly. An immediate plummet into sweet slumber. The problem always comes later, when I wake after only an hour or two, suddenly alert, restless, and filled with an undefinable sense of dread. This can last for several more hours before I'm able to fall back asleep. Sometimes that falling-back-to-sleep part never happens.

Chronic insomnia, my doctor calls it. I've officially had it since my twenties, although it started long before then. Over the years, I've done the sleep studies and kept a sleep journal and tried every suggested remedy. Removing the TV from my bedroom. Reading an hour before bed. Hot showers and chamomile tea and sleep stories droning on in the darkness. Nothing works. Not even sleeping pills strong enough to sedate an elephant.

Now I just accept that I'll always be awake between one and four a.m. I've grown accustomed to those dark, quiet hours in the middle of the night, when it feels like I'm the only man in the world not asleep.

Rather than waste them, I try to put those wakeful hours to good use, keeping an eye on things while everyone else sleeps. In college, I roamed dormitory halls and circled the quad, making sure all was well. When Claudia and I shared a bed, I'd watch her sleep, unnerving her every time she woke to find me staring at her. Now that it's just me, I spend that long, lonesome stretch of night looking out the window. A one-man neighborhood watch.

Dr. Manning, the last in a long line of therapists stretching back to my teens, said it stems from a combination of guilt and anxiety.

"You can't sleep," she told me, "because you think you might miss another chance to stop something terrible from happening. And that whoever took Billy will eventually come back to take you."

She said it with the utmost sincerity, as if I hadn't already been told that a dozen times before. As if that all-too-obvious assessment would somehow allow me to sleep through the night. I pretended it was some major breakthrough, thanked her profusely, left her office, and never returned.

That was seven years ago and, contrary to what I let Dr. Manning believe, I still can't sleep.

Right now, my insomnia is manageable. I catch up on rest with midday naps, snoozing on the couch as the evening news murmurs in the background, sleeping in on Sundays until noon. That'll change when the school year starts in September. Then I'll have to be up by six, whether I've slept or not.

Tonight, though, is still mid-July, allowing me to roam from room to room. I've done nothing to the house in the week since I moved in while my parents moved out, and the place now has a disjointed, temporary feel. As if all of us—my parents, the movers, me—gave up halfway through. Most of my possessions, including half my clothes, remain in boxes stacked in corners of empty rooms, waiting to be unpacked. They're joined by everything my parents left behind—furniture that was either too big to fit into their downsized Florida condo or too unloved to make the trip.

In the dining room, chairs surround an empty space where a table should be. In the kitchen, the cabinets have been raided of most plates, utensils, and glasses, leaving only mismatched stragglers behind. In the living room, the sofa remains, but the matching armchair in which my father falls asleep every evening is gone. As is the TV. And the grandfather clock. And at least one end table, although the crystal bowl that once sat atop it now rests on the beige carpet.

Each time I notice it reminds me that I need to do something with the place. I can't let it stay like this for much longer. But I also have no desire to settle in for real, which would make this feel less like a temporary situation and more like the sad, permanent move I fear it is.

Until last week, it had been almost thirty years since I lived here full-time. I didn't go back to school the fall after Billy vanished. Rather, not the school I'd been attending. The one with familiar halls and teachers I knew and friends I never saw during the summer even though we lived only a mile or so apart. Instead, my parents sent me to a private school in upstate New York where no one knew who I was. Or what had happened in my yard. Or how I'd rarely slept a full night since.

It was a relief living in a creaky dormitory, surrounded by boys who were blissfully incurious about me. I used that to my advantage, blending in with the crowd until I graduated. No one noticed me, and I made every attempt to keep it that way. The few close friends I did have were still kept at arm's length when it came to Billy. Even though I told no one about him, they couldn't help but notice how gloomy I got right before the holidays or summer breaks—and how happy I was to be back at school when they ended.

I think my friends assumed I hated my parents. The truth was that I hated this house. I hated being reminded of what happened here. I hated waking up in the middle of the night, looking out my bedroom window, and seeing the same patch of grass where Billy vanished. Most of all, I hated the guilty feeling that overcame me every time it happened.

Billy was gone.

I was still here.

Somehow, that didn't seem right.

When it came time to choose a college, I picked one even farther away from home. Northwestern. There, it was even easier to blend in with the crowds of students tramping through golden summers and brutal winters. I fell in with a group of misfits. The same kind of video game geeks and comic book nerds who are popular now but definitely weren't back then. Even among them, I was bit of an outcast, preferring books to Game Boys, quiet gatherings to parties.

It was at one of those small gatherings that I met Claudia, who'd tagged along with a friend of a friend. We found ourselves standing next to each other in a corner, pretending to enjoy our lukewarm beer.

"The upside to huge parties," she said, unprompted, "is that their sheer size provides good cover for introverts like us. Here, we just stand out."

I eyed her over the rim of my plastic cup. She was pretty, in a bookish way. Brown hair. Willowy frame. Shy smile.

"What makes you think I'm an introvert?" I said.

"Your expression," she replied. "Your demeanor. Your body language. The fact that you're standing here with me, president of Introverts Anonymous."

I grinned, surprised and delighted to be so easily pegged. "Yet you talked first."

"Only because I have a weakness for guys in glasses."

That single sentence gave me enough courage to ask her out on a date. We went for deep-dish pizza and beer, that most clichéd of Chicago first dates. Not a cliché was what I told her as we walked back to campus—that the summer I was ten, my best friend was taken from a tent in my backyard and never seen or heard from again.

"Jesus," she said, appropriately shocked. "Who was your friend?"

"Billy Barringer."

Claudia recognized the name, of course. Everyone had heard of Billy.

The Lost Boy.

That's what the press started calling him in the weeks following his abduction, when you couldn't turn on the news without hearing about it. And it's what he continues to be called in those shadowy, conspiracy-laden corners of the internet that still talk about him. To them, Billy has entered the realm of urban legend, even though what happened isn't as mysterious as those girls who vanished from that summer camp or as terrifying as that group of teenagers killed in a cabin in the Poconos.

Billy's case still resonates because it happened in a quiet suburban backyard, which is generally recognized as one of the safest places in America. And if it could happen here, it could happen anywhere.

That night, fueled by nerves, too much beer, and Claudia's lovely, searing gaze, I told her all of it.

About how, in the middle of the night, someone crept into my backyard, sliced open the tent in which we slept, and snatched Billy out of his sleeping bag.

About how I'd slept right through it, unaware of what had happened until I woke the next morning and glimpsed the sun through a slash in the tent that definitely hadn't been there the night before.

About how weird those first few morning hours were, when none of us quite knew the gravity of the situation, our confusion outweighing our fear.

About how the police were just as lost, unable to find even the smallest clue about who might have taken Billy. Or why. Or what happened to him after that.

About how no one knows anything after all these years. And how we'll likely never know. And how it all feels like my fault because I was *right there* when it happened. And how sometimes the guilt is so strong that I find myself wishing it had been me who was taken.

"But you weren't," Claudia said. "You're here, now, with me."

She kissed me then, my heart exploding into a thousand butterflies. In that moment, I swore that I would remain there, with her, for as long as possible.

That turned out to be seventeen years, during which both of us graduated. Me first, then Claudia two years later. We stayed in the Chicago area, where she got a job with the parks service and I found a teaching gig at a private school not unlike the one I'd attended. I was never the most popular teacher. A far cry from the cool ones you see in movies, whose passion is so infectious that students end up standing on desks reciting poetry. I showed up, gave my lessons, guided bored teenagers through *Great Expectations* and *To Kill a Mockingbird*.

Our life together might not have been exciting, but it was good.

Until it wasn't.

Now I'm here, moving through a dark house half filled with boxes containing remnants of that once-good life. I retrieve my phone from the charging station in the kitchen (another tip for insomniacs: sleep with your phone in another room) and tap out a text.

can't sleep. of course

I pause, then type what I'm really feeling.

i miss you, Claude

I send the texts before I can change my mind, even though I know they make me sound completely pathetic. Not at all how I envisioned myself at age forty. Especially the part about living in my childhood home. This was my parents' idea, sprung on me when they announced they were finally taking the plunge and moving to Florida.

"You'll be doing us a favor," my mother said when I initially resisted. "Selling a house like this is such a headache."

What she meant but couldn't bring herself to say is that she knew I was going through a rough patch, both emotionally and financially, and that they were happy to help, even though I'm far past the age of needing help from my parents. At least, I should be.

I relented and moved into the house after getting them settled into their new condo outside Orlando. I've been here ever since, caught between adulthood and adolescence. Some days it feels like my parents will be home at any minute, carrying in groceries, my mother announcing that she bought that flavor of Ben & Jerry's I like so much. Other times it feels like I've been hurtled into the future, to a time in which both are long gone and I've inherited everything.

At the end of the hallway, past the mudroom and the laundry room, is what used to be my father's study and now serves as my makeshift office. The boxes in here are opened—a half-hearted feint at unpacking. My father left the bookcases but took the desk, forcing me to use my laptop propped on a battered coffee table I found in the basement.

I flick on a lamp, sit at the coffee table, and open my laptop. I tell myself that I have no idea what I'm looking for. That this is just mindless web surfing until I get tired or the sun comes up, whichever arrives first.

But I know full well where I'm going, typing in the address with the unthinking ease of someone slipping back into a bad habit.

The National Missing and Unidentified Persons System.

NamUs, for short.

An online database of people who've gone missing, been taken, vanished into thin air.

I know the statistics well. Each year in America, more than half a million people are reported missing. Although the vast majority are quickly located, alive and well, some aren't so lucky and end up on NamUs. Those who remain missing after a year or two or more eventually become cold cases.

Then there's someone like Billy. A case so cold it's now a block of ice.

As I type in Billy's name, I can't help but think about the presence I detected in the driveway. Feeling it was like being an amnesiac hit with a thousand memories at once. A sudden awakening, as surprising as it was comforting. A sense of long-forgotten familiarity.

And enough to make me think, for a slice of a second, that it was indeed Billy.

That he was alive.

That he had returned.

But Billy is still unaccounted for, a fact confirmed for me when his page appears on the NamUs website. At the top is his case number, his name, and his photograph, under which sits a red bar and white letters spelling out that most horrible of words.

Missing.

The picture had been taken in the school gymnasium the previous October. Somewhere in my parents' condo is a framed portrait of me in front of that same smudged blue backdrop. In my photo, I'm grinning wildly, exposing teeth too big for my mouth, my polo shirt rumpled and my hair gelled into submission.

Billy's school photo is the opposite. In it, he appears uncharacteristically subdued and formal. His mouth teeters on the cusp of a frown, like he wanted to be anywhere but there. I'm certain his mother, and not Billy, picked out his dark blue shirt and green necktie. She probably even tried to tame his unruly hair, to no avail. The cowlick poking up from the back of his head is the photo's most disarming feature.

Near the picture is the date Billy disappeared and what he was last seen wearing. Black T-shirt, blue shorts, white sneakers.

Accurate, yes, but only scratching the surface. I know, for instance, that the black T-shirt had a small white stain on the chest, the shorts were made by Umbro, and the sneakers had come off an hour before we went to sleep and were still in the tent when I woke up. The last thing he ate were two s'mores my mother had made in the oven because she thought having a campfire in the backyard was too dangerous. I even remember Billy's last words.

Hakuna matata, dude.

Lower down on Billy's page, a series of age-progression photos shows how he might have looked over the years. At fifteen, at twenty, at twenty-five. Using his school photo as a starting point, they all disconcertingly picture him in that same blue shirt and green necktie, as if they're the only clothes he's ever worn, magically expanding with the rest of his body as he grew taller, wider, older.

The last photo suggests what he would have looked like five years ago, at age thirty-five. His face is fuller, though the almost-frown remains. His hair, finally tamed of its cowlick, is darker and thicker. I've seen this picture before. Too many times to count. Each time, I'm struck by how strange it is to see someone I think of as forever young looking thoroughly middle-aged. It's the same jarring feeling I sometimes get when I look in the mirror. Those fine lines on my face and the gray hair at my temples and in my patchy beard make me think, *When the hell did I get so old?*

Only, with Billy, the question is, *did* he get this old? Is it possible that he's still alive today, living in complete anonymity, blending in with all the other middle-aged men out there? I doubt it. If Billy was alive—if he truly still existed—wouldn't it be known by now? Wouldn't Billy himself reveal it to *someone*?

In case he does, there's a police contact at the bottom of the page. It's changed multiple times in all the years I've been coming to Billy's NamUs listing, including since my last visit. Currently, the contact is Detective Ragesh Patel, a member of the local police department and the only son of Mitesh and Deepika Patel, who live two doors away. A noticeable demotion. The contact used to be someone from the FBI, telling me that not even the authorities think Billy will ever be found.

In some ways, I get it. Everyone—including his own family—thinks Billy is dead. There was even a memorial service, held a year after his disappearance. I attended, sweaty and itchy in a suit bought just for the occasion, staring at a silver-framed photo of Billy that sat atop an empty coffin. Everyone else, meanwhile, stared at me, the kid who *hadn't* been taken. I felt the entire church quietly assessing me, wondering what made me different enough that a kidnapper would choose Billy over me. In that moment, I so badly wanted the roles to be reversed. For Billy to still be alive and for me to be anywhere but there, a feeling that grew more pronounced once Mrs. Barringer started screaming. Full-on, chest-heaving wails so loud inside the church that they rattled the stained glass windows.

I close the NamUs listing and do a Google search of Billy's name. The most recent link is to the website of an armchair detective who's gained quite a following discussing unsolved cases. I click it and am immediately confronted by two photos.

The photos.

The two images most associated with the strange case of Billy Barringer. They're famous in certain parts of the internet. Well-known enough that every true-crime blog, podcast, and website uses them. Understandable but still unnerving, seeing how both were taken in my backyard.

One shows an orange pup tent on a patch of lawn that's been

fenced in by a perimeter of police tape. Snapped by a *Star-Ledger* photographer who snuck into the backyard without my parents' permission, the photo has become the defining image of the Billy Barringer case. The picture is angled in a way that highlights the vertical slit in the tent's side, the gash puckered open by the same breeze that causes the police tape to buzz like telephone wire. For thirty years, that slight gap—and the darkness beyond—has made people lean in and look closer, straining for a glimpse into a place where something horrible occurred.

Even me, who had been inside that tent mere hours before the photo was taken, yet who knows as little about what happened as everyone else.

The other picture is the last known photograph of Billy, snapped on the Fourth of July, 1994. It shows him eating a wedge of watermelon, pink juice dripping from his lips like he's a vampire. It's far more endearing than his dour school picture, which is why I think the media glommed on to it. In it, he looks like a regular kid, when in truth, Billy was anything but regular.

Someone stands next to him, completely cropped from the photo except for a sliver of bare arm nudging Billy's at the edge of the frame.

That's me.

My parents, immediately concerned about how I'd be affected by my friend's abduction, made sure to cut me out of the snapshot before it was released to the press. In doing so, they created an ironic reversal of the situation.

Billy, the Lost Boy, was seen literally everywhere, his image almost as prominent that summer as O. J. Simpson and the white Bronco. And I became invisible. Just a bit of skin belonging to another boy. Because I was a juvenile, that's how both the police and the media referred to me back then.

"Another boy."

As in "Ten-year-old Billy Barringer was camping in the backyard with another boy when he was taken in the middle of the night," which happens to be the first sentence on the website now open on my laptop. I keep reading, although it's nothing I haven't seen a thousand times before. There's a brief introduction about who Billy was, where he lived, what he was doing the night he went missing, and what happened after everyone realized he was gone. Scattered throughout are more references to me as "another boy," "a neighbor," "Billy's best friend." All the euphemisms strike me as silly, considering how the website names nearly everyone else, including my parents.

Fred and Joyce Marsh.

Much like our homes at the time, their names sit side by side with those of Billy's parents, Blake and Mary Ellen Barringer. After all, it was our yard Billy vanished from. And it was my parents' care into which he had been placed.

The only other notable name not mentioned—on the website or anywhere else I've seen—is Andy Barringer, Billy's younger brother. Seven at the time, he was also left alone by the press, meriting barely a mention.

Like most things I've seen about Billy's disappearance, there's an air of judgment to the piece. That's always been the case. In the weeks following the abduction, much was made about how a boy could have been taken from a suburban backyard without anyone seeing it happen. Everyone from the nightly news to the *New York Times* to *Unsolved Mysteries*, which aired a segment about it that fall, had the same questions. "How could this happen?" they asked. "How did no one notice?"

Unspoken but abundantly clear is that the neighborhood was to blame.

Especially my parents.

And especially me.

The small scraps of blame that weren't laid at our feet went instead to the authorities, who never figured out what happened to Billy.

Every agency you can think of, from the local police to the FBI, got involved at some point. The only certainty these disparate authorities could agree on is that sometime between 11 p.m. on July 15 and 6:30 a.m. on July 16, someone created a thirty-eight-inch slice in the left side of the tent and pulled Billy through it.

What happened after that was—and still is—a mystery.

A close examination of the gash indicated it was made outside the tent. Because it was a clean cut, police assumed a new or recently sharpened knife was used. The narrow width of the slash made them conclude it was a kitchen knife and not a hunting knife, which has a thicker blade.

This intel was enough to prompt a search of every house on the cul-de-sac from top to bottom. I remember sitting in the kitchen with my parents and an FBI agent, listening to the clomp of footsteps over-head as investigators upstairs went from room to room. At the time, I didn't know what, exactly, they were looking for. All I knew was that my parents were scared, which made me scared as well.

The search yielded multiple knives from every home on Hemlock Circle. After they were tested, not a single one could conclusively be pinpointed as the same knife used to slash my tent.

With the searches came interviews. Everyone in the neighborhood had to endure more than one round of questioning. Local cops led to state police detectives, which became FBI agents.

No one reported hearing or seeing anything suspicious, largely be-cause the backyards of Hemlock Circle are big blind spots. I've always thought of the cul-de-sac as like a circular Trivial Pursuit game piece, with each tract of land one of those colored wedges you insert when you give a correct answer. Every house, meanwhile, sits at a slight angle from the neighboring homes. All of that, coupled with privacy hedges bordering every yard, means no one in Hemlock Circle can easily see into a backyard that's not their own. The only people who could have witnessed something useful the night Billy vanished were me and my parents. But their bedroom sat at the front of the house, offering a view of the cul-de-sac and not the yard behind it.

As for me, well, the website I'm looking at sums it up like this: "The other boy in the tent claimed to have seen and heard nothing."

One word in that sentence gnaws at me.

Claimed.

As if I possibly could have lied to the police about that.

As if I don't care what happened to Billy, when in truth I would do anything to learn what fate befell him.

Yet there's nothing left to be done. Despite all the searches and interviews, the only trace of Billy's whereabouts came after a K-9 unit followed his scent for a mile through the vast forest that surrounds the cul-de-sac. The trail ended at an infrequently used access road that bisects the woods, connecting two bigger, busier roads, making police think Billy had been led from the tent to a waiting car.

What happened after that—or who did it—well, no one knows. There were no signs of a struggle, either inside the tent or out of it. No one reported hearing screams or cries for help. No blood was found in our yard. No fresh footprints, either, mostly because the grass had been mowed the afternoon of July 14 and was therefore too short for someone's shoes to make much of an indentation. Trace evidence belonging to more than a dozen people *was* found in the yard, thanks to the Fourth of July party my parents had thrown earlier that month.

It could have been any of us.

It could have been none of us.

Over the years, there've been plenty of suspects, none of which hold much water because all of them are improbable at best, impossible at worst.

Take, for instance, Unlikely Suspect No. 1: Fred Marsh.

My father.

He was the first person the police considered because, why not?

The crime took place on his property, after all, under his watch. What became very clear very early on is that he never, ever would have done such a thing. He's a decent man. A *good* man. Devoted husband, professor of sociology at Princeton, a man so careful about abiding by the law that he's never even had a speeding ticket. Plus, my mother—no slouch herself in the decency department—had sworn that he was asleep beside her the entire night. And why would a homemaker and longstanding member of the PTA lie about such a thing?

Suspicion fell away from my father almost instantly, moving on to Unlikely Suspect No. 2: Billy's father, Blake Barringer.

Because the slash was made on the side of the tent that faced the Barringer house, authorities assumed Billy's kidnapper came from that direction. This led to police wondering if Mr. Barringer was to blame. Just like with my father, that went nowhere.

Blake Barringer, a pharmaceutical sales rep, was away on business in Boston that night. Dozens of witnesses saw him at the hotel bar, nursing a Sam Adams until close to eleven p.m., and checking out the next morning after his wife called to tell him Billy was missing. It was impossible for him to drive home, kidnap his son, and then drive back to Boston.

Also, he had no known reason to hurt his son, and appeared just as distraught by Billy's disappearance as the rest of the family. Besides, most abductions by parents are the result of custody disputes, and the Barringers remained married until Blake's death in 2004.

Unlikely Suspects No. 3 through 16 were everyone else on Hemlock Circle. Not counting me and Billy, a total of fifteen other people were present on the cul-de-sac that night. All of us were investigated in one way or another. None of us had any reason to hurt Billy—or any idea of who did.

That void was filled by the dozens of people who, over the years, have said they know what happened. Sickos, attention-seekers, and, in some cases, literal psychopaths have said they kidnapped Billy. Or murdered Billy. Or saw Billy bagging groceries in their local ShopRite. To date, seven men have come forward claiming to be him. Every pronouncement and confession was investigated. None were true, leaving those of us who knew and loved Billy with nothing but dashed hopes and unanswered questions.

By now, most everyone agrees the likeliest suspect is an outsider. Someone who swept into Hemlock Circle, took Billy, and left just as quickly and quietly. The website open on my laptop is a big proponent of that theory. It details how someone—no one quite knows who—claimed to have seen a strange man in camouflage roaming the cul-de-sac closest to Hemlock Circle the day before Billy vanished. But authorities have never been able to tie Billy's abduction to similar crimes. It didn't match the patterns of any known serial killer twenty years before 1994 or in the thirty years since. In FBI interviews of people incarcerated for abducting and killing young boys, none admitted to having anything to do with it.

Thirty years later, that's where things stand. No culprit. No answers. Nothing but the sad, brutal fact that Billy is still gone.

I close the laptop and go back upstairs. In the bedroom, I reach for the pen and notebook again. The sole remedy for my insomnia that actually seems to do some good. Two therapists ago, I was told that if something's on my mind, churning through my thoughts into the wee hours of the morning, the best thing to do is write it down. In doing so, I allow my brain to put off thinking about it until later, like a mental snooze button. It doesn't always work, but it's better than nothing.

I open the page I wrote on earlier.

Had The Dream again.

Beneath it, I add, *Billy is NOT out there.*

I gingerly place the notebook and pen on the nightstand and check the clock. A little before four. Still a chance to get at least a few hours of sleep.

Yet when I close my eyes, my thoughts drift back to the true-crime website I'd been reading. While better written and researched than others I've seen, it still didn't tell the whole story. For one, it insinuated that Billy's abduction came out of nowhere. That the twenty-four hours before he vanished were like any other day that summer. That there were no storm clouds on the horizon, portending imminent doom, or events in the neighborhood that, in hindsight, foreshadowed tragedy.

Most of that is correct. It *had* been a typical New Jersey summer. Sunny. Lazy. A little muggy for my mother's taste, but pleasant.

Yet there's more to the story. There always is. In truth, the day Billy vanished had been anything but ordinary.

And I knew something was off the moment I woke up.

Friday, July 15, 1994
8:36 a.m.

E than senses something's wrong even before his eyes snap open. Lying in a tangle of sheets intermittently kicked off and pulled back on in his sleep, he hears Barkley pawing at the bedroom door he's only recently been allowed to close at night. Before this summer, his mother made him leave it open so she could easily check on him during the night, making sure he wasn't staying up too late. Something Ethan swore was no longer necessary. Only after an assist from his father—"He's ten, Joyce. Give the boy some privacy."—did his mother relent. Since the end of the school year, he's been allowed to close his door each night before going to bed.

Now, though, as his beagle continues to sniffle and scratch, begging to be let out, Ethan reconsiders his decision. Maybe, he thinks, leaving the door open another year isn't such a bad idea after all. At least then Barkley could come and go as he pleases, allowing Ethan to sleep in.

As he kicks off the sheets and slides out of bed, Ethan notices the unmistakable scent of pancakes and bacon slipping through the crack beneath the door. No wonder his dog wants to be let out. The smell of his favorite breakfast makes Ethan eager to leave, too.

He opens the door, letting Barkley bolt down the stairs to the kitchen. Ethan's about to do the same when he's stopped by a realization as sudden as it is confusing.

Today is Friday. His mother only makes pancakes and bacon on Saturdays. Why would his father be doing it this morning while his mother's at work?

The answer comes to Ethan when he enters the kitchen, finding not just his father but his mother, too. A rarity for weekdays so far this summer. Since she started working, his mother has been gone by the time he wakes up most mornings during the week. A strange reversal from how it was during the rest of the year, when his father left early. His dad taught a few summer classes, but those weren't until the afternoon, leaving him to fix Ethan's breakfast.

Even more strange was the night before, when Ethan's mother returned to the office two hours after dinner. He and his father had been watching a rerun of *The Simpsons* when she came into the living room, car keys jangling in her hand, and said, "I need to go to the office real quick. I left something there."

Ethan, only half paying attention, heard his father say something to the effect of "Now? Can't it wait until morning?"

"I'll be just a minute," his mother said before hurrying toward the garage.

It ended up taking more than thirty minutes. Ethan knows because by the time she'd returned, *The Simpsons* was over, and an episode of *The Sinbad Show* had started. Now he wonders if her presence here this morning has something to do with her leaving last night.

"Morning, sport," his father says from behind that morning's *New York Times*. At his elbow sits a steaming mug of coffee and a plate stacked with pancakes.

Standing at the stove, Ethan's mother says nothing.

While it's never been spelled out for him, Ethan knows deep down that he's had a mostly carefree existence. He lives in a nice house surrounded by other nice houses, in a nice neighborhood made up of other nice neighborhoods. He gets whatever toys he wants, even if he's forced to wait until Christmas or his birthday to receive them. His parents buy a new car every two years. They've been to Disney World twice. On the rare occasions he worries, it's either about something trivial—an upcoming math test, getting picked last in gym class—or in the form of vague, abstract fears. Death. War. Quicksand.

But seeing his mother in her apron, spatula in hand, silently cooking like it's Saturday when it definitely is not, fills Ethan with an anxiety he's rarely experienced in his young life.

"What's wrong?" he asks.

"Nothing's wrong, sport," his father says, still hidden behind the newspaper.

"But you're both home."

"Why is that so unusual?" His father at last lowers the *Times* to give what Ethan has come to know as the Professor Look. Calm face. Probing eyes framed by tortoiseshell glasses. Left eyebrow raised so high it resembles the curve of a question mark. "This is where we live."

"You know what I mean," Ethan says, scooting his chair forward as his mother sets breakfast in front of him.

"He wants to know why I'm not at work," she says to his father, as if Ethan's not there at all.

"Are you sick?" Ethan asks. "Is that why you're home?"

"I don't work there anymore."

"Why not?"

Ethan's mother looks to his father. A wordless exchange in which he knows they're debating how much to tell him. It ends with his father nodding and his mother saying, "They no longer need me."

Even though the strain in her voice makes it clear she doesn't want to talk about it, Ethan needs to know more. She'd started the job in May—forcing an adjustment that was huge for a kid accustomed to his mother being around before and after school and all day during the summer. The first time Ethan came home from school to an empty house was both scary and exhilarating. Sure, he was only alone for an hour. And yes, he'd ended up watching TV and eating Goldfish crackers like he always did. But much like closing his bedroom door each night, that small bit of freedom made him feel more grown up.

Second in his thoughts, but equally important, is the fact that with his mother being home all day now, there'll be no need for his babysitter, Ashley. To Ethan, that is worse than losing his freedom. It means he probably won't get to see Ashley at all for the rest of the summer. And he *loves* seeing her.

"Are you going to get another job?"

"I don't know." His mother picks up a piece of bacon, considers eating it, gives it to Barkley instead. "We'll see."

In Ethan's experience, that almost always means no. But he's not ready to drop the subject.

"I think you should," he says. "Or maybe ask for your old job back. Maybe you can do something else there."

"This is for the best," Ethan's mother says, using another favorite euphemism for no. "Besides, I don't want to go back there."

"Why not?"

"I can't really talk about it."

Ethan's father lowers the newspaper again. "Can't or won't?"

"It's complicated," his mother says as she carries the skillet to the sink and fills it with water. A stalling tactic even Ethan knows won't work out. Fred Marsh is persistence personified.

Sure enough, his father waits until the faucet stops running before saying, "You told me you were let go because of budget cuts. What's so complicated about that?"

Rather than answer, Ethan's mother grabs a Brillo pad and starts to scrub.

"Joyce, what aren't you telling me?" his father says. "Did something happen last night?"

At the sink, Ethan's mother nods toward Barkley, who's at the sliding door to the patio, snout against the glass. "Take him outside," she tells Ethan. "He probably needs to pee."

Ethan, staring at the half-full plate in front of him, starts to argue but thinks better of it. Something weird is going on with his parents.

"Go on, sport," his father adds. "Just for a minute. Breakfast will still be here when you get back."

Ethan opens the door and Barkley zooms outside, his tail bouncing as he tears through the yard, scattering birds. Ethan follows, the patio's sun-warmed paving stones hot beneath his bare feet. In the cooler grass of the lawn, he finds the stick he and Barkley played with the day before.

"Here, boy," he says, immediately drawing Barkley's attention. "Fetch!"

He tosses the stick high into the air, watching it spin as it arcs across the lawn and lands on the edge of the woods that border the backyard. Barkley romps after it as Ethan glances toward the house. Inside, his parents sit at the breakfast table, caught in mid-argument. Seeing them like that tightens the knot of worry in Ethan's stomach.

Divorce is another one of his vague fears, although less abstract than the others. He's seen what happens when parents split. Three years earlier, the house next door had been occupied by Ethan's former best friend, Shawn. When his parents got divorced, their house was put on the market and Shawn was forced to move to Texas with his mother. Ethan hasn't heard from him since.

He worries the same thing could soon happen to him, even though neither of his parents seems too angry as he watches them through the patio door. His father's sporting the Professor Look again, which Ethan knows comes with many meanings. Curiosity. Impatience. Frustration.

His mother's expression is easier to read. She simply looks sad.

Ethan turns away, facing the rest of the yard. He spots Barkley still at the edge of the woods, the game of fetch forgotten. Instead, his dog peers into the trees, body rigid. When he growls, it sounds so unlike Barkley that it sends a chill down Ethan's spine.

"What's wrong, boy?" he says. "What do you see?"

It must be a squirrel, he thinks. Or one of the other animals that emerge from the woods at all hours of the day. Ethan can only remember one other time when his dog growled—at Fritz Van de Veer during the Fourth of July picnic, for reasons no one could understand.

"Come here, boy," Ethan says, trying to coax his dog away from whatever's in the woods. When that doesn't work, he goes to Barkley, crossing the yard to the point where freshly mowed grass meets the forest's edge. A clear line of demarcation. Past it, the woods stretch for miles, interrupted only by an access road that cuts through it.

Recently, Ethan's been allowed to venture with Billy to the road, about a mile away, but no farther. Which is fine by him. He has no desire to go beyond it. It's not that he's scared, exactly. He's just never felt the need to explore the woods any farther, mostly because he already knows what's there. Lots of trees. Lots of rocks. Oh, and the Hawthorne Institute, which Ethan knows nothing about beyond the fact that it exists and that he's not allowed to go there.

"Stay away from that place," his mother once told him during an autumn walk in the woods.

"Why?"

"Because it's private property and it would be trespassing, which is illegal."

"But what's there?" Ethan asked.

"Nothing you'd be interested in."

Ethan took her word for it and continues to stay away. Unlike other kids his age, he doesn't find the forbidden tantalizing. He suspects the institute is just like where his dad works, only stuffier.

A noise sounds behind them, startling Ethan and Barkley both. They whirl around in unison, the empty woods suddenly forgotten, focusing now on the emerald lawn stretching between them and the house.

Sitting in the grass a few yards from the hedge that separates Ethan's lawn from Billy's is a baseball.

Ethan picks it up, noting the grass stains and Barkley's bite marks from dozens of previous times the ball has been thrown into his yard. So far this summer, it's been an everyday occurrence. A secret code, passed between Ethan and his neighbor.

And the message is always the same.

Billy wants to play.

THREE

Scriiiiiiiitch.

I bolt awake at eight a.m., breathless from The Dream.

Twice in one night.

Not a good sign.

At least The Dream isn't echoing through the bedroom like it did hours earlier. That's due to both the sunlight pouring through the windows and the roar of a lawn mower tearing across the front yard.

Most suburbs run with the precision of a Rolex, and Hemlock Circle is no different. Mondays are trash day, during which everyone wheels their hulking bins of garbage to the curb in the morning and drags them back to the garage in the evening. The same is done with the recycling every other Friday.

Tuesdays are when the landscaping crews arrive, swarming the cul-de-sac in ear-splitting cacophony. Lawn mowers, weed whackers, leaf blowers. Especially leaf blowers. If suburbia had an official sound, it would be the agitated whir of compressed air blasting across patios and driveways, clearing them of any cut grass blades or stray leaves that dare to rest on their surfaces. When the leaf blowers cease, the resulting silence feels momentarily unnerving. Too quiet. Too abrupt.

For now, though, the lawn mower keeps on trucking, moving from the front yard to the back as I shower, dress, and head downstairs to the kitchen to make coffee. As it brews, I try to shake off my latest encounter with The Dream, which has haunted me since the day after Billy's disappearance.

It's always the same, beginning in darkness that's just starting to recede. My surroundings soon grow clearer. Enough for me to see that I'm inside my old tent. The one Billy was snatched from when I was ten.

But Billy's still there, asleep beside me.

Above him, running the height of the tent, is a long gash.

Sensing the presence of someone just outside, I peer into the slash, finding only darkness beyond. Whoever it is, I can't see them, despite knowing they're *right there*.

Then I hear it.

Scriiiiiiiitch.

The sound of the tent being sliced, even though that part's already happened. It's a delayed noise, just like the way you see the lightning before you hear its accompanying thunder.

That's when I wake up. Every damn time. The horrible *scriiiiiiiitch* lingering a moment in whatever room I happen to be in.

Why I keep having The Dream and what any of it means is a mystery I'd love to solve. At first, I assumed it meant that when the tent was slashed, I was at least conscious of it happening, if not fully awake. But I have no memory of hearing it happen. No vague recollection of opening my eyes and seeing the gash in the fabric.

I honestly still don't know what to make of that. A stranger entered *my* yard, sliced through *my* tent, took *my* best friend. Is it possible I could sleep through all of that, noticing nothing, remembering absolutely nothing? The insomnia-racked me of today would say no, but ten-year-old me was a different story. Back then, I slept like the dead.

So the question is: Did I really hear something, see something? Or is The Dream imagined memory, formed by things I know? The tear in the tent. Billy gone. An unknown person responsible for both.

I tried my hardest to answer that question and give the police at least some small clue about what had happened. With my parents' consent, I was put under hypnosis a week after Billy disappeared, in the hopes some forgotten tidbit would bubble up from the dark depths of my subconscious. When that didn't work, I was taken to a dream analyst, who had me talk about The Dream and every other one I could remember having since the night Billy was taken. That also led nowhere.

After that, we all had to make peace with uncertainty. Maybe I didn't see anything, maybe I did. Maybe it was too traumatic for me to process and so I sliced it from my memory, with only The Dream to intermittently remind me of this self-edit.

Everyone understood but Mrs. Barringer, who convinced herself— and tried to convince me—that the key to finding Billy was buried somewhere in the dark recesses of my brain. One morning a month after Billy had vanished, she lurched into my yard. Worry had aged her so much that she looked like a stranger. Someone to fear.

Mrs. Barringer had dragged Billy's younger brother into the yard with her, likely too afraid to let him out of her sight. Andy, seven at the time, couldn't bring himself to look at me or his mother. He simply stared at the grass, scared and ashamed.

"Ethan," Mrs. Barringer barked, her mouth turning into an O of surprise, as if even she was shocked by how harsh she sounded. She dropped Andy's hand and hobbled toward me, her footsteps slick-swishing through the grass. "You need to tell them," she said, gently this time. "Okay, sweetie? Just tell the police what you remember about that night."

"But I don't remember anything."

Mrs. Barringer was within arm's reach now. I took a backward step toward the house, but she latched onto my shoulders with both hands. Her grip was tight and rough. The complete opposite of her still-soothing voice.

"You have to remember *something*. Even if you don't think you do. You couldn't have slept through the whole night."

Her grip on my shoulders became a pinch. She started shaking me, lightly at first, but growing more violent with each passing second. Soon I was being jerked back and forth, my head bobbing uncontrollably. Even though I was young and scared, I knew what Mrs. Barringer wanted from me. I wanted the same thing myself. Some clue, no matter how small, that might help find Billy.

But I remembered nothing.

I knew *nothing*.

"I'm sorry!" I cried. "I'm so sorry!"

At that point, my mother rushed outside and pulled me away from Mrs. Barringer's grip.

"He doesn't know anything, Mary Ellen," she said, not without kindness. I'm certain she saw a bit of herself in Mrs. Barringer's unhinged state. The way she gazed at our neighbor, my mother seemed to understand that, had it been me who was taken, she would be the one in *their* yard, shaking *their* son, pleading for information.

I'm taking that first, blessed sip of coffee when I realize the noise outside has stopped. No lawn mower. No leaf blower. In their place comes the jaunty chime of the doorbell. I answer it, finding one of the lawn guys on the front porch.

"Are Mr. and Mrs. Marsh home?" he says, using a rag to wipe sweat from his brow.

"They just moved, actually."

"Are you the new homeowner?"

"No," I say, because technically I'm not. Which makes me wonder what, exactly, I am. "I'm their son. I'm staying here until my parents put the house on the market."

It dawns on me that he might already know this and is gearing up to politely request payment for the lawn he's just mowed. I try to spare him the chore by saying, "How much do I owe you?"

"Nothing," he says. "Your parents paid in advance for the entire summer. I'm here because there was something in your yard this morning. It was no problem today. But in the future, I'd really appreciate it if you made sure your kids don't leave sports equipment in the grass when we come to mow."

"I don't have kids." I squint, confused. "What sports equipment?"

"This."

The man digs into a deep pocket of his cargo pants. He removes his hand and holds it out so I can see it.

There, resting in his cupped palm, is a baseball.

Friday, July 15, 1994
8:56 a.m.

illy looks at the baseball in his hand, surprised by how battered it's become after just a few weeks of use. The once-white leather is now a dull gray and scuffed with dirt and grass stains. There are even a few teeth marks from the couple of times Barkley found it before Ethan could. That might happen again today if he's not careful. Billy can hear the dog with Ethan on the other side of the hedge.

He knows it's weird. The way he crouches behind the hedge, listening to Ethan play with Barkley in the yard next door. Other boys would just pop through the greenery and say hello, but where's the fun in that?

No, Billy prefers to do it his way.

The weird way.

Hidden behind the hedge, gripping the baseball, waiting for the perfect moment to spring his secret code.

The first time he tried it was the first day of summer vacation. Already bored by ten a.m., he decided to run next door and ask Ethan if he wanted to go exploring in the woods. Billy's still not sure why he opted to make a game of it. But once he saw the baseball sitting on his dresser, untouched since he got it months earlier as a birthday present, he knew that was what he needed to do with it.

Ethan was confused at first. He'd brought it back to Billy, asking if it accidentally went over the hedge while he and Andy were playing catch. As if that were an everyday occurrence in the Barringer back-yard. It wasn't. Andy sometimes tossed a ball back and forth with their dad. But Billy? Never.

"I threw it there on purpose," Billy told him.

Ethan scrunched his eyes. "Why?"

"I dunno. I wanted it to be, like, a secret message. Whenever you find the ball in your yard, it means you need to come over and find me. I saw it in a movie. A man who moved into a haunted house kept find-ing balls left by a ghost."

"Why would a ghost do that?"

Billy sighed then, as if the answer was obvious. "So the man would know he was there."

Ethan shook his head and passed the ball back to him. "That's weird," he said, but not in a bad way. Not like Ragesh Patel or the other older boys on the school bus who spit the word at him like an insult. Ethan meant it as an observation.

Or so Billy likes to think.

He knows he's not like other boys his age, and sometimes that bothers him. Sometimes he even wishes he could be different. Not so prone to flights of fancy or fits of imagination. Not as much of a nerd, to use another word thrown at him on a regular basis, even though Billy thinks of nerds as being super smart, which he is not. He's okay at English and loves reading, but he completely sucks at math. All the other not-smart boys he knows make up for it by being athletic. An-other area in which Billy is hopeless.

"He's eccentric," he once heard his father say to his mother when Mrs. Jensen called them in for a parent-teacher conference because she was concerned about Billy's inability to fit in with the rest of his class. "I don't understand why that's such a bad thing."

"It's not bad, necessarily," his mother said. "But I worry. This world isn't kind to boys who stand out."

That was three years ago, and even though they'd moved to a new house, a new town, and a new school since then, Billy still found himself unable to fit in. He'd feel completely alone if it weren't for Ethan, who never seems to mind Billy's eccentricities. Which is why Billy thought it was fine to try out his baseball-as-secret-message bit on his best friend. And why he's kept it up every day so far this summer.

Well, every day except yesterday.

Yesterday was special.

But today Billy is back to his regular routine, ready to toss the ball while Ethan's still in the backyard. A stealth delivery. As if the ball had indeed been placed there by a ghost.

Peering through the hedge, he sees Ethan in the middle of his yard, shooting a concerned look at Barkley. The dog's at the edge of the woods, growling.

"Come here, boy," Ethan calls.

When Barkley doesn't come, Ethan goes to him. Billy watches his friend cross the yard, waiting until he's at the trees. In one swift, silent motion, Billy stands, tosses the ball over the hedge, and listens to it hit the ground.

Then he runs.

Again, weird.

Since he knows Ethan will see the baseball in two seconds, he might as well stay. Yet Billy hurries back to his house, running through the open back door and up the stairs to his bedroom.

There, he sits—and waits for Ethan to find him.

FOUR

stare at the baseball, which now sits on the kitchen counter. Pristinely white with red stitching, it looks brand-new.

This, I think, is a coincidence.

It has to be.

Billy is still gone. He hasn't come back. And he absolutely wasn't outside last night, roaming the cul-de-sac, despite that brief tingle of recognition I'd felt at the time.

No, this ball belongs to someone else. Some neighbor kid playing catch who overthrew, lost the ball in my yard, then lost interest after that. That's the only logical explanation. Yet I know of only one kid in the neighborhood, and I doubt he's even old enough to play catch.

Still, I grab the ball, head outside, and cross the grass to the house on the right. With any other neighbor, I'd go up the sidewalk to the front door and ring the bell. Because this is Russ, I squeeze through the hedge separating our properties, emerging like Bigfoot into the Chens' yard.

As I'd hoped, Russ is already outside, drinking coffee on the back patio. It's a perfect morning for it, the July heat being kept at bay by a soft breeze bringing scents from Mrs. Chen's garden. Rose and freesia and honeysuckle.

Russ waves when he sees me and lifts his mug. "Want some?"

"Just had a cup."

"Cool," Russ says, in that chill surfer-dude way of his. Something he acquired after I left for private school. Before that, he'd been angsty, agitated, always fidgeting.

Then again, nothing about Russell Chen bears any resemblance to his ten-year-old self. He'd been a scrawny boy. Awkwardly so. His noodle-thin limbs, coupled with his shortness, made him appear younger than he was. He still does, only now it's in a way that inspires envy. Tall and muscular, he looks nowhere near his actual age of forty. His face is free of worry lines, and his thick chest strains against a polo shirt branded with the logo of his sporting goods store.

Russ and I were friends as kids, although not like Billy and me. He was the third wheel we'd sometimes grudgingly let tag along. Then Billy was gone, and it was only the two of us, pushed together by the fact that we were neighbors and our parents were suddenly terrified to let us out of their sight.

I'll never forget the first time we hung out without Billy. He'd been missing for three weeks by then, and I tried to temporarily bury my sadness and fear by playing basketball at the hoop set up in the driveway. Russ popped through the hedge and asked if he could join me. I told him no, that I wanted to be on my own.

"I know you'd rather be with Billy," he said. "But right now, I'm your only option."

Even back then it struck me as unbearably sad for a boy to know he was no one's first choice for a friend. But I also thought it was brave of Russ to acknowledge it.

"Sure, you can play," I said.

We spent the rest of the summer shooting hoops in my driveway, and stayed in touch after I went off to private school. We remained friendly during college, although by then we had almost nothing in common. Whereas I shrank into myself, Russ expanded, both in size and social status. Star football player. Homecoming king. Even modeled for a bit after college. Yet I still made a point to hang out with him every time I returned home for holidays or summer breaks. Seeing Russ was a much-needed reminder that not every boy on Hemlock Circle left or disappeared.

The few times he did leave, he soon found himself back here, most recently after his father passed away and Russ and his wife, Jennifer, moved in to take care of his mother. That was five years ago, and they've had one child since with another on the way.

"Is that for Benji?" Russ says, gesturing to the baseball in my hand.

"It's not his? The lawn guy found it in the backyard. I thought that maybe Benji tossed it there."

"He's four," Russ says. "If he can pitch like that already, then Jen and I don't need to worry about paying for college."

Jennifer emerges onto the patio, holding a coffee mug in one hand and helping their son down the back steps with the other. "Worry about what?"

"Ethan found a baseball," Russ says. "Thought it was Benji's."

I hold out the ball so Jennifer can have a look. She shakes her head. "Not his. Benji has a ball, but it's, like, twice that big. Toddler-sized. Where'd you find it?"

"The backyard."

Jennifer lowers herself into the chair next to Russ, cradling her growing stomach. "Maybe it's from someone who came to look at the Barringer place."

Billy's old house has changed hands multiple times since his family moved away in the mid-nineties, with no one staying there for very long. All of them were couples without kids or families with teenagers. Apparently, no one with a child wanted to risk another disappearance. The last owners, Bob and his partner, Marcel, had lasted five years before putting it on the market six months ago. A FOR SALE sign has been planted in the front yard ever since.

"I haven't seen anyone go near the place," I say.

Benji tugs on my arm, wanting to see the ball for himself. I kneel and hand it to him, nervous in that way I always get around anyone under a certain age. Kids strike me as being so helpless, so fragile, and Benji is no exception. Not for the first time, I wonder how Russ and Jennifer don't appear racked with anxiety every second of the day. Once, during a visit shortly after Benji was born, I asked Russ why he didn't seem nervous now that he was a father.

"Oh, I'm nervous as hell," he told me. "I've just gotten really good at pretending I'm not."

Right now, Russ is all smiles as he watches Benji try to throw the ball. It sails about a foot before plunking onto the flagstone patio, proving that it definitely wasn't Benji Chen who tossed the ball into my yard.

Having exhausted his curiosity about the baseball, Benji ambles to his father and climbs onto his lap. "What's in there?" he says, eyeing Russ's mug.

"Coffee. Want a sip?"

Jennifer playfully swats his arm. "Don't you dare!"

In that moment, they are a picture-perfect family. Father, mother, son, all enviably adorable, with another child arriving soon. A girl, Russ told me as we drank beer on this very patio two nights ago. Seeing the three of them together, at ease and happy, reminds me of what I could have had—but chose not to.

It was me who didn't want kids, although for a time I'd thought it was something both Claudia and I agreed on. I remember everything about the moment I realized I was wrong, from the ecru walls of the restaurant to the scent of the grilled salmon that had just been placed in front of me. A zingy mix of lemon and woodsmoke. I was reaching for my glass of wine when Claudia, out of nowhere, said, "I want to have a baby."

I froze, my fingers still wrapped around the stem of the wineglass, unable to respond.

"Ethan, did you hear me?" Worry had edged into Claudia's voice. She knew her words were like a hand grenade tossed into our marriage. Now she was bracing herself for the explosion.

"I heard you," I said quietly.

Claudia leaned forward, uncertain. "And?"

"You told me you didn't want kids," I said, which was the truth. After a month of dating, right before it got really serious, we decided to lay all our cards on the table. The biggest one—the make-or-break one—involved not wanting children. "We agreed on that."

"I know. We did. And I was fine with that. I really was." Claudia looked at her lap, where I assumed her hands were bunching her napkin under the table. A nervous tic that I knew so well. Until that moment, I'd thought I knew everything about her. "But for the last few years, I've started to think that maybe I do."

"What changed?"

"Me," she said. "*I've* changed. At least, my thinking has."

I sighed then. A sad exhalation. Because my thinking *hadn't* changed, although it was clear Claudia hoped it secretly had.

"You're upset," she said.

Yes, I was. But not with her. I couldn't be mad at Claudia for feeling the way she did. I was scared about what it meant for our marriage.

"I'm surprised, that's all."

"I know," Claudia said. "And I'm sorry. I should have told you sooner."

"Why didn't you?"

"I guess I thought it would pass. But the longer I've thought about it, the more I realized I want it. I can't stop thinking about our legacies.

What we'll leave behind when we're gone. Right now, that's nothing. But if we had a family . . ."

Claudia's voice trailed off, forcing me to fill the void. "We *are* a family. You and me."

"No, Ethan," she said. "We're just us."

Then she started to cry, right there in the middle of the restaurant, and I knew that our marriage was in deep trouble.

I'm wrenched from my memories by the appearance of Russ's mother emerging from the house wearing a floppy straw hat and clutching a trowel caked with dried dirt. In her seventies, she still moves with effortless grace.

"Hi, Mrs. Chen," I say, just like I did when we were kids.

"Hi, Ethan," she calls back before continuing to the gladiolas waving in the breeze at the patio's edge. "Are you remembering to water your mother's flowers?"

"Yes."

A lie. I haven't watered anything—inside or out. Still, it pleases Mrs. Chen, who nods and says, "You're a good son. Just like my Russell."

Russ cringes at the compliment, which makes me wonder if he's thinking about his older brother, Johnny. The bad son. The son who might have eventually become good if he hadn't died of a drug overdose when Russ was nine.

That was the first great loss on Hemlock Circle.

"Hey, I thought of someone else you could ask about the baseball," Russ says. "The Wallaces."

"Why?" I scoop up the ball Benji had thrown/dropped, confused why Russ thinks I should go to a house on the other side of the cul-de-sac. Especially since the only person there now is gruff Vance Wallace.

"Ashley's back. She and her son moved in last month."

"I didn't know that," I say, trying to hide the surprise flashing through me like heat lightning.

Ashley Wallace is back on Hemlock Circle.

"Your parents probably didn't mention it because they know you had a huge crush on her back in the day," Russ says, grinning.

"I did not."

"You totally did. We all did."

Jennifer shoots him a look. "Oh, did you now?"

"Did I say 'we'?" Russ stalls with a sip of coffee. "I meant Ethan and Billy."

"He meant that none of us did," I add. "She was older."

Five years older, to be exact. Not much of an age difference now, but completely out of my league when I was ten and, despite my present-day denial, hopelessly in love with Ashley Wallace. With good reason. Ashley was fun and funny and, at that stage of my life, the prettiest girl I'd ever seen. Also, she was cool in a way a slightly dorky ten-year-old could only aspire to be. She wore T-shirts bearing the names of bands I'd never heard of but wanted to listen to. Smashing Pumpkins. Violent Femmes. Her favorite was white with black letters inside a black rectangle that simply read "NIИ."

"What does that mean?" I once asked.

She half smiled. "Nine Inch Nails. They're awesome."

The next week, when my parents took me to Sam Goody and said I could buy whatever CD I wanted, I grabbed *The Downward Spiral*. My father stopped me before I could reach the register. Eyeing the parental advisory sticker slapped on the case, he said, "Whoa now. A bit too grown-up for you, don't you think, sport?" I didn't think that, yet I dutifully put the CD back and picked up the *Forrest Gump* soundtrack, not because I wanted it but because it was a two-disc set and therefore cost my parents more money. A hollow victory.

But the real reason I liked Ashley was the fact that she was nice. Not fake nice, like some of the girls at school, or condescending nice, like most of those girls' parents. Ashley was genuinely kind. Any boy my age couldn't help but fall in love with her a little.

"I guess I'll ask her, too," I say, suddenly anxious at the prospect. It's been almost thirty years since I last saw Ashley Wallace, and when it comes to people, I've found that sometimes memories are best left undisturbed.

"Good luck, buddy," Russ says with a wink.

I shake my head, wave goodbye, and cut through the yard to the sidewalk circling the cul-de-sac. I turn left, which takes me past first my house, then the old Barringer place, the route bringing forth the memory of making this same trek after I woke to find Billy gone.

In that initial confusion, with the tent zipped shut but a gash in its side, I first thought Billy had torn it open. A ridiculous notion for several reasons, but I was ten.

And once the idea was in my brain, I couldn't shake it, leading me to next come up with reasons why he'd rip his way out of the tent. The only one I could think of was a bathroom emergency. So I left the tent the proper way—unzipping the front flap, crawling outside, standing once I was on the grass—and headed indoors. The house was silent when I came inside, with my parents still sleeping upstairs and Barkley doing the same on the living room couch. Hearing the patio door slide shut woke him, setting him into a frenzy of barking that immediately woke my mother.

"You're up early," she said as she crept downstairs, a robe thrown over her nightgown.

"Where's Billy?"

My mother replied with a tired shrug. "He's not outside?"

"No."

I didn't think to tell her about the state of the tent, and how there was now a slice in the side big enough for a toddler to walk through. I was more concerned with finding out where Billy was. Worry had started to creep in, even though I didn't quite know it at the time.

"I'm going to check the bathroom," I said.

"The one upstairs is empty," my mother said, which made me head down the hallway past the kitchen to check the first-floor powder room. It, too, was empty.

While I did that, my mother had stepped outside, presumably to make sure I wasn't mistaken and had somehow overlooked Billy sleeping in the tent beside me. A sign even she wasn't thinking clearly in that moment.

"What's this?" she said when I joined her in the backyard. She was by the side of the tent, peering through the sliced fabric the exact way I had done minutes earlier, only from the inside.

"I think Billy did it."

Unlike me, my mother knew the damage to the tent hadn't been the work of a ten-year-old boy. "Ethan, run over to the Barringers' and see if Billy is there."

That made as much sense as anything else. It certainly seemed reasonable that Billy would go home to use his bathroom instead of ours. Or that he'd had trouble sleeping in the tent and opted to return to his own bed.

For reasons I'm still not sure about, I went back into the house and left through the front door instead of simply slipping through the hedge into the Barringers' backyard. I suspect that, deep down, I knew something horrible had happened, kicking off an avoidance of our backyard that persists to this day. That's how I found myself tracing the curve of the sidewalk, turning up the walk bisecting the front yard, and hopping up the three steps to the front door.

Mrs. Barringer answered the door. Seeing me there, without her son, sent a hand flittering to her throat.

"Where's Billy?" she said.

"He's not here?"

"No, Ethan. He's not with you?"

When I shook my head, fear sparked in Mrs. Barringer's eyes. Seeing her silent panic made clear the unnerving fact I'd been trying to suppress since waking up in the tent.

Billy was gone.

Thirty years later, he's still gone, as is his family; the house they once occupied now stands empty. I pause on the sidewalk, struck by how utterly abandoned the place feels. It's not surprising no one wants to buy it. The shutters have been faded by the sun and the windows are as dark and empty as the eyes of a corpse. The only sign of life is the flowers lining the front walk. Bright and in full bloom, it's clear they're the work of Mrs. Chen, Hemlock Circle's expert gardener. She probably couldn't bear the sight of unattended plants and took it upon herself to care for them.

After one last look at Billy's house, I continue to the next one on the cul-de-sac—the Van de Veer residence.

Fritz Van de Veer and his wife, Alice, were the first to settle on Hemlock Circle after it was built in the late eighties. They were soon followed by the Wallaces, the Patels, the Chens, and my family. Of the six original houses, only the Barringer place has been home to more than one family. First the Remingtons, who spent three years there before they got divorced and moved away, then the Barringers, then several other families who came and went. That turnover, while normal for most neighborhoods, is unusual in a place like Hemlock Circle, where few people ever leave.

Make no mistake, it's weird that five out of the six families living on the cul-de-sac when Billy vanished remain here thirty years later. Even the Barringers, who had every reason to leave, stayed a few years after their son's disappearance. The night before they left for Florida, I asked my parents why they had stayed here for so long. Why everyone had stayed.

My father cited the diverse neighborhood, its cleanliness and quiet, its excellent schools and low crime rate, what happened to Billy notwithstanding. Situated a stone's throw from Princeton and halfway between New York and Philadelphia, its location made it one of the most desirable neighborhoods in the country.

Despite the way he talked, I know the real reason that's kept every family here all these years. No one wanted to be the first to leave, lest it make them appear suspicious. Now that my parents have finally felt comfortable enough to move, I wouldn't be surprised if others did as well. Especially Vance Wallace, who lost his wife to cancer a few years ago and, until Ashley moved back in, had lived in that big house all alone.

To get to the Wallaces', I must pass the Van de Veers'. As I do, I spot Fritz Van de Veer rounding the house, a garden hose in hand. Even though he's watering flowers, Fritz looks like a businessman on Casual Friday. Pressed khakis. Crisp white shirt tucked in to show off his still-trim figure. The only sign that he's been retired for years are his sneakers, which are the same gleaming white as his shirt.

Fritz is soon joined by his wife, Alice, who's clad in a floral sundress and sandals. She's as slender and elegant as the last time I saw her, which might have been more than a decade ago. Like her husband, her hair is a shade of beige that refuses to betray her age. Not quite blonde, not quite gray. Standing side by side, the two of them give off distinct Pat Sajak–and–Vanna White vibes.

I step closer to their yard, stopping next to the hedge separating their property from the old Barringer house. "Hi, Mr. and Mrs. Van de Veer," I call out, sounding like I'm thirty years younger and not the same age they were when Billy was taken. Such formality can be forgiven. As the only couple on Hemlock Circle without children, Fritz and Alice rarely entered my childhood orbit. Other than appearances at our annual Fourth of July party, I can't remember another time in which the Van de Veers were at our house. Nor can I recall ever setting foot in theirs.

Then again, after Billy, the general mood of Hemlock Circle changed. The neighborhood grew more somber, less friendly. Russ's parents stopped celebrating Chinese New Year with an open house, and Ashley's halted their Memorial Day pool parties. The Patels still celebrated Diwali, but only with close friends and family. Even my parents stopped their Fourth of July picnic, opting instead to take me on vacations to national parks and notable historical sites.

"Ethan, hello!" Alice squeals as her husband waves with his hose hand, sending a stream of water arcing across the lawn. She dodges it on her way to the sidewalk, where she presses both of her well-manicured hands to my cheeks. "It's been ages since we last saw you. Hasn't it been ages, Fritz?"

Behind her, Fritz nods. "It has."

"Now you're all grown up! You must be, what now, thirty?"

"Forty," I say.

"No!" Alice says, gasping then giggling. "Oh, that makes me feel positively ancient."

She gives my arm a playful swat that might be seen as friendly but could also be considered flirtatious. For clarification, I look to Fritz, who offers none. Instead, he says, "I see you've been making the rounds this morning."

"What do you mean?"

"Going from house to house," Fritz says, again gesturing with the hose, the water splashing first toward the Chens', then the old Barringer place, before stopping in the direction of the Wallace house next door.

"Oh," I say, a bit unnerved. Has Fritz Van de Veer been watching me? If so, maybe he also saw who tossed the baseball into my yard. I hold it up for him to see. "Just trying to find the owner of this. It was in my yard this morning."

Alice briefly eyes the ball. "Strange for something like that to show up."

"Have you seen anything else strange recently?"

"Can't say I have," Fritz says before turning to his wife. "Sweets, could you go inside and pour me a glass of lemonade? I'll be there in a sec."

At first, I'm not sure what surprises me more—that Fritz calls his wife "sweets" or that he can't get his own damn lemonade. What ends up surprising me the most is when Alice dutifully nods, gives me a wave goodbye, and heads inside.

"I assume you *have* seen something strange," Fritz says once she's gone. "Otherwise you wouldn't be asking."

I debate how much to tell him, knowing there still might be a logical explanation for what I saw last night and that the ball in my yard might have nothing to do with the garage lights flicking on and off at all the houses on Hemlock Circle. Deciding it's too complicated to share, I simple say, "No, Mr. Van de Veer."

"No need to be so formal, son. Call me Fritz."

"Fritz," I say, the name feeling weird as it springs off my tongue. "I'm just getting a feel for the neighborhood now that I'm back."

He nods in a way that makes me think he doesn't believe me. "You plan on staying a while?"

"Maybe. I haven't decided yet."

"It'd be a shame if you didn't," Fritz says as he aims the hose at a hydrangea bush dominating the corner of his yard, its blue blooms quivering in the water's spray. "This place wouldn't be the same without someone from the Marsh family living here. I was sad to see your parents go. They settling in okay?"

"They are, yes."

"Good to hear," he says. "Next time you talk to them, give your mother my regards."

Fritz cuts the water and starts gathering up the hose. I nod goodbye and resume heading to the Wallaces', my encounter with the Van de Veers already fading from my memory. Since I didn't see much of them when I lived here as a kid, I suspect we'll have even fewer interactions now that I'm back. It isn't until I reach the Wallaces' front steps that I realize something odd about the conversation.

Why did Fritz Van de Veer mention my mother but not my father?

After throwing her half-eaten breakfast in the trash and shoving the syrup-streaked plate into the dishwasher, Joyce Marsh tells her husband that she's going to go outside. Their argument earlier had been intense but brief, and even though everything since has been smoothed over—for now, at least—Joyce needs to put some distance between the two of them or else she'll admit everything.

That there is indeed more to the story of how she lost her job.

That she can't ever tell him all of it.

"Rejoining the Gaggle?" Fred says as she trades her house shoes for a pair of canvas slip-ons by the mudroom door.

He's referring to the other wives of Hemlock Circle, who often gather for a few minutes each day in the yard of whoever happens to be out there first. Today, it's Trish Wallace, who's using a spray bottle to spritz the lilies that line her front walk. Deepika Patel, who lives next door, has already joined her, and Joyce knows it'll be a matter of minutes before the others make their way over.

No one's quite sure when the gatherings began. It certainly wasn't planned, and there's no organization to it. Just a group of friends and neighbors spotting each other across the cul-de-sac and stepping outside to say hello. Still, Fred insists on calling it the Gaggle, in a way that sounds more condescending than Joyce thinks he intends. As if they're all just a bunch of gossips with nothing better to do. She chalks it up to jealousy on his part. The men of Hemlock Circle never gather like this.

"Might as well," she says with a sigh. "Time to get back in the habit, I guess."

Once outside, she sees that in addition to Trish, Deepika, and Misty Chen, Mary Ellen Barringer has joined the group. A surprise. Her next-door neighbor rarely participates in the Gaggle. At least, she didn't used to. Maybe that's changed since Joyce stopped taking part.

Making her way across the cul-de-sac, she can't help but think about how jarring it is to not be going to work anymore. Yes, she'd only been there two months, but it was long enough to fall into a comfortable routine. Right now, for instance, she'd be settling at her desk with a cup of coffee after a five-minute chat with Margie, the senior assistant. Margie's there right now, likely chatting with whoever they brought in to take Joyce's place. Joining the Gaggle on the Wallace lawn makes her feel . . . Well, she's not sure how she feels. "Failure" is too strong of a word, but it feels akin to that. Disappointment, she guesses, that she's so easily slipped back into her old routine.

"Look who's back," Trish says. "Day off?"

"Permanently off," she replies. "It just wasn't a good fit with my schedule. You know how it is."

Joyce smiles through the lie. If she can't tell her husband anything, she's certainly not going to tell these women. Because, condescending though it may be, there is some truth to the name Fred gave the group.

"A mother's work is never done," Trish says as the others nod in agreement. Their bobbing heads make Joyce wonder if they're silently judging her for trying to have a job while also maintaining a home.

On Hemlock Circle, the women aren't expected to work. They don't need to. It's an expensive neighborhood in an expensive corner of an expensive state. They all live here because they can afford it, thanks to their husbands. They are the wives of professors and scientists, engineers and bankers. Everything they could possibly want is provided for them.

"It's better this way," Misty tells Joyce. "Ethan needs you at home. Just for a little longer."

Joyce would beg to differ. Lately, Ethan acts like he doesn't need her at all, which is one of the reasons she decided to get a job. She misses the days when he depended on her for everything. Now that he doesn't, there's a void she had hoped employment would fill.

"I suppose you're right," Joyce replies, declining to debate the point with Misty, whose bright smile and perfect skin betray no hint that in the past twelve months she's endured one of the worst things a mother can go through. Poor, troubled Johnny. Such a tragedy.

"Right about what?"

Joyce spins around to see Alice Van de Veer has joined the group. The last person she wants to see right now. From the tight-lipped smile Alice gives her, Joyce wonders how much she knows. Not just about what Alice's husband, Fritz, has been up to, but Joyce's role in all of it. She doubts Fritz outright told Alice anything, but wives have ways of finding things out. Even things they shouldn't know.

"Alice is a good woman," Fritz once said as they rode in his car. "The less she knows, the better."

"Being there for your kids," Trish says offhandedly, clearly assuming Alice wouldn't understand. She and Fritz are the only household on Hemlock Circle without kids, which makes them unofficial outsiders, even though they were the first to move here.

"Of course," Alice murmurs.

Changing the topic, Trish Wallace leans in close and says, "I don't know if I should even mention this. It's probably nothing. But someone's been roaming the neighborhood."

She goes on to tell them that some man—a stranger—was spotted walking between Hemlock Circle and Willow Court the previous afternoon. She heard it from Sally Seitz, who's lived on Willow for as long as Trish has been on Hemlock.

"He came from the woods?" Mary Ellen says.

Trish nods. "Apparently. Sally heard he emerged from the woods behind Willow before walking over here, to Hemlock. She also said he was wearing camouflage. If that's not suspicious, I don't know what is."

Or it could all be nothing, Joyce thinks. It's not illegal to walk in the forest surrounding the cul-de-sac. All of it is preserved woodlands, purchased by the county with grants from the state in the late eighties, when New Jersey realized it was going to run out of undeveloped land if something wasn't done about it. Hence the thick wall of trees behind her house. A whole mile of forest until the access road, and then another mile after that until the Hawthorne Institute.

"Maybe it was a hunter that got turned around," she suggests.

"Hunting's not allowed in these woods," Trish says.

"A hiker then."

Joyce assumes people hike there all the time. One of them stumbling into a backyard is unusual, yes, but nothing to get worked up over.

"Do you think he was casing our houses?" Alice says.

"We need a good neighborhood watch program," Deepika chimes in. "I've been saying that for years now."

"Just keep your eyes open, ladies," Trish says with finality. "This world gets crazier every day."

The Gaggle disbands after that, with the women retreating to their various homes. Standing alone on the asphalt of Hemlock Circle proper, Joyce stares at the house she shares with her husband and son. It looks so big from the street. A much larger house than she ever thought she'd live in. Built by the same developer at the same time, all the homes on Hemlock Circle look slightly similar, with brick fronts and dormer windows on the second floor and two-car garages.

The North Jersey neighborhood she grew up in was filled with tall, narrow homes crowded close together like books on a shelf. She always assumed she'd settle down in a place similar to that. Instead, she's here, in what's technically the suburbs but feels more remote than that. Like the cul-de-sac is an island unto itself. Not for the first time, Joyce wonders if she's worthy of a place like Hemlock Circle. If she deserves to be here. Right now, she feels like she doesn't.

She knows the other ladies of the Gaggle would say otherwise. That being a homemaker is just as vital as any other job. *You're the damn glue that keeps the household together,* she imagines Trish Wallace saying.

That may be true. But Joyce wants more than that. Why does she have to just be the glue? Can't she also help build the house?

Right as she's about to go inside, Joyce hears her name being uttered from the yard next door. It's Mary Ellen Barringer, standing at the end of the privacy hedge, looking as hushed and serious as always. Joyce tries to pretend she doesn't hear her and keeps marching through the front yard. She's not in the mood for Mary Ellen. It's not that she doesn't like her neighbor. She does—in small doses. But now that Ethan and Billy Barringer have become inseparable, those doses are getting bigger and bigger.

Mary Ellen says her name again, louder this time, and Joyce has no choice but to stop in the middle of the lawn, plaster on a smile, and pivot.

"Hey, Mary Ellen," she says.

"Do you still think it's a good idea to have Billy stay over tonight?" her neighbor says, as usual getting right to the point.

"I don't see why not. Ethan loves the weekly campout."

"You don't think it's dangerous? With that man walking around?"

Joyce studies Mary Ellen, wondering at first if she's making a joke about how ridiculous everyone else in the Gaggle acted about the stranger allegedly roaming the neighborhood. From their reaction, you'd think Trish Wallace had told them Bigfoot was in their midst.

"Oh, that," Joyce says. "It's silly, right?"

"It's not silly," Mary Ellen says, making it clear she isn't joking. Of course she isn't. In Joyce's experience, Mary Ellen Barringer is deadly serious about everything. "Someone is out there. Planning God knows what. We should all be worried until he's caught."

But he's done nothing wrong, Joyce thinks. *If he even exists at all. It's more likely Sally Seitz made it up just so she'd sound important.*

"I think we need more information before we start getting too worried," Joyce says. "Besides, it's not like the boys will be camping in the woods. They'll be in our backyard the whole time. It's perfectly safe."

"Do you really think so?" Mary Ellen says.

Joyce flashes the same kind of tight smile Alice gave her. "There's nothing to worry about. Everything will be just fine."

Twenty-four hours later, Joyce will regret every word. But right now, in this moment, she fully believes what she says—at least about Ethan and Billy camping in the yard. Everything else remains maddeningly worrisome. Especially when she reaches the front door of her house and notices that one neighbor remains outside. Someone who hadn't been there earlier.

Fritz Van de Veer.

Dressed in a black suit, he stands next to his open garage, simply staring at her from across the cul-de-sac. Joyce does the neighborly thing and waves—just in case someone is watching from one of the other houses.

Fritz doesn't wave back.

Instead, he lifts a finger to his lips, his message from the other side of Hemlock Circle silent but frighteningly clear.

Don't tell a soul about last night.

FIVE

My steps are slow as I climb onto the Wallaces' front porch, so preoccupied am I by what kind of friendship Fritz Van de Veer had with my father. If they had one at all beyond simply being neighborly. The fact that he singled out my mother but not my father suggests they weren't on the best terms, which I find impossible.

Everyone likes my father. He's as decent as he is nice. The kind of father I wanted to make proud, which is partly why I got into teaching, although a prep school English teacher is a far cry from being a professor at Princeton.

Maybe that doesn't impress Fritz. Or maybe it makes him insecure. Or, more likely, it's nothing at all, and Fritz only mentioned my mother because she used to sometimes chat with Alice and the other wives at various spots on the cul-de-sac. Concluding that must be the reason, I ring the bell at the Wallace house.

The door is answered by a boy of about ten with unruly brown hair and dark-framed glasses sliding down his nose. He peers up at me through the smudged lenses, looking both curious and slightly annoyed to be pulled away from whatever ten-year-olds do nowadays.

"How may I help you?" he says in a manner so precociously serious it would be amusing to everyone else but me. Instead, my general mood is unease. The fact that I'm uncomfortable around kids shocks everyone who knows I'm a teacher. "Of teenagers," I always remind them. "Not children."

I hold out the baseball and say, "Um, hi. Does this belong to you? I found it in my yard and thought it might be yours."

"It's not," the boy says without looking at the ball. His gaze stays firmly on me, curious.

"Henry? Who are you talking to?"

The woman's voice rising from inside the house makes me stand a little straighter. Although it's different from the last time I heard it, there's a warmth there that's instantly familiar.

Ashley.

"A stranger," the boy, apparently Henry, calls back.

"Tell him to please go away."

Henry looks up at me, unsmiling. "I'm supposed to tell you to please go away."

"So I've heard."

Suddenly Ashley is there, coming up swiftly behind Henry, too preoccupied with putting in an earring to notice me at first. When she does, there's a moment in which she recognizes the boy she once knew in the man I've since become and tries to mentally process if we're one and the same. When she concludes it's a match, a wide smile spreads across her face.

"Ethan? Is it really you?"

An awkward few seconds follow in which Ashley opens her arms for a hug as I attempt a handshake, forcing both of us to change tactics. The result is a partial embrace that leaves Henry looking confused.

"So you're *not* a stranger?" he says.

"This is Ethan Marsh, honey. I used to be his babysitter. A long, long time ago."

"Thirty years," I add, prompting a grimace from Ashley.

"That long? My God."

She smiles shyly, as if embarrassed by the passage of time. There's no need to be. Dressed in dark jeans and a tangerine blouse, she's as beautiful as I remember. The same Ashley, yet also different. Her hair's slightly darker now—a light brown instead of the cool blond of her teenage years—and her face and figure are thinner, more angular, like she's been slightly hardened by life. I have, too, but it's taken the opposite toll on my appearance. I'm softer, as if my body is trying to cushion life's blows.

"I haven't seen you since . . ."

The way Ashley's voice trails off tells me she remembers exactly when we last saw each other. Billy's memorial service. Because the church was packed, we didn't get a chance to sit together or even speak. But when the service had ended, I caught Ashley's eyes as she was leaving. She gave me one of the saddest smiles I've ever seen, waved, and was gone.

"What are you doing here?" she says now.

"Do you mean right now? Or in general?"

Ashley laughs. "Both, I guess. Your parents just moved, didn't they?"

I briefly bring her up to speed on my past few months. My parents' move to Florida and me staying in the house until I settle into my new job teaching English lit at a nearby private school.

"Similar story," Ashley says when I'm done. "Dad's not doing so well, and Henry and I needed a fresh start, so we came back here. I'd invite you in to catch up, but I'm showing a house in fifteen minutes, and we need more time than that. Rain check?"

"Absolutely," I say. "I actually just came by to see if this belonged to Henry."

Like her son, Ashley doesn't glance at the baseball in my hand. "I don't think he's thrown a ball in his entire life."

"I'm uncoordinated," Henry says.

Ashley shoots him a surprised look. "Who told you that?"

"Everyone."

"Even your grandpa?"

"*Especially* Grandpa."

As if summoned, Vance Wallace lumbers into view behind Ashley and Henry, barking out a half-confused, half-ornery "Who's calling me?"

"No one, Dad," Ashley says with a sigh. "We're talking to Ethan Marsh."

"Ethan?"

Mr. Wallace comes to the door, a little slower than I expected, but looking as pugnacious as I remember, even though he's now pushing eighty. A former boxer, he opened several regional gyms in the eighties that had done well for many years before he sold them all to a national chain. Now he looks like a cross between a retiree and a drill sergeant. Big arms, big chest, big belly, a tan that can't be natural. As he gets closer, though, I notice a slight vagueness in his gaze. Even though his eyes are locked on mine, it seems like he's looking past me instead of at me.

"Your parents make it to Florida in one piece?" he says.

"They did."

"Good. We're going to miss them around here." He spots the baseball I'm holding. "What's that?"

"It's a ball, Dad," Ashley says nervously, giving the impression this isn't the first time she's had to help him identify everyday objects. It makes me wonder what exactly she meant when she said Vance wasn't doing well.

"I know that," he snaps. "I wanted to know why he had it."

"Found it my backyard," I say. "I'm just trying to return it to its rightful owner. Any ideas where it could have come from?"

"You ask your neighbor?" Mr. Wallace says.

"Russ? Yeah, I just came from there."

"Not him." He gives an agitated point toward Billy's house. "Your other neighbor. The Barringer boy. I saw him outside last night."

"Dad," Ashley says, her voice low with concern. "Billy wasn't outside last night."

"He was so. I saw him running through the backyard."

"What time was this?" I say, my interest suddenly piqued.

Mr. Wallace thinks it over for a slice of a second. "A little after two."

Despite the hard heat of the day, a chill washes over me.

That was roughly the same time I watched the light above the Wallaces' garage flick on for no discernible reason.

I look to Ashley, whose expression is rightly skeptical—in addition to pinched, worried, and unbearably sad. "Billy hasn't been around in decades, Dad," she says. "You know that."

"And I know what I saw, dammit."

Ashley takes her father by the arm. "Let's get you inside. Remember what the doctor said about needing your rest." To me, she flashes an apologetic look before saying, "I really need to get going. Catch up later?"

"Sure," I say. As nice as it is to see Ashley again, all the memories and feelings of nostalgia are so overwhelming that I'm honestly relieved our reunion has been cut short. There'll be plenty of time to catch up later. Besides, all I can think about is what Mr. Wallace just said—and how it supports my own experience last night.

I wave goodbye to Henry and, baseball in hand, head home. Rather than use the sidewalk, I cut across the cul-de-sac itself, curving around the planter in the middle of the circle. At my own yard, a flashback hits when I step onto the curb. Me in the driveway last night sensing someone else outside, present yet hidden. And the only person I thought of is the same person Mr. Wallace claims to have seen in his backyard.

Is there even the slightest possibility that both of us could be right?

Inside the house, I head straight to my father's study. There, I open my laptop and bring up Billy's NamUs listing. Still missing. But just because the database says it doesn't mean it's accurate. It just means that no one—not even the authorities—knows where he is.

That leaves a chance, however small and improbable, that Billy is alive.

That he returned to Hemlock Circle last night.

That he could still be here right now.

I scan the laptop screen, seeking out the police contact listed on NamUs. Next to Ragesh Patel's name is a number to call with any information regarding the case. Without thinking, I grab my phone and dial.

Ragesh answers on the second ring with a harried "Detective Patel. What's the nature of your call?"

I pause, jarred by how different he sounds since the last time we spoke. Gone is the teenage snark I've always associated with the older kid who once lived two doors down from me. In its place is a voice that's deeper, gruffer, and extremely tired.

"Hey, Ragesh. It's Ethan Marsh. From Hemlock Circle."

Ragesh spends a moment doing the same thing I just did. Trying to match a name with a voice that's changed dramatically. He probably pictures me as a the gangly, gawky ten-year-old I used to be and not the no-longer-gangly-but-still-slightly-gawky forty-year-old I've become.

"Ethan, hi," he says. "How can I help you?"

"I'm calling about Billy Barringer."

"What about him?" Ragesh says, hesitation drawing out the question to twice its length.

"Have there been any updates?"

"Why are you interested in Billy's case?"

A baffling question. He was taken from my backyard while he slept next to me. Why *wouldn't* I still be interested?

"I just moved back into my parents' house," I say. "Since being here's brought back a lot of memories, I figured I'd see if there was any news."

Not a lie, but far from the complete truth.

"What have you heard? How much do you know?" Ragesh says, lowering his voice.

I go numb. There *is* news. Important news, from the way Ragesh sounds. And for a second I allow myself to think that what I felt last night and what Mr. Wallace saw were real. That the impossible has indeed happened.

Billy's *back*.

"I haven't heard anything," I say. "What's going on?"

"Yesterday morning, human remains were found in the area." Ragesh pauses and the whole room tilts. "A boy. Probably around ten years old. They're still checking dental records, but I'm pretty sure we found him, Ethan. We found Billy Barringer."

SIX

illy is dead.

While I'd assumed that was the case, it feels different when that assumption is confirmed. Because deep down, I never wanted to believe it. For decades I'd harbored faint hopes and what-ifs. Now that I know I was wrong all this time, it feels like I'm floating. A strange, weightless sensation that hit the moment Ragesh broke the news on the phone and that has stayed with me the rest of the day.

From the way the others look, I can tell they feel the same. Russ keeps a tight grip on the side of the sofa, as if he's afraid of sliding off. Ashley, squeezed between the two of us, simply looks nauseated.

The only person seemingly unaffected by today's news is the bearer of it: Ragesh Patel, who volunteered to stop by with more details when he got the chance. At 7:30, he finally arrived and now speaks calmly and slowly, a far cry from the teenager with the cruel voice and mocking laugh of my memories. He's changed so much that when he came to the door, I barely recognized him. He's larger now, thick in both chest and stomach, and strands of gray pepper his hair and his full beard. Back when he was the neighborhood bully, his face was angular and clean-shaven, all the better to show off his perpetual sneer.

"I can't talk long," he says. "I probably shouldn't even be talking to you at all. We haven't told the media yet because Billy's family still hasn't been notified. We reached out yesterday to the state hospital where Mrs. Barringer is being cared for. They said a doctor would tell her, but that it's highly unlikely she'll comprehend what he's saying. As for Andy Barringer, he's MIA. The last contact information anyone seems to have for him is more than ten years old. He was in a brief relationship with one of his mother's nurses back then. She's tried to reach out, but I'm not sure if she got ahold of him or not. So this is all very classified information—which doesn't leave this room."

He doesn't need to explain further. It's clear this is a favor to me, Ashley, and Russ.

"What about the rest of the neighborhood?" says Russ, who's shrunken himself so the three of us can fit on the sofa. It makes him look oddly fragile. Just a boy getting bad news. "The others should hear this, too."

"And they will," Ragesh says. "Very soon. But we don't want this news leaking to the press before we locate Billy's brother. So you can't tell anyone. Not that I can share very much. The state police's Criminal Investigations Bureau has taken charge."

I study Ragesh's face. If he's annoyed about being pushed aside, he doesn't show it.

"All I'm allowed to say is that yesterday morning, a set of human remains were found in the area. A forensic anthropologist examined them and concluded that they appear to be the remains of a male juvenile."

"Are you certain it's Billy?" I say, clinging to the idea that Ragesh could be wrong.

"Dental records now confirm it's him. Which we already knew. Based on the condition of the remains and where they were found, it was clearly Billy Barringer."

All the air leaves my lungs, taking with it that last bit of hope. For a moment, it feels like I'm drowning. I force myself to inhale before saying, "Where was he found?"

"The base of the falls at the Hawthorne Institute," Ragesh says with the abruptness of someone ripping off a Band-Aid. With good reason. The institute sits just two miles away, separated from my backyard by a stretch of woods.

And Billy had been there this whole time. So close yet so beyond rescue.

The weightless sensation grows worse, to the point where I press my feet against the floor just to make sure I haven't lifted off the sofa. To counter it, I close my eyes and picture the falls. Rushing water colored a turbulent white pouring over a granite cliff into a lake of indeterminant depth. All of it created not by nature but by man more than a hundred years ago.

Growing up, I'd heard rumors that the lake was bottomless. That, long ago, people would jump in and never resurface. That their ghosts haunted the falls, floating like strips of fog around the cascading water. Suburban legend, but apparently with enough truth to it that my parents forbade me from ever going there. To this day, I've only seen the falls once.

With Billy and the three other people in this room.

On the afternoon before Billy disappeared.

"How did Billy end up there?" I keep my eyes closed as I say it, as if that will make the question easier to ask. It doesn't. Because part of me doesn't want to know, even though I need to, if only to see if it's better or worse than my imagination. "Do you think he could have fallen in and drowned?"

As the words still hang in the air, I realize the unlikeliness of such a scenario. While it's possible that Billy returned to the falls on his own, sneaking away under the cloak of darkness, that isn't the case. The side of the tent had been sliced open, which is reason enough to think Billy didn't leave of his own accord. What seals the deal for me, though, are his sneakers. They were still in the tent when I woke up the next morning. If Billy intended to walk two miles through a heavily wooded area, he certainly would have put on his shoes.

"That's unlikely," Ragesh says. "Both the forensic anthropologist and investigators at the scene found evidence that suggests foul play."

A pall settles over the room, during which I hear nothing but the dull hum of the central air unit and a blue jay screeching from the elm tree in the front yard.

Foul play.

"I can't share any details, but it's believed he was killed first and that his body was weighed down and tossed from the top of the falls into the lake below."

Beside me, Ashley claps a hand over her mouth. "I think I'm going to be sick."

She rushes to the powder room in the hallway off the kitchen, the memory of visits thirty years ago showing her the way. I follow Ashley out of the room and hover in the hallway, far enough to give her some privacy but unfortunately close enough to hear her retching behind the closed door.

When she emerges a few minutes later, Ashley spots me and freezes. Then her face crumples and she reaches for me, pulling me into a hug both desperate and sad. Weeping at my shoulder, she says, "Oh, Ethan. All this time, I liked thinking he was still alive. I knew it wasn't true, but it was nice having that thought to cling to."

I wrap my arms around her, unable to keep the memories at bay. Of the two of us a week after Billy had gone missing. By then, every parent in town was terrified to let their children out of sight for even a second. I was allowed to go outside and play, but only in the front yard, where I'd be in view of others in the neighborhood.

That's where I was sitting that afternoon, not playing. Not by a long shot. Instead, I smoothed my hand over the grass, plucked a few strands, and watched them catch the breeze and fly away. Each time a blade lifted from my fingertips, I thought of Billy, who had in essence done the same thing.

Flown away.

Vanished.

Even though no adult—not the police, not even my parents—had told me so, I also knew the likelihood was high that Billy was dead. A horrible thing for a ten-year-old boy to deal with.

Yet that's what I was thinking about when a brown Camry, shining like a polished penny in the light of the mid-afternoon sun, pulled up to the curb. I stood and instantly started backing toward the house. Despite staying mum about Billy's probable fate, the adults around me had plenty to say about stranger danger. I was on the verge of running when the passenger-side window lowered, revealing Ashley behind the wheel.

"You got a new car," I said, because it was true. Her parents' other car had been a boatlike blue Chevy Malibu.

"Yeah," Ashley said. "Now, are you going to stare at it all day or are you going to get in?"

By then my mother was outside the house and stalking toward the car. She looked so strange in that moment. Her eyes gleamed with terror, yet her mouth was twisted into an angry snarl, her teeth literally bared. It made her seem both vulnerable and vicious. It was, I assumed, what mother bears looked like when someone got between them and their cubs.

"Ethan, get away from that car!" she yelled as she thrust her arm in front of me, as if that alone could shield me from the evil she thought rested inside that idling Camry.

"Hi, Mrs. Marsh," Ashley said through the open window.

My mother practically melted with relief. The terror left her eyes and her face went slack. Only the arm thrown across my chest remained, and even that soon dropped to her side.

"I thought you were a stranger," my mother said with relief.

"I'm just saying hi to Ethan." Ashley paused, mulling something over. "I could take him to get some ice cream. Give you some alone time."

With anyone else, I'm certain my mother would have said no—or at least considered it for more than five seconds. But since it was Ashley, her reply was instantaneous.

"Thank you," my mother said. "That would be wonderful."

I climbed inside, making sure to fasten my seat belt. Worry fluttered in my stomach. It was, to my recollection, the first time I'd ever been in a car without an adult behind the wheel. A scary thought, but also exciting.

"Can you drive?"

"Obviously," Ashley said as she eased the car away from the curb. "My dad taught me this spring."

"I meant legally."

This time Ashley, who I knew to still be fifteen, said nothing.

"Where are we going?" I asked once she'd steered us out of Hemlock Circle.

"*Not* for ice cream." Ashley set her jaw and stared straight ahead through the windshield. "I wanted to talk to you. About Billy."

I shifted in the passenger seat, annoyed and sad and guilty. I'd wanted to forget about Billy. Just for a little bit. Which made me feel even more guilty—and more annoyed and sad that I couldn't escape that guilt.

"What have the adults been telling you?" Ashley said.

"That he was taken."

I turned to look out the window, watching the neighboring homes and lawns. The way they slipped by and vanished from view made me think about Billy. I knew I'd see those houses and yards again when Ashley turned around and brought me home. But Billy? I knew in my gut that I'd never see him again. A realization so awful that I began to bawl right there in the car.

"I think he's dead," I said with a sorrowful sniff.

"Who told you that?"

"No one. I just know that he is."

Ashley slammed on the brakes, bringing the Camry to a rocking stop in the middle of the road. "Look at me," she said.

I didn't. I couldn't. Not with tears streaming down my face and snot dripping from my nose. I wanted Ashley to think I was older, tougher, wise beyond my years. Instead, I looked like the weak crybaby I truly knew myself to be.

"Ethan," she said, softer this time. "Look at me."

I did, resisting the urge to flinch when Ashley returned my gaze. The pity in her eyes made me feel so utterly pathetic. But then she reached over and pulled me to her.

"Don't think that," she said. "You hear me? Don't ever give up hope, Ethan. If you keep thinking Billy is alive and safe, then that's what he is. Even if it's just in your mind. Even if you never find out what happened to him."

Now here we are, repeating that moment, only with our roles reversed and both of us faced with the stark reality that any hope we still had is now gone. Ashley pulls out of my grip, breaking the spell of memory. She steps away from me, swiping at the mascara-stained tears running down her face. "Fuck, I'm a mess right now."

"Everyone is," I say.

"Not you. You're handling this so well."

If only she knew about The Dream. And the insomnia. And the guilt and the grief and the long line of therapists stretching back to my early teens who, despite their valiant efforts, couldn't help me one damn bit.

"Looks can be deceiving."

"I guess we should go back in there," Ashley says, looping an arm through mine. "Getting bad news is always easier with a buddy."

We return to the living room, squeezing onto the sofa next to Russ again as he says, "What kind of evidence did they find?"

Ragesh clears his throat. "I'm not at liberty to say."

"*How* was he found?" I say as I shift on the sofa. Something about this doesn't feel right. Billy had been missing for thirty years, with no clue as to where he was or what had happened to him. Then he was suddenly found two miles from here—not long before I thought I'd sensed his presence outside.

"By two scientists with the state Department of Environmental Protection," Ragesh says. "They were taking water and soil samples. Routine stuff they do all the time. In one of the samples, they found a bone fragment. That prompted them to dredge the lake. That's when they found Billy."

"But didn't they search that area decades ago?"

Ragesh shakes his head. "It's my understanding that they didn't."

"Because of the institute?" Ashley says, referring to the Hawthorne Institute, which sits on the same land as the falls and the lake. A hundred acres total. All of it once the property of Ezra Hawthorne, the last remaining member of a family whose old money stretched back to the days of the *Mayflower*.

While a stone's throw from Princeton University, the Hawthorne Institute was separate from those hallowed halls of higher learning. It was quiet, unassuming, and private. Exceedingly so. For decades, it flew under the radar because no one quite knew what it was, what they did there, or why they needed so much land.

Even though I've only been there once, I vividly remember how strange the place seemed. A stone mansion surrounded by several barns and other outbuildings. Surrounding that was the lake and the falls, formal gardens, and thick clusters of trees, all of it by design. An idealized version of nature that couldn't happen without planning. Like a Central Park that hadn't seen a tourist for decades.

"More like because Ezra Hawthorne was so rich they looked the other way," Russ says.

Ragesh presses his lips together until they form a flat line. "I don't know why it wasn't searched back then. But, clearly, it's being searched now."

"Aren't the institute grounds private property?" I say.

"Yes and no," Ragesh says as he runs a hand through his formidable beard. "It's government land now. Green space. The institute closed in the late nineties when Mr. Hawthorne died. He donated the land to the county, with the stipulation that it remained untouched. No tearing down buildings or turning it into a public park or anything like that. So it's technically public land that's still very much off-limits. The only time people are allowed there is when they occasionally rent the mansion out for private parties and weddings."

"What about back then?" Russ says. "What did they do there?"

He'd asked a similar question thirty years ago, as we stood at the edge of the falls. Only Billy had an answer, and the memory plants a seed of unease in my already-roiling stomach.

Ragesh shrugs. "I don't know. Whatever it was, the institute kept it secret. Very few people had access."

Yet we were there.

All four of us.

It had been Billy's idea, and the rest of us went along with it because we had nothing better to do. We were just a group of kids in the thick of summer, listless in our suburban world of nice houses and manicured lawns. It was natural to want to push against the boundaries our parents had drawn for us.

We ended up getting more than we bargained for. Billy most of all. Possibly more than I ever could have imagined.

"Do you think this has something to do with that day?" I say, because one of us needs to. "We were there. And Billy ended up there again—this time dead—less than twenty-four hours later. That can't be a coincidence."

Ragesh, who'd been standing this whole time, kneels until he's eye level with those of us on the couch. It's a disarming gesture, which is surely the point. Something taught at the police academy to put people at ease.

"I understand why you'd jump to that conclusion," he says, although it's not a jump at all. It's a half step at best, taking me from one fact—our presence at the falls—to another: Billy's body was found there. "But there seems to be no correlation between what happened that afternoon and Billy's abduction."

"Other than you, does anyone else investigating this thing even know we were there that day?" I say, jarred by the realization that none of us talked with each other about what happened that day after Billy was taken. "I mean, all those years ago, did anyone tell the police about that afternoon?"

"I didn't," Ashley says. "I think I mentioned we were all in the woods, but not specifically where."

"Same," Russ says.

And it was the same with me. Despite being interviewed by so many cops, detectives, and agents that they became a blur of blue and khaki, I never mentioned we'd been at the falls or on the grounds of the Hawthorne Institute. I'd like to think it's because I was scared of getting myself and others in trouble, but I know the real reason is because I felt guilty. Just like I'm sure the others did. About what happened while we were there. About how we treated Billy. And while it feels inexcusable in hindsight, back then I didn't think what happened that day had anything to do with Billy's disappearance.

That's no longer the case.

"So the police back then didn't know we were there," I say. "Or that Billy was there. Do they know now?"

We all look to Ragesh, the actual cop in the room, who nods and says, "I mentioned it today."

"And everyone still thinks it's unrelated?" I say.

"Our gut instinct—*my* gut instinct—is that there's no reason to think Billy's death is connected to anyone associated with the institute."

Ragesh stands, done with trying to put us at ease when I need it now more than ever. The pernicious floating sensation resumes. Caught off balance, I lurch to the side, bumping shoulders with Ashley. She reaches for my hand and gives it a reassuring squeeze.

"Why not?" I say.

"Because technically we didn't do anything wrong that day," Ragesh says. "Yes, we were somewhere we shouldn't have been. But we were just a bunch of kids messing around. And we didn't see anything forbidden or suspicious."

"But don't you think it's the least bit strange that's the place where Billy ended up?"

"It *is* strange," Ragesh concedes, "if you don't stop to consider that a lake in a remote area where few people have access is the most convenient place in a ten-mile radius to dump a body."

Next to me, Ashley blanches. "Jesus, Ragesh. You don't need to be so blunt about it."

"Murder *is* blunt." Ragesh crosses his arms and stares her down. "Billy was taken from the tent, killed, and his body was dumped in a lake. That's the brutal truth."

"Brutal" is the perfect word to describe it. Billy was just a boy. And what happened to him is so brutal that, like Ashley earlier, I think I'm about to be sick. I take a deep breath and swallow hard, determined to keep it together at least until everyone else leaves.

"Are there any suspects?" Ashley says.

"None that I'm allowed to tell you about," Ragesh says, inadvertently answering her question. Yes, there are indeed suspects.

Russ leans forward, elbows on his knees. "What about the stranger who'd been seen in the neighborhood?"

"That was all conjecture. No one knows if there was really someone roaming the woods."

"But it still could have been him, right?"

"We're looking into every possibility," Ragesh says.

"You mean the state police?" Ashley says.

"Correct. Detective Cassandra Palmer is in charge of the investigation. Currently, she's overseeing the search of the institute grounds, but I'm sure all of you will be hearing from her soon."

My wooziness grows at the prospect of yet more questioning. Other than the fact that we were at the institute—which Ragesh insists isn't important—there's nothing I can tell the authorities now that I couldn't thirty years ago.

Nothing I can remember, that is.

I take another deep breath and lean back on the sofa. Maybe because she senses my weariness—or because she's feeling the same way—Ashley asks Ragesh, "Is there anything else?"

"That's about it."

About.

Meaning there *is* something else, and Ragesh is either unable to tell us what it is or unwilling to. I suspect it's the former, because he adds, "I'm sorry. I know all this is a lot to take in, especially with no real resolution."

That fact is one of the many things I'm grappling with right now. For decades, all I wanted was an indication of what had happened to Billy. Now that I have an answer, it feels both horrible and inadequate.

The knowledge of Billy's death only begets an even bigger mystery: Who did this to him? Why? For what purpose? Without those answers, all that's left is a sense of mournful disappointment. After thirty years, there should be more.

More information.

More justice.

More fucking closure.

Instead, all we can do is carry on with our day, which for Ashley and Russ means returning to their families. I walk them both to the door.

"Thanks for telling us what you could," Russ tells Ragesh on his way out. "We appreciate it."

At the door, Ashley gives me a quick squeeze and a peck on the cheek. "It's nice to have you back, Ethan. Don't be a stranger."

She leaves, and it's just me and Ragesh, who remains in the living room, his arms crossed.

"What's going on, Ethan?"

"What do you mean?"

"You damn well know what I mean," he says. "You called me asking about Billy barely twenty-four hours after his body was found. That's a coincidence I think is worth discussing."

I plop back onto the sofa, stunned by yet another wallop of surprise. I think about how suspicious he sounded on the phone earlier. *What have you heard? How much do you know?*

"You think I *knew* Billy had been found when I called you earlier?"

"I'm not saying that," Ragesh replies, though it feels like that's exactly what he's saying. "But I do find the timing of your call very interesting. Something had to have prompted it."

"Other than being back in the house where it all happened? That's reason enough, don't you think?"

"You've been back a week. I checked." Ragesh wags his finger at me, a gesture that's both absurd and taunting. In that moment, the stoic detective he's become flickers enough to reveal a glimmer of the bully he'd once been. "So I suspect something else made you think to call about Billy's case."

He's right, of course. But to tell him that would mean having to explain how, for the briefest of moments, I'd thought Billy was outside circling the cul-de-sac in the middle of the night. Faced with the choice of appearing suspicious or merely mentally disturbed, I pick the latter.

"I thought I sensed him," I say slowly, fearful Ragesh the bully will show himself again. "His presence. In my yard."

I tell him everything. About The Dream, the garage lights, the sudden, strange sense that Billy was outside with me. That last part makes me weak with shame. That I really thought, even for the briefest of moments, that Billy was still alive, that he was here, that he was, I don't know, waiting for me.

Ragesh lifts a brow. I can't tell what it signifies. Amusement? Condescension? Concern?

"And in the morning," I continue, "this was in my yard."

I slip into the kitchen, grab the baseball, and give it to Ragesh. He turns it over in his hands and says, "It's just a ball."

"The same kind of ball Billy threw into my yard almost every day that summer before he—" I almost say *vanished*, but catch myself, replacing it with something more accurate. "Died."

Yet even that's not quite right. Billy didn't just die. He was murdered. Something I can't yet bring myself to utter. Just thinking it causes another sickly twist in my stomach.

"Well, Billy didn't put it there," Ragesh says as he hands the ball back to me.

"I know that. Now. But I didn't last night. Or this morning. *That's* why I called you."

Ragesh looks like he believes me. Or maybe it's all an act. Another thing he learned during his journey from teenage asshole to local cop. Make people think you're on their side, keep them talking, wait until they trip up.

"Do you think someone is messing with you?" he says.

"It's possible. But I don't know why. Or who would even know to do it."

No one else knew about the meaning behind the baseball. Just me and Billy, both of us pinkie swearing to keep it a secret.

"Maybe to remind you," Ragesh says.

"I don't need reminding. I remember enough about what happened."

"But not everything."

The smirk that follows makes it clear Ragesh knows all about the gaps in my memories from that night. Because of course he does. He's probably read every interview and report about the case.

But the smirk is also a reminder that Ragesh and I are not friends. We never were. Far from it, in fact. Thirty years ago, the rest of us boys on Hemlock Circle went out of our way to avoid him. Unlike a lot of bullies, Ragesh never physically hurt us. He specialized in emotional torment. Insults. Name-calling. Learning the things we were most self-conscious about and bringing them up constantly. Like Billy's eccentricities and Russ's scrawniness. Back then, Ragesh could never peg my individual weakness. Now he knows.

"I remember what really happened that day," I say.

"I already told you—"

"That your gut tells you it's unrelated to Billy's murder. Yeah, I know. And I think you're wrong. And I think you know why."

Like a spent candle, Ragesh's smirk flickers and goes out.

"Listen, what went down that afternoon was unfortunate," he says. "I'm not going to deny that. And I regret literally all of it. But it likely had nothing to do with what happened to Billy later that night."

"How can you be so certain?"

"Because if it did, Billy never would have come home that afternoon," Ragesh says. "But he did. He made it home later that day, completely unharmed and none the worse for wear. Hell, you were with him that night. Did he seem upset about it?"

Memories appear in my mind like Polaroid pictures coming into focus. The tension in the tent that night. The fight we'd had once it reached a breaking point. My immediate apology and Billy's attempt at a smile that never quite took spark.

Hakuna matata, dude.

"No," I say, because it's easier than trying to explain all that transpired between the two of us that night. "He seemed fine."

"See?" Ragesh says, his I-told-you-so glare softening into something that resembles pity. "I know this is harder on you than on the rest of us, Ethan. I know that for you it's . . . complicated. But leave the investigation to the cops. Right now, you should just focus on mourning your friend."

I stay on the couch after Ragesh leaves, held in place not by the seasick swaying of the living room, though that still remains, but by thoughts of that final night in the tent with Billy. I hadn't lied to Ragesh. Not entirely. Billy really did seem fine with the behavior of the others at the institute that day. Russ and Ashley and Ragesh. It was only me he had issues with.

Because I was his best friend.

And I had run away like the others.

Leaving Billy alone to fend for himself.

I can still hear the echo of his voice as I fled with the others. How desperate he sounded. How lonely and sad and scared.

Ethan, don't leave me! Please don't leave me!

SEVEN

Once darkness has settled over Hemlock Circle like a funeral shroud, I reach for my phone. Even though I'm not supposed to, I feel the need to tell Claudia about Billy. More than anyone, she understands how much what happened to him has affected me.

The phone rings five times before going to voicemail. Rather than making me miss her, the sound of her voice telling me to leave a message at the tone is soothing. It feels like old times.

"Hey, it's me," I say, knowing there's no need to clarify. "Um, I just got some news about Billy."

I tell her about Billy's remains being found and how he's been dead this entire time and why the police think it's murder. I get so lost in the telling that I drone on for too long, not stopping until her phone decides I've talked enough and cuts me off with an abrupt beep.

I'm about to call back and continue, but decide against it and Face-Time my parents instead. A simple phone call would suffice, but lately my mother prefers video calls, even though she has yet to master the nuances of them. When she answers, she holds the phone at a too-close angle that cuts off both her chin and the bulk of her forehead.

"Hey, honey," she says. "Is something wrong with the house?"

The question, delivered with both urgency and resignation, tells me two things—that I get my anxiety from her and that she doesn't think too highly of my adulting skills. Both of which I have neither the time nor the headspace to think about right now.

"No," I say. "I just—"

The image on my phone shakes when my father enters the room wearing a turquoise polo and a white visor. I wonder if, as a former professor of sociology, he realizes it's taken him only a week to turn into the clichéd Florida retiree.

"Hey, sport," he says. "How's it going?"

"You look tired," my mother adds. "Are you sure nothing's wrong?"

I don't know what to say because I'm not sure why I called. I can't tell them about Billy, like I did with Claudia. My parents have connections here, and they'll surely spread the word if they find out. It's best to stay quiet for now.

"I just wanted to see how you were settling in," I say. "People around here have been asking."

"Great," my father says. "Everything's unpacked."

My mother nods proudly. "And we met some of the neighbors."

She jostles the phone, giving me a glimpse of the giant Monet print that had once hung in the living room. Seeing it now grace the walls of a different location is a surreal reminder of how much things have changed recently. Too much. I suddenly long to reach into the phone, yank my parents through the screen, and have them hold me the way they did when I was ten and Billy first vanished.

The feeling pulls me to the edge of confessing the forbidden. *They found Billy.*

I even get the first word out.

"They—"

The sound of the doorbell prevents me from saying the rest. Perfect timing.

"Someone's at the door," I say. "But things are great here. That's why I called. To say you don't need to worry about me."

I end the call and answer the door, finding Russ on the front steps carrying a bottle of bourbon. "We're getting trashed," he announces.

Having no reason to disagree, I invite him inside. We sit at the kitchen island, the place where I used to eat lunch, scarfing down grilled cheese sandwiches or burning the roof of my mouth on Chef Boyardee ravioli fresh out of the microwave. Now I set out a pair of rocks glasses and let Russ dole out two generous pours. Because the news about Billy left me with zero appetite, I also grab some Chex Mix so I'm not drinking on an empty stomach.

"Here ya go," Russ says as he slides a glass toward me, the bourbon inside sloshing to the rim. He lifts his in a toast. "To Billy."

"To Billy," I repeat, clinking my glass against his.

Then we both drink, Russ downing half his glass in a single gulp. I take only a sip, relishing the soothing warmth it brings to my chest.

"Did you break the rules and tell anyone yet?" Russ says.

"No," I lie, thinking it best to leave out my call to Claudia.

"Me, neither. I wanted to at least tell my mom, but figured it's best to stay quiet for now. She's not a gossip, but I think she still chats with Alice Van de Veer and Deepika Patel a lot." Russ pauses to take another gulp of bourbon. "Do you really think this has something to do with what happened that day?"

"Maybe," I say, which is the best answer I can give. "If it doesn't, then it's an awfully big coincidence."

Russ grabs a handful of Chex Mix but makes no move to eat it. "So you think, what? That Billy saw something at the Hawthorne Institute he shouldn't have seen, so someone there took him from your tent, killed him, and hid the body?"

"I know it sounds paranoid."

"Extremely," Russ adds before finally tossing back the Chex Mix.

"But it's at least a possible reason for who took Billy."

The lack of a suspect is one of the many things that kept the case burning in public memory. I've spent decades trying to think of who could have done it, always coming up empty. But now knowing *where* Billy was taken puts *when* he was taken in a scary, new light.

"Even if the police don't think it is?" Russ takes another gulp of bourbon and swallows hard. "Ragesh was right, you know. We didn't see anything strange that day."

"*We* didn't see anything," I say. "But maybe Billy did after we left. No one knows what went on at that institute, Russ. Don't you think that's odd? That we live two miles from that place but have no clue what they really did there?"

Russ says nothing for a good long while after that. Not until his glass is empty. As he pours himself another round, he says, "Just be careful with that kind of thinking. I mean, I understand why you'd connect that place to what happened to Billy. But if the police don't think they're related, maybe that's the truth."

I crunch some Chex Mix and wash it down with bourbon. "Then who do you think did it? And why?"

"I still think it was the stranger in the woods. Someone who took Billy, killed him, then went far, far away from here."

"Doesn't that seem a little too simple?" I say.

"It's better than your conspiracy theory." Russ pauses, a boozy flush to his cheeks that suggests this isn't his second bourbon of the night. "If Billy hadn't—"

He stops himself, prompting me to say, "Disappeared."

I cringe at the euphemism for what we now know to be true. Billy was murdered. To call it a mere disappearance doesn't come close to the horribleness of the situation.

"Right," Russ says. "If that hadn't happened, do you think we'd be friends now?"

"Of course," I say, even though it's not entirely the truth. Before

Billy was gone, our interactions were forced at best. I didn't actively dislike Russ, but he wasn't exactly fun to be around, either. Young Russ was easy to frustrate and quick to anger. At school, his playground temper tantrums had earned him the unflattering nickname Wuss.

Then again, Russ has chilled considerably since then. Far more than myself. And I'd like to think that whether or not a tragedy had befallen Billy Barringer, he and I would have found each other anyhow.

"I agree," he says. "What about Billy? If things were different, would the two of you have stayed friends?"

I take a drink and sigh. "I doubt it."

Even though it breaks my heart to say it, I know it's the truth. Billy and I were too different to last beyond a few more years. It would have been one of those fleeting friendships born of loneliness and close proximity, not of a shared bond or common interests. I think about our last waking moments in that tent, how at the time it felt like we'd already turned a corner in our friendship, each of us heading in separate directions. Even more, I remember how we both tried to pretend it wasn't happening.

Hakuna matata, dude.

"That doesn't mean I don't miss him," I add. "Don't you?"

"Honestly? I barely remember him."

I take a quick glance at Russ's drink. He's downed half of it in the span of a minute. Still, the brusqueness of his answer is more than just the alcohol talking. A fact Russ confirms by adding, "I'm sorry if that sounds cruel. But it's true. It was so long ago. Decades."

"But he was your friend," I say.

"He was *your* friend. I was just allowed to tag along sometimes."

I nod, guilty as charged. "I'm sorry about that. We should have included you more."

"I'm not trying to make you feel bad, man," Russ says. "I'm just pointing out that you have more memories of Billy than I do. When I think about him, all I really remember is what happened to him. Not that I spend much time thinking about it at all. Before today, it had been a long time since Billy Barringer crossed my mind."

Over the years, there have been days, even weeks, in which, like Russ, I didn't think about Billy. But then I'd have The Dream, remember what happened, and feel guilty all over again. I see it as the least I can do. Isn't it my duty to remember? Don't I owe Billy that much? Doesn't Russ?

"I get why you're not as impacted by what happened as I am," I say. "But I assumed you at least thought about him from time to time."

"Do you ever think about Johnny?"

Russ peers at me over the rim of his glass, clearly drunk but his question coming out stone-cold sober. It makes me realize this isn't about Billy at all. It's about Johnny Chen and what happened to him and how today's news is dredging up all the bad memories Russ has about his brother.

"Sometimes," I say, hedging, for the truth is I don't think of Johnny Chen much at all. On the rare occasions I do, it's in an abstract way, with me thinking less about Johnny than how his death affected Russ.

"Name one thing you remember about him," Russ says.

I don't even try because I know I can't, proving his point and making me feel like an awful person. Rightly so. Me expecting Russ to mourn Billy as much as his brother is just pure hypocrisy.

"Shit, Russ, I'm sorry."

"It's okay," Russ says, swatting at the air like there's a fly in the room. "I don't expect you to miss Johnny as much as I do. Just don't expect me to do the same with Billy. I'm sad about what happened to him. I really am. But that sadness has its limits. Something you need to remember, my friend."

Although he's drunk and slightly slurring his words, Russ's message is clear. He'll mourn Billy to a point. As much as any neighbor would. But he won't let it consume his life. Just like I shouldn't.

"I'll try," I say.

"Good." He downs the rest of his drink and stands, swaying in the middle of the kitchen. "Because let's face it, buddy. We've both had our share of loss and we've both mourned too much."

After his brother died, Russ thought the house would feel bigger. There was, after all, one fewer person inside, ceding more space to the others. Instead, the whole place seemed to shrink. The ceilings felt lower, the walls closer together. Russ found himself ducking when he passed through doorways, even though there was no need.

It took him awhile to realize what had happened. Johnny's presence was so huge in their lives that the house had expanded to accommodate it. Now that he is gone, it has reverted back to its intended form—a house of small people.

And Russ is the smallest of them all.

The only part of the house that still feels normal-sized is Johnny's old bedroom, which Russ assumes is because his brother's presence can still be felt there. Nothing about the room has changed in the year since his death. The same posters hang on the walls and the same academic trophies crowd the dresser. First place in the science fair six years running. Math bowl champ. Spelling bee champ. Quiz bowl champ.

Russ eyes them all as he quietly closes the door behind him and tiptoes across the room to the window overlooking the backyard. He's not supposed to be in here. His mother's orders. Ever since Johnny died, she's treated his bedroom like a shrine, and if Russ is caught up here, the punishment will surely be swift. It always is. Double the chores tomorrow. Maybe no TV for the night. Certainly no playing his SEGA.

But right now, Russ's mother is working in the flower bed that's become her pride and joy. He sees her from the window, elbow-deep in dirt, a floppy sun hat on her head. Now that she's returned from gossiping with the other wives of Hemlock Circle, she'll be gardening for the rest of the morning, giving him plenty of time to sit in his brother's room and inhabit the space the same way he imagines Johnny did when he was alive.

Russ first snuck into his brother's room a few days after Johnny's funeral, when his father had returned to work and his mother was still too grief-stricken to pay him much mind. Left to his own devices, Russ slipped inside, closed the door, and lay down on the bed, pressing his weight into the mattress and bringing the pillow to his face, searching for a hint of Johnny's scent. When Russ detected it—a small whiff of sweat and Calvin Klein cologne—it felt like his heart had been cracked wide open.

A year later, the heartbreak is less acute. A small ache instead of full-blown pain. Russ feels twinges of sadness as he roots through his brother's belongings. Clothes and books and CDs that had been tossed into dresser drawers, discarded in the closet, kicked under the bed. He's searching not for reminders of Johnny but for things that might show him how to take his place.

If he can do that—fill the Johnny-shaped hole in their lives—then maybe the house will start to feel its normal size again and the people inside it will return to their old selves.

Russ shoots another envious glance at the scholastic trophies Johnny accrued over the years, knowing he'll never come close to winning something similar. He's an average student, whereas his brother was a genius. But Russ knows he can emulate Johnny in other ways. His tallness. His confidence. His presence in the neighborhood. Everyone on Hemlock Circle knew and liked Johnny, coming out to say hello when they saw him roaming the cul-de-sac with Ragesh Patel, his best friend and next-door neighbor. Now that's something Russ can achieve. Not with Ragesh, who's older and, honestly, got meaner after Johnny died. But it might be possible with Ethan Marsh, their neighbor on the other side, although Russ has had little luck in the past. Although they've grown up next door to each other, Ethan seems indifferent at best, annoyed at worst.

"Why doesn't Ethan like me?" he once said to his mother. A mistake, it turns out, because her response was brutal in its honesty.

"He does like you," she said, adding after a pause, "But he'd like you more if you didn't get so angry all the time."

Russ hated that his mother made a good point, and reacted accordingly by proving her right. "I don't get angry!" he shouted before storming upstairs to his room and slamming the door behind him.

Thinking about it now fills him with shame and, yes, anger. Although Johnny was the smart one in the family, Russ isn't stupid. He knows what the other kids say about him behind his back. How quick he is to anger. How easy it is to get him upset. Wuss, they call him. Now *that's* stupid. "Russ" and "wuss" don't even rhyme.

What those kids don't understand is that Russ can't help it. There are always so many thoughts rolling through his brain that he gets overwhelmed and melts down. He imagines them as marbles, cracking into each other and careening off the inside of his skull. A near-constant stream of motion and color and distractions.

He knows it's a problem because his parents told him so. "Too many thoughts," his mother said, tapping her head. "Bad to have so many."

Russ cringes as he remembers that moment, just like he cringed when it happened. He wonders, not for the first time, if his mother can hear herself. If she knows just how stupid she sounds, with her clipped English and accent so pronounced that other kids at school make fun of it when they think he isn't around. One time, it made him so angry that he punched the wall in the boys' bathroom until his knuckles split open. When his mother picked him up from school, saw his bandaged hand, and demanded to know what happened, he lashed out at her rather than admit other kids were mocking her.

"Why can't you just sound normal?" he yelled.

"I do sound normal," his mother insisted.

But he also knows it's easier to blame his mother than to admit the truth: He does have mood swings and anger issues. He doesn't like that he gets so mad so often. He tries not to let it happen. But with all those thought marbles swirling through his head, there are bound to be violent collisions.

The only solution he can think of is to continue to try to be more like his brother. The good parts. The Johnny who never got angry. The Johnny who was kind and confident and smart. As for the other aspects of his brother's personality—addict, secret keeper, control freak spinning out of control—well, Russ doesn't want to think about those. He certainly doesn't plan on emulating them.

Having completed his search under Johnny's bed and finding nothing that would teach him how to be more like his brother, Russ takes a peek between the mattress and the box spring. He doesn't expect to find anything. He only looks because Petey Bradbury at school once said it's where his brother keeps girlie magazines.

Running his hand under the mattress, Russ is surprised to discover there is something there. Magazines, yes, but not the kind he was expecting. These have names like *Muscle & Fitness* and *Men's Health*, and on the covers are men with gleaming pecs and sculpted torsos. Most of them are white. None are Chinese. But all of them are huge.

After a quick glance outside to make sure his mother is still in the garden, Russ smuggles the magazines from Johnny's room into his own. Although he's convinced their existence says something about his brother's life, he's unable to understand what that something is. Maybe Johnny, tired of being admired only for his smarts, had wanted to become more athletic. And maybe that's something Russ should aspire to as well.

Safe in his room, he flips through the magazines, spotting not just pictures but articles on proper diet, protein intake, the correct way to do a squat, the amount of weight required to make biceps bulge. Overwhelmed yet intrigued, Russ starts with the article that seems to be the most basic—a tutorial on the best way to do a push-up.

With the magazine spread open on the floor in front of him so he can follow along, Russ gets into position. Arms stiff. Legs straight. Back and torso rigid. He lowers himself to the floor, pauses, then pushes upward, arms straining.

One.

Five.

Ten.

When he's done, Russ feels exhausted but also oddly satisfied. The burning ache in his arms fills him with a sense of accomplishment he rarely experiences. Which is why he does another set, even though he's out of breath and his arms feel like wet noodles.

One.

Five.

Ten.

Russ collapses on the floor, the magazine sticking to his sweat-slicked cheek. He's breathing even harder now and mildly worried his arms might fall off from strain. Yet he feels good. No, he feels better than that. He feels strong. He feels confident.

Maybe this is the feeling Johnny was looking for when he took the pills that ultimately killed him. And maybe it's what Russ has been seeking all this time. Not a way to replace Johnny, but a means by which he can become his own person.

Russ peels the magazine off his face and starts another set.

One.

He knows what he'll do when he's done.

Five.

He'll go outside, ask Ethan to play, will him into becoming his friend.

Ten.

Then his anger will fade, he'll continue to get bigger, his mother will start to see him as more than just an inferior version of the son she lost.

And everything—his house, his life, his family—will feel normal again.

EIGHT

*S*criiiiiiitch.

I knew The Dream was coming.

Considering the events of the day, how could it not?

I'd prepared for it by keeping the TV on and not switching off the bedside lamp, all so that I'd know immediately where I was when The Dream startled me awake. What I didn't expect was how The Dream would linger just a beat longer than normal. Long enough for me to not just sense the person lurking on the other side of the tent but *hear* them as well.

The soft rustle of clothing.

Shifting feet on the grass.

Slow, labored exhalations.

Then I wake up and, despite my preparation, experience a moment of disorienting panic when my eyes snap open and the ominous sound of The Dream fades.

I sit up and reach for the notebook. When I find a blank page, I scribble something my very first therapist told me. On a night like this, I need the reminder.

The Dream is just a manifestation of guilt and grief. It is not real. It cannot hurt me.

That may be true, but it certainly lingers long after I turn off the TV and bedside lamp. Lying in the darkness, I fear that closing my eyes will send me straight back into The Dream, where it will reset and begin anew. So I keep them wide open as the hour grows later and later.

By the time two a.m. has come and gone, I slide out of bed and go to the window. A light is on over the garage of the house on the other side of the cul-de-sac.

The Wallace house.

Just like last night, I strain to see what set it off. Also like last night, there appears to be nothing there. The Wallaces' driveway is empty. Staring at that illuminated patch of asphalt, all I can think of is Vance Wallace and what he said earlier.

I saw him outside last night.

But something triggered that garage light before scurrying away. I know because the light soon goes out, leaving Hemlock Circle dark once again.

Until the light over the Patels' garage starts to glow.

I grip the windowsill when it flicks on, knowing deep down that it's happening again. A creeping, unseen something is circling the cul-de-sac, this time in reverse. Unlike last night, I don't wait for the light to click off at the Patels' and come back on at Russ's house a few seconds later. Instead, I pull on a pair of joggers, go downstairs, and grab my phone. In seconds, I'm out the front door. By then, the light over the Chens' garage is just clicking on.

I halt in the front lawn, watching it glow just above the hedge separating our properties. The someone—or something—that set it off is likely on the other side of that hedge this very second, waiting to cross into my yard.

I reach into my pocket for the phone, wondering if I should call the police. They'll want to know there's a potential prowler in the same neighborhood where Billy Barringer was abducted. Then again, whoever it is might be gone by the time the cops arrive. In fact, they might have already left. The light above Russ's garage flicks off, indicating there's no one near his driveway. It's possible whoever was there became aware of my presence and fled.

Or they could simply be waiting for me to go inside.

Or, worse, waiting for me to come closer to the hedge.

I shove my phone back into my pocket and clench my fists, pretending I know how to swing a punch when the truth is I've never hit anyone, ever.

I start moving again, taking a hesitant step across the lawn.

Then another.

Waiting for someone to ease through the hedge.

Praying that it doesn't happen.

Fearing that it will.

I continue across the lawn like that.

Step, wait, step, pray, step, fear.

Deep inside the hedge, something moves. I hear it rustling, the sound drawing me closer when common sense tells me I should be doing the opposite. Getting away and going back inside and calling the damn police.

But it's too late. I'm already here. Inches from the hedge as the rustling gets louder.

When a rabbit darts out, close enough that I can feel the prickle of its fur on my shins, I yelp so loud I fear it's awakened the entire neighborhood. It certainly startles the rabbit, which zips across the driveway. I run in the opposite direction, around the rear corner of the house, not stopping until I realize where I am.

The backyard.

Halfway between the house and the woods.

Standing in the exact spot where my tent had been that night.

I suck in a nervous breath. I can't remember the last time I stood in this backyard. Definitely years. Maybe even decades. All this time, I've purposefully avoided it, afraid to confront the memories being here would bring.

Now here I am, back at the scene of the crime, and my first thought is how the yard has barely changed in the past thirty years. It remains a tidy swath of grass stretching from the back of the house to the edge of the woods. The magnolia tree directly behind the house is bigger, of course, its branches now brushing the siding and roof. But everything else looks exactly the same. Even the grass where the tent once sat. A shock. Considering how unholy this spot is in my mind, it feels like it should be nothing but scorched earth.

I kneel and run my hand over it, the freshly cut blades tickling my palms as the green, earthy scent does the same to my nostrils. Beyond the lawn, the forest is alive with noise. Crickets and cheepers and birds that hunt in the dark. Fireflies lazily dance in the trees, as bright as the stars sparkling in the cloudless sky.

It's all so peaceful.

And menacing.

I stand and start walking toward the forest, inexplicably drawn to it. I peer into the dark cluster of trees, horrified by the knowledge that almost thirty years ago, on a night very much like this, someone emerged from these woods. They stood next to the tent where Billy and I slept. They sliced the tent, grabbed Billy, and—

I force myself not to think about the rest. It's too horrible to imagine.

To distract myself, I pull my phone out of my pocket and consider calling Claudia again. Instantly, I decide against it. Not twice in one day.

As I drop the phone into my pocket, I notice something strange. The sounds coming from the woods have stopped. No crickets. Or cheepers. Or birds of prey hurtling through the night with a flap of their wings. Even the fireflies, so bright a moment ago, appear to have fled.

In their place is silence and a tickle on the back of my neck that tells me I'm not alone.

Someone else is here.

In the yard.

Right behind me.

I spin around and see—

Nothing.

There's no one else around. It's just me and the grass and the magnolia tree, its moon shadow stretching across the lawn to my feet. My gaze follows it back to the house, which sits silent and dark, casting its own rectangular shadow onto the backyard.

And in that darkness, barely visible on a patch of grass that only seconds earlier had been empty, is another baseball.

NINE

I t's a joke.

After a night spent awake thinking about it, that's the only explanation I can come up with for this second baseball, which is identical to the first.

I know it's a different ball because the one the lawn guy found yesterday remains in the living room, where I showed it to Ragesh. Sitting cross-legged on the carpet, I now stare at both baseballs, obsessing over who could have placed one in the yard unnoticed as I stood mere feet away. How did I not see them? Had I been so distracted by the woods and thoughts of Billy that I completely missed someone rushing through the yard, dropping the baseball along the way?

Beyond the mystery of who put it there is this question: Why? There seems to be no purpose behind it other than to remind me of Billy's secret message. Not that I need reminding. I remember it well.

So someone is playing a prank. A cruel one. Someone who knows Billy was taken from this yard—which, thanks to the internet, is everyone—and decided that the discovery of his body would be the perfect time to fuck with the person living here. Which happens to be me.

But, according to Ragesh, very few people outside the police know Billy has been found. Just me, Russ, Ashley, and whoever they secretly told. If they told anyone at all.

When you subtract those who don't know the meaning of the baseball left in my yard, that leaves only two people who could have done it: me and Billy.

As I go upstairs and take a shower, I consider what my next step should be. Since the appearance of the baseballs has occurred during nights when the lights mysteriously flicked on above the garages of Hemlock Circle, I assume the two are related. Perhaps whoever's leaving the baseballs is triggering the lights on their way to my yard. Still unknown is how they've managed to remain practically invisible while doing it. Along with who they are and why they're doing it.

The only way to find out any of those things is to catch them in the act. Luckily, I have an idea for how to do that—not to mention a friend who can help.

I dress quickly, head downstairs, and grab my phone and car keys. I'm halfway to the garage when the doorbell rings. I reverse course and head to the door, determined to tell whoever it is to go away. But when I open it, I find Ashley on the front stoop with Henry standing a few feet behind her, a book in his hands.

"Hi!" she says in that too-bright way used by people who know they're intruding. "Are you doing anything right now?"

"I was just about to head to the store."

A frown crosses her face. "Oh, okay. Never mind then."

"Do you need help with something?"

"I need a favor, actually. A pretty big one." Ashley bites her bottom lip, stalling. "I need to take my dad to the doctor. He's . . . in pretty bad shape this morning. Normally, I'd leave Henry with Alice Van de Veer, but she's not home. And since he doesn't really know the Chens or the Patels, I was wondering if you could watch him for a few hours."

Behind her, Henry pushes his glasses higher onto his nose so he can gaze at me with undisguised skepticism. Which is fine, since I'm doing the same to him.

"I'm not very good with kids," I say.

"He's well-behaved, I swear," Ashley says. "You won't have any trouble."

"I've been told I'm inconspicuous," Henry adds.

It's still not a good idea. I have never been alone with a child since, well, I was one myself. And I'm daunted by the prospect of keeping Henry occupied—of keeping him *safe*—for even the smallest amount of time.

"Are you sure there's no one else?" I say.

Ashley comes closer and whispers, "I know this is sudden and, well, a lot right now. But what's happening to his grandfather is scary, and I want to shield Henry as much as possible. Please. You're my only hope."

I give Henry another wary look, thinking about when I was his age and how Ashley watched me every weekday until Billy was taken. If she could do it at fifteen, then I can manage the same thing with her son now.

"I guess I can watch him for a little bit," I say.

"It'll be two hours, tops. You won't even need to feed him lunch."

That's a relief, seeing how I have no idea what kids eat nowadays.

Ashley kneels in front of her son, straightening the collar of his polo shirt and smoothing the sleeves. "Ethan's going to watch you while I take your grandpa to the doctor. You two are going to go to—"

"Russ's sporting goods store," I say.

"Exciting!" Ashley says, feigning enthusiasm. "Isn't that exciting, Henry?"

Henry looks as excited as a cat facing a bathtub full of water. "Can't we go to the library instead?"

"I'll take you to the library when I get back," Ashley says. "How does that sound?"

"Acceptable, I guess." Henry turns to me, his shoulders slumped in resignation. "Well, Mr. Marsh, I guess I'm coming with you."

Ten minutes later, we're heading to Russ's store. The mood in the car is awkward at best. I'm at a loss over what to say to a ten-year-old I've met only once, and Henry clearly has no idea what to make of me. So we ride in silence, me staying five miles under the speed limit.

"You doing okay back there?" I say to Henry, who I relegated to the backseat because I'd once read it's safer there.

In the rearview mirror, I see him look up from the book he's reading. Part of the Goosebumps series. *The Werewolf of Fever Swamp*.

"I'm fine, Mr. Marsh," he says.

"You can call me Ethan, you know."

"I prefer to keep our relationship formal, if you don't mind."

I suppress a chuckle. Who *is* this kid?

"So, um, do you want me to call you Mr. Wallace?"

Only as I'm saying it do I realize that Henry might not have the same last name as his mother. I'm assuming there's a father in the picture somehow, even though it's clear he and Ashley are no longer together. Henry provides no clues, for his answer is a calm "You may continue to call me Henry."

"Right. Henry." I stall, trying to think of anything else I can say to this kid I barely know. "I can turn on the radio, if you want. What kind of music do you like?"

"My mom picks what we listen to," Henry says, which makes me pleased that some things about Ashley haven't changed. She always was fanatical about her music. Back when she was my babysitter, we spent a few afternoons by the pool at her house. I'd swim while she ate Fla-Vor-Ices and listened to the radio. Whenever a song came on she didn't like—anything by Ace of Base, for example—she'd switch to a different station with a prickly "That's enough of that shit."

I turn on the radio and find a nineties station playing "Creep" by Radiohead. Ashley would approve. After that comes "What's the

Frequency, Kenneth?" by R.E.M., another keeper. By song's end, we're at the store.

"Can I look around?" Henry says, still clutching his book as we enter.

I scan the inside of the store, overly cautious. "Sure, I guess. Just don't touch anything."

Henry looks at me, affronted by the suggestion. "Please," he says indignantly. "I'm not a nine-year-old."

Then he's off, disappearing around a table stacked with baseballs as I go look for Russ. Instead, I find a salesclerk, whose eagerness tells me I'm the first customer of the day.

"Need help finding anything?" she asks.

Like Russ, she's good-looking and fit, making me wonder if it's a requirement. That, in order to work here, you must be hale and hearty, like someone who not only owns a canoe but actually uses it on a regular basis.

"Is Russ here?"

The clerk's shoulders droop. I've literally just asked to speak to the manager. "I'll get him," she says.

I survey the store as I wait, ashamed to realize I've never been here before despite Russ owning it for almost a decade. I'm impressed. It's bigger than I expected, and stuffed to the rafters with things I didn't know people actually needed or used. Kayaks and canteens. Life vests and paddles. Backpacks the size of a toddler. Hanging from one wall is a row of mountain bikes.

The other side of the store is a riot of camouflage. A surprise. There can't really be a need for so much camo in a town as yuppified as Princeton. Yet here it is, covering everything from boots to hoodies to full-body suits that I assume come in handy only for hunting or jungle warfare.

Seeing all those splotches of forest green and dirt brown makes me think of the stranger allegedly seen roaming the neighborhood in camo the day before Billy was taken. The stranger no one found. Why did he feel the need to camouflage himself? Was he hunting in the woods? If so, *what* was he hunting?

"Ethan?"

I spin around to see Russ, whose bloodshot eyes and rough red skin signify a hangover. However many bourbons he had last night, they certainly did a number on him.

"What are you doing here?" he says.

"Shopping," I say. "I'm thinking about buying a camera for the backyard. One of those night-vision things."

"A trail cam?"

"Is that what they're called?"

Russ nods. "You strap it to a tree and it'll take pictures of the wild-life that passes by. Is there something in your yard?"

"Yeah," I say, not daring to admit the truth.

That it's not some*thing* coming into the yard.

It's some*one*.

Which I can't mention to Russ. He made it clear last night that I shouldn't let Billy's murder consume me—and that if it does, he's not going to join me.

"Well, I have plenty in stock," Russ says. "Everything from cheap basics to state-of-the-art. Follow me."

He leads me deeper into the store, past the bikes and kayaks and a mock campsite on a patch of fake grass. It's elaborate for a store dis-play. There's a circle of rocks spewing red and yellow cellophane flames, two canvas camp chairs, a cooler, a grill, a lantern. Plopped in the mid-dle of it all is an orange tent that looks exactly like the one I had as a child.

The one Billy was taken from.

I never saw it again after that day. The police took the tent and ev-erything inside it. Our sleeping bags. Our pillows. Even the pair of Air

Jordans I'd kicked off before going to sleep. All of it was evidence that, after endless inspection and examination, yielded nothing about what actually happened that night.

The tent in the store sets my pulse racing in what I can only assume is a fit of PTSD. Like the baseballs in my yard, its presence feels like a prank. I turn to Russ, wanting to accuse him of insensitivity at best, cruelty at worst. But I know he didn't set up this fake campsite just to mess with me. One, he wouldn't do such a thing and, two, he didn't even know I'd be coming to the store today. The tent being here is without a doubt a coincidence.

"It's cool, right?" Russ says. "Jen helped me set it up."

I stare at the display, its charm eclipsed by a sense of déjà vu. I barely notice how a fan hidden inside the fake firepit gently crinkles the cellophane flames. Or that a speaker shaped like a rock emits the light chirp of birdsong. All I can focus on is the tent itself and how I fear that if I close my eyes, there'll be a slash in its side when I open them.

Then the tent begins to move—a tiny quake that brings with it a confounding realization.

Something is inside.

The tent's front flaps start to open, and I brace myself for the sight of Billy. Not gone. Just misplaced for the past thirty years. Looking not like he does in those age-progression photos on his NamUs listing but exactly the way he did the last time I saw him.

While a little boy does eventually emerge from the tent, it's not Billy. It's Henry, who looks up at me uncertainly as he says, "Hi, Mr. Marsh."

"Oh, hey," Russ says. "You're Henry, right?"

"Hi, Mr. Chen."

Henry gives a little wave that Russ doesn't see because he's too busy eyeing me with confusion. "Is he with you?"

"Yeah." I do a little shimmy, trying to shake myself back to the present. "Ashley needed me to watch him for a few hours. I told him he could look around, but not to touch anything."

"I needed a quiet place to read," Henry says, holding up his book.

"It's all good," Russ says. "Do you like camping?"

"I've never experienced it." Henry stands and brushes his knees, as if he had just moved across the forest floor and not fake grass in the middle of a strip mall store. "But as a reading space, the tent is quite satisfactory."

"Good to hear," Russ says before clapping his hands together. "Now, let's look at those trail cams."

Henry and I follow him away from the campsite display to a shelf at the back of the store filled with boxes of trail cams.

"How much are you looking to spend?"

A very good question. Until my teaching job starts in a few weeks, I'm not exactly flush with cash. Then again, I don't want to buy something so cheap that it barely works.

"I guess I want the best one."

"Music to my ears," Russ says with a grin before taking a box down from the shelf and showing it to me. "Our top model. Most trail cams need an SD card to save the pictures on. This one comes with an app and uses Bluetooth to send 4K images directly to your phone. It's motion-activated, of course. A deer or something steps in front of the camera and, click, a picture of it goes right to your phone."

I scan the back of the box, reading the camera's features. It has night vision, which is a must, and a range of a hundred feet. Definitely enough to catch the person dropping baseballs there. The camera also has different settings, including one for direct sunlight and a sports mode with a faster shutter speed.

"How much is it?"

Russ quotes the price, which prompts a low whistle of shock from me. My first car cost less.

"I've got plenty of cheaper options," Russ says. "It all depends on what you're trying to do. Are you just mildly curious that something's coming into the yard? Or do you want proof of it?"

Definitely the latter. Yes, I could simply stay up and stake out the backyard all night. It's not like I'll be missing out on much sleep. But I *might* miss whoever's doing this. They've been surprisingly stealthy so far. Even though it costs a small fortune, this trail cam is my best hope at catching the person entering my yard.

"I need proof," I say. "I'll take this one."

TEN

Russ ends up taking pity on me and applies his employee discount. Even with the additional ten percent off, the purchase puts a major dent in my savings. And now that the camera's removed from its box, and thereby unreturnable even to a friend like Russ, buyer's remorse has kicked in big-time.

"Where are you going to put it?" Henry asks as we stand in the backyard.

I study the camera in my hands. Roughly the same shape and size as a paperback book, it seems too small to do all the things it claims to be capable of. But there's one advantage to its compactness: It can be attached to almost anything.

"I'm not sure," I say, scanning the yard for an appropriate place. I settle on the magnolia, mostly because it seems to offer the most expansive view of the rest of the backyard.

With Henry's help, I strap the trail cam to the tree, pointing it toward the forest that borders the yard. We place it at chest height, which is what the instructions recommend. It makes sense, though. Too low would catch only the bottom half of someone entering the yard. Too high might allow them to slip, undetected, under the camera's eye, eluding it altogether.

I turn on the camera and download its corresponding app to my phone. Then I tell Henry to leap in front of the camera, pause a moment, then jump out of view. When he does, the camera lets out a click so light no one would be aware of it unless they knew what to listen for. It's followed a second later by another sound—the phone in my hand letting out a sharp *ping!*

I check the app, which has sent me a photo of Henry in front of the camera, slightly blurry as he prepares to spring out of frame.

Well, it works, although the blur could be a problem. If whoever's coming into the yard never stops moving, there's a chance the blur might render them unrecognizable. After consulting with the instructions, I switch the camera's settings from regular to sport, which should produce a crisper image. Then I ask Henry to pass in front of it again.

"Mr. Marsh, why do you need a camera in your backyard anyway?" Henry asks as he jumps into frame, pauses, leaps away again.

My phone sounds a second time.

Ping!

"I think someone's been coming here at night," I say as I check the app again. This time, the image of Henry is crystal clear. "And I want to find out if it's true or not."

"Why do you think they're doing it?"

That's a very good question. One I hope the trail cam will help me answer. "No idea," I say honestly.

"And you don't know who it is?"

"Nope," I say, feeling foolish about how, two nights ago, I'd thought it might be Billy, returning after thirty years. But then I remember how Vance Wallace also claimed to have seen him outside at around the same time, and my sense of foolishness fades.

"Have you seen anyone in your backyard?" I ask Henry.

He shakes his head. "Not really. Just some squirrels and birds. Oh, and a hawk. I don't like the hawk because it tries to eat the birds and squirrels."

"But never any people?" I say.

"No," Henry says. "Grandpa has, though."

I lower my phone, intrigued. "Who has he seen? Did he say?"

This time, Henry responds with a slow, uncertain nod. Knowing what I'm about to ask next, he says, "But he made me promise not to tell anyone. Especially my mom."

"What can't you tell me?"

Henry and I both freeze at the sudden appearance of Ashley coming around the side of the house and into the backyard. She gives us a curious look, her head tilted, a hand on her hip.

"What Henry's reading," I say, trying to cover for the kid and doing a shit job of it. Surely Ashley knows what kind of books Henry likes. He had one with him when she dropped him off this morning. But in the moment, it's the only thing I can think of.

"Those?" Ashley says incredulously. "They're harmless. Besides, I remember you liking those at his age."

She's wrong. It was Billy who was obsessed with the Goosebumps books. He was always trying to get me to read them, but I declined, saying I wasn't interested. In truth, I was too scared. The covers alone gave me the creeps.

"Can I get another from the library now?" Henry says.

"Yes, you *may* get another," Ashley says as she tousles her son's hair. "Did you and Ethan have fun?"

Henry studies me a moment, as if tallying the pros and cons of our morning together. Apparently, it's a draw because he says, "It was adequate."

Ashley rolls her eyes and gives me a headshake that's partly to apologize and partly to say, *Can you believe this kid?* "That's better than awful," she tells Henry. To me, she says, "Thanks again for watching him, Ethan. I owe you."

Putting a hand on Henry's shoulder, she leads him out of the back-yard and past the side of the house. I head inside, curious to see how well the trail cam performs when there's not a ten-year-old boy stand-ing directly in front of it. Parked at the sliding glass door that leads to the patio, I watch the yard and wait. Five minutes later, a squirrel emerges from the woods. After a few tentative steps onto the grass, it begins to bound across the lawn, its tail twitching. When it passes in front of the camera, my phone lets out a telltale alert.

Ping!

I check the picture on the app. With Henry out of the frame, I get a better sense of the camera's view—a clear square of grass stretching from the base of the magnolia tree to the cusp of the woods. In the center of the frame is what set the camera off—the squirrel, caught in mid-leap, as if it's flying.

Satisfied the camera works, I set my phone down on the counter and make a cup of coffee. As I stir creamer into the steaming mug, the phone erupts into noise again.

Ping!

I take a sip of coffee and reach for the phone. The camera has now sent me a picture of a cardinal pecking at the ground, its red plumage bright against the green grass. I set the phone back down on the counter.

Ping!

I pick it up again, check the app, see a picture of both the squirrel and the cardinal, warily eyeing each other on opposite sides of the frame.

Ping! Ping! Ping!

Jesus, did the backyard suddenly turn into a zoo?

I grab the phone again, expecting to see the squirrel, the cardinal, or some combination of both. Instead, on the app are three pictures of a woman I've never seen before standing in the backyard. In her early forties, she's dressed like a lawyer. Tidy hair. Tailored suit. Starched white shirt. Slung over her shoulder is a purse as big as a diaper bag.

The first image is of her looking at the woods behind the house, her back turned to the camera, her purse prominent at her hip. The second catches her in profile as, now aware of the camera, she spins around to face it. The third picture is the most arresting—her staring with curiosity directly into the camera, her lightly glossed lips forming a bright smile.

I do my own turn, whirling from the coffee maker to the patio door. The woman now stands on the other side, cupping her hands against the glass as she peers inside.

"Hi!" she says brightly. "Didn't mean to sneak up on you there. I was just checking out your camera. Looks fancy!"

Cautiously, I approach the door. "Can I help you with something?"

"Oh, my bad. Of course." The woman presses a set of credentials against the glass, allowing me to see that she's with the state police. "I'm Detective Cassandra Palmer. Do you have a minute to chat?"

Now her surprise appearance makes more sense. Ragesh had said Detective Palmer would be coming around to talk to us.

"I assume you're Ethan?" she says when I let her inside.

"I am."

"Fantastic. Always good to check first, you know?" The detective nods to the kitchen table. "Mind if I sit?"

"Sure," I say as she pulls out a chair and gingerly settles into it. "Coffee?"

Detective Palmer beams. "That would be swell, actually. Thank you."

As I fill a second mug, I notice Detective Palmer looking through the kitchen doorway to other parts of the house. Surveying the decor—or, rather, the lack of it—she says, "Are you moving in or out?"

"Little of both," I say. "My parents moved out. I'm moving in. Temporarily."

Detective Palmer smiles politely, as if she doesn't believe me. I don't, either.

I join her at the table and slide the coffee her way. She takes a lip-smacking sip and says, "So, Ethan, as you've likely already guessed, I'm here to talk about the Billy Barringer case." Detective Palmer pauses to enjoy another sip. "That's why I was poking around outside, by the way. I wanted to get a good look at the crime scene."

Hearing those words to describe my backyard is jarring, especially when they're uttered so cheerily. And even though I know abduction is itself a crime, I find myself asking, "Do you think Billy was killed in the yard?"

"Gosh, no." Detective Palmer jerks her head toward the lawn beyond the patio door. "If he had been murdered there, the forensics team would have found evidence. Blood spatter, maybe bone fragments. Billy was definitely killed in the woods and his body disposed of in the lake. But let's not dwell on the gory details."

Too late, I think as I take a sip of coffee. Detective Palmer does the same, content to wait for me to speak next.

"So, um, I guess you want me to go over everything I remember about that night."

"Oh, there's no need for that," Detective Palmer says. "I know Billy's case forwards and backwards. It's what got me into law enforcement, actually. I was twelve when it happened, and I remember it just like it was yesterday. I grew up not too far from here, believe it or not. In Somerville. And that summer, I remember most people only wanted to talk about O.J. But me? I was obsessed with finding out what happened to Billy."

That makes two of us. The only difference is that Detective Palmer got to choose her obsession.

"No, I'm interested in what you *couldn't* remember back then," she says. "I don't suppose the memory bell has rung much since then?"

I look down at my coffee to avoid making eye contact. I know I should tell her about The Dream, even though it's unclear if it's a memory or just a combination of imagination and nagging guilt. Also, there's no new information contained in it. Just the tantalizing possibility that I might have been awake when the tent was sliced open and Billy was taken. Which I guess is reason enough to talk about it.

"I have a recurring dream," I say, still staring into my mug, alarmed by the way my reflection ripples and wobbles on the coffee's mud-brown surface. Is that how I look to Detective Palmer? Is it how I look to everyone?

"About Billy?"

"About that night."

I describe The Dream in as much detail as possible, right down to that unholy *scriiiiiiiitch* before I wake.

"Interesting," Detective Palmer says when I'm done. "And it's the same every time?"

"Always."

"I'd ask if you've tried to unpack what it all means, but I assume you have."

I respond with a solemn nod.

"Do you have any idea who might have taken Billy?" Detective Palmer says.

"I don't," I say. "I didn't see anything."

"I wasn't asking if you saw who did it. I want to know who you *think* did it."

I take another sip of coffee, thinking it over. For thirty years, I've pondered that very question, usually while lying awake in the middle of the night. While various possibilities have crossed my mind, none have ever quite stuck.

"Ethan?" Detective Palmer says when twenty seconds pass without a response from me.

"Still here," I say, although part of me remains deep in thought.

Who *do* I think took Billy? The question was always so hard to answer because I never knew why Billy had been taken—or what happened to him afterward. Now that I know the latter, I can infer the former.

"Someone at the Hawthorne Institute," I say.

Detective Palmer crosses her arms and leans back in her chair. "An intriguing answer. I'm curious why you think that."

And I'm surprised by her curiosity. Billy's bones were discovered there. Isn't that enough?

"Because we were there that day," I say. "At the falls. Did Detective Patel tell you that?"

"He did, yes."

"And did he also tell you what happened?"

"He told me that as well," Detective Palmer says.

"Yet you don't think it's related to Billy's death?"

"We're looking into every possibility."

It's the same thing Ragesh said. Obviously, the official line. One that feels created to placate suspicious people like me, even though I have every reason to be suspicious.

"You are now," I say. "But that wasn't the case thirty years ago. Do you know why the institute's grounds weren't searched back then? Was it because Ezra Hawthorne was filthy rich?"

"He was, yes," Detective Palmer says. "And he made many generous donations to places throughout the state, including the governor's campaign fund."

I roll my eyes. "Of course he did."

"But I don't think that had anything to do with it. You have to remember, Billy's trail seemed to end at the access road in the woods, a mile away from the institute, leading everyone to think he was taken to a car waiting there. And considering the institute grounds are surrounded by a perimeter wall, it was assumed no one could easily trespass onto the property."

"But we did," I say. "Me, Billy, three other people. We all trespassed with no problem."

"A fact none of you mentioned until yesterday." Detective Palmer's expression can only be described as "not mad but disappointed." With her tilted head and lips *this* close to forming a frown, she looks like a kindergarten teacher who just caught someone trying to sneak a second chocolate milk. "Had my colleagues known this all those years ago, they would have included the institute grounds in their search."

Shame presses down on my rib cage, to the point where my breathing starts to get shallow.

"What did they do at the institute?" I say.

"I'm not sure. It's my understanding they did research."

"What kind of research?"

"*Private* research," Detective Palmer says. "The kind the public isn't privy to."

"But you have some idea, right?"

Detective Palmer grips her coffee mug and turns it slowly. "From what I've been able to gather, it was just a bunch of eccentrics. Very smart, very rich eccentrics. Certainly not the type of people who would kidnap and murder a little boy."

"Well, you asked me who I think killed Billy and I told you," I say. "Since it's not the answer you wanted, I guess we're done here."

"We're on the same team, Ethan," Detective Palmer says, and this time it sounds genuine. "We both want to catch who did this and find some justice for Billy. So, let's try again: Who do you think did it? Someone *not* associated with the Hawthorne Institute."

I stare over her shoulder, to the backyard beyond the patio door and the woods beyond that. Someone emerged from that forest, sliced the tent, and pulled Billy out of it and into the woods. Whoever it was then killed him and threw his body over the falls. Just thinking about it makes me queasy. And that's without considering the very real possibility that, had the killer approached the tent from a different angle and slashed the other side, it likely would have been me who was abducted and killed.

"There were—" My mouth has gone dry, making it hard to talk. I gulp down some coffee and start again. "There were rumors of a stranger roaming the neighborhood the day before Billy was taken. Someone who came out of the woods."

"And you think he might have done it?" Detective Palmer says.

"Maybe," I say. "Some serial killer who later went far, far away from here."

"Unfortunately, that's highly unlikely. Over the years, every known serial killer, kidnapper, and killer of children has been interviewed and asked about Billy Barringer. I've mentioned him to at least a dozen myself."

I try to picture Detective Palmer, with her chipmunk cheeks and Girl Scout troop leader smile, interviewing a serial killer in a maximum-security prison. It's impossible.

"Not a single one has confessed to the crime, which they love to do, even if they didn't commit it," she continues. "No one has even hinted that they were in a hundred-mile radius at the time. So the culprit was either a psychopath who's killed only once—a sick, thrill-kill situation—or a serial offender we don't know about or who hasn't yet been caught, or it was—"

"Someone from here," I say.

I can tell I'm right when Detective Palmer locks eyes with me from across the table. Now I understand why she doesn't think the Hawthorne Institute had anything to do with Billy's death. She suspects it was someone closer to home.

"This wasn't done by someone on Hemlock Circle," I say.

"I understand why you think that. I know it's hard to believe one of your friends and neighbors is a killer."

"It's impossible."

"Even when you consider the details of what happened that night?" Detective Palmer stands and goes to the patio door. Pointing to the yard, she says, "You and Billy were asleep in a tent. Something you did throughout that summer, right?"

I swallow, my mouth suddenly dry again because I know what she's getting at. "Every Friday night."

"So it wasn't a secret," Detective Palmer says, stating it not as a question but as the undeniable fact it is. "Now, consider how you didn't notice when Billy was taken. Yes, you might have been awake for it, based on your recurring dream, but that seems more because of the sound of the tent being cut open and not any other noises."

She pauses, giving me a chance to figure it out for myself. When I do, it feels like I've been punched.

"Billy didn't scream," I say.

Detective Palmer nods, pleased at my deduction skills. "Nor did he yell for help or put up a fight. You didn't hear anything. Your parents claimed not to have heard anything. No one on this cul-de-sac heard anything. Now why do you think that is?"

This time, no pause is needed for me to put it all together.

"Because Billy knew who it was."

"And he willingly left the tent and followed them into the woods," Detective Palmer says. "*That's* why I'm convinced it was someone who lived here and not some stranger who just happened to enter your yard and see a tent with two ten-year-old boys inside."

I'm not as convinced. It's not unreasonable to think that someone outside of Hemlock Circle was responsible. As for the lack of a scream or calling for help, maybe Billy was in shock when he was pulled from the tent. Or maybe he never woke up until he had been carried into the woods and it was too late.

"But this is a good neighborhood," I say. "Filled with good people."

"They might seem that way on the surface," Detective Palmer says.

"But when you're in my line of work, you tend to see people for who they really are. Most of them are good, I'll grant you that. Upstanding citizens who only want to do the right thing. I deal with the small percentage of people out there who don't do the right thing. They hurt. They kill. Sometimes for reasons beyond comprehension. These kinds of folks? They're definitely not good people."

"What would you call them?"

For the first time since she appeared in my yard, Detective Cassandra Palmer looks deadly serious. "They're monsters."

B illy doesn't believe in monsters, but he does believe in ghosts.

Well, he wants to believe.

He *mostly* believes.

He knows almost everything there is to know about them, the bulk of it gleaned from his favorite book, the gloriously named *The Giant Book of Ghosts, Spirits, and Other Spooks*. Yet a single, persistent seed of doubt continues to exist. Because although the book is filled with illustrations and, yes, even actual photographs of ghosts, the only thing in Billy's mind that would prove their existence beyond a doubt is to see one himself.

Billy assumes most boys his age—and even those a lot older—would be scared by the idea of seeing a ghost. Not him. Billy's the opposite. He fears *not* seeing one, because then it means he'll always slightly doubt their existence.

And he wants so desperately for them to be real.

Because if they are, he thinks he'll feel less alone.

Other than Ethan, Billy doesn't have many other friends. He guesses Russ Chen counts, even though he's usually annoying. As does his brother, Andy. Also annoying. But that's about it. In the past, Billy had tried to expand his circle of friends, mostly by trying to fit in. He pretended to be into baseball and video games and even begged his mom to buy him the same kind of clothes cool kids at school wore. Billabong board shorts and GAP tees and G-Shock watches. The only thing she agreed to was a pair of Air Jordans just like Ethan's. But when Billy wore them to school, nothing changed. He was still seen as weird.

If he was noticed at all.

But then he found *The Giant Book of Ghosts, Spirits, and Other Spooks*. He stumbled upon it one day in the school library while searching for a book about sharks because he needed to write a paper about them for science class. The size of a phone book, it was indeed giant. On the cover was an illustration of a blue-white entity hovering over a cemetery.

Staring at it, Billy felt a shiver of . . . something. It wasn't fear, exactly. But it was close. Tremulous curiosity. Enough for him to want to put the book back on the shelf. Instead, he opened it, and in that moment his entire world opened as well. Flipping through the book, reading page after page of spirits with names like djinn and stafie, he realized he wasn't the only one who didn't feel seen. That the world was filled with entities who were here but invisible, present but ignored. In fact, there were enough of them to fill an entire book. A giant one.

Thus began his fascination with ghosts of all stripes. Eventually, he grew to love them. Even the scary ones that scream in the night or are rumored to steal souls. Billy understands that all they really want is to be seen, acknowledged, noticed.

Just like him.

He checked the book out of the library and took it home, careful to hide it from his mother, who wouldn't approve. When he had to return it, he checked it out again. Then again. Then multiple times after that until, on the last day of school, Mrs. Charbrier, the school librarian, told him he could keep it.

"You've earned it," she said, smiling as she pried the library sticker from the spine and slid the book across the checkout desk. "When someone shows a book this much love, they deserve a copy just for them."

That was more than a year ago, and Billy's parents still don't know about his copy of *The Giant Book of Ghosts, Spirits, and Other Spooks*. He'd like to keep it that way. His father doesn't mind his obsession with ghosts. He even encourages it, going so far as to help him dress up as one for Halloween last year. But his mother would absolutely freak out if she found the book, which is why Billy takes great care to hide it. He moves it around every few days, shuffling it from the back of his underwear drawer to his desk to under the bed.

He knows she's just concerned about him, but her concern can also be overbearing. She wouldn't understand that he sees ghosts as, no pun intended, kindred spirits. That when he opens *The Giant Book* and sees illustrations of all these scary, fantastical, misunderstood spirits, it feels like they could be the friends he lacks.

At least, some of them could be. Billy completely understands that not every ghost, spirit, and spook mentioned in the book exists in real life. About half of them are from myth, movies, or other books by authors he's still too young to read. Lovecraft and Poe and King.

Now Billy pages through his book, a pencil in hand, circling the ones he believes are real.

Poltergeists? Circled, because there've been about a thousand incidents involving them.

Banshees? Also circled, for the very same reasons.

The Headless Horseman doesn't get a circle because he's from a story, though Billy suspects that something similar to him is real.

If Ethan or Billy's brother or even his father were to ask him why he suspects ghosts exist, he'd probably tell them that there are so many listed in his giant book that it would be impossible for all of them to be made up. That's simply the law of probability, which he'd just started learning about before school let out for the summer.

Now all he needs to know for certain is to see one for himself.

And Billy knows just the place to make that happen.

ELEVEN

By nine p.m., I'm sprawled across the couch, half dozing through an episode of *Ted Lasso* I've watched at least a dozen times before. On the floor, an empty beer bottle sits next to a paper plate with uneaten crust from the pizza I ordered for dinner. Friends had warned me there'd be a phase in which I let myself go, ignoring all healthy habits and basic hygiene. I didn't believe them at the time. But now, after a week of eating takeout dinners and performing the bare minimum of dressing and bathing, I know it to be true. I've now hit a point somewhere beyond letting go. Abandonment.

Even though I could use a shower, a shave, and a vegetable, I remain where I am, letting my eyelids flicker and close. Maybe I'll sleep through the entire night this way. That would be a welcome change of pace.

I'm on the cusp of sleep when my phone chirps out a noise.

Ping!

Startled, I reach for the phone sitting a few feet from the beer bottle. Activity from the trail cam died down once dusk descended, with the birds retreating into the trees and the squirrels going to wherever squirrels go. Opening the app now, I'm greeted with a picture of

moonlit lawn and, at the edge of the woods, an opossum with its glowing eyes unnervingly aimed straight at the camera.

The view from the trail cam is different at night. More ominous.
Deep pockets of shadow border the frame, tinted a sickly green by the
night vision. The grass itself is rendered gray, like dirty snow. Beyond
the lawn, barely visible in the darkness, is the forest, the trees there tall
and blurry.

I set my phone face down on the floor and check the bottle for any
remaining drops of beer.

Ping!

I eye the phone as the alert from the trail cam shoots a thin glow
across the living room carpet. I ignore it, telling myself it's just the
opossum again. Or something similar. A deer. A raccoon. A fox.

And ghosts.

I'm struck by a memory of Mrs. Barringer coming to our door one
summer, right before I returned to school for the fall semester. By
then, I knew they were moving out of the neighborhood. I'd heard my
parents whispering about it one night. It was too hard on them, my
mother had said. Especially Mrs. Barringer. Hemlock Circle now held
too many bad memories. Where they were going—and when—I had
no idea. All I knew was that it felt like I was partly to blame. That my
inaction that night in the tent meant the Barringers didn't just lose a
son, but that they were also losing their home.

So I was surprised when Mrs. Barringer showed up holding something rectangular wrapped in tissue paper.

"I thought you should have it," she said as she handed it to me.
"Billy would have wanted you to."

I tore off the tissue paper, revealing a book. The front cover was an
illustration of a translucent figure floating over a cemetery. Above it,
written out in bold purple lettering, was the title.

The Giant Book of Ghosts, Spirits, and Other Spooks.

I turned the book over in my hands, uncertain if I wanted it.

Taking something that belonged to Billy felt wrong for a hundred different reasons. I didn't want to see this book every day and be reminded that he was gone, that it was my fault.

"That's so thoughtful, Mary Ellen," my mother said, deciding for me that the unwanted gift was something I had to accept. "What do you say, Ethan?"

"Thank you," I dutifully replied.

I went upstairs and put the book on the top shelf of my bookcase, its spine facing the wall so I couldn't see the title. I never touched it after that. Not once. It might still be in my room, buried under decades of dust.

Thinking about it now brings forth another memory, jarring in its suddenness. Like a movie that's been spliced together wrong, jump-cutting from one scene to another.

My last Halloween with Billy, trick-or-treating in our respective costumes. I'd dressed as Sam Neill's character from *Jurassic Park*, braving the crisp October night in khaki shorts, denim work shirt, red neckerchief. Billy had gone as a ghost, complete with gray face paint, powdered hair, and plastic chains dripping from his limbs.

Afterward, we sat in my kitchen eating candy. Although Billy had washed his face, traces of his makeup remained. Pale rings surrounded his eyes, and a streak of gray ran down his cheek. Munching on a fun-sized Snickers, he said, "What would you do if you ever met a ghost?"

"Scream and run away," I said. "Wouldn't you?"

Billy shook his head. "I'd try to talk to them. That's all they want, really. To be acknowledged."

"But what if they tried to kill you?"

"Most ghosts can't hurt you," Billy said, as if it were the most logical thing in the world.

That, plus his obvious sincerity, prompted me to say, "You know ghosts aren't real, right?"

"Yeah, they are."

"Then why don't we see them everywhere?" I said. "Why aren't there, like, ghosts walking down the street? Or in the supermarket?"

"First of all, a lot of ghosts are invisible, so you can't see most of them," Billy said, making his point by stabbing the air with his candy bar. "Second, they *are* everywhere. I bet there are ghosts roaming these woods right now."

The very thought gave me a full-body shudder. Unlike Billy, I'm not a fan of ghosts, then or now. I spent that Halloween night burrowed under my covers, too scared to even glance at my bedroom window for fear I'd spot a ghost on the edge of the woods.

"All ghosts really want is for you to know they're there," Billy continued. "They're not intentionally trying to scare people."

"Well, I think everyone's scared of ghosts."

"Not me," Billy said proudly.

Ping!

The alert stops the memory cold, and I grab my phone again, this time annoyed. Whatever animal is in the backyard, I'd love it to leave. But when I open the app, I don't see an animal.

I see Vance Wallace.

He stands between the magnolia tree and the woods, seemingly oblivious to the camera. He's dressed like a man who's been startled awake—pajama bottoms, gray T-shirt, hair standing off his head at multiple angles. Slippers cover his feet. Grass clippings from yesterday's mowing cling to the soles.

I'm outside in thirty seconds, tentatively crossing the lawn. When Vance spots me, he lurches my way. Up close, he looks addled. It's the only way to describe it. There's no recognition in his eyes, even though he saw me yesterday and stares directly at me now.

"Mr. Wallace?" I say. "Are you okay?"

"Did you see him?" he says in a voice too quiet to be a bark and too gruff to be a whisper.

"See who?"

"That Barringer boy."

Unlike Vance Wallace, I do whisper. "Mr. Wallace, Billy's dead."

Vance reaches out and seizes my forearm in a death grip. His mind might not be all there, but Mr. Wallace's muscles are working just fine.

"I saw him," he says. "I followed him here. He's back."

He turns to face the woods, now crowded with shadows. I see nothing in the gloom. Just trees stretching for miles, turned pale from the moonlight.

"Are you sure it wasn't a deer or something?" I say.

"That was no deer," Vance growls. "The Barringer boy is up to no good."

In the distance, I hear the slap of footsteps on the grass. Turning, I see Ashley running around the side of the house with Henry straggling behind her. Instinctively I know why she's here and why she brought her son with her. Much like Mary Ellen Barringer when she crept into my backyard with Andy, Ashley doesn't want to leave her son unattended.

"Dad?" she says, out of breath from exertion and exasperation. "You're not supposed to leave the house without telling me."

"But I saw him again."

"We've gone over this. You didn't see anyone."

"I did, dammit!"

"Let's get you home." Ashley tries to take his arm, but Vance shakes her off.

"I can walk home on my own, for God's sake. Stop treating me like a fucking baby, Trish."

Behind her, Henry gasps. Ashley's reaction is even worse. Her eyes go wide, shimmering with hurt. That same pain slips into her voice as she says, "It's me, Dad. Ashley. Mom's no longer with us."

Mr. Wallace stares at her a moment, confusion writ large on his face. The expression soon falls away, replaced by something approaching abject terror. He opens his mouth to speak, but Ashley shushes him and tells him it's okay. She reaches for him again, and this time Mr. Wallace lets her do it.

As they leave, Vance turns around to stare at the woods.

"I'm not lying," he tells me. "Something is out here."

"That's enough, Dad. Let's go back to the house." Ashley pauses to give me an over-the-shoulder glance. "You, too, Ethan. I could use the help."

TWELVE

While Ashley gets her father resettled in his room, I'm down the hall, making sure Henry gets back into bed. Not a problem, it turns out. Henry's a far cry from how I acted when I was his age and bedtime rolled around. I'd wheedle and cajole and beg to stay up just five more minutes. Ironic, seeing how I now long for a full night's sleep.

Henry, maybe anticipating a similar situation in his later years, simply crawls under the covers and grabs a book from the nightstand. He's moved on to a different volume in the Goosebumps series, *The Ghost Next Door.*

"Won't you get scared reading that before bed?" I say.

"No," Henry says. "It's just fiction. Also, I like reading about ghosts and monsters."

"I had a friend who liked that, too. He was obsessed with ghosts."

"Billy Barringer," Henry says, the name sounding foreign coming from someone so young.

"How do you know about him?"

Henry pushes his glasses higher onto his nose. "My mom told me about him. She said he was a good kid who disappeared, which is why I should always tell her where I'm going."

I shouldn't be surprised that even Ashley has turned Billy's story into a cautionary tale, yet I am. Surely Billy meant more to her than that. Or maybe she's like Russ, limited in both memories and mournfulness. When it comes to Billy, maybe everyone is.

Everyone but me.

"Don't stay up too late reading," I say as I switch off the overhead light. "Sleep is important."

When I reach the doorway, Henry stops me.

"Mr. Marsh, do you think I'm weird?"

I turn to face him, surprised by how young he looks half under the covers, bathed in the warm glow of his bedside lamp.

"Do you?" Henry prods when I don't have a quick answer.

I cringe. The truth is that, yes, I think Henry is weird, but to tell him would be cruel. Then again, I don't want to lie to the kid. Too much of childhood is spent being lied to by adults because they think it'll spare your feelings.

"Does it matter if you are?" I say.

Henry nods. "A little."

"To who?"

"Whom," he says, correcting me. "And I guess the answer is other people."

"Like kids your own age?" I say.

"Yes," Henry concedes. "I should have been more forthcoming."

Hearing someone so small use such a big word—correctly, even—makes me smile. Sometimes weird isn't so bad.

"I'll let you in on a little secret," I say as I cross the room and sit on the edge of his bed. "Something most people don't realize until they're older. But everyone is a little weird. Some people hide it more than others, but it's true. Everyone is weird."

"Including you?"

"Including me," I say, trying not to give too much thought to how true of a statement it really is.

"So I shouldn't care that I'm a little weird?"

"All you should care about is being yourself," I say. "No matter who that person is. Some people might not like you for who you are, but a whole bunch will. I promise."

I pat his leg beneath the covers and take my leave. Again, Henry stops me at the doorway, this time to say "Good night, Mr. Marsh" with a formality that makes me feel compelled to play along.

"Good night, Mr. Wallace."

Henry nods, pleased, and I leave the room. In the hallway, I find Ashley leaning against the wall right outside Henry's door, where she no doubt heard every word.

"You're good with kids," she says.

"Am I? I've never thought so."

"You're a pro. It's shocking you don't have one of your own."

I follow her downstairs to the kitchen, where she opens a cupboard and pulls out two shot glasses and a bottle of tequila. The tilt of her head is a question. *Should we?* My answer is yes, especially if we're going to continue talking about children.

I take a seat as Ashley moves about the kitchen, placing the bottle and glasses on the table before pulling some limes from the fridge. With her back toward me as she slices them, she says, "Did you and your wife want kids?"

"She did," I say. "I didn't."

"I can see that."

Claudia couldn't. Not that I was, to borrow from Henry's vocabulary, forthcoming with the reason I didn't want kids. When we argued about it, which was often toward the end, I refused to tell her. It was only during our final argument that I revealed all.

"Tell me why you don't want to have a child," she said.

"There's no specific reason."

"There has to be, Ethan."

"Lots of couples choose not to have kids, for a whole slew of reasons."

"Is it me?" Claudia said, her voice wounded.

"Of course not. I think you'd be an amazing mother."

I tried to pull her into a hug, but she slipped out of it and stalked to the other side of our bedroom. "Then why? You know I want a baby. You just said I'd be an amazing mom. I think you'd be an amazing dad. We have good jobs. We're financially secure. There's absolutely no reason why we shouldn't at least try except for something you're not telling me."

"I just don't want to be a father," I said. "Isn't that reason enough?"

"Honestly? No."

"Well, it should be. But I guess in this situation, my feelings don't matter."

It was a shitty thing to say. I realize that now and probably did then, but the heat of the moment had made me angry. With Claudia, yes, but mostly with myself for refusing to be honest with her, even though it made her more upset with each passing minute.

"You won't tell me what you're feeling!" she yelled, her eyes wide and shining with newly formed tears that had yet to fall. "And you have no idea how much that hurts. I'm your wife, Ethan. You shouldn't be afraid to share anything with me."

"Even if it's something you don't want to hear?"

"Especially that. Because how can we fix it—together—if only one of us knows what the problem is?"

"There is no fixing it," I said. "*That's* the problem."

"Then just tell me. *Please.*" Claudia stared at me from across the room. One of the tears had slipped free and was sliding down her cheek. "Ethan, I need to know why you don't want kids."

I wearily dropped onto the bed, knowing I was about to break my wife's heart.

"Because kids disappear," I said, the truth feeling not like a weight had been lifted from me but like it had suddenly been doubled.

Claudia touched my cheek and kissed my forehead. "I understand," she said softly, and I believed her. She knew what happened to Billy. She knew how much it had fucked me up. And she knew that, because of it, I would never, ever change my mind.

"I'm sorry," I whispered.

"I know," Claudia said.

Then she left our bedroom for the very last time.

"Here we are," Ashley says, jerking me back to the present by setting a plate of quartered limes and a saltshaker on the table in front of me. She pours us both a shot. We lick our hands and sprinkle them with salt before licking it off, downing the tequila, and ending with a suck of lime wedge. The tequila, cheap but strong, burns its way down my throat. I bark out a cough. Ashley slaps the table.

"God, I needed that," she says. "I bet you never thought you'd be doing shots with your old babysitter."

"I can honestly say I never did."

"Life is full of surprises, isn't it? I mean, I never thought I'd be back living in this house. I bet you didn't, either. You, of all people, had every reason to stay far, far away."

"There weren't many other options," I say, pointedly not getting into the why and how of it all. It'll take more than a shot of tequila to get me talking about *that*.

"It's scary how little the place has changed." Ashley looks around the room, and I know she's really gesturing to what's beyond the kitchen walls. To Hemlock Circle. "The houses are the same. The people are the same. In some ways, it's like I never left. When all I wanted to do was get the hell out and never come back."

"Why didn't you?"

"Dad needed me," Ashley says. "I mean, he needed me after my mom died, and I stayed a few weeks, but no more than that. I knew how easy it would be to get sucked back into life here, and I refused to do it. But then Dad started forgetting stuff and getting confused, and it seemed to get worse and worse every time I visited. Once Deepika Patel found him standing at her door saying he couldn't remember which house he lived in, it became inevitable."

She refills the shot glasses and we do it all over again. Lick, shoot, suck. This time, I manage to refrain from coughing, but the tequila loosens me up enough to say, "So all that stuff your father said—about seeing Billy in your yard and following him into mine—is just his imagination?"

"More like confusion."

"Are you sure?"

"Of course." Ashley gives me a curious look. "Are you drunk already?"

"No. I just thought—" I stop myself, trying to think of a way to say it without sounding crazy. And delusional. And utterly pathetic. "I thought I sensed Billy's presence. A few nights ago."

"Where? In your house?"

"The backyard. And all around Hemlock Circle. I've . . . seen things."

"Is that why you bought that camera?"

"Yup," I say. "To try to figure out what's going on. Because ever since your father said he's also seen things, I've been wondering if—"

"It's true?" Ashley says, her tone making it clear she's skipped past crazy and delusional and gone straight to thinking I'm pathetic. "Oh, Ethan. It's nice to think about those we love still being near after they're gone. Unfortunately, it doesn't work that way."

"How can you be so sure?"

"Because it's science. As for what my dad's been saying, you can't believe any of it. I hate to say something like that about my own father, but it's true. He's not well. Which is why I had to come back, even though it was the last thing I wanted to do."

"What about Henry?" I say. "Does he like it here?"

"I think so? We'll see how it goes when he starts school. As you've noticed, he's kind of an odd kid."

"There's nothing wrong with that," I say. "Being different was a liability when we were his age. Now, it's a badge of honor."

"Still, I worry. He's so sensitive. Smart as hell. Certainly smarter than me. But kids can be so cruel. Since it's only me looking after him, I'm in a constant state of fear that I'm going to fuck it up."

We do a third shot. After humiliating myself a moment ago, I need it. This time, I don't even bother with the salt and lime. It's just the tequila, knocked back without hesitation.

"Where's Henry's father?"

"He's not in the picture," Ashley says as she takes an extra slurp of lime. "Hasn't been from the start. He doesn't know Henry exists. And I, well, I don't exactly know who he is."

"Oh," I say, wishing I could take back the question. "I didn't mean to—"

"No, it's fine." Ashley twists the lime wedge until it's just pulp. "It is what it is. Mom had just died, and I was in LA, where I'd been living since college, still fooling myself into thinking I could make it in the music business. But out there, thirty-five is considered ancient. I was competing for internships with twenty-year-olds. The whole time, I kept on being the same stupid party girl I was in high school and college. Nothing numbs disappointment quite like alcohol. And then, oops, I got pregnant and had no idea which one of the multiple anonymous douchebags I'd hooked up with was responsible. In short, I was a total fucking mess."

"It doesn't seem that way now," I say.

"You can thank Henry for that. As soon as I saw the plus sign on that home pregnancy test, my whole way of thinking changed. It wasn't just about me, you know?"

I can't help hearing the echo of Claudia in my memory the night she told me she wanted to have a baby.

We're just us.

As if that wasn't enough.

"Do you ever regret it?" I say. "Becoming a parent?"

Ashley shakes her head. "Not for a second. Raising a boy like Henry isn't easy. Not in the least. And I know I didn't need to go through with it. I had options. But every time I look at him, I know I brought something good into the world."

"So what's next?" I say, my brain buzzing from too much tequila. "You plan on staying here awhile?"

"Not sure." Ashley screws the cap back onto the tequila bottle. "My dad's not getting any better. And something will need to be done about it sooner rather than later. After that, who knows? Turns out, there are worse places to live than Hemlock Circle. How about you?"

"I have no idea. Especially now that Billy's been found. There are too many memories to know what to do with them all."

"I thought I was going to get away from all this," Ashley says, which is exactly what I've felt all week but haven't been able to articulate. "It's like it was destined or something. That, no matter how far I ran, this place insisted on dragging me back here."

Friday, July 15, 1994
11:52 a.m.

God, I hate it here," Ashley says, cradling the receiver between her neck and shoulder as she wraps a Band-Aid around her thumb. She'd been playing guitar—well, *trying* to play—and hit a string at the wrong angle, slicing her thumb in the process.

"It's not *that* bad," says Tara. "I'd kill to live in your neighborhood."

This makes Ashley feel a wee bit guilty, because Tara lives in town, in a modest house next door to a dentist's office. She once complained that she can never open her bedroom window in the daytime because of the whine of the dentist's drill. Ashley guesses that's worse than waking to the wives of Hemlock Circle gathered beneath her window, which is what happened this morning.

Today, instead of their usual gossip and giggling, the women spoke in hushed tones, which Ashley took to mean they were talking about one of their kids.

A favorite topic of conversation.

Look, she gets it. Hemlock Circle exists in a kind of bubble. Part of a larger neighborhood, yes, but also on its own, surrounded by woods like some outcast in one of those stuffy books she's forced to read in English class. Hester Prynne. That's what the cul-de-sac reminds her of. Hester fucking Prynne, but minus the scandal. Nothing juicy ever happens here. Sure, there was what happened to Johnny Chen, but that was more sad than anything else.

Ashley still gets depressed thinking about Johnny. She'd had a bit of a crush on him when she was younger, and they waited for the school bus together at the end of the street. Now he's dead, and sometimes she still can't believe it. An overdose? At his age? That's how rock stars die. Not cute, shy, studious boys like Johnny.

Which explains the lowered voices from the ladies of the cul-de-sac whenever they talk about their kids. It denotes seriousness, especially when it involves something that affects all of them. As an only child, Ashley doesn't know how she feels about being lumped in with the other neighborhood kids like they're distant cousins seated together at a wedding reception. She has nothing in common with the others save for the fact that they all live in the same place. She doesn't even like them very much.

Well, that's not true. She likes Ethan Marsh, who's a good kid, even though she sometimes catches him staring at her like she's Claudia Schiffer or something. She lets it slide because it's in an innocent, awe-struck way. Not like the leering of Ragesh Patel. A few weeks ago, Ashley spotted him hiding in the woods, watching her house. It creeped her out so much she told her dad, who marched next door and yelled at the Patels to, in his words, "keep your Peeping Tom son away from my house!" Ragesh denied it, of course, but Ashley knows what she saw.

As for the other kids on Hemlock Circle, she has little patience for huffy Russell Chen, who gets upset at the littlest things when he occasionally comes over to play with Ethan while she's watching him. Ashley barely knows Andy Barringer, the youngest of them, but has a soft spot for his brother, Billy. He's a weird kid, which makes her worry about him. In this world, weird kids are bully magnets, and she fears life will only get worse for Billy if he doesn't lower his freak flag a little bit.

"This world gets crazier every day," Ashley heard her mother say this morning, which piqued her curiosity enough to lure her out of bed and closer to the window. Maybe they weren't talking about one of the neighborhood kids after all. But by the time she got close enough to listen in, the group had broken up, with the women going back to their cooking and cleaning and whatever other forms of suburban drudgery they do every day.

Ashley vows to not live like that. She has plans. Short-, medium-, and long-term.

The short one is to scrape up enough money to go to Woodstock in August. Doable if she saves every penny of her babysitting money and can convince her parents she's going to the Poconos with Tara and her family and not driving to upstate New York with Tara and her cousin to crash a music festival. The lying part is easy. She does it to her parents all the time. It's the cover-up that causes her the most concern. While her parents and Tara's moms aren't friends, there's always the risk they'll run into each other at the Stop & Shop or the movie theater in downtown Princeton.

Also simple is her medium-term plan: graduate high school and peace the hell out of here. She's not the best student. School bores her and, frankly, she's too lazy to apply herself to things she doesn't care about. But Mrs. Daniels said her grades are decent enough to get her into college, which is all Ashley needs to know.

As for her long-term plan, well, that's not so easy. Her father has made it clear he wants her to go to Rutgers, major in sports science, then work at his gyms. Ashley hasn't yet summoned the courage to tell him that's not going to happen. But she will, once she figures out what she wants to actually do with her life. She knows it'll have something to do with music. She's just not sure what. She can't sing to save her life, and the only instrument she knows how to play is the guitar—poorly. But marketing or PR is a possibility, which is why she perks up when Tara says, "By the way, I hear Steve Ebberts is going to be at the party tonight."

The party in question is being hosted by Brent Miller, whose parents took his little sister to Cape May for the weekend. Ashley's already told Tara she's not going. The last time she saw Brent Miller was at Sherri Benko's graduation party, and he got so handsy she had to knee him in the balls. He's lucky it wasn't worse. Ashley is stronger than she looks. That happens when your dad owns several gyms. She's been lifting weights since she was ten. She's not huge. Not like those badass women on *American Gladiators* with necks the size of tree trunks who can lift, like, a Volkswagen Beetle. But she's sinewy.

"Are you sure?" Ashley says, holding the receiver to her ear now even though her thumb still throbs.

"Positive," Tara says.

Well, this changes things. It's not that Ashley has the hots for Steve or anything like that. In truth, he's kind of weird-looking and a bit of a jerk. But his older brother works for Warner Music, and she's more than willing to pretend to like Steve if it helps make a connection to the industry, no matter how thin.

She's not going to date him. She refuses to wrap her life around a boy. But she can go through the motions if she has to.

"Can you give me a ride?"

"No can do," Tara says. "My moms are taking the car to visit my aunt in Pennsylvania."

"Then how are you getting there?"

Tara sighs. "I'm not. Unless you can take me."

"I'll think of something," Ashley says, with the kind of finality that shows she means it.

And she does. She knows the party, a possible hookup with Steve Ebberts, Woodstock, college, and a career in music are all necessary steps toward her real goal, which is to not live like her mother and the other women of Hemlock Circle. She loves her mom, and she has no issue with the others, but their lives disappoint her. Raising kids. Keeping house. Gossiping on the lawn. It all seems so orderly, so banal. And Ashley wants to get messy. Not too messy. Not like Courtney Love. Just messy enough to know, when she's on her deathbed, that she lived.

No regrets.

That's the kind of life she wants.

Even if it means leaving Hemlock Circle and never looking back.

In the hall, Ashley hears her mother calling up the stairs. "Ash? You up there? It's time to go to work, honey."

Ashley checks the Swatch around her wrist. Shit. She needs to be at the Marsh house in two minutes.

"Tara, I gotta run," she says before hanging up and swiping the bloody tissue and Band-Aid wrapper into the trash. She slips on a pair of Keds and runs downstairs, shouting "Bye, Mom!" on her way out the door.

Although she could have easily gotten a summer job at one of her dad's gyms, Ashley instead jumped at the chance to babysit Ethan Marsh. The hours, each weekday from noon until five, are far better than at the gym, which would have required her to be up at the butt crack of dawn each morning. Also, if she worked at the gym, her father would know exactly how much she got paid, which would have made it harder to sock away money in secret like she's been doing all summer. In a few weeks, the money Joyce Marsh is paying her—in cash, no less—will cover the entire cost of the Woodstock trip.

Ashley traces the curve of the cul-de-sac to the Marsh house and skips across the lawn to the front door. When it opens, she expects to be greeted by Ethan, happy as usual to see her. Instead, it's Mrs. Marsh at the door, blinking at her in confusion. Ashley's equally confused. Shouldn't she be at work?

"Oh dear," Mrs. Marsh says in a way that makes Ashley's heart start to sink in her chest. "I completely forgot to tell your mother."

Ashley's heart drops another few inches. "Tell her what?"

"I'm so sorry, but we won't be needing you anymore this summer."

"Oh," Ashley says. "Is it something I did?"

"No, you're wonderful," Mrs. Marsh says. "Ethan adores you. It's just, well, I'm no longer working. And since I'll be home all day, it doesn't make sense to also have a sitter for him. I'm sorry for not letting you know sooner."

In that moment, Ashley sees her short-term plan for the rest of the summer blow away like dust in a strong wind. No more hiding her earnings from her parents. No more Woodstock. Still, she doesn't want to make Mrs. Marsh feel like shit, so she says, "I get it. It's fine."

"It's not fine," Mrs. Marsh says. "We made an arrangement for the entire summer, and I'm sure you were counting on that money. I can give you what we would have paid you this week, and if we ever need someone at night, you'll be the first person we call."

"That's nice," Ashley says as she mentally recalculates how much it'll take to get to Woodstock. "I really appreciate it."

"Thank you for understanding."

Mrs. Marsh then surprises her by pulling her into a hug. Ashley lets her do it, waiting for the awkwardness to end. Instead, it only gets more awkward.

Because that's when Joyce Marsh starts to cry.

At first, Ashley remains frozen in place, hoping it'll stop. When it becomes clear the crying won't end anytime soon and, in fact, is only getting worse, she takes control of the situation.

"Let's get you inside," she says, knowing how the wives of Hemlock Circle gossip, her mother included. And the sight of Joyce Marsh weeping on her front stoop will spur plenty of that.

Inside, Ashley leads Mrs. Marsh to the kitchen, sitting her down at the island where she normally serves Ethan his afternoon snack.

"Can I get you something to drink?" she asks, as if her job has changed and she's now Mrs. Marsh's babysitter.

"Thank you, no." Mrs. Marsh takes a deep breath and wipes her eyes. "This is so humiliating."

"I understand," Ashley says, even though she doesn't. Her main source of income, not to mention her summer plans, have just been shot to hell. If anyone should be crying, it's her.

Mrs. Marsh reaches for a paper napkin and uses it to blow her nose. "That's sweet of you to say. Still, I'm sorry you had to see that. It's just, well, I'm upset because I was fired."

She barely gets that last word out before she starts weeping again, this time in great, heaving sobs that start to worry Ashley. Is Mrs. Marsh having a nervous breakdown? Should she yell for help? Also, where the hell is her husband? He usually doesn't leave for the university until 12:30.

"There, there," Ashley says, struck by how useless it sounds. Has that ever helped anyone?

"God, I'm so pathetic," Mrs. Marsh says between sobs. "I know I should be grateful for what I have. A good husband. Ethan. This house. But I just wanted to contribute, you know? And now I feel so . . . useless."

Her tears flow even harder now, and Ashley realizes there's nothing else to do except be Mrs. Marsh's friend. So she hops onto the stool next to Mrs. Marsh, puts an arm around her, and lets her cry against her shoulder.

As Ashley watches her neighbor weep in her perfectly appointed kitchen, she renews her promise to herself that she'll never end up like Mrs. Marsh or any of the wives on Hemlock Circle. She won't be dependent on her husband. She won't burst into tears because she feels inadequate. Most of all, no matter what happens, she'll get the hell out of suburbia.

And nothing is going to stop her.

THIRTEEN

Although only half the cul-de-sac separates Ashley's house from my own, it feels a lot longer with three shots of straight tequila in me. I sway slightly as I navigate the sidewalk in front of the Wallaces', almost tripping over the strip of flower bed running beside it. At the driveway, the security light above the garage kicks on, the sudden brightness startling me.

I stand there a moment, trying to gauge the range of the light's motion sensor. How close does one have to get to trigger the light? To test it, I move backward twenty paces and wait until the light over the Wallaces' garage clicks off.

Then I take a step.

And a second.

On the third, the light flicks on again.

I estimate that I'm about twenty feet away. Not as close as I thought was needed to activate it. Twice now, I've watched the garage lights on Hemlock Circle turn on, seemingly triggered by nothing. But just because I didn't see anyone doesn't mean they weren't there. It's very possible the lights were set off by someone twenty feet away in the opposite direction, toward the backs of the houses.

But who was that someone?

According to Vance Wallace, it was Billy. "I saw him running through the backyard," he said—a statement I'd like to dismiss but can't. Not after sensing Billy in my backyard around the same time Vance claimed to have seen him.

There are also the baseballs to consider. No one else knew about them. Yes, Ragesh does now, but he didn't until I told him after the first one appeared in the yard. Before that, the only people aware of their existence—and their meaning—were me and Billy.

Then there's the unnerving fact that one ball had been placed un-noticed *while I stood there*. How could I not see someone enter the yard and drop a ball there? How was that even possible?

I picture the way Vance Wallace looked an hour ago as he stood in my backyard. Not only confused and disheveled, but something else. Something more troublesome. He looked haunted—a fact made worse by what he mumbled to me.

I saw him. I followed him here. He's back.

Despite Ashley's assurances that it's the disease slowly eating away at her father's mind, I can't help but think something else is at work here. Something too strange and scary to be real.

I stop again, this time in front of the former Barringer residence, reminded of the trail cam. It had sent three alerts to my phone earlier tonight. The first was an opossum. The third was Mr. Wallace, led into my yard by someone he claimed to be Billy.

Between them was another picture. One I never bothered to check—a regrettable choice because it might show me who Vance Wallace followed into the yard.

I dig the phone from my pocket and open the trail cam app, which still displays the befuddled form of Mr. Wallace standing in the yard, his gaze aimed at the trees. The image makes my heart thud dully in my chest. Whatever he was looking at could be in the previous picture.

My finger starts to tremble as I resume swiping it across the phone's screen. And when I check the picture on the app, it's through eyes half closed in an anxious squint.

Not that there's cause for any of it. Because the image transmitted from the trail cam shows . . . nothing. Just the gray-green lawn spreading to the woods and the thicket of trees beyond it.

I keep scanning the image, searching for what triggered the trail cam. But I can't find anything that could have done it. There are no animals to be seen. Not a night bird or a large bug or even a falling leaf.

I'm about to close the app when I spot something at the forest's edge, faintly visible among the trees.

A shadow.

A human-shaped one.

Which doesn't mean it's really a person there. For all I know, it's always there, cast by the slant of moonlight through the trees. I swipe between the three pictures the trail cam took within a couple minutes of each other. The shadow only exists in the picture showing the empty lawn, destroying my theory that it's a consistent thing.

Whatever this is, it *moved*.

I bring the phone closer to my face, trying to see if it might be an animal standing on the cusp of the yard. A deer, most likely. Although the shadow is barely distinguishable from the rest of the night-shrouded woods, I can still make out its general shape. Head, neck, rounded shoulders.

This is no deer.

It's a person.

A short one, from the looks of it. Based on the nearby trees, I estimate the shadow to be about four and a half feet tall. About the height of a child. But not just any child. I'm struck by a memory of being in the fourth grade and learning about weights and measures. Our teacher, Mr. Richardson, lined all of us up against the wall to see how tall we were. My height then was four and a half feet.

So was Billy's.

I hurry the rest of the way home, my sneakers scuffing the sidewalk. Inside, I head upstairs, not stopping until I reach the door to my old bedroom. I can't remember the last time I set foot inside. Just like the backyard, I've avoided the bedroom for years, for all the same reasons. Too many memories. Ones I'd love to forget. It takes all the effort I can muster to twist the handle and open the door. Once I do, I cautiously peer inside, as if my younger self is waiting for me there.

Stepping inside feels like being hurtled to the past in a time machine. Nearly everything about the room is the same as it was when I was ten. Same wallpaper of cowboys, horses, and pines that I picked out during a weird Western phase when I was six. Same twin bed. Same desk by the window where I'd look out onto the backyard instead of doing homework.

And the same bookshelf.

It fills the wall opposite the bed, still as tall as I remember. When I was young, I needed a step stool to reach the top shelf. Now, no stool is required, but it's still a stretch.

The book I'm looking for is easy to find. It's the one with its spine facing inward. I pull it down, wipe away what seems like a half inch of dust, and examine the cover.

The Giant Book of Ghosts, Spirits, and Other Spooks.

I sit at my desk, filling a chair built for someone thirty years younger, and open the book. Inside are page after page of vibrant illustrations. Some of them have been circled in pencil, presumably by Billy.

I leaf through the book, noting how it's been organized alphabetically, starting with Amadlozi, figures from African folklore, and ending with Zuijin, Japanese spirits that are said to guard the gates of shrines.

I flip back and forth among the pages, encountering revenants and wraiths and a standard apparition dressed in old-timey clothes and surrounded by a bluish-green glow right out of *Scooby-Doo*.

Then one illustration stops me cold.

It depicts a humanoid figure the same color as a shadow but with two white pinpricks for eyes. The spirit in the illustration isn't translucent, like a stereotypical movie ghost, but it's not completely solid, either. A human-shaped storm cloud.

I compare the illustration to the image on my phone. While the shadow captured by the trail cam doesn't have white eyes—or any eyes at all—the rest of it appears very similar to the picture in the book.

Adding to the intrigue is how, like some of the other entries in the book, Billy had circled it with pencil.

Shadow Person.

I look to the margins of the page, which sends fear dripping down my spine like droplets of ice-cold water. There, Billy had written something that might have been innocuous at the time but is all too unnerving now.

This is real.

FOURTEEN

It's midnight, and I'm at the laptop in my father's study, where I've spent the past hour scrolling through one paranormal website after another. As a result, my head is spinning. It turns out that shadow people aren't as easy to classify as their name suggests. They might be ghosts, or they might be imaginary, summoned by those who suffer from night terrors. Or they might be nothing at all. Just peripheral vision playing tricks on those who claim to see them.

Adding to the confusion is that, if the internet is to be believed, there are several subcategories of shadow people. Most, it seems, don't harm anyone. They just like to hide in corners and watch you, sometimes to the point of stalking. Others cause not physical harm but a sense of extreme fear and unease with their presence alone. And still others attack, sometimes beating and choking sleeping victims.

I'll admit to getting a shiver when I read that part, and feeling slightly better about being an insomniac.

Some shadow people roam, oblivious to the humans around them. Some only appear in the same spot. There are even shadow animals, though it boggles the mind how that works. As for what the trail cam picked up, it appears to be what's known as a forest shadow person.

If it's anything at all.

I'm not convinced that the trail cam snapped a picture of a shadow person, for a gazillion different reasons. It could be a glitch in the trail cam or the silhouette of an animal that just happened to look human in that moment or any of a hundred different things. Just because Billy wrote in a book thirty years ago that shadow people are real doesn't mean they are.

Or that he became one.

Then again, what if he did?

Because something weird has been happening outside. That's undeniable. Which is why I continue to scroll through paranormal sites with the restless intensity of a teenager looking at online porn. I search for plain old ghosts next. A mistake. There are literally thousands of websites about ghosts. So many that it brings on a stinging pain just behind my eyes.

I try to blink it away as I scan the search results, clicking one at random. It turns out to be a long list of all the different types of spirits known throughout the world. A *very* long list. Less than half of which I recognize. Wraiths and shades. Djinn and mylingar. Poltergeists and phantoms and apparitions out the ass.

After another hour of scrolling, clicking, and reading, I think I have a decent grasp on the situation. Well, *a* situation. One that would make anyone I shared it with worried about my mental state. Honestly, I'm a bit worried myself. As a teacher of English lit, I'm well acquainted with ghosts. Hamlet's father, requesting vengeance. The mind-shattering spirits of Shirley Jackson's Hill House. All the phantoms and spooks that sprang from Poe's imagination. But those were all made up. Just stories. What I'm contemplating is something else entirely.

Something utterly, impossibly real.

From my admittedly slapdash research, I've gathered that most ghosts have a purpose beyond scaring the shit out of people. In many cases, that purpose is to complete some form of unfinished business here on earth so they can move on. But that often requires help from the living, who can be oblivious to a ghost's presence or needs. To get their attention, ghosts sometimes resort to that most clichéd of actions.

They haunt.

Which isn't necessarily the kind of haunting you see in movies or gothic novels. Slamming doors and rattling chains and shrieking like a banshee down castle corridors. Ghosts are more subtle than that. They're also patient, sometimes waiting for the right moment in which to spring into action.

For Billy, this would be the perfect moment. Events beyond my control have brought me back here, to the place where Billy disappeared. The same is true of Ashley, who never thought she'd return to Hemlock Circle. It's slightly different with Russ and Ragesh, who never truly left, but even in their cases, life has kept them tied to this place.

All four of us were with Billy hours before he was taken. Now we're back on Hemlock Circle for the first time in thirty years.

At the exact moment Billy's body is found.

On what will soon be the anniversary of his death.

Looking at it from that angle makes it seem like not fate exactly, but something in the same ballpark.

What if it's all the work of Billy?

A crazy notion, no doubt prompted by his stupid ghost book and all the stupid websites I've spent the night skimming. But according to those websites, there's also some logic to it. If the primary goal of a supernatural entity is to resolve unfinished business on earth so it can retreat to the other side, then it stands to reason that Billy needs us to find out who killed him and why.

It's even possible that's the reason Billy's remains were found now and not five, ten, twenty years ago. That *he's* the one who allowed them to be found, because he knew the four of us had returned to Hemlock Circle.

More likely, it's just me he was waiting for. His best friend who left and never looked back. It would explain the lights going on and off around the cul-de-sac—not to mention the baseballs in the yard. That also could be Billy, resorting to one of his old tricks to gently nudge me in this direction.

What to do next, I have no idea. The consensus suggestion of the websites I've consulted is to try to establish communication. Carefully, of course. Make a mistake and all sorts of things could go wrong. And one of the most common mistakes is to approach communication without utter sincerity.

I shut my laptop, pull out my phone, and call the only person I know I can talk to about something so strange. I count the rings, knowing there'll be five of them before the call goes to Claudia's voicemail.

"Hey," I say after the beep. "It's me again. I know I shouldn't be calling you like this. But I have to tell someone or else I'll go crazy. Maybe I already am."

It's not until I say it out loud that I realize it might be true. Maybe everything that's happened the past few days, combined with the events of the previous years, have led me to insanity. It would explain a lot, including why I'm calling Claudia at one in the morning. Yet I keep talking, compelled to try to make some sense of it all.

"I think Billy might be haunting me, Claude." I pause, picturing her weirded-out reaction. "I know, it's ridiculous. But weird things are happening that I can't—"

Ping!

At first, I assume I've again exceeded the limit of Claudia's voicemail system and been cut off. The realization that I'm wrong comes a few seconds later, when I hear the familiar impatient beep from Claudia's voicemail. Only then do I understand the first noise.

It was an alert from the sole app open on my phone.

The trail cam has just taken another picture.

I freeze, the phone still pressed to my ear, paralyzed by—what?

Uncertainty?

Maybe.

Fear?

Definitely.

Because what if this is indeed real? What if I open the app and see Billy's ghost standing in front of the trail cam?

That thought alone is frightening enough, but there is also the bigger picture to consider. I don't know how to live in a world in which ghosts are a reality. Does this mean I'll start seeing more of them? Will they also try to contact me? Even more daunting, will I be able to contact them?

Bracing myself, I open the app. Instead of Billy, I see bare lawn and the forest rising behind it, with nary a shadow person to be found.

But something triggered the camera's motion sensor, and I need to find out what it is.

I leave the study and head to the kitchen, where I grab a flashlight from the cluttered all-purpose drawer. Outside, I step cautiously into the backyard and sweep the flashlight's beam across the grass and into the woods. The light catches something just beyond the tree line.

A blur.

Something in motion.

The sight of it elicits a yelp from me and more motion from whatever the hell is moving through the trees. In that moment, all I can think about are the stories about the falls and the lake and the ghosts of people who've died in it drifting over the water like fog. Is that what happened to Billy? Is he this blur of gray?

No, it turns out. For the thing in the woods quickly takes shape, turning from a gray blur into what's clearly a startled deer. In the flashlight's glare, I can easily see its white tail bobbing as it springs deeper into the woods.

Mystery solved, I remain in the yard, waiting. For what, I'm not exactly sure. Billy, I guess, stepping into the yard in ghostly form. Or floating. Or doing whatever ghosts do. Maybe he's here right now, invisible in the shadows, quietly biding his time until I notice him.

I look back on everything that has happened in the past few days—the lights, the baseballs, the shadow in the woods—and wonder, not for the first time, if there could be a rational explanation for all of it. If so, I haven't found it yet. Which, I suppose, is what makes something supernatural. That complete lack of rationality.

There's a chance that some of it could simply be my imagination, fueled by guilt, grief, and a form of magical thinking. Then, of course, there's Vance Wallace's unfortunate condition, which confuses his brain into thinking he's seeing things that aren't there. Even the baseball appearing in the yard while I stood there could have a logical explanation.

I shoot a glance to the old Barringer house, where a corner of the second floor is visible over the hedge. A single window there faces my backyard. Maybe someone tossed the ball from there, although I don't know who could have done it. No one currently lives there, and no Barringer has been inside since the mid-nineties. But it's at least a hint of an explanation. I'm sure I can think of similar hints for every single strange thing that's happened. It doesn't matter that my gut tells me the opposite, that it's all been the work of Billy himself.

I'm in the process of turning back toward my house when I hear something.

A rustle in the woods.

Light yet oddly loud in the otherwise silent darkness.

With it comes the same presence I felt two nights ago. This time, it's unmistakable.

Billy.

And not a memory of him. It really, truly, utterly feels like he's here with me right now.

With the flashlight gripped tight in my fist, I rotate toward the woods again.

Slowly.

So very slowly.

Slow enough that I can feel my thoughts changing from fearful to curious to borderline hopeful. What if it's really him? What can I possibly say after all these years?

I'm sorry, for starters. *I shouldn't have said what I said and done what I'd done. And I definitely should have helped you, even though I had no idea you needed it.*

Instead, once I'm facing the woods, the flashlight aimed at the trees, all I can think to say is "Billy? Are you out there?"

At first, there's nothing. Just the white noise of insects and the faint flicker of fireflies and a stillness so vast it's suffocating.

Then I spot a faint rustle in the trees and hear a whisper of leaves. Something emerges from the woods, low to the ground.

A baseball.

I lower the flashlight until it's latched onto the ball. I stare, hypnotized, as the ball continues to roll across the lawn toward my feet.

When it knocks against the toe of my shoe, I run.

Into the woods, crashing through underbrush, searching for the person who just put the ball in my yard.

But there is no person on the edge of the woods.

Just me.

Spinning in circles as the flashlight beam shudders through the forest, illuminating the ground, the trees, their branches drooping with leaves.

I return to the yard and pick up this new baseball, which in reality looks decades old. The leather is slightly yellowed, and the red stitching is frayed in spots. Turning it in my hand, I see a few grass stains and teeth marks likely made by a dog.

It is, I realize, the very same baseball Billy threw into my yard when he was still alive.

Gripping it now, I understand everything.

Billy *is* back.

He's been out here for days, trying to get my attention any way he can. Roaming the cul-de-sac, flicking on lights, tossing baseballs into my yard. And the meaning is the same now as it was thirty years ago.

It's time to play.

After eating lunch but before going out to play, Ethan takes a quick shower—another recent development. Until May, he'd been forced by his mother to take baths every evening. Something he used to like because baths inspired playful thinking. He'd imagine he was a sea monster or a shark or sometimes, flat on his back under the water, a person drowning. But ever since Russ Chen said he only took showers, the very idea of a bath made Ethan feel babyish, and so he begged his mother to let him switch to showers.

Once clean, Ethan dresses quickly—a neon-green T-shirt, cargo shorts, his white Air Jordans now scuffed gray from overuse. The reason for his speediness is simple: He doesn't want to be around his mother anymore. She'd acted strange all morning. Angry. Not at him, which should have been a refreshing change but in fact only unsettled Ethan. He knows it's because she lost her job. That much is obvious. What eludes him is what he can do about it.

Ethan senses his father felt the same way because he left for work earlier than normal—an act that seemed to make his mother angrier. It only got worse when Ethan asked, for the second time that day, when Ashley was coming over to babysit him.

"She's not," his mother snapped. "You're stuck with me now."

Yet Ethan can hear Ashley downstairs. Another reason for his speed. Maybe his mother had a change of heart and decided he can still have Ashley as a babysitter.

Downstairs, he understands that's not what's happening. What is, he doesn't know. Because his mother is seated at the kitchen island, her head on Ashley's shoulder. As Ethan gets closer, his heart seizes in his chest.

His mother, he realizes, is crying.

"Oh!" she says when she spots him, and quickly tries to dry her eyes, as if that will make Ethan forget what he's just seen.

But then Ashley swoops in, blocking Ethan's view of his mother. "Hey, buddy," she says. "Why don't you go outside and play? I'll meet up with you soon, okay?"

Ethan reluctantly heads outside, giving his mother a quick backward glance as he goes. She's composed herself in the few seconds he was with Ashley and now looks more embarrassed than sad. Yet the image of her weeping sticks with Ethan as he stands in the backyard, his imagination filling with all sorts of dire scenarios. The main one from that morning—his parents' imminent divorce—is quickly usurped by others. Illness and death and having to move.

He's so occupied with terrible thoughts that he doesn't notice when Russ Chen squeezes through the hedge separating their yards. Ethan only becomes aware of him when Russ speaks, squeaking out a nervous "Hey, Ethan."

"Hey," Ethan says absently.

"What's going on?"

Ethan finally turns to look at his neighbor, struck as usual by how awkwardly skinny he is. All legs and arms and knees and elbows. Not for the first time, Ethan wonders how Russ stays upright on such thin limbs.

"Nothing," he says, which is the opposite of the truth. Everything, it seems, is going on, and he understands none of it. "I was going to Billy's to play."

"Cool," Russ says. "I'll come, too."

Ethan knows Billy won't like that. But he doesn't have the will-power to resist. "Sure," he says as he scoops up Billy's baseball and carries it through the hedge and into the Barringers' backyard.

There, he finds not Billy but his younger brother, Andy, lazily run-ning a Matchbox car over the grass. Andy perks up when he sees the two older boys.

"Hi, Ethan! Hi, Russ!"

"Is Billy around?" Ethan asks, knowing the answer is yes. If Billy threw a ball into his yard, it means he's surely home.

A window on the second floor opens. Billy's bedroom, Ethan real-izes. Through the window screen, Billy calls down to the yard, "I'll be right there!"

When he emerges from the house twenty seconds later, Ethan tosses him the baseball. "Here's your ball back."

Billy lunges for it, misses, and watches chagrined as the ball plops onto the grass. Then he spots Russ on the edge of the yard. A moment passes in which Ethan and Billy have a full conversation without say-ing a word, exchanging looks that only a best friend can interpret.

What's he doing here?

It's not my fault. He invited himself.

Why couldn't you get rid of him?

Please just deal with it.

"So, do you guys want to play?" Russ says in such a way that Ethan can't tell if he understands the silent exchange with Billy or remains completely oblivious.

"We're not playing," Billy says. "We're *exploring*."

This is news to Ethan, who assumed they'd be playing hide-and-seek or Teenage Mutant Ninja Turtles. "Where?" he asks.

Billy shrugs, as if he hasn't given it any thought. "The woods."

Ethan looks to the trees bordering the swooping curve of Billy's yard. His parents don't like him going into the woods without telling them first, something he can't do today because it might mean he'll see his mother crying again.

"Can't we just stay in the yard?" he says.

"Do you see any places to explore in this yard?"

Ethan checks both sides of the lawn, for reasons unknown even to him. Obviously, there aren't. "No," he says.

"Exactly," Billy replies.

Next to Ethan, Russ pipes up. "I'll go exploring!"

"Me, too," says Andy, abandoning his Matchbox car in the grass.

Billy kneels before his brother and puts a hand on his shoulder. Although he complains about Andy's annoyingness all the time, Ethan's never once seen Billy treat him with anything but affection. Being an only child, Ethan suspects he wouldn't be the same way. He can't imagine having a sibling. Sharing space. Sharing toys. Sharing parents. He gets the luxury of always being the center of attention.

"Only big kids can go," Billy says, as if they're teenagers and not a mere three years older than Andy.

"But I can act like a big kid."

"I'll play with you when I get back." Billy then invokes the phrase he's been using constantly since he and Ethan went to see *The Lion King* three weeks earlier. "Hakuna matata, dude?"

Andy nods, dejected. "Okay."

Then the three of them begin the march across the yard. First Billy, then Russ, then a reluctant Ethan. There's something off about Billy today that he can't quite pinpoint. He's normally less determined, less self-assured. If Russ weren't with them, he'd ask Billy what's going on. But Russ *is* with them, a fact Billy no longer seems to mind as they pause at the tree line.

"You ready?" he asks.

"Totally," Russ says with an enthusiasm that makes Ethan roll his eyes.

"Ethan?"

Billy looks his way, the curious glint in his eyes worrying Ethan. Something is definitely up.

"I guess," Ethan says, resigned to endure whatever it is Billy clearly has planned. "Let's go exploring."

FIFTEEN

After groggily going through the motions of normal life—coffee, breakfast, shower—I'm back at the laptop by nine a.m., this time examining Hemlock Circle as it looks on Google Maps. From above, it appears as a series of circles within circles, like a target.

The bull's-eye, if you will, is a small circular island of plants in the dead center of the cul-de-sac. There's a Japanese maple, some stubby evergreens, swaths of ivy. Surrounding it is the street itself, which juts into the circle between the Wallaces' and the Patels'. The outer circle is made up of the property lots—a thick band of green lawn on which sit six homes.

Surrounding all of it is the forest, which thins out a quarter mile behind the Wallace house, where it's replaced by a state road with another, less-wooded residential area on the other side. I move the map in the opposite direction, nudging it northward until the screen is filled with the green of the woods behind my house.

I don't stop until a brown rectangle breaks through the green.

The Hawthorne Institute.

At least I think it is. The land surrounding it is more overgrown than I remember it being, with swaths of pixelated green obscuring what resides there. Even when I zoom in, it's hard to make out individual buildings or other details. Almost as if it's forbidden to see them from any angle.

Or maybe I'm just so exhausted I can't see straight.

I barely slept a wink during the night, too occupied by thoughts of Billy, of ghosts, of *Billy's* ghost. Now I'm running only on fumes and caffeine as I stare at the satellite view of the area, trying in vain to bring it into focus.

One of the things that kept me awake all night was this idea that Billy needs me to help him move on. That he's spent the past thirty years in a ghostly limbo, waiting for my return. Since his remains were found there—and because it's where we went to explore the day he vanished—the falls and the Hawthorne Institute seem like the most logical place to start.

I return to my old friend Google, beginning my search with Ezra Hawthorne. For someone worth a billion dollars when he died, his digital footprint is shockingly small. The search yields just a few archival photos showing a man whose looks barely changed over the years. A picture of him taken in the sixties bears a striking resemblance to one snapped in the nineties. In all of them, his overriding feature is paleness. White hair, white skin, white teeth. When that's combined with the fact that he seemed only to have been photographed while wearing a black suit, a person couldn't be faulted for thinking Ezra was actually a walking corpse.

Yet he lived for almost a hundred years, according to his meager Wikipedia page. Born in 1900, died in 1998. And that's about it for pertinent information contained in his listing, which mostly details his status as the only child of Elsa Hawthorne, who was the only child of steel magnate L. B. Hawthorne. The institute is mentioned once, in a sentence so vague it could mean literally anything.

Hawthorne founded the Hawthorne Institute in 1937, and remained its head and primary benefactor until his death. It closed shortly thereafter.

There's no link to a separate entry for the institute, nor is there any hint of what went on there. The rest of the page is just Ezra Hawthorne's biography, outlined in brief snippets.

Education: Princeton University
Occupation: Philanthropist and philosopher
Personal life: Never married

Only under the entry for religion do things get interesting. There, it reads, "While Hawthorne never publicly affiliated himself with any organized religion, he was known to dabble in the occult."

That last word glows like neon on my laptop screen.

Occult.

A far cry from how Detective Palmer described Ezra Hawthorne. She merely called him eccentric and said that his institute was a place of research. But this makes it sound like it was something else.

Something sinister.

Then again, it might not be true at all. Wikipedia has given the sentence a "citation needed" tag, indicating there's nothing to back it up.

Yet the word "occult"—and all that it implies—sticks with me as I do another Google search, this time for the Hawthorne Institute. It yields hundreds of results. Very few are places in the United States. None are in New Jersey.

I search again, this time including the zip code. That brings up one entry: Hawthorne Farms.

I click it and am brought to a section of the county park system's website. At the top of the page is an image of what could pass for a royal estate in the British countryside. Walls of mountain stone, leaded windows, slate roof. And while the accompanying text makes no mention of an institute, I'm certain this is the place. I know because it says the mansion and grounds are available to rent for weddings and private functions, which Ragesh mentioned the other day. Apparently, dubbing it a farm is better for bookings than calling it an institute.

Lower on the page is a sampling of photos taken at such events. One shows a room filled with men in suits bearing a cadaverous appearance similar to Ezra Hawthorne's. Another pictures that same room decked out for a wedding. Beneath it is a photo of a bride and groom posing with the falls in the background. My stomach clenches when I see it.

Billy is in that photo.

Not visible.

Certainly not a shadow person lurking at the edges of ghostly mist hovering among the rushing water.

But he's there nonetheless. Just beneath the lake's surface. His presence known to no one.

I stare at the faces of the happy couple and wonder a hundred different things. Could they feel Billy's presence while smiling for the camera? Did they sense him the same way I do when I enter the backyard?

Unable to look at what's become of the place now, I resume my search for signs of what it used to be. Rather than futilely Google for a few more hours like I did last night, I remember how Claudia, in her work for a far different parks department, used a subscription-based newspaper archive whenever she needed to do a historical deep dive into one of the places she oversaw.

Five minutes and one credit card charge later, I'm scanning more than a century's worth of local newspapers, most of them long gone.

The Hawthorne Institute yields several hits from the kind of hyper-local weekly newspapers that used to flourish everywhere but barely exist nowadays. I choose one at random and see it's from late October 1963. A notice in the social calendar informing readers of upcoming events, in this case a lecture about Harry Houdini to be held on Halloween night for invited guests at the Hawthorne Institute. There is no follow-up article.

Most of the other search results are similar event listings or tersely innocuous recaps. "The Hawthorne Institute hosted the Amazing Kreskin at a private dinner on Saturday," reads one entry from 1972. "Hawthorne Institute holds annual meeting," goes another from 1985.

Among the most recent items are obituaries for Ezra Hawthorne, in which the institute is mentioned but dwarfed by flashier topics such as his family and his philanthropy. Not long after those are articles heralding his bequeathing of the institute's land to the county. Nearly all of them describe Ezra as "eccentric" or "reclusive" or, in one, "controversial," although, like Wikipedia's mention of the occult, there's nothing to support the statement. Just like there's nothing to suggest what really went on at the Hawthorne Institute and if anyone there would have had a reason to harm a ten-year-old boy.

That's where my mind keeps going, even though I agree with Russ that it makes me seem paranoid. Maybe I wouldn't feel this way if the institute grounds had been searched after Billy was taken. But they weren't, most likely because Ezra Hawthorne paid someone off. Since Billy's body was found there—and because I don't buy into Detective Palmer's theory that the killer was from Hemlock Circle—the only conclusion I can come to is that his murder was somehow related to our time at the Hawthorne Institute.

The big unknown about that day is Billy's whereabouts between the rest of us leaving the institute grounds without him and his arrival in my backyard later that evening. A span of more than five hours. I have no idea how long he was at the Hawthorne Institute or what he saw or who he talked to. He didn't share any details in the tent that night because he was mad at me and I was mad at him, and both of us, I suspect, were also angry at ourselves.

But if Billy's death is somehow related to being at the Hawthorne Institute, is it even possible that he could have seen or heard something he shouldn't have? I won't know until I see the place for myself.

Which means the next step is to go there. I'll likely discover nothing by retracing our steps to the institute and back, but that's not really the point. If Billy wants me to do it—and I'm pretty sure he does—I will. I owe him at least that much.

Before closing the website, I narrow the search to things published within a five-year window of Billy's abduction. A last-ditch attempt to learn something useful about the place during that time. I don't find much. The Hawthorne Institute's social calendar slowed noticeably in the nineties. Instead, I only see tiny mentions lumped in with others in listings of library donations and property tax assessments.

Exactly one item piques my interest, in a crime blotter from July 1992. Someone living near the institute filed a noise complaint, saying they heard a scream coming from the property in the middle of the night.

Because Hemlock Circle is the closest residential area to the institute, my guess is that the complaint came from here. I doubt my parents would have done it, even though we were firmly ensconced on the cul-de-sac by then. Besides, I think I'd remember hearing a scream from the woods when I was eight. Who made the complaint—and the source of the scream—remains unknown. The newspaper never bothered to follow up on it.

I assume that lack of detail will be evident in the news item immediately preceding it, from June of the same year. I give it a half-hearted scan, uninterested in a listing of places where local students have been assigned to do mandatory volunteer service. But then I see that the

Hawthorne Institute was one of them—a revelation that brings a spike of adrenaline.

I'm hit with another when I read the very familiar names of the two students sent there.

Johnny Chen and Ragesh Patel.

While I'm not surprised the two of them did volunteer work—it was required, after all—I'm shocked that a place as secretive as the Hawthorne Institute took part in the program. Only once, it seems, because a search for mentions of it in similar listings from other years comes up empty.

That strikes me as odd.

Very odd.

A private institute doing unknown research let two teenage boys volunteer there. Then it apparently never happened again. Making it weirder is the fact that Johnny died of a drug overdose the next summer. Even though one likely has nothing to do with the other, it does make me wonder what kind of work Johnny and Ragesh did at the Hawthorne Institute—and how much Ragesh really knows about the place.

Whatever it is, it's more than he's let on, both now and thirty years ago.

Ragesh sits on a log in the woods behind Johnny Chen's house, wondering if today will be the day he finally smokes his first joint. He's had it for more than a year, kept in an Altoids tin stuffed in a back corner of his underwear drawer. He's lost count of the number of times he's entered this forest, come to the same downed tree where he and Johnny used to sit together, and pulled out the joint, prepared to smoke and toke. Yet he never gets the nerve to actually do it. Johnny gave him the joint, after he switched to stronger stuff a few months before he died, and Ragesh is afraid that once it's smoked, it'll be official.

His best friend is gone.

And never coming back.

Ragesh knows that already. He's not a fucking idiot. But he also knows that if he keeps the joint tucked in that Altoids tin, in some ways it'll feel like Johnny never left.

He jabs the joint between his lips, the twist of paper now brittle from the dozen or so prior times he's done it, and thinks about what to do next. He knows what Johnny's answer would be. *Smoke 'em if you got 'em, bro,* he'd say in that exhausted way Ragesh knew came from being the older son of strict parents who demanded perfection. Straight A's, star student, extracurriculars out the ass so you'd look well-rounded enough to get into Harvard or Yale. (Not Princeton, though. When you live a stone's throw from an Ivy, attending it feels like going to your local community college.)

Ragesh doesn't face such pressure. His older sister, Rani, took care of all that for him. Miss Perfect is currently at Oxford, enjoying the first year of her Rhodes Scholarship. Since his parents have zero expectations for him, Ragesh can spend the summer doing nothing, like he always does. It's why he's never felt the urge to get messed up the way Johnny did. A couple of stolen beers are all he needs to have a good time. Not Johnny, though. He always seemed lost in himself, haunted by something. For him it wasn't just about having a good time. It was about escape.

"You're seriously not curious what it feels like?" he once asked as the two of them sat on this very log, Ragesh sipping a lukewarm Zima and Johnny smoking weed. Before Ragesh could answer, Johnny said, "I wanna show you."

"I'm good."

"Please," Johnny said. "Just a taste."

Relenting, Ragesh waited to be passed the joint. "Open your mouth," Johnny told him before inhaling. He did, letting out a grunt of surprise when Johnny leaned in and placed his parted lips against Ragesh's. Once the smoke passed from one mouth to the other, Johnny remained there, kissing him.

Panic rang through Ragesh's brain, slicing through his Zima buzz and whatever high the pot was providing. He didn't know what to do because he wasn't quite sure what was happening. Was Johnny kissing him for real? Was it a joke?

Ragesh didn't freak out until Johnny reached up and started running a hand through his buzz cut. That's when he knew his friend wasn't just dicking around. He was truly, seriously kissing him.

"What the fuck, dude?" Ragesh yelped as he leapt from the log and stood a good ten paces away.

The look in Johnny's eyes went from dazed to devastated in half a second. "I didn't mean it," he said. "It's the weed."

Ragesh told him it was cool. That he shouldn't worry about it. But things weren't the same after that, even though both of them pretended they were. Six months later, Johnny was dead, and the only thing Ragesh has left of him is this stupid joint, which probably isn't even any good anymore.

If Johnny were there right now, Ragesh would tell him that he hadn't meant to freak out, that it was okay if he was into guys or whatever, that he even kind of liked the kiss, even though he's pretty sure he's *not* into guys. Most of all, Ragesh would ask Johnny if the overdose was intentional and if it had anything to do with his reaction that day.

But Johnny isn't there, and all Ragesh can do is whisper "Smoke 'em if you got 'em, bro" before pulling out his lighter and flicking the flame to life.

Just as he's about to place the fire to the joint's tip, Ragesh hears voices echoing through the trees. Three of them, from the sound of it. Ones he knows well. Sure enough, Johnny's brother, Russ, appears in the distance, ahead of the Marsh kid and behind the older of the Barringer nerds.

Ragesh pockets the joint and the lighter. Not because he's worried the boys will narc on him. They wouldn't dare. But he also doesn't want to remind Russ that his big brother was a pothead before moving on to the stuff that would soon kill him.

By the time the boys spot him, Ragesh is standing on the log, knowing how tall it makes him appear. Towering over them, he enjoys the nervous way they look when he says, "What are you losers up to?"

"Nothing," says the Marsh kid, whose name he can never remember even though they live across the cul-de-sac from each other.

"And we're not losers," says Russ, who knows he can talk back to Ragesh because of the Johnny connection.

Only the Barringer kid, Billy—that name Ragesh can remember—gives what amounts to a real answer. "We're exploring," he says with such innocent pride that it makes the Marsh boy cringe a little.

Ragesh hops down from the log and sneers. He doesn't really know why. They're just kids, doing stupid kid things. He and Johnny marched through the woods doing the same thing when they were that age. But even as he decides to let them pass, he can't keep himself from saying, "There's nothing to explore here, dipshit."

A voice cuts through the forest. The voice of a girl. One older than the boys.

"Leave him alone, asshole."

Ragesh sees Ashley Wallace marching his way, looking like she wants to deck him. He lifts his hands in innocence. "I was just having some fun."

"You were picking on a kid, which is, like, so pathetic." Ashley turns to the boys and says, "I told your mom I'd keep an eye on you, Ethan."

Ragesh slaps his thigh. Ethan. Of course. He can't believe he forgot that. Yet he notices the wounded way the kid talks.

"So you're still my babysitter?"

"For today, yeah." Ashley's shoulders rise and fall. "I guess."

"We're exploring," Billy announces.

Ashley shoots Ragesh a mean look and says, "So I've heard. Lead the way."

The four of them continue pushing through the woods, and Ragesh, having nothing better to do, goes with them. He checks out Ashley as she walks, taking in her long legs in her too-short shorts and how her shirt sometimes rides up to give glimpses of her tanned lower back. Looking at her, he wants to feel desire. Or even just basic

PG-rated attraction. But as usual, he can only think about the way Johnny's lips felt against his and how part of him wanted to kiss back and how now that will never, ever happen.

Ragesh sidles up to Ashley, scratching the back of his head, not because it itches, but because he knows it makes his bicep look bigger and hopes Ashley notices that fact.

She does, and it looks like she's impressed.

"There's a party tonight at Brent Miller's house," he says.

"I know."

"You wanna go?"

"Like, together?" Ashley says before grimacing, like she's completely incapable of hiding her disgust.

"Forget it." Ragesh pauses before reversing course. "Actually, no. Do you not want to go with me because of what I said to Billy back there?"

"Partly, yeah. Picking on kids half your age doesn't make you cool, Patel. It makes you pathetic."

Even as Ashley's words make him wince, Ragesh can't help but ask, "What's the other part? Is it because of the thing in the woods?"

He hates to bring it up, mostly because it's totally humiliating, even weeks later. But he hates the idea of Ashley being repulsed by him even more. He knows it's fucked up, but he needs her to like him, because if she does, then maybe he'll be able to like her back and not feel so . . . Well, he doesn't know how he feels. All he knows is that he hates it.

"Behind your house," he adds when Ashley doesn't answer.

"I know what you mean," she snaps. "And yes, that's part of it. Can you blame me? You were spying on me—"

"I wasn't. I swear."

"Probably jerking off."

"That definitely wasn't what was happening," Ragesh says.

"Then what were you doing?"

Thinking. That's what Ragesh was doing. Standing in the woods thinking about Johnny and how he'd fucked things up between them so much that he suspects Johnny decided to kill himself. But he can't tell Ashley that. He can't tell anyone.

"Nothing," Ragesh says. "Just clearing my head."

Ashley snorts, clearly not believing him. "Sure. Right."

Ragesh looks away, more humiliated than he thought he'd be and regretting every decision he's made in the past ten minutes. He should have just let these twerps keep walking, lit his joint, and let all his bad thoughts fade into nothingness. Instead, he's here, marching through the woods with three boys and a girl who hates him, going God knows where. Checking his surroundings, he realizes they're deep into the forest now. Even though he's certain he's been this far before, nothing looks familiar.

"Where the hell are we?"

"I don't know," Ashley says with a sigh. "Hey, Billy, since you seem to be guiding us here, how far are we going, exactly?"

Up ahead, Billy says, "Another mile."

"Uh, why?"

They've reached a clearing in the woods, the trees giving way to a narrow strip of land before rising again on the other side. Billy turns around to answer, backing into the clearing as he does so.

"Because that's—"

Ragesh hears the car before he sees it. A loud bleat of a horn, followed by the screech of tires skidding to a stop along the blacktop. That's the moment he realizes the clearing is actually a road cutting through the forest.

And that Billy had almost backed right onto it as he was talking.

And that the car—a Ford something or other with a startled driver behind the wheel—had just barely missed him.

SIXTEEN

The forest is quiet and dark.

Unnervingly so.

I'd expected chirping birds and prancing critters and sunlight streaming through the trees. A cartoon, basically. Something from those Disney VHS tapes still sitting in the basement in their white plastic clamshell cases. Instead, I walk in near silence, the only sound made by my own footsteps as I move through the trees. Above me, a canopy of leaves blocks out much of the sun. What little light there is comes in bright splotches that dapple the forest floor.

I have only a vague recollection of the last time I walked these woods, the day Billy vanished. In my memory, it's brighter, more open. Then again, there were five of us clomping through the woods, making no attempt to be quiet. Now there's only me, the crash of my footfalls breaking the otherworldly hush of the forest.

Between them is another, lighter sound that I first think is an echo of my steps. But something is off about them. They're not quite in sync with my movements, not to mention they seem quieter than an echo.

I stop, lift my right foot, and stomp once on the leaf-covered ground. The sound it makes reverberates through the woods a moment before quickly fading. Now that I know what the echo of my footsteps sounds like, I continue walking.

One step.

Five steps.

Ten steps.

On the eleventh, I hear the sound again.

I stop. A halt so sudden that all noise made by me instantly ceases. Yet there's another sound in the forest. A single, almost imperceptible shush of leaves coming from somewhere behind me.

Hearing it creates a cold drip of anxiety that runs directly down my spine. Yes, it could be an animal. But animals, far more scared of us than we are of them, don't just stop when there's a human present. They run, scurrying through the underbrush and making all sorts of noise as they go.

But this? This sounds like footsteps. Quiet, unobtrusive ones timed to match my own.

I'm not alone in these woods.

Someone else is with me.

I slowly turn in a complete circle, scanning the forest for signs of where they are—and who it could be. But I see nothing. It's just me and the trees and the ragged weeds filling the ground around them.

Which means whoever's here doesn't want to be seen. Definitely *not* a good sign.

I remain completely still, even as my mind races, thinking of reasons why someone would follow me into the woods while trying hard not to make their presence known. As usual, I go to the worst-case scenario first: Someone wants to do me harm.

A maniac hiding in the woods. Preparing to do to me what someone else did to Billy.

That leads to another, worse thought.

That it's Billy himself, his long-ago Halloween prediction coming true in the most twisted way.

I bet there are ghosts roaming these woods right now.

I resume walking. I don't have a choice. I'm in the middle of the forest and must go somewhere. So I forge ahead, each step I take matched by a similar, slightly quieter one a half second later.

One step.

Five steps.

Ten steps.

Then I run.

Terrified that I'm being chased—by a killer, by Billy, by anything— I crash through the woods, dodging low-hanging branches and leaping over logs, fully aware it's borderline-ridiculous behavior. I don't know what I'm running from. Or if I need to be running at all. Yet instinct keeps me moving. Not slowing, I risk a backward glance, trying to see who or what or *if* anything is behind me.

I see nothing.

Still looking backward, I burst through a line of trees and out of the woods. A startling transition that makes me whip my head around to face forward. A second passes in which I think I've reached the falls, its dark water spreading before me. I skid to a stop, arms pinwheeling to steady myself, as if one wrong move will send me tumbling over them.

But I'm not at the falls. Not even close.

I'm still a mile away, at the road that sits between my backyard and the Hawthorne Institute. The sight of that asphalt cutting through the forest—as clear a reminder of civilization as there can possibly be—makes me wonder if Detective Palmer is right about Billy knowing who sliced open the tent.

If so, it means he went willingly into the forest, coming to this very road. What did he feel at that moment? Did he have any inkling of what would happen here?

Then there's my biggest question: Was he scared?

God, I hope not. I hope it was quick and painless and so sudden that he never knew what was happening.

Catching my breath now at the road's edge, I think about the police dogs that followed his scent here. It's common knowledge that the dogs couldn't track Billy farther than that, leading everyone to think he was taken to a waiting car and whisked far away. What's not as well-known is that Billy had been here earlier in the day with four other people.

Me and Ragesh, Ashley, and Russ.

I can't keep from thinking that we're to blame for the misunderstanding. That our presence in the woods confused the dogs and sent them back the way they came. All those different scent trails crisscrossing the road, some of them with Billy, some of them not. As a result, everyone thought Billy's journey ended right here.

In truth, it was only the halfway point.

E than watches it all unfold like a movie in slow motion. Billy edging close to the road. The car honking its horn and screeching to a stop. Ashley shrieking as she runs to Billy, pulling him away from the road, mouthing an apology to the driver as the car slowly moves on.

"You need to watch where you're going!" she yells at Billy.

Billy, visibly shaken but none the worse for wear, nods. "I'm sorry. I was distracted."

"Just be careful." Ashley sighs as she looks at the rest of them. "All of you. Me and Ragesh will be in deep shit if something happens to one of you."

"I'm not their babysitter," Ragesh protests.

"Hate to break it to you, doofus, but you're just as responsible for their well-being as I am. It's called maturity. Look it up."

As they bicker, Ethan stares at the road slicing like a knife through the forest. His parents don't allow him to wander this far, and Ethan has never had the desire.

"Maybe we should head back," he says, knowing they're now a mile deep in the forest and run the risk of getting lost if they go any farther.

The others keep moving, crossing the road without a second of hesitation. Even Billy, who appears to have forgotten about the car that almost just hit him. He now looks even more eager to get to the other side and explore the deepest, darkest regions of the forest. Pausing in the middle of the road, he turns to Ethan and says, "Are you coming?"

Ethan doesn't know how to answer. Nothing about this afternoon has gone according to plan. He had simply wanted to hang out with Billy. He certainly didn't think Russ or Ashley or Ragesh would be involved. He's still confused as to why they're here and nervous about what they collectively plan on doing.

"I think we should go back," he says again, proud of himself for sounding more insistent this time.

But Billy's completely across the road now, joining the others on the shoulder. Seeing his friend—his *best* friend—standing with Ragesh, the guy who bullied his way into their group, and Russ, who he doesn't even like, makes Ethan ache from betrayal. Billy should have sided with him. He should have *stayed* with him. Yet there he is, impatiently shifting his weight to one leg and crossing his arms in an unconscious mimicry of Ragesh's stance.

"We don't have all day," Ragesh says.

"Yeah," Russ adds, sounding like a weak echo of the older boy.

Billy stares at him across the road, which is barely big enough to fit two cars yet feels as wide to Ethan as a river. "Come on," he says. "I want to keep going."

Ethan turns around, studying the expanse of forest they've already traveled, as if he can trace their path all the way back to his house, where his mother might still be crying. Faced with the unsettling memory of seeing her weep, Ethan knows he's not yet ready to go back home.

"Fine," he says. "I'm coming."

Standing with his toes on the edge of the asphalt, Ethan looks both ways, even though there are no longer any cars near them. He's about to break one of his parents' cardinal rules: *Don't go past the road.*

He knows they'll be mad if they find out.

No, not mad.

Furious.

They might even ground him, which has never happened precisely because Ethan knows it will be torture if it ever does. So he minds his manners and does his chores with only a minimum of complaining. In short, he behaves. But this? This is the opposite. It's willful misbehavior.

And his parents can never, ever know.

"Then come on already," Ragesh says.

Ethan nods, looks both ways once more, and then sprints like a startled deer over the road. The others are on the move before he's all the way across, which makes him simultaneously sad and angry. Especially at Billy, who's again taken the lead. Ethan thought they'd be walking together, the way best friends do. But Billy forges ahead like they barely know each other.

"It's this way," he says.

"What is?" Ethan asks, hoping the sound of his voice will remind Billy that he's here, that it was just supposed to be the two of them. He considers the possibility that Billy's also mad at him, likely because he let Russ tag along. If so, he doesn't look too upset about it now as Russ marches right next to Billy. The spot where *he* should be, Ethan notes with bitterness.

"The Hawthorne Institute," Billy says.

The answer is a surprise to Ethan, who has never set foot on the institute grounds and doesn't think Billy has, either. Honestly, he didn't think people could walk there. Ethan's parents certainly don't want him going there. Its existence is one of the reasons they forbade him from crossing the road in the woods.

Yet he's now marching right toward it. The fact leaves him feeling so apprehensive that not even Ashley's sudden presence at his side can lighten it.

"Hey," she says. "You doing okay?"

Ethan gives a weak nod. "Yeah."

"You know, you can tell me if you're not," Ashley says. "And if you want to turn back, I'll go with you."

The idea is both tempting and humiliating. While Ethan has no desire to keep going, he also doesn't want to be the scaredy-cat who needs his babysitter to walk him home. What would Billy think of him? What would Ashley? Ethan worries that if he turns around now, it will somehow diminish his standing in their eyes. And while he doesn't care what Ragesh or Russ think of him, the way Ashley and Billy see him matters.

"We can keep going," he says.

"You sure?"

"I'm sure," Ethan says, even though he's not. But it's either this or lose face in front of the only two people he wants to impress.

Ashley jabs him with her elbow, seemingly pleased, which Ethan thinks means he made the right choice. That assumption only grows when Ashley continues to stay by his side as they follow the others deeper into the forest.

Ethan knows they've reached the institute grounds when he spots a stone wall up ahead. Even though it's far in the distance, seen only in half glimpses through the trees, Ethan's stomach clenches at the sight. It's tall, at least eight feet high, and topped with curls of razor wire. As they approach, he can see evenly spaced signs warning them to keep out. Pointless, really. The wall's presence is warning enough.

Beyond it, the forest seems to continue undisturbed, as if the wall itself is just a mistake and there's nothing on the other side. But there is. Ethan hears it. A rush of water that grows louder with each subsequent step.

Billy, Ragesh, and Russ reach the wall first. Russ peers up at it and asks, "Is this it?"

"Yep," Billy says.

Ragesh gives the base of the wall a light kick. "How do we get past it? You didn't bring us all this way just to see a stupid wall, right?"

"There's more," Billy says, standing a few paces down the wall from everyone else. "This way. Follow me."

The others do as instructed, and start crunching their way over dead leaves that have been blown into piles against the wall. Only Ethan pauses to wonder why Billy knows just where to go. Again, he considers suggesting they turn around. Now that they're at the wall, there's nowhere else to go. He runs a hand along the stone, noting how thick the wall seems, how impenetrable, as if whatever sits on the other side is best left alone. Ethan is happy to do just that. Yet everyone else keeps walking, following Billy's lead and sticking close to the wall.

"Keep up back there," Ragesh calls, prompting Ethan to hurry to catch up.

He finds the others clustered around a break in the wall, the stones that used to be stacked there now strewn across the ground. Ethan can't tell if the breach was caused by natural forces or if someone knocked it down. All he notices is that there's a two-foot gap big enough to sneak through.

Which, to his astonishment, Billy does.

"That's not a good idea, Billy," Ashley says, making Ethan relieved he's not the only one nervous about what's happening. "Maybe you should come back."

"Or maybe we should join him," Ragesh says, pushing past her and joining Billy on the other side of the wall.

Russ follows suit, slipping through the gap and standing next to Billy on the other side. Billy turns around to give Ethan an expectant look.

"Aren't you coming?"

Ethan remains where he is, uncertain. Again, he wonders what Billy will think of him if he refuses. He's noticed the way Russ has been by Billy's side the entire time, and he worries it will continue after they leave this place. Until today, Billy tolerated Russ—barely. The only reason Russ came along is because Ethan allowed it. Yet the two of them now look like the best of friends as they stand shoulder to shoulder on the other side of the wall.

"Sure," Ethan says.

Next to him, Ashley gives a disapproving frown. "I guess that means I'm coming, too. We might as well all trespass together."

They step through the gap and join the others. Billy walks ahead of them, leading the pack. He seems intent on reaching a particular destination, and Ethan thinks he knows what it is by the steady rise of the land beneath their feet and the sound of rushing water that's grown unnervingly loud now that they're on this side of the wall.

The falls.

Ethan's heard of them, of course. The boys at school whisper stories about a mysterious waterfall that everyone seems to know about but very few people have actually seen. The falls are said to be haunted, in addition to being cursed. Two claims that made him doubt the place even existed.

But it does.

And to judge by the thinning of the forest in the distance, it's just ahead. Through the trees, Ethan sees blue sky and nothing else, making him aware of their elevation. So much higher than the ground in front of them. He'd assumed they were moving toward the base of the falls. Now he knows better. Now he knows they're approaching the top.

Soon they're there, emerging from the woods onto a rocky out-cropping. On the left, water rushes past them before cascading into the lake below. Standing so close to it fills Ethan with fearful fascination.

The waterfall itself is only about ten feet wide. But what it lacks in size, it makes up for in force. The water doesn't slip over the falls. It *roars*. A sound Ethan can feel in his sternum just as surely as he feels the spray of water on his skin.

Ethan nudges forward until he's between Russ and Billy at the front of the outcropping. A move he instantly regrets. Now that he's a mere foot from the edge, the drop seems even bigger and more menacing.

Instead of a slide into the lake at an angle, the falls plummet straight down for at least thirty feet. Maybe more. When he dares to look down, Ethan sees that the water below is a churning white and that a fine mist hovers over the surface. The lake could be a foot deep there; it could be fifty. There's no way to tell.

The height, steepness, and power of the falls unsettle Ethan. It feels dangerous here, especially with nothing to keep them from slipping off and falling into the abyss.

"How many people do you think drowned in here?" Ragesh says. "I've heard at least a dozen."

"Bullshit," Ashley says. "If someone died here, we would know about it."

Ragesh puffs out his chest, clearly annoyed to be corrected. "I meant, like, a hundred years ago."

"This wasn't here a hundred years ago. It's all landscaped. It's not like the Grand Canyon."

It might as well be to Ethan. He's awed by it. All this is within walking distance of his own backyard and he never even knew it. And while it's still technically part of the suburbs, it feels like the end of the earth.

Adding to the strangeness of the falls is what lies beyond it. From the outcropping, the grounds of the Hawthorne Institute stretch out before them like some storybook kingdom. Directly below is the lake, which widens as it moves away from the falls, the water settling into a flat mirror that reflects the sky. It eventually splits into several small streams that meander across the property. Here and there, stone bridges arc over the water.

Nestled beside the lake is a meadow that slants upward to a vast area dotted with trees and various structures that Ethan can't make out from this distance. He can only see walls of wood and stone.

Beyond them is a stone-walled mansion that looks as big as a library. It reminds him of the building at Princeton where his father's office is located. It's got the same look. Old. Stately. A little bit creepy. Ethan doesn't like visiting his father at work because the floors creak and everything echoes. He doubts he'd like being inside that mansion even less.

"What is that place?" he says to no one in particular.

"The Hawthorne Institute," Ragesh says.

"What do they do there?" Russ asks.

"Scientific shit," Ragesh says. "It's a research center."

"Yeah, but what kind of research?"

"*I* know what they do."

This is said by Billy, who's inched away from Ethan and closer to the edge of the outcropping. Too close, Ethan thinks. Right on the cusp of dropping over the falls. But Billy doesn't seem to notice that as he stares in the distance.

"They talk to ghosts," he says.

SEVENTEEN

The wall, when it appears in the distance, sends a shudder of recognition running through me. It looks just as imposing now as it did thirty years ago. Maybe even more so, thanks to its obvious lack of upkeep. Some stones have broken off, leaving behind dark crevices slick with moss. At the top, rust clings to the teeth of the razor wire. It all suggests something not just forbidden, but truly dangerous as well.

Once I reach the wall, I follow the path blazed thirty years ago, looking for the gap we had passed through. It's still there, making me think both stewards of the land—first the Hawthorne Institute, now the county—either don't know about it or don't care.

Passing through the gap in the wall, I get the same nervous chill I'd felt as a child. I shouldn't be doing this. Not now, not then. The biggest difference between these two journeys is my fitness—or lack thereof. When I was ten, I was barely aware of the ground sloping higher as we approached the falls. Now forty and in only semi-good shape, my legs ache as I trudge onward. By the time I reach the outcropping, I need a minute to catch my breath. Then I peer over the falls and lose it again.

Billy was here all this time.

While I grew up, grew older, went to college, met Claudia, got married, Billy remained right here, unable to do any of those things. The unfairness of it—the downright cruelty—brings a tear to my eye that I quickly wipe away.

Although there's currently no police activity at the base of the falls, signs of their recent presence are everywhere. On the lake, a small inflatable dinghy sits moored to a rock, the unsettled water from the falls making it bob slightly. On the shore, yellow police tape has been stretched along the lake's edge. A bit of procedural overkill that nonetheless reminds me I'm looking at a crime scene.

Rescue vehicles have left large tire marks on the grass, including two parallel ruts in the ground that lead right to the water. I can think of only one vehicle that would need to get that close: the van that carted away what was left of Billy.

Sobered by that thought, I turn my attention to the rest of the grounds. The place has grown in considerably since the last time I was here, with the forest encroaching on all sides. Thirty years ago, I could see most of the outbuildings, even though I was too high up to tell what they were. Now, though, I can barely make out anything through the trees. Maybe the people who pay to have their weddings here prefer it that way.

The only structure that can easily be seen is the mansion. Even among the increased growth, it's too big to miss. Looking at it now, I remember what Billy said about the place.

They talk to ghosts.

Scanning the institute grounds from my perch, I see no one else around. No cars. No people. Even though I know the area isn't completely abandoned, it feels that way. As if the police, having recovered Billy's body, decided to pack up only what they needed and left the rest behind.

I wonder if the same is true of the institute itself. While the mansion is put to occasional use for weddings and parties, I assume there are areas where guests can't go. It's a big place, likely containing rooms that haven't been touched since the institute closed. Is it possible that, just like the police here at the lake, the people who worked at the Hawthorne Institute left things behind?

I leave the outcropping and start to make my descent to the rest of the institute grounds, relying on the memory of my long-ago previous visit. There's no path down. Just a steep, densely wooded slope studded with rocks and waist-high weeds. I step carefully, gripping tree trunks and ducking under branches. The whole time, I listen for noises like the ones I heard on the way here. The echo of footfalls that aren't my own. If someone followed me to the road, I see no reason why they wouldn't continue to do so here.

But no one is following me.

At least, no one I can see.

That—and the fact that I hear nothing as I resume walking now— makes me think what I heard back there really was an echo of my footsteps. Or my imagination getting the best of me.

Or maybe it was just an auditory hallucination. Considering everything I've experienced in the past few days, that's the likeliest explanation. That guilt, grief, and a lack of sleep have at last broken my brain.

But then my phone pings in my pocket, reminding me that at least some of this is real. Trail cams don't capture hallucinations. Whatever it just sent me is real and currently in my yard.

Henry, it turns out.

I open the app, and there he is, standing in front of the camera with a big grin on his face and a sheet of paper in his hands. He's written on it with Magic Marker.

Hi, Mr. Marsh!

I see it and smile. Ashley's right. He *is* a good kid, and the tinge of worry I feel for the boy is nothing compared to what she must endure every single minute of every single day. Life is hard. There's no point denying it. The world is often brutal and cruel, and it only seems to get harder as time marches forward. The pressures and dangers kids face today are so much worse than when I was that age. I can't imagine how parents like Russ and Ashley handle the anxiety. I don't have the emotional bandwidth for it. Something Claudia never understood.

Now that the phone is in my hand, I think about calling her, just to tell her I'm currently marching down a wooded hillside, surely getting poison ivy as I go. Claudia was the outdoorsy one in our marriage, constantly dragging me to one park or another to, in her words, "experience nature."

"I'd like to experience my couch," I'd tell her. "And my television."

But I've already called too much in the past few days. I cringe when I think about the voicemail I left last night. *I think Billy might be haunting me, Claude.* So I send a text that's short, sweet, and one hundred percent true.

walking in the woods and thinking of you

Once the phone's back in my pocket, I continue my descent to the rest of the Hawthorne Institute grounds. The forest thins where the land flattens. There's even a gravel path that I remember from thirty years ago. I take it now, going in the opposite direction of the route we followed back then. I wouldn't mind avoiding the things we encountered that day.

I follow the path's winding route past a field of wildflowers and over a stone bridge that spans a tributary of the lake. On the other side, in an area that had once been a meadow but is now slowly being overtaken by trees, is a barn that looks as old as the land itself. Its wooden walls are unpainted and sun-bleached, and the whole thing leans slightly on its stone foundation, looking like it could be toppled by a stiff breeze.

The barn's door is ajar, a sliver of darkness tantalizing not for what it reveals but for what it hides. Curiosity draws me closer, and I find myself leaving the path to peer through the crack.

The barn's interior is a web of shadows broken only by the occasional slash of sunlight leaking through gaps in the walls. I smell more than see what's inside. Dried hay, likely baled decades ago. Dust. The warm, earthy scent of old wood. There's something else, too. Something distinctly unpleasant.

I spot the source on the barn floor, sitting in the strip of light coming through the open door behind me.

A tin can.

Now that's odd.

The can's been opened, its flip-top lid hanging on by a jagged thread. Even from a few feet away, the stench wafting out of it tells me what it had once contained.

Tuna.

Surrounding it are footprints that spread in all directions. Some are pointed toward the door, others deeper into the barn. Mine do a little bit of both, toes aimed at the barn as I take several quick backward steps away from it.

It hadn't occurred to me that there might be squatters on the property. But now that it's clear there are, it makes perfect sense. The Hawthorne Institute is an isolated place, all but abandoned save for the occasional wedding or private event. Someone could live here undisturbed for days, possibly weeks. And while it's unclear just how long these footprints have been here, I don't want to stick around to find out.

Back on the path, I quicken my pace, going over another bridge and past a semicircle of statues, the ground surrounding them choked with weeds. I round a corner and am stopped cold.

This is the place we'd stumbled upon thirty years earlier.

The place I'd been hoping to avoid.

Staring at it now—the granite walls, the wrought iron gate—I'm struck by a single, all-consuming thought.

This is where I betrayed Billy.

The sound of Ragesh's braying laugh is so loud it spooks a nearby flock of birds. They take flight in a flurry of startled cries and flapping wings, soaring over the falls. By the time they've passed, so, too, has Ragesh's laughter.

"I hate to break it to you, but ghosts don't exist," he tells Billy.

"Yeah, they do," Billy says with such conviction that even Ethan feels embarrassed for him, which then prompts feelings of guilt. Billy's his best friend. He should have his back. But Ragesh is right: Ghosts don't exist. Besides, Billy didn't have Ethan's back when they were all gathered on opposite sides of the road. The slight still stings even now that they're next to the falls, clustered close together on the outcropping in a way that makes Ethan claustrophobic.

"Can we just go?" he says, the words so meek he wonders if anyone has heard them. Ethan doubts it, because now Ragesh is talking.

"Prove it," he says.

"I can't," Billy replies. "I haven't seen one yet."

"But you want to, right?" A cruel glint flashes in Ragesh's eyes. "I know a place where that could happen."

Ashley cocks her head to give him a look. "You just told him ghosts don't exist. Make up your mind."

"Maybe Billy can help with that," Ragesh says. "Maybe where we're going will turn me into a believer. Come with me . . . if you dare."

He walks away, heading back into the trees without another word, as if he knows the others will follow. Which they do. Billy and Russ eagerly, Ashley slowly while emitting a sigh. Ethan again brings up the rear, grudgingly trailing behind them as they descend through the forest. He doesn't understand why they're moving deeper onto the property instead of turning around and going home. Nor does he understand why they're even here. Why did Billy bring them to this place? Is it really to look for ghosts?

Last but certainly not least in his thoughts is this: What will happen if they get caught? Ethan assumes it won't be good. But that's nothing compared to how his parents will react when they find out he's disobeyed them, which they surely will if they're caught. And his mother is upset enough over losing her job.

When they reach flat land and a gravel path meandering over the grounds, Ragesh turns left. "It's just up ahead," he says.

Sure enough, a structure sits around the bend. It's backed against the trees and flanked by a pair of giant willows, so it's hard for Ethan to see what it is as they approach. Only when they're directly in front of the structure does it become clear.

A mausoleum.

Built of marble and granite, it sits wide and squat in the dappled shadows of the willow trees. The front is adorned by two columns, around which climb tendrils of ivy. That and the drooping leaves of the willows brushing the peaked roof give the impression that the whole place is quickly being overtaken by nature.

Instead of a solid door, a simple wrought iron gate secured by a rusted latch covers the mausoleum's entrance. Ethan looks past the gate and into the mausoleum itself. It's dark inside. A discomfiting blackness that reminds him of a cave, inside of which waits something terrible. In this case, though, he already knows what that something is.

Dead people.

"It's so cool," Billy says, even though that's the last word Ethan would use to describe it. Mysterious? Yes. Creepy? Definitely. Scary enough to make him want to turn around and go the other way? Absolutely.

Billy, though, takes a step closer to the mausoleum. "Who's buried there?"

"Beats me," Ragesh says. "Why don't you go look?"

To Ethan's surprise, Billy does, shuffling to the iron gate and peering between the bars. "I can't tell. It's too dark to see."

"Ask your ghost friends," Ragesh says.

"They're not my friends," Billy says, adding, "Yet."

Ethan again feels a twinge of embarrassment for his friend. Billy's so sincere and so fully believes what he's saying that he can't see how everyone else thinks it's ridiculous. Especially Ragesh, who joins Billy at the gate. He lifts the latch, which emits a rusty creak as it rises from its cradle. Another creak comes when Ragesh yanks the gate open. Holding it ajar, he looks at Billy and says, "Maybe you should go inside."

"No," Ashley says. "Billy, don't do it."

"It won't be for long," Ragesh says, needling. "Just for a second."

Ashley crosses her arms and glares at him. "Why don't *you* get inside?"

"Because I'm not the one eager to make friends with a ghost."

"I'll do it." Billy flicks his gaze toward Ethan. "If he goes with me."

Ethan's stomach twists. With its iron bars and thick stone walls, the mausoleum more resembles a prison than a grave. Peering into the darkness, he's hit with a disturbing thought: Is the gate there to keep people out? Or to keep whoever's interred there in?

"No," he says.

He sees the others staring at him the same way they did when the road stretched between them, him on one side, them on the other. Just like then, he feels a palpable sense of shame. Like he's failing them somehow. Especially Billy.

"Come on," he says. "It'll be fun."

"But I don't want to." Ethan wishes he'd been able to put it a different way. One that makes him sound sensible, if not brave. Instead, he comes off childish and whiny. Younger than even Andy Barringer. "Can't we just go home?"

"Sure," Ragesh says. "Once someone spends at least a minute inside this mausoleum."

He stares at them, his expression a dare. One Billy wants to accept. The only thing holding him back is his best friend.

"Please?" he says to Ethan. "It's kind of cool."

"It's not," Ashley tells him. "And just because Ragesh dares you to do something doesn't mean you should."

"But I want to."

"And I don't," Ethan says.

Russ, silent this whole time, suddenly pipes up. "I'll do it." He takes a long step forward, his puny legs stretching to bring him to Billy's side. "I'll go if Ethan's too afraid."

"I said I'm not scared!"

From the looks they give Ethan, it's clear Billy and Russ don't believe him. Russ's expression, like Ragesh's, is a silent challenge. *Prove it then*, it seems to say. Billy's look is more complicated, revealing dejection tinged with disappointment and, yes, pity. Ethan feels a twinge of recognition when he sees it. He's worn that expression plenty of times, including today. But to see it now from someone else brings a sobering realization.

Billy is embarrassed for him.

Shame burns Ethan's cheeks, and the twist in his gut becomes red hot. This isn't how it's supposed to be. It's Billy who's embarrassing, with all his talk about ghosts. Of the two of them, Ethan is the cooler one. The normal one. Or so he thought. But the longer Billy looks at him that way, the more Ethan begins to doubt it.

"I'm going, too," he says, hoping he doesn't sound as scared as he feels.

Ashley grabs his arm before he can join the others. "You don't need to do this," she whispers. "Peer pressure is bullshit, and only dumbasses go along with it."

Ethan pulls out of her grip and doubles down on the obvious lie. "I want to do it."

He joins Billy and Russ at the entrance to the mausoleum. Its interior remains as dark up close as it did from a distance. A chill emanates from the gloom, brushing Ethan's face. When he closes his eyes, he smells earth, water, decay.

"Right this way, boys," Ragesh says as he widens the gate. It opens about two feet before age and rust keep it from budging another inch, no matter how mightily Ragesh tugs. Still, it's enough room for them to slip past, which Billy does, continuing to display a fearlessness Ethan never knew existed. He doesn't even pause before stepping through the gate and disappearing into the mausoleum. Right behind him is Russ, proceeding with slightly more hesitation. Before going in, he turns around to make sure Ethan's still behind him, that he's watching, that he's not chickening out.

"Gnarly, right?" Russ says before slipping inside.

Ethan can't agree. Nor can he match Russ's feigned enthusiasm. He's only doing this to preserve his suddenly precarious friendship with Billy.

Still, he pauses in the doorway, nervous even though he tells himself he shouldn't be. Nothing inside can hurt him. Yet it *feels* like it could. That the unknown dead resting inside might not be so dead after all. That they might be capable of reaching out and grabbing whoever dares to invade their final resting place.

Beyond the gate, Billy and Russ shuffle around the interior of the mausoleum, their shoulders touching. For something that looks so big on the outside, it seems so small on the inside. All that space, Ethan knows, has been taken up by the dead, leaving little room for the living.

Before he can think about turning back, Ethan moves past the gate and into the waiting darkness of the mausoleum.

At first, he thinks it's fine. Weird but fine. There's a little bit of light coming through the half-open gate. There's air that, although musty and stale, remains breathable. Best of all, there are no dead bodies. At least none that are visible. Those remain behind marble slabs in the walls.

Four of them, Ethan counts. Two on each side. In the dim light trickling in, he can make out the name of the one closest to the door.

ELSA HAWTHORNE
BELOVED MOTHER

Seeing those words etched into the slab and knowing a corpse rests just behind it fills Ethan with a deep sense of dread. So does the fact that still more lie hidden behind the three other slabs, which Billy and Russ are straining to read. They bump into him as they move about the mausoleum, reminding Ethan how small the space is. About the same size as the first-floor powder room in his house, which isn't very big at all.

He notices other things, too. How water has gathered in a corner, dirty and stagnant. How a single dried rose petal floats atop the puddle like a boat adrift. How the smell gets worse the farther back he goes. A sickly combination of mildew and dust. How at the back wall, the light coming through the gate doesn't even reach him. It's nothing but shadow there.

To make matters worse, a tortured groan rises behind them, snapping Ethan to attention. He whirls around, gaze skimming the marble floor, where the shadows of the gate's bars start to stretch.

Beyond the bars is Ragesh, silhouetted by the sun as he slams the gate shut. It rattles from the force, raining down bits of rust and flecks of iron. The gate's still trembling as Ragesh pushes downward on the latch, which hits the cradle with a dull clang.

He's just locked them inside.

Ethan rushes to the gate. He grips the bars and pushes, growing alarmed when they don't budge. Panicked, he looks outside to Ashley, only slightly relieved to see that she's already on the case. Stalking toward Ragesh, she wears an expression of pure fury.

"Hey, asshole," she says. "Stop being a complete dick for once in your life."

"I'm just messing with them a little," Ragesh says.

"Well, how about you don't. Open the gate."

Ragesh huffs with annoyance. "Fine."

But the gate doesn't open. Watching through the bars, Ethan sees Ragesh fiddling with the latch, seemingly unable to lift it.

"Stop messing around, Ragesh," Ashley says.

"I'm not."

"What do you mean?"

"What the hell do you think I mean?" Ragesh snaps. "The latch is stuck."

Billy and Russ cluster around Ethan, pressing against the gate. Ethan is far from claustrophobic. He loves being inside his tent, and when he and Billy play hide-and-seek with Andy, he's willing to cram himself into the tightest hiding spot. But the mausoleum, the stuck gate, and the two boys pushing against him on both sides are all too much for Ethan. A low simmer of panic takes hold, and all he wants to do is leave.

Now.

Only there is no exit. Ashley has joined Ragesh in trying to move the latch. Both of them tug upward, their arms straining, exertion turning their faces crimson.

"Shit," Ashley says. "It's not moving. What do we do?"

"I don't know," Ragesh says, panicked.

"Well, figure it out."

"Why me?"

"Because," Ashley says, "you're the dipshit who just trapped three boys in a goddamn mausoleum."

One word of that sentence—trapped—normally would send panic sparking through Ethan. But Ashley barely gets it out before Russ says, "I'm not trapped. See?"

Moving sideways, he slips between the bars like water through a grate. One of the benefits of being scrawny. Free of the mausoleum, he stands behind Ashley and Ragesh as they size up the space between the bars. They then do the same to Ethan and Billy.

"Do you think you can squeeze through?" Ashley says.

"Maybe," Ethan says, even though he doesn't think so. He's bigger than Russ in every way, and Billy is bigger than him. Not by much. Centimeters. But that could make all the difference. "We can try."

This time, Ethan goes first, approaching the bars from the side. He slides his shoulder between two of them, both surprised and relieved to find that it easily fits. It's the same with his knee, the leg twisted so that his toes point outward.

Things get trickier when Ethan's halfway through. The combination of his chest, butt, and head proves to be too much, and he finds himself caught halfway inside the mausoleum, halfway out of it.

"Don't panic," Ashley tells him. "Just turn your head."

Ethan does, pushing his face between the bars, wincing as the coarse iron scratches across his ears. Like someone's scouring them with the Brillo pads his mom uses. But once they clear the bars, the rest of his head is free. Now all he has to worry about is the other two-thirds of his body.

"Stand as straight as you can," Russ advises.

Ethan takes a deep breath, makes himself as straight and thin as possible, and slides the rest of the way out.

The others applaud. All but Billy, who peers between the bars like a dog in the pound. "I don't think I'll fit," he says.

"You will," Ethan says. "Just do what I did."

He guides Billy through it, starting with one shoulder and one knee. As Billy pushes his head between the bars, there's a moment in which Ethan fears he won't make it. The bars seem to catch on Billy's ears, pinning them against his head. Billy keeps pushing forward, all but forcing his head through, his ears scraped scarlet.

"You can do it," Ethan says when Billy pauses. "Just suck—"

He's interrupted by a voice cutting across the grounds, as loud as a shotgun blast. "Hey! You kids shouldn't be here!"

Ethan whips around to see someone in the distance, hurrying up the path. He looks official. Dark suit. Tie flapping as he runs, his dress shoes scuffing along the gravel.

"Shit!" Ragesh yelps. "Run!"

He takes off, sprinting away from the mausoleum and going back the way they came. Russ follows, his skinny legs pumping. Panicked, Ethan doesn't know what to do as the man in the suit keeps yelling for them to stop and his body keeps insisting he run. So he spins in place like a broken toy, bumping into Billy, who's still trying to wriggle his way out of the mausoleum, his body at an angle now, the gate's bars slicing across his chest and back.

Ashley latches onto Ethan's arm. "Let's *go!*" she says with a tug. "Grab Billy."

Ethan does, snagging Billy's hand and pulling as hard as Ashley's pulling him. Each tug only seems to lodge Billy tighter between the bars, his eyes widening as if they're about to pop out of his head.

"Stop," he hisses. "I can't move."

That's when Ethan realizes the awful truth of the situation.

They are in a place where they absolutely shouldn't be.

The others are leaving or have already left.

And Billy is completely stuck.

EIGHTEEN

On the outside, little about the mausoleum has changed in the past thirty years. It still rests in the shadows of the trees, the giant willows weeping onto the pitched roof. The only noticeable difference between then and now is the fat padlock on the gate, hanging from chains looped around the bars. Even though it's likely because of what happened thirty years ago, I can't help but have the same thought I did then: Is all this effort to prevent someone from entering—or the dead inside from escaping?

The other obvious change has nothing to do with the mausoleum, but with me. There's no way I'd fit between those bars now. I'd be lucky to get a leg through.

Yet there's something inside that I'm curious to see, so I venture off the path and approach the gate. Peering through the bars is an addition made since the last time I was here—a narrow box of granite placed directly on the mausoleum floor.

I aim my phone's flashlight into the darkness, sweeping it across the stone until I spot the name carved into it.

EZRA HAWTHORNE

While I'm not surprised that Mr. Hawthorne chose the institute grounds as his final resting place, I do find the plainness of it interesting. The man was rich as sin, and his family spent a fortune turning this piece of New Jersey woods into their own private estate. Yet he's buried inside a simple granite box that doesn't even include the years in which he was born and died. The only other writing I can see is an epitaph, etched a few inches beneath his name.

DEATH IS MERELY AN ILLUSION

I have no idea what that means. That Ezra Hawthorne believed in an afterlife? Or that there is no such thing and those who believe in it are fools? It makes me think about Billy. Dead—but also not. I wonder what Ezra would have thought about *that*.

I leave the mausoleum and move on, my steps quick against the gravel path. After I round another bend and pass a hedge maze that's seen better days, the mansion comes into view.

The structure sits large and stately against the rolling lawn. Wide and rambling, it bears no particular architectural style, making it seem like a building out of time. Something from a movie. Other than its size, the most striking feature about the Hawthorne mansion is its silence. The place is *quiet*. The only sounds I hear as I approach are my own footsteps, startlingly loud amid the overall hush. It makes me instinctively start to tiptoe, which might not even be necessary. I haven't seen or heard signs that anyone else is around.

Still, I try to make myself as inconspicuous as possible once I draw close to the mansion. Sneaking up to a window in the back, I cup my hands to the glass and look inside. It appears to be some kind of sitting room, with wingback chairs and a velvet sofa surrounding a low coffee table. A tapestry hangs from one wall, while another is filled with a large landscape painting.

The room itself looks to be empty—until a woman pops into view just on the other side of the glass. In a shaky voice, she says, "Whoever you are, please leave."

Startled, I leap away from the window, raising my hands like a burglar caught mid-theft. Not the look I want to go for. I drop them to my sides and say, "Hi! Sorry! I just wanted to take a look at your event facilities."

I have no idea how the lie arrived so quickly, but thank God it did, for the woman calms slightly. She points to her right, my left. I look that way and see a red door tucked into the rear of the building. I nod and make my way there, reaching the door thirty seconds before the woman opens it.

Standing in the doorway wearing a lavender pantsuit and a wary smile, she says, "I'm sorry, but we're closed."

"I just want to take a quick look around."

"Do you have an appointment?"

"No," I say. "I just saw this place online and felt like coming over to check it out for myself."

The woman takes in my sweaty, bedraggled appearance. "How did you get here? There are no other cars in the lot."

"My Uber dropped me off at the front gate."

Since the property is bordered by a stone wall, I'm fairly confident in my assumption that a gate sits at the front entrance. I'm less certain that said gate is currently open. Still, the woman offers another smile and says, "Well, we normally only give tours to those who schedule in advance. But since you're here, I suppose a quick look around won't hurt."

She ushers me inside to a plain, narrow corridor. Hurrying ahead of me, she gives me several over-the-shoulder glances. "I'm Lonette Jones," she says in the same way cops use the full names of kidnap victims in press conferences to try to humanize them in the eyes of their abductors.

"I'm Ethan," I reply, realizing a little too late that I probably shouldn't use my real name. "Ethan Smith."

"Is your event a wedding or a private party?"

"Wedding," I say, the lie popping out.

"Perhaps you can make an appointment and return with your fiancée."

"She's really busy right now." I cringe. Why do I keep talking? "But if I like what I see, I'll absolutely make an appointment and bring her along."

"Well, here we are," Lonette says when the corridor empties into an entrance hall that kind of resembles *Downton Abbey*. There's a similar faded grandeur to the place, which is stuffed to the rafters with mahogany, velvet, brocade. Evenly spaced portraits adorn the walls, hanging above side tables on which vases of flowers sit. Wooden beams crisscross the high ceiling, and sunlight streams in from tall windows.

The area is dominated by a staircase that sweeps upward to the second floor. Beneath it, a wide doorway leads to what looks to be a ballroom. I glimpse parquet floors, gilt trim, an unlit chandelier dangling like a massive cobweb.

Like the mansion's exterior, nothing inside the place seems overtly sinister. It's just a lot of finery purchased with old money. The only oddity comes in the form of a large oil painting near the front door. It depicts a young man in a dark suit, his gaze searing. Behind him is a gnarled tree on one side and a stone obelisk on the other.

"Ezra Hawthorne," Lonette says with a sigh when she catches me staring at it. "He lived here."

I move closer to the painting, noticing that both the tree and the obelisk bear strange markings. One is clearly a star. Another resembles a figure eight knocked on its side, which I know to be a sign for infinity. Most of the others, though, are foreign to me.

"What do those symbols mean?"

"Beats me. All I know is that brides hate it. But we're not allowed to take it down. Mr. Hawthorne stipulated it in his will." Returning to tour mode, Lonette drifts to the doorway of the ballroom. "This is a flexible space. It can be used for the ceremony or as a reception hall if the ceremony takes place outdoors."

I turn away from the painting and eye the stairs. "What's up there?"

"The second floor is off-limits to all guests, although we do allow wedding photos to be taken on the staircase."

While nothing in the area suggests that this used to be the Hawthorne Institute, let alone what they did here, I suspect remnants of that time still exist somewhere in this mansion. Maybe I'm wrong and there's nothing left to see. Or maybe it's all been relegated to the forbidden second floor. I decide to ply Lonette for more information.

"Didn't this place used to be a school at some point?"

"Yes, the Hawthorne Institute."

"What was their focus?"

Lonette seems taken aback, as if she's never been asked before. Maybe she hasn't. I assume that on most tours people are too busy checking out the amenities to care what the place was in the past.

"I don't really know. I've only been managing the event space for two years." Lonette lowers her voice to a whisper. "The rumor is that it was some kind of cult."

I try to appear unruffled, even as the word "occult" flashes through my thoughts like a neon bar sign.

"Do you think it's true?"

"No," Lonette says with a shrug. "But I can see why people would say that. Especially if they've been in the basement. It wasn't just the land and mansion that were donated to the county. All the furniture was, too. They just stuffed it all in the basement. It's creepy as heck, if you ask me."

I did ask her, and whether she intended to or not, Lonette has told me exactly where to look. Forget the second floor. I need to find my way into the basement. I even think I know how to get there: a closed door located directly beneath the main staircase.

While thinking of ways to get to it, I allow Lonette to lead me through the rest of the tour. In addition to the ballroom, I'm shown the preparation areas for the bride, groom, and other members of the wedding party; the kitchen facilities that caterers use; and the dining room where receptions can be held if the ceremony takes place in the ballroom.

The room I peered at through the window is where cocktail hours take place. Next to it is what Lonette refers to as "the recovery room," a small antechamber where guests who've drunk a bit too much can sober up. Soon we're back in the entrance hall, where Lonette hands me her card and recommends I return with my fiancée, after making an appointment.

"May I use your restroom?" I say, which is what I should have asked when she caught me at the window. It would have saved both of us some time.

Lonette points to a short hallway just past the door that I assume leads to the basement. "It's down the hall on the left."

I stroll toward the hallway, aware she's following my every move. Pretending to be confused, I pause at the door beneath the staircase.

"Further down," Lonette calls before I can open it. "And on your *left*."

I flash a sheepish grin and head toward the bathroom door, moving so slowly that Lonette gives up watching and retreats into her office. That's when I make my move. Hustling to the door beneath the staircase, I crack it open, slip inside, and quietly close it shut behind me.

I spend a moment in complete darkness, fumbling for a light switch. When I finally hit it, I see steps leading down to what's clearly a basement.

Jackpot.

At the bottom, I find myself in a massive stone-walled chamber that's been stuffed to the rafters with furniture, crates, and decades of detritus. It's all haphazardly arranged, with chairs on top of tables, shelves crammed full of curios, boxes stacked to teetering heights. Dust covers everything in thick layers. There are cobwebs, too, which fill the corners. All combined, it makes me feel like I've just entered the world's most haunted antiques store.

Stepping among the junk, I'm hit with a cold draft that makes the hair on the back of my neck stand at attention. Lonette is right: This place *is* creepy as heck.

Not helping is how half of the furniture is covered by drop cloths darkened with dust, looking unnervingly human-shaped. Not unlike the shadow people in Billy's book. I try to ignore them as I whip out my phone and start taking pictures, starting with the nearest shelf. I snap pictures of the grab bag of items placed there. A ceramic phrenology bust. A box inlaid with jewels. A wooden Ouija board.

Next, I open a nearby box, almost coughing as I get assailed by a cloud of dust. I quickly rifle through the books inside, spotting everything from leather-bound encyclopedias to an alleged book of spells. More books are in the next box I open, including an ancient-looking copy of *Gray's Anatomy*, *Walden* by Thoreau, a battered paperback of *House of Horrors*.

Since searching each box could take all day, I move to a pair of wooden trunks sitting side by side. Inside both are stacks of framed photographs. I quickly remove them and start taking pictures of each one, not stopping to notice what they depict. Most seem to be of long-ago events that took place in this very mansion. Groups of old white men in black suits staring at the camera. Gold plates at the bottom of the frames tell me the year they were taken, starting with 1937 and ending in 1998.

As I aim my phone at a photograph from 1993, one face stands out from the rest—a teenager posed beside a man who looks to be almost eighty years older. The older gentleman is clearly Ezra Hawthorne, and not just because he's dressed like the man in the portrait by the front door. I've seen enough photos of old Ezra to recognize him.

I also recognize the teenager next to him.

Johnny Chen.

Although I know he volunteered here, seeing him so obviously familiar with Ezra Hawthorne makes me gasp in shock—a sound loud enough to be heard through the closed door at the top of the stairs. From above, I hear Lonette say, "He's down there." It's followed by two sets of footfalls on the stairs.

I keep clicking, quickly capturing the photographs from the remaining years. I've just finished taking a picture of 1998 when Lonette enters the basement. With her is Ragesh Patel, and he's none too happy to see me.

"Hey, Ethan," he says with pronounced annoyance. "You're going to need to come with me."

Ethan continues to pull on Billy, just as Ashley continues to pull on him. He feels stretched by the twin strains. On the verge of snapping.

Come on! Ethan tries to yell to Billy, but no words come out. He's too startled, too scared, too distracted by the sounds of people running, some away from the mausoleum, one toward it. Meanwhile, Ashley keeps tugging, the force of it pulling Ethan's hand from Billy's.

Their grip breaks.

Billy thrusts his hand toward Ethan's, their fingers inches apart. The gap widens as Ashley starts to drag Ethan away from the gate.

"Wait!" Ethan yelps, not sure if she can hear him. *"Wait!"*

He wrenches free of Ashley's grip as she keeps running, unaware that Billy can't join them, that he's trapped, that he's about to be caught.

"Get out of there," yells the man in the suit, now only a hundred yards away. Everything about him is big. He's tall and formidably built.

Turning back to the mausoleum, Ethan sees Billy still flailing between the bars. He then checks for the others, confirming that they're fleeing or—in Ragesh's case—already gone. Russ and Ashley are far down the path, springing for the woods like spooked deer.

Ethan goes the opposite direction, edging back toward the gate, wanting to help Billy. Needing to.

The man in the suit's closer now. So close Ethan can see the anger on his face as he snarls, "I told you yesterday to stay away."

Ethan freezes when he hears it, stunned.

Billy has been here before.

Without him.

The betrayal he felt earlier roars back, this time tenfold. He wonders why Billy hadn't told him he'd visited this place before. He wonders what else Billy hasn't told him. He wonders if, right now, he and Billy are even friends.

The events of the day landslide through Ethan's thoughts. Billy's need to explore. The others joining in one by one. Him by the road as Billy stood with Ragesh and Russ, literally siding with them. Finally, this moment, in which he realizes Billy had led them to the falls and the Hawthorne Institute even though he'd been warned the day before that no one should be here.

Now they're in trouble.

Well, Billy is.

Ethan will be, too, if he doesn't run.

He takes a halting backward step as the full weight of that hits him. *He* could get in trouble. For something he didn't even want to do. For something that, in all honesty, is Billy's fault.

He didn't want to come here.

He didn't want to cross the road or sneak through the wall or see the falls.

And he definitely didn't want to step inside that mausoleum.

All of that was Billy.

Ethan takes two more backward steps, widening the distance between him and Billy as the suited man reaches the mausoleum.

Clocking Billy's predicament, he says, "Jesus Christ. What have you been up to?"

Ethan sees nothing else after that, for he starts to pivot, turning his back to the mausoleum and staring at the expanse of path ahead and the retreating forms of Ashley and Russ. Then, without giving it any more thought, Ethan runs to join them. As he hurtles forward along the path, he hears Billy begging him to stop.

"Ethan, don't leave me! Please don't leave me!"

NINETEEN

Are you going to arrest me?" I ask Ragesh once I've been led like a felon to his car.

"I could," he says. "I probably should."

"Technically, I wasn't trespassing. Lonette let me in."

"Because you lied," Ragesh says. "And she called the cops the first chance she got. She thought you were trying to rob the place."

The very idea is ridiculous. Me? A burglar? I can't even do a decent job of sneaking around. "Well, I wasn't."

"Then why did you come here?"

"I just wanted to look around."

Ragesh sees right through the lie. Not that it takes a detective to do so. It's clear I was up to something. "For what?"

I don't know because Billy didn't tell me. Since I doubt Ragesh will believe that one, I choose a more logical response. "Any sign that the Hawthorne Institute had something to do with Billy's death."

"We already went over this, Ethan. There's likely—"

"No connection? So everyone says. But how am I supposed to believe that when no one will tell me what went on here? Even though you know at least some of it."

Ragesh starts the car. "I have no idea what you're talking about."

"You volunteered here in 1992," I say, gesturing past the wind-shield to the stone mansion looming before us. "You and Johnny."

"Where did you hear that?" Ragesh says, either annoyed or im-pressed that I know. I can't quite tell.

"Let's just say I've been doing some research. So I suggest we cut the crap and tell each other what we know."

Ragesh appears to consider it as he steers the car away from the Hawthorne mansion and down a narrow drive. Up ahead is the stone wall and, to my delight, an open gate. At least I got one thing right today.

"Okay, deal," Ragesh says once we're past the gate. "Let's put all our cards on the table. Quid pro quo. Why are you so adamant that Billy's murder is somehow tied to the Hawthorne Institute?"

"Because that's where he was found."

"And I already told you that if you're trying to dispose of a body, that's as good a place as any."

"But we were there that day," I say, even though Ragesh doesn't need reminding. "Billy longer than the rest of us."

"Did he ever mention what happened then?"

"No," I say, still too ashamed to tell Ragesh about the argument Billy and I had in the tent that night and how I wish I could take back every word I said. If Billy had revealed any details about earlier in the day, I would share them. But he didn't. The only thing Billy made clear was how much I had betrayed him.

"Okay," Ragesh says. "Your turn. Ask me anything."

I'm at a loss as to where to start. There are so many questions I want answered. Eventually, I opt with one that's bothered me since Ragesh told us Billy's remains had been found.

"The other night, you said you knew Billy's death wasn't an acci-dent because there was evidence of foul play. What kind of evidence?"

"There were fractures on Billy's ribs and skull," Ragesh says. "Based on the damage, the forensic anthropologist thinks it's likely he died from blunt force trauma to the chest and head."

He pauses, checking to see if I'm okay. I'm far from it. The whole car seems to quake. Like it's just been rear-ended, even though there are no other vehicles around.

"While it's possible his injuries were caused by a fall, it's also un-likely," Ragesh continues.

"Why?"

"Divers found a piece of fabric in the mud with Billy's remains. Like he had been wrapped in a blanket or something before he was thrown over the falls."

I feel another quake. Worse than the first one. Because I now doubt that Billy's death was quick and painless. It was likely the oppo-site, a fact that leaves me momentarily speechless.

Ragesh gives me a sympathetic look. "Sorry you asked?"

Yes.

And no.

Because the way I see it, the likely nature of Billy's murder elimi-nates a bunch of suspects, chiefly everyone on Hemlock Circle. No, I haven't forgotten Detective Cassandra Palmer's theory about why Billy didn't scream or call for help. I just continue to disagree with it. Because I can't imagine how someone who knew Billy could do that to him. Which means his killer wasn't from the cul-de-sac.

"Tell me what you know about the Hawthorne Institute," I say.

"There's not a whole lot to tell. I was there for exactly an hour."

"That's it?" I say. "But you were a volunteer."

"More like guinea pig," Ragesh says. "Johnny's the one who signed us up. He said he wanted to see what the place was like."

"And what was it like?"

"Pretty much the same as it is now. Very old. Very stuffy. Lots of guys in dark suits sitting around reading. As soon as we got there, they separated Johnny and me, taking us into two different rooms. Mine was all white. Johnny later told me his was the same. We both sat at a table divided by a partition so I couldn't see who was on the other side."

"Did you ever see who it was?" I say.

"No." Ragesh does a little shimmy, as if he's still freaked out by the memory. "I just heard them. It was a man who told me he was going to hold up cards with shapes on them and that I needed to guess what they were by using ESP or something. I could take as much time as I needed, just as long as I concentrated on the card I couldn't see."

"How many were there?"

"Fifty."

"Did you get any right?"

"Don't know," Ragesh says. "I was never told if I was right or wrong. We just moved on to the next card. When we were done, I was sent home and never went back. I finished up my volunteer work at the library, reshelving books."

I look his way. "And Johnny?"

"He went back," Ragesh says quietly. "A lot. Even after we finished our volunteer duty."

I pull out my phone and swipe to the image of that photograph from 1993. The picture quality is terrible. In my haste, I hadn't bothered with things like focus or centering the frame, resulting in a photo that's slightly askew. Still, by zooming in I'm able to see the important part: Johnny Chen and Ezra Hawthorne.

Looking at them again, I pick up on details I missed the first time, such as the way Ezra's pale, clawlike hand rests on Johnny's shoulder. Or how Johnny's dressed in a black suit identical to the one Ezra is wearing.

"Did Johnny ever tell you what he did there?"

"No," Ragesh says. "I assumed it was the same thing. Weird tests and experiments. But Johnny liked the place. By the end, it was the only thing that seemed to make him happy."

The end? At first, I don't understand what Ragesh means by that.

But then I check the photo again, this time zeroing in on the gold plaque and its date. The same year Johnny died. For all I know, this might be the last photograph taken of him.

I study the strange expression on Johnny's face. He looks vaguely nervous. Like he's not entirely comfortable being there.

Choosing my words very carefully I say, "Do you think what happened to Johnny could have had something to do with his time at the Hawthorne Institute?"

Ragesh pounds on the brakes, bringing the car to a skidding stop in the middle of the road. The force of it throws me forward a moment before the seat belt tightens, jerking me back against the seat. I tug it away from my neck as Ragesh turns to me, his face hard.

"Do *not* drag Johnny into this conspiracy theory of yours. No one else had anything to do with his death. Johnny was . . ." Ragesh's voice deflates, like air hissing out of a balloon. "He was messed up, okay? He was going through some stuff—a lot of stuff—and turned to drugs because of it. Then he died. And there are still days when I think about it and get so mad at him for what he did to himself. But that's the key here. Johnny did it to himself. The Hawthorne Institute had nothing to do with it. Just like it had nothing to do with what happened to Billy."

"I'm sorry," I say, and I truly am. His reaction reminds me that I'm not the only person on Hemlock Circle who lost a friend.

Ragesh resumes driving. "You're forgiven."

A tense silence fills the car, becoming so stifling it makes me want to crack open the window. After a few minutes, it gets so unbearable that I feel compelled to break it.

"Detective Palmer thinks someone from Hemlock Circle killed Billy," I say. "Do you agree?"

"Not exactly."

"Since you don't think it was one of our neighbors—and you don't think it was someone from the Hawthorne Institute—who do you think killed Billy? The stranger in camouflage people saw the day before?"

"It definitely wasn't him," Ragesh says.

"How can you be so certain?"

"One, because I know how rare that kind of thing is. Yes, it can happen, and does in often tragic ways. But the odds of it happening in your backyard are one in a million." Ragesh stares straight ahead, a firm grip on the steering wheel. "Two, I know because the stranger in camouflage was me."

Because he's still focused on the road, Ragesh misses the look of utter shock on my face. It's only me who witnesses it, my slack-jawed reaction caught in the side mirror and reflected back to me. Accompanying it is a sinking disappointment. While it was never proven that a stranger was roaming the neighborhood the day before Billy was taken, the idea provided a distorted form of comfort. It was easier to believe a nameless, faceless bogeyman took Billy than consider the likelihood that it was someone from Hemlock Circle.

"Why didn't you tell anyone?"

"Why would I?" Ragesh says. "It's embarrassing to admit that I was roaming the woods, got turned around, and ended up in a backyard on Willow Court instead of my own. It's even more embarrassing to know the whole neighborhood freaked out about it."

"But you lived there," I say. "Why would anyone think you were suspicious?"

"Are you seriously asking me that?" Ragesh points to his face. "Look at the color of my skin, Ethan."

I nod. "Point taken."

"I suppose the camouflage also had something to do with it," Ragesh concedes. "But I looked slick in camo. Still do."

I think about the day we all went to the falls and the Hawthorne Institute. Ragesh hadn't been part of the group until we stumbled upon him sitting in the forest.

"What were you doing in the woods?"

"Thinking," he says. "Johnny wasn't the only person going through some shit. I was, too. And being in the woods helped clear my head. But to everyone else, it seemed shady. Like whoever saw me leave the woods at Willow Court. Or Ashley, who was convinced I was spying on her. God, the way her dad reacted. He told my parents I was a Peeping Tom. Talk about embarrassing."

"Ashley's single now," I say. "If you're interested."

"I don't think my husband would approve."

Thrown off guard, I do a surprised jolt in my seat. Ragesh clocks the movement, smiles, and says, "Surprised?"

Very, I think. "A little," I say.

"Told you I was going through some stuff back then," Ragesh says.

"How long have you been married?"

"Eight years."

"Congrats," I say. "And your parents? Are they cool with it?"

"They weren't at first," Ragesh says. "But they came around eventually. It helps that I found myself a nice Indian boy. Lately, my mother's biggest complaint is that he's a better cook than she is."

Despite not knowing him that well as a kid—and not particularly liking what I did know—I'm happy for Ragesh.

"I'm sorry, by the way," Ragesh says.

"For what?"

"Lots of stuff. I was a little shit back then. Mostly because I was scared and confused and sad. That's not an excuse. There isn't an excuse for some of the things I did."

"Like locking us in a mausoleum?" I say.

Ragesh cringes. "Yeah, that. Although, just to be clear, it's not my fault the latch got stuck. But mostly I'm sorry for not trying to, I don't know, help you back then."

"There was nothing you could have done."

"I could have been nicer," Ragesh says. "At the very least, I should have talked to you or tried to take you under my wing. Because of all the people on Hemlock Circle, I knew what it was like to lose a best friend."

Looking at Ragesh, I imagine him going through the same things I did. The grief. The guilt. The wondering all these years if such a friendship was sustainable. The only difference between us, other than the state of our marriages, is how we handled losing our best friends. He became a bully, channeling his anger into cruelty before mellowing out and changing his ways. I chose a different path.

I fled.

Yet here we both are, in a car that's currently hugging the curve of Hemlock Circle as Ragesh brings it to a stop in front of my house.

"Thanks for the ride," I say. "And, you know, not arresting me."

"No problem," Ragesh says before letting me out. "Just do me a favor. Stay away from the Hawthorne Institute."

I assure him I will, mostly because I know he *will* arrest me if I'm found there again. I'll have to make do with what I saw, which isn't much, and the other photographs I captured with my phone. That's exactly where I start looking once Ragesh drives off. Sitting in the living room, I scroll through them, pausing at each one.

Most are creepy in the way that almost all old photos are creepy. Groups of long-dead people staring at the camera, their poses stiff, their smiles forced. Not that the people involved with the Hawthorne Institute smiled often. These were serious men, and their mirthless expressions matched that. The result is that no face stands out, not even Ezra Hawthorne's. They become pale blurs, the men pictured in, say, 1942 interchangeable with the ones from forty years later.

Many of the photos are group shots of different gatherings that took place in Ezra Hawthorne's mansion. I can tell because I recognize some of the places Lonette showed me on the tour. The grand hall. The ballroom. One photograph was even snapped at the falls, the water a white cascade behind two men wearing black robes over what I know to be black suits.

Those suits, by the way, are omnipresent. Every person in every photo wears them. That's not so unusual in the pictures dating back to the forties and fifties. Suits were common back then, worn everywhere from the dinner table to the movies. It's only in the photos from the eighties and nineties that it starts to get weird. By then fashion rules had changed to the point where men only wore black suits to funerals.

Of all the photos, only two are unusual enough to warrant closer scrutiny. One, of course, is the picture snapped at the falls, mostly because of the black robes. Hooded and cinched shut with rope, they're undeniably sinister. Maybe the Hawthorne Institute *was* a cult.

The only thing keeping me from fully embracing the idea is that I doubt a cult could have passed unnoticed here, no matter how much money they had. In other states, sure. But not New Jersey. Especially not this part of New Jersey, with its rich colonial history and all the Episcopalian trappings that come with it.

Another reason I don't completely buy the cult thing is that no other photo depicts anything close to that. The other one that catches my attention does so in a different way. Taken in 1969, it's of Ezra Hawthorne and three men. They're at a table, seated around an honest-to-God crystal ball. Ezra's mouth is open mid-word, his eyes aimed toward the ceiling, as if he's addressing someone hovering there. Looking at it, I can only think of Billy.

They talk to ghosts.

Is that indeed what's happening in this picture? If so, how did Billy know that—and is that why he insisted on going there two days in a row, once alone, the other with a group?

Curious, I swipe through the remaining photos, slowing when I get to the one that features Johnny Chen. The one after it was taken in 1994, the same year Billy was killed. I don't expect it to show me anything regarding his death. I'm just interested to see what might have been taking place back then.

The photo ends up being just like most of the others, a group shot taken in the entrance hall. The big difference is that, instead of all men in black suits, two women have joined the group, bringing with them much-needed pops of color.

I zoom in on them, starting with the one on the left. She appears to be in her fifties and boasts a midlife sass that's evident even in a photograph.

When I move to the woman on the right, my heart stops. Seeing her is so disorienting it feels like I've fallen through the floor and am now plummeting into the basement. A free fall so dizzying I think I might faint.

I know who this woman is, just as surely as I know that she's still alive. What I can't fathom is why she was at the Hawthorne Institute.

Mostly because the woman is my mother.

Joyce remains at the kitchen island long after Ashley has gone. In the afternoon silence, she can't help but feel foolish. What kind of woman confides in her teenage neighbor? Weeping while doing it, no less? No wonder Ashley volunteered to watch Ethan for free. She probably wanted to get as far away as possible. Joyce can't blame her. If she had been in Ashley's shoes, she would have done the same thing.

Left all alone, Joyce surveys the kitchen and sighs. This, it seems, is where she's destined to be. Her mother certainly thought so. She was of the generation that believed a woman's place is in the home, so that's where she stayed. Joyce remembers being a little girl and watching her mother toil all day. Cleaning and laundry, ironing and cooking. It never seemed to end. Since all the mothers in the neighborhood did the same thing, Joyce had grown up not knowing there were other options even after she went to college, which to her was simply a place where women made friends and met their future husbands.

Joyce did both, joining a sorority and meeting a handsome senior named Fred Marsh during her first mixer. When they got engaged by the end of her freshman year, there seemed no need to continue her studies, and so Joyce quit school and ended up doing the same thing as her mother.

For a time, she found contentment in making sure her family was cared for. She took pride in driving Ethan to school, attending his silly class plays in which he had one line, spending an entire evening making dozens of cupcakes for the school bake sale. No, she wasn't running a business or curing the sick or doing one of the millions of jobs that women do every day. But she'd learned from observing her mother that domesticity was important. It *mattered*. Without homemakers, who would run the PTA? Or volunteer on field day? Or shuttle hordes of kids from one extracurricular activity to another? In short, who would keep things flowing in that way that looks effortless but in truth is exhausting?

Certainly not the men, Joyce thought.

But she wasn't prepared for how lonely it all felt in between one obligation and the next. That's something she wished her mother had warned her about. The long, quiet hours when she wasn't needed. Those were the times when Joyce got to thinking that maybe she wanted more. Not a bigger house or a better kitchen or a nicer car. She was happy with what she had, and grateful for all of it.

What Joyce wanted was a sense of accomplishment outside of her home and her family. She wanted a purpose beyond the needs of her husband and her son. So, after discussing it with Fred, she took the first job she could find.

At the Hawthorne Institute.

Before starting there, she'd been only vaguely familiar with the place. She was told by the wife of one of Fred's colleagues that it was full of crackpots who did things like stare at animals and try to read their minds. It was all completely harmless, she assured Joyce. Just weird.

Joyce took the job anyway. A low-level secretarial job. An assistant to an assistant. Still, she liked it. She liked how the office smelled of fresh coffee in the mornings and how she and Margie, the senior assistant, would sometimes eat their lunch outside by the falls, gazing at the water crashing into the lake below. She enjoyed the studious quiet of the place. It felt like working in a library.

Yes, there was some weirdness, starting with the fact that everyone but she and Margie wore black suits. Joyce assumed it was to emulate Ezra Hawthorne, who, despite founding and funding the institute, made himself scarce. She'd only glimpsed him three times. The first was to welcome her the day she started working there. The second was a week later, when a group photo was taken in the vast entrance hall.

The third time was when everything went wrong.

Joyce technically reported to Margie, who reported to their boss, who had the ear of Mr. Hawthorne. When Joyce noticed something strange, she knew not to ask. That was the first thing Margie told her: Don't ask questions. Just keep your head down, do what needs to be done, ignore the rest. Still, Joyce couldn't help but be curious about the odd symbols tattooed on a visitor she was asked to fetch coffee for. Or the strange music she sometimes heard coming from the second floor. Or that time she spent an afternoon typing up transcripts of Rorschach tests conducted on blind people.

"Why would they do that?" she asked Margie. "It's such a waste of time and resources."

"Mr. Hawthorne has all the money in the world," Margie said. "If he wants to waste it on this silliness, he can be my guest as long as he pays me."

And pay he did. Joyce's salary was almost twice as much as similar assistant jobs in the pharmaceutical companies that dotted the area. That alone made up for the weirdness. Joyce enjoyed having money of her own. Money she had *earned*. She and Fred had a joint account, which she could tap whenever she wanted, for whatever she wanted. Yet she always felt weird buying her husband Christmas presents or birthday gifts with money he had made. So the first thing she did with *her* money was use it to buy Fred a watch for his birthday, which was coming up on the eighteenth.

Ironic, seeing as how it ultimately led to her getting fired.

Not wanting to risk Fred finding it at home, she kept the watch in the top drawer of her desk at work. She had intended to bring it home with her the night before and then drop it off at the engraver's on her way to work so it would be ready by Monday. Only she'd forgotten to do that, a mistake she realized while washing dishes after dinner. She grabbed her keys and told Fred, "I need to go to the office real quick. I left something there."

"Now?" he said. "Can't it wait until morning?"

It really couldn't. "I'll be just a minute," she said, hurrying away before Fred could ask any more questions.

On her way to the Hawthorne Institute, she worried the front gate would be closed and that all this sneakiness would be for nothing. The gate ended up being open, but the institute itself was completely dark and the front door locked. Not having a key herself, Joyce went around to the back, hoping that maybe one of the rear doors was open.

Halfway there, she heard the chanting.

At first, she thought someone was listening to a CD of those Gregorian chants that are inexplicably all the rage right now. But the sound quality was too clear to be coming from a recording.

This was live.

Joyce almost turned around and left. In hindsight, she should have done exactly that. But curiosity got the best of her, and she tiptoed around the corner of the building to see what could possibly be going on.

Sitting in her kitchen in the bright light of day, she gets a chill thinking about what she saw, even though she still doesn't understand any of it.

The chanting.

The robes.

The blood.

It was all so unexpected and surreal and, yes, terrifying that she almost screamed. Instead, she forced the sound down and backed away—literally bumping into her boss. This time, she did attempt a scream, which was stifled when her boss slapped a hand over her mouth.

"You shouldn't be here," he hissed as he pulled her away to the front of the building. There, he unlocked the front door and led her inside to his office, which overlooked the back garden. Although the blinds were blessedly closed, sparing Joyce from another glimpse of what was happening outside, she still heard the chanting as her boss sat her down.

"What did you see?" he asked.

"Not much," Joyce said.

But it was enough to make her dizzy. So very dizzy. It dawned on her that she could be in shock.

"What were they doing?" she said. "What *is* this place?"

Instead of an answer, she was told she was being fired.

Now, eighteen hours later, she sits in her all-too-familiar kitchen, still unable to comprehend just what it was she had witnessed. Not having any answers is bad enough, but even worse is how she's not allowed to tell anyone about it. Not even her husband. Her boss made sure of that when he forced her to sign that piece of paper before escorting her out of the building.

Joyce remembers staring at the sheet, trying to speed-read all that fine print, confused by, well, everything.

"What is this?" she asked.

"An NDA."

Joyce had frowned at the paper, confused. "A what?"

"A nondisclosure agreement. In short, it means you can't mention a word of what you saw tonight to anyone."

"Not even Fred?"

"No," her boss said. "Not even your husband."

That seemed way too extreme for her. How could she tell anyone about it when she didn't even know what she saw?

"And—" Joyce hesitated, afraid to ask the question that was nagging at her. "What will happen to me if I do tell someone?"

"Mr. Hawthorne will sue you."

"Can he do that?" she said.

Her boss flashed a smile that was in no way friendly. "Mr. Hawthorne has enough money to do whatever he wants. If he wants to sue you, he will. And he'll make sure he wins. His lawyers are very good at keeping his secrets."

Joyce had no more questions after that. With a trembling hand, she signed the paper that guaranteed a lifetime of silence, went back to her office, and quickly gathered her things, including the stupid watch she'd bought for Fred.

Thinking about it now makes her want to start crying again, mostly because she knows she'll never give it to him. On Monday, she'll return it to the store and get back her money, which she'll quietly deposit into the joint account.

The watch is now a luxury she can no longer afford on her own.

TWENTY

I continue to stare at my phone, studying the picture of a picture. I zoom in on my mother. A long-ago version of the woman she is now. Her hair is the chestnut brown I remember from my youth, and her face is narrower, the skin tighter.

Looking at it, I'm hit with a jarring thought: I'm older now than my mother was when that photo was taken.

Even more jarring is the fact that she never told me she worked at the Hawthorne Institute the summer Billy vanished. Knowing it now changes everything I've thought about that place, about that time, about *her*. Did she know what went on there? Was she aware that Billy had been there? That *I* had been there? Most of all, I wonder if there are other things she hasn't told me about that summer.

Yet I'm also mad at myself. I'm her son. I should have known where she worked. The fact that ten-year-old me was so self-centered that I couldn't be bothered to find out fills me with so much shame it brings heat to my cheeks. They remain red as I steady myself with a deep breath and FaceTime my mother.

"Hi, honey!" she says when she answers, bobbling the phone enough for me to see she's working on a jigsaw puzzle.

"Is Dad there, too? I need to talk to both of you."

My mother summons my father into the frame, and the two of them sit shoulder to shoulder, like they've done all my life. The familiar sight brings with it years of memories, to the point where I see them not just as they appear now, but as they did ten, twenty, thirty years ago. They are simultaneously young and old, an idea that carries over to myself. I feel both childlike and utterly ancient.

"They found Billy's remains," I announce, still uncertain if I'm allowed to be telling them and beyond caring if I'm not. "Two miles from our house. He was murdered."

A moment passes in which my parents sit as if spellbound while memories of that time come at them from all sides. I know because I felt the same thing. The past crashing like a wave into the present.

"That poor, poor boy," my mother eventually says.

Nodding in agreement, my father says, "Does his family know?"

I tell them the same answer I was given. That Mary Ellen Barringer's doctors were told, which isn't quite the same as telling her, and that Billy's brother currently can't be located. Then I utter the words I've been dreading to say.

"We need to talk about that night."

Until now, I never once considered my parents suspects. They had no reason to hurt Billy. They *loved* Billy. Most of all, they love me, and I know they would never purposefully do anything to cause me pain. But suspicion has a way of breaking through even the strongest barriers. It slips through the cracks, seeping in drip by drip. That's what finding out my mother worked at the Hawthorne Institute has done to me: let in enough doubt that I can no longer avoid it.

"Of course, sport," my father says, his voice earnest, as if he not only knows what's coming but expected it decades ago.

That doesn't make what I'm about to do any easier. There's a dull thud at my temples. A headache coming on. I try to ward it off by tilting my head back and pinching the bridge of my nose.

"I'm going to ask you this only once. So please be honest with me." I pause, tremulous, fighting the urge to hang up. The very last thing I want to do right now is pose this particular question to my parents. A willfully ignorant part of me thinks I'm better off not knowing. I've gone thirty years without answers. What's another thirty more?

But I also think I've earned the right to ask. I was there when it happened. In that tent, inches from Billy. I deserve if not answers, then at least the opportunity to seek them out.

"Did either of you do something to Billy that night?"

I huff after saying it. A small, guilt-ridden exhalation riding the words like a punctuation mark. It's made even more noticeable by my parents' silence, which lasts seconds but feels like hours.

"Ethan," my mother says, the disappointment reverberating through those two terse syllables making me feel like the shittiest son in the world. "How could you ask such a thing?"

"It's okay, Joyce," my father says.

"It's *not* okay."

"He's naturally curious. He's not accusing us of anything."

My mother sniffs. "It certainly feels that way."

"It doesn't mean I think you killed Billy," I say. "It just means I need to hear you say that you didn't."

"I understand, sport," my father says, his voice patient and his expression calm. "We both do. And I swear to you that neither your mother nor myself had anything to do with what happened to Billy."

I exhale, releasing the breath I hadn't known I was holding in.

I believe him.

Truly and deeply.

"Thank you," I say, on the verge of tears for reasons I can't quite fathom. Maybe it's relief. Or guilt. Or some combination thereof. Or maybe it's simply because seeing my parents in a different home in a different state makes me miss them. I lower the phone so they can't see me wipe away the tears that are threatening to fall. When I raise it again, I'm all business, ready to tackle why I called them in the first place.

"There's a reason I had to ask. Billy's remains were found on the grounds of the Hawthorne Institute." I pause to register my mother's look of surprise. "I know you worked there for part of that summer. What went on at that place?"

"I was just a secretary." My mother looks to my father, who gives a nod, urging her to continue. "But one night, I saw something. Something I wasn't supposed to see. So they fired me."

I remember when she lost her job because it was clear how much it upset her. I can still recall, with vivid clarity, the moment I walked into the kitchen to find her literally crying on Ashley's shoulder.

There is, of course, another reason it stands out in my mind.

That was the day Billy was taken.

"Mom, what did you see?"

My mother shakes her head. "I can't tell you. He swore me to secrecy. He made me sign something promising I wouldn't tell anyone. Not even your father. He said I'd be sued if I did."

Another memory slithers into my thoughts. Something the man in the suit said as we fled the mausoleum. Something intended not for the rest of us but solely for Billy.

I told you yesterday to stay away.

The ever-increasing ticking in my heart switches from fear to an unwieldy combo of dread and excitement. Billy was on the institute grounds the same day my mother saw something so sinister they fired her. Is it possible Billy saw something similar? Did someone at the Hawthorne Institute go to even greater lengths to silence him?

"This is important, Mom," I say. "I need you to tell me what happened."

There's an extended moment of silence as my mother considers it. Her face gets distorted, her mouth twisting as if she's physically trying to keep words from coming out of it. She looks to my father for reassurance, which he offers without hesitation. Seeing it brings a punch of sadness that I once had a relationship as loving as theirs. Now it's gone.

"A ritual," she eventually says.

I lean forward, peering into the phone. "What kind of ritual?"

"I don't know, Ethan. But it was terrifying."

The rest of the story rushes forth like water from a broken dam. For twenty unbroken minutes my mother talks, telling me about her job, her coworker Margie, the strange place that was the Hawthorne Institute.

"I was just so happy to be working that I didn't really stop to think how weird it all was," my mother says at one point. "But looking back on it now, it was like something out of *The Twilight Zone*."

After mentioning buying my father a watch for his birthday and leaving it in her desk, necessitating a nighttime trip to the office, my mother gets to the heart of the story. "The incident," she calls it, using air quotes to express its importance.

Without a key to the front door of the Hawthorne Institute, she went to the rear of the mansion, hoping to find an unlocked back door. Instead, she found the area behind the mansion aglow with firelight.

"Torches," my mother says. "They were placed in a large circle on the grass behind the mansion."

She tells us that inside the circle were Ezra Hawthorne and several other men, all dressed in black robes. They, too, were arranged in a circle, surrounding a small fire and chanting in a language she couldn't place.

"Latin?" I say.

My mother shakes her head. "No. Something different. It sounded, I don't know, almost primal. But that wasn't the worst part. Ezra Hawthorne held what appeared to be a copper plate. There was something on it."

"What?"

"I shouldn't tell you. I'll get in trouble."

"I'm not going to tell anyone. I swear. Now, please, what was on the plate?"

My mother pauses a bit longer before forcing out the words. "A heart."

I stare at my parents, suddenly woozy, their faces on my phone's screen blurring in and out of focus. While I don't know what I was expecting, it certainly wasn't *that*.

"I couldn't tell from what," my mother continues. "Human or animal, I don't know. It was slick with blood, like it had just been removed. Mr. Hawthorne picked it up with his bare hands and lifted it over the fire."

"Then what did he do?"

My mother tells me she doesn't know, because she was already trying to run away, only to come face-to-face with her boss. Although he wasn't taking part in the ritual, it was clear he knew it was going on, especially once he took my mother inside to his office and fired her.

"He made me sign something forbidding me from talking about it with anyone," she says. "An NDA. Legally binding. I was told that if word got out that I talked, Mr. Hawthorne would sue me. I know, I know. Saying you're going to sue someone is usually an empty threat. But I knew this was serious, especially after what I saw. A man like Ezra Hawthorne would go to extreme lengths to make sure that stayed a secret."

"Extreme," I say, the word a bombshell in my thoughts, obliterating them until a new one emerges.

All this time, I'd harbored a vague theory that someone associated with the Hawthorne Institute abducted and killed Billy because of something he'd witnessed after I and the others abandoned him at the mausoleum.

But what if that wasn't the case?

What if it had nothing to do with what Billy potentially saw and everything to do with what my mother actually did see? Yes, the Hawthorne Institute made her sign an NDA and threatened to sue if she talked. But what if they thought that wasn't enough? How far would they go to ensure her silence?

That brings forth another, far more frightening theory.

Maybe Billy wasn't the intended target.

Maybe I was.

The idea sends me slumping against the sofa, my mind reeling. I think about Billy and me tucked into our individual sleeping bags and how indistinguishable we must have looked in the darkness. I picture a person in a black suit—maybe Ezra Hawthorne, maybe one of his followers—still clutching the knife used to slash the tent, blindly grabbing Billy while thinking it was me. I imagine him carrying Billy through the woods and not realizing his mistake until they reached a car parked on the access road halfway between here and the institute.

I force myself not to think about what likely happened after that.

"Mom, other than the NDA and mentioning a lawsuit, were you threatened in any way?"

"No," my mother says. "Frankly, that was enough. I could tell that my boss meant every word."

I furrow my brow. "You keep mentioning this guy. What did he do there?"

"He was Ezra Hawthorne's right-hand man. The institute was named for Mr. Hawthorne, but everyone knew that my boss was the one who really ran the place."

Which makes her boss the person most invested in making sure everything that went on there remained a secret. If the institute did have something to do with Billy's murder, he would know about it. In fact, it's likely he's the one who orchestrated it.

"Mom," I say. "I need you to tell me. Who was your boss?"

Billy starts to cry the moment the retreating forms of Ethan and the others vanish in the trees. Something about the way he can still hear the rapid crunch of their footfalls long after they've disappeared eclipses his fear, replacing it with disappointment and sadness.

They abandoned him.

All of them.

Even Ethan.

That thought—of being left behind by his best friend—brings the tears, which in turn brings shame. He should be fighting. He should be trying to squeeze himself through the bars. He should be doing anything but standing there sniffling, especially now that the man in the suit has him by the arm.

"Hey, there's no need for all that," he says. "I'm not going to hurt you."

Billy wipes his eyes and looks up at him. It's the same man he saw yesterday, the one who sent him scrambling when he was spotted at the falls.

"But I'm still in trouble, right?" he says.

The man eyes Billy, stuck between the bars of the gate like the world's worst jailbreaker. "Right now, I'd say you've got a bigger problem on your hands."

With the man's help, Billy finally gets free of the bars. All it takes is patience, sucking in his breath as much as he can, and a little maneuvering he didn't get a chance to do before Ethan and the others fled.

"Well, now that that's been taken care of, would you mind telling me why you're here again?" the man says. "I told you not to come back. You should have had enough sense to stay away."

What he doesn't understand is that it was impossible for Billy to stay away. Not after what he'd been told by Johnny Chen the previous summer, when they both found themselves in the woods at the same time.

Billy had just started exploring the forest on his own, curious about what he might find there. What he found was Johnny sitting on a stump with a dazed look in his eyes.

"Hey there, Billy boy," Johnny said, capping his words with an odd chuckle even though they hadn't been that funny. "Whatcha doing?"

"Just looking," Billy said.

"For what?"

"Ghosts."

A year later, Billy's still not sure why he told the truth. He guesses it's because he thought Johnny would understand. He was also in the woods, after all, making Billy hope that maybe there was someone else on Hemlock Circle as curious as he was.

"Intriguing," Johnny said. "There are definitely ghosts out here, but not where you think."

He then told Billy about the Hawthorne Institute, a place Billy never knew existed. Now that he did, he wanted to learn everything about it.

"Is it haunted?" he asked Johnny.

"Not in the way most people think about hauntings," Johnny said. "It's more like a place where ghosts come to visit. The people there, they talk to them. So I've been told. I've never seen any myself."

Billy's eyes widened to the point where he imagined they were as big as saucers. "You've been there?"

"Plenty of times. Going there used to distract me from things I didn't want to think about. Not anymore, but it helped for a little while."

Billy, who also had things he sometimes didn't want to think about, said, "How do I get there?"

He listened, rapt, as Johnny gave instructions on how to reach the Hawthorne Institute. Cross the road that cuts through the woods. Go a little bit farther until you reach the stone wall. Crawl through the hole in the wall and keep going until you hit the falls.

"From there, you'll see the institute," Johnny said.

The conversation ended then, and Billy never got a chance to talk to Johnny about it again. For soon he was dead. Drugs, Billy's mother told him in that worried way of hers, as if just mentioning it might cause it to happen to someone else.

For the rest of last summer, Billy had no desire to find the Hawthorne Institute himself. Thinking about the place made him sad because it reminded him of Johnny, the only person who'd taken him seriously when he talked about ghosts. Ethan certainly doesn't. Sure, he pretends to be interested, but Billy can tell he doesn't believe in them. Not the same way Billy does.

When this summer rolled around, though, his sadness about Johnny had faded, and Billy was ready to explore. He began gradually, making quick treks into the woods, going a little bit farther each time until he reached the road. Then he started exploring beyond it, eventually finding the stone wall Johnny had mentioned.

Then, yesterday, he'd found the breach in the wall and, without hesitation, pushed through it. After that, curiosity took over, pulling him all the way to the top of the falls, where he finally laid eyes on the Hawthorne Institute.

What he saw disappointed him.

The place was huge, yes, and undeniably interesting. Yet he'd been expecting something different. Something spookier. Still, he was debating whether to explore farther when the man in the suit spotted him.

"Hey, you!" he yelled. "You're not allowed to be here! Go away and don't come back!"

Billy ran.

All the way home.

Afraid he was being followed but too afraid to look behind him to find out.

Now Billy knows the man is right. He should have had enough sense to stay away. Instead, he returned. And this time he brought others.

"Let's go," the man says, giving Billy a nudge that's surprisingly gentle for someone so huge. "I need to find out what to do with you."

He leads Billy along the gravel path, heading toward the mansion he'd seen from the top of the falls. As they approach it, Billy expects to feel nervous or afraid. Instead, by the time they get to the mansion itself, a kind of anticipatory curiosity has taken over.

This is where they talk to ghosts.

And he's about to go inside.

The man in the suit guides him through a red door in the back of the mansion and down a long hallway. It leads to a vast entrance hall with a huge staircase and a creepy oil painting of a man surrounded by weird symbols.

The only other person there is a woman who pokes her head out of an office door. Peering at Billy, she says, "What do we have here?"

"Trespasser," the man in the suit says. "Where's the boss?"

The woman gestures to the stairs. "His office. This is either going to make his day or ruin it."

Off they go, across the entrance hall and up the steps to an office on the second floor. "Hope you're ready, kid," the man tells Billy before they go in. "Because you have a lot of explaining to do."

The fear Billy had felt earlier comes roaring back at full force. He shouldn't be here. Not alone. He wishes more than anything that Ethan were here with him. Anger, sadness, and disappointment mingle with his fear, threatening to overwhelm him. He feels tears start to form again, although he's not sure which emotion has summoned them.

Or maybe it's a new one, sneaking up on him like a ghost.

Loneliness.

That's what Billy feels in this moment. So terrifyingly, utterly alone.

The man in the suit nudges him into the office, where Billy sees another man in a similar black suit. He's standing behind a desk, his back turned as he looks out a window overlooking the gardens at the back of the mansion.

"Hello there, Billy," he says. "I hear you're very curious about this place."

Billy's hit with a wave of confusion. How does this man know his name?

The answer arrives when the man turns around, revealing himself to be Billy's neighbor.

"Mr. Van de Veer?" he says, stunned. "What are you doing here?"

"Please, son," Mr. Van de Veer says. "Call me Fritz."

TWENTY-ONE

In the evening, when Alice Van de Veer opens her front door to find me standing there, I wonder how much she knows about her husband's job at the Hawthorne Institute. Is she aware of everything that went on there? Or would she be as surprised as I was when my mother, after much coaxing, finally uttered the name Fritz Van de Veer.

My shock stemmed from Fritz's appearance more than anything else. I assumed he was a banker or a used-car salesman. I'd always sensed a slight slipperiness lurking just beneath his affable exterior. Now I intend to find out just how slippery he truly is.

"Well, hello, Ethan," Alice says, beaming. "What a pleasant surprise!"

A surprise? Maybe. But my being here is anything but pleasant. In fact, the Van de Veer house is the last place I want to be.

"Is Fritz home?" I say. "I need to talk to him."

"He is." Alice disappears into the house, her voice echoing within its depths. "Fritz? Ethan Marsh is here. Come say hi!"

Mr. Van de Veer soon appears, dressed as if for a corporate picnic. Tommy Bahama shirt, chinos, and penny loafers, which I didn't even know they made anymore. The clothes and the beige blandness of his hair and skin make him eerily inconspicuous. I suspect that's the reason I missed him in those photos hanging inside the Hawthorne Institute. After ending the call with my parents, I looked through them again, finding Fritz in ones dating back to the early eighties, just another face blending in with all the others.

Seeing him now, I need all the willpower I have not to punch him square in the jaw and then start kicking him the moment he hits the floor. Both my hands have curled into fists on their own accord. I stuff them into my pockets to keep them from swinging.

If my hunch is correct, then he took Billy, possibly because he thought it was me. And while I don't think Fritz did the actual kidnapping, I do suspect he's the one who set it all in motion.

"Ethan, hey," he says. "I was just going to treat myself to a scotch. You want one?"

"What I want," I say, "is for you to tell me if Billy Barringer was your intended target or if it was me."

Fritz freezes. The only noticeable motion comes from his eyes, which ping-pong with fear, and his mouth, which collapses into a frown.

"I don't know what the hell you're talking about, son," he says.

"Yeah, you do. Just like you knew all this time that Billy's body was on the grounds of the Hawthorne Institute."

All the color leaves Fritz's face. "It was?"

If his surprise is an act, it's a very convincing one. I almost believe he really didn't know.

"Maybe you should tell me everything—and I mean literally everything—you know about the night Billy Barringer vanished."

"Not here," Fritz says, sneaking a glance into the house. "Your place. I'll tell Alice I'm going for a walk."

Ten minutes later, he's cutting across the cul-de-sac. I watch his approach from the bedroom window, his face blurred by the encroaching dusk but the rest of him perfectly clear. He's adjusted his wardrobe since I left his house, wearing a gray windbreaker over his gaudily printed shirt and swapping the loafers for a pair of sneakers. They flash white in the deepening gloom as he steps purposefully into the yard.

"They found Billy at the institute?" he says when I meet him at the front door.

"Yes. In the lake."

I open the door wider, signaling for him to enter. Fritz shakes his head and says, "Can we stay outside? I think I still need some fresh air."

"The backyard then," I say, certain he also doesn't want to have this conversation in full view of the rest of Hemlock Circle.

Fritz follows me as I walk stiffly through the foyer, past the dining room, and into the kitchen. There, I open the patio door and we step into the backyard. It's dark here, the only light a rectangle of brightness spilling through the glass of the patio door. Fritz edges away from it, stopping in a shadowy patch of grass, his hands shoved into the pockets of his windbreaker. Whether he's aware of it or not, he's chosen to stand on the exact spot where my tent was located the night Billy was taken.

I join him there, my senses sharpened by nervousness. I feel the grass sinking beneath my sneakers, smell the aftershave Fritz splashed onto his cheeks this morning.

"I assume your mother told you she once worked at the institute," he says.

"She did. She also told me what she saw—and that you fired her because of it."

"She shouldn't have done that," Fritz says. "There's no expiration date on that document she signed, so it's still binding. But since old Ezra's been dead for more than twenty-five years, I guess it doesn't matter anymore."

"Sounds like Mr. Hawthorne had a lot of secrets. Big ones. Big enough to maybe kill to keep hidden."

Fritz jolts, possibly from confusion, probably from surprise. "That's a mighty big accusation, Ethan. Irresponsible, too."

"But is it wrong?"

At first, Fritz says nothing, his sudden plunge into silence a stark contrast with the noise coming from the woods. The symphonic chirp of crickets and the droning chorus of cicadas. I wonder if Billy is with them there now. Blending in with the shadows. Quietly watching. Waiting for justice.

"What's your goal here, son?" Fritz finally says.

"The truth."

"In my experience, men who say they want the truth end up wishing they had settled for the lie."

I'm not one of them. Thirty years of knowing nothing about what happened to Billy has me primed for the facts, no matter how brutal they may be.

"Let's start with the Hawthorne Institute," I say. "What went on there?"

Fritz straightens his spine and clears his throat. "The institute was devoted to the study of parapsychology. Are you familiar with the field?"

I am, slightly. A week ago, I would have dismissed what I've heard as pseudoscience. Now, having experienced some of it myself, I'm less doubtful.

"Give me your definition," I say.

Fritz pulls a pack of cigarettes from a pocket of his windbreaker. After tapping one out and lighting up, he says, "Parapsychology is the belief that there are forces at work beyond the easily proven ones we encounter every day. Extrasensory perception, telepathy, clairvoyance. I'm sure you've occasionally been hit with a sudden sense of déjà vu. Have you ever wondered why?"

"Can't say I have."

"Well, Ezra Hawthorne did," Fritz says, exhaling a stream of smoke that hovers in the still, humid air. "From a very young age, he wondered about many such things. He didn't think the way most people do. He was more attuned to what's beyond the things we see and know to be fact. He told me once it was because he emerged from the womb stillborn. For a full minute, there was no life in his infant body until, suddenly, there was. Because of that, he said, a piece of him always remained tethered to the afterlife."

I give him a look. "That sounds like bullshit."

"It might have been," Fritz admits. "But he believed in things like that. Because he was blessed with both money and an estate with plenty of privacy, he created a place where people could study unexplained phenomena without mockery or skepticism. That was the purpose of the institute. To provide room, board, and research space for those trying to explain the unexplainable. Why can some people sense things more than others? How can someone seemingly read minds, predict futures, move things without laying a finger on them?"

My mind's eye returns to the photograph of the men in robes and what my mother said she saw.

"And occult rituals? Where do those come in?"

"Occult." Fritz makes a disapproving sound. "Mr. Hawthorne despised that word. He said it was simply a label people put on practices they either feared or failed to understand. After all, something called occult by one person could have deep, religious meaning to someone else. It's all in how you perceive it."

"What did my mother perceive the night you fired her?"

Fritz looks past me to the forest at the edge of the yard, almost as if he can see the two miles to the Hawthorne Institute, where Ezra Hawthorne and his robed cohorts continue to circle a fire.

"That was unfortunate," he says. "Your mother was mistaken about what she saw. I suppose that was to be expected. It looked far more sinister than it really was. The institute had a policy in place for such situations, which was instant termination and a nondisclosure agreement. It avoided a lot of explaining on our part and a lot of unwanted scrutiny from the outside world. As a result, your mother has held a grudge against me for the past thirty years."

"I don't think it's a grudge," I say. "I think she was scared of you— and that place."

"She had no reason to be."

"She witnessed a satanic ritual."

"Satanic?" Fritz does an incredulous headshake, as if he can't believe I'm so dumb. "That was a ritual practiced by a small sect of Druids in the fourth century BC. It was an offering to the earth, expressing gratitude for what it provides."

"By 'offering,' you mean sacrifice."

"No," Fritz says, the tip of his cigarette flaring orange as he takes a drag. "I mean a pig's heart I procured from a butcher right before the ceremony began. Ezra Hawthorne had many eccentricities, like requiring all men at the institute to wear a black suit like he did, but he abhorred violence. He never would have ordered me to harm a child, which is what you've been insinuating. Nor would I ever have resorted to such a thing."

"So he was a pacifist."

"Yes. Ezra was a jack-of-all-trades when it came to religion, master of none. If he had any deep-seated spiritual beliefs, he never shared them with me. But I do know he kept an open mind about all of them. He attended Catholic Mass, studied the Quran and the Torah, spent a month living with Buddhist monks in Tibet, and, yes, conducted ancient Druid rituals. All in an attempt to expand his understanding of the universe."

"And what was your role in all of this?" I say. "How did you end up at the institute?"

"Me? Like almost everyone who found their way there, I was seeking answers."

"Did you find them?"

Fritz shakes his head. "But I've learned to live with the uncertainty. Working for Ezra Hawthorne helped with that, even though, outside of the occasional test or group study, I didn't take part, nor did I want to. I was just an administrator. I kept the place running smoothly so Mr. Hawthorne and the others could focus on their research."

"Who else did research there?"

"Plenty of established scientists and psychologists who wanted to explore a niche interest without fearing ridicule by their colleagues. Don't ask me for specific names. Even though the place closed long ago, I can't give them to you."

"I know one name," I say. "Johnny Chen."

Fritz eyes me through a stream of smoke, surprised. "Yes, there was a year in which he spent a lot of time at the institute."

"But he wasn't a scientist or psychologist. He was just a teenager. Why was he there?"

"Johnny took part in a group study of ESP. While his results showed no promise in that area, he displayed a curiosity about the place and the work we did there. Because of this, Mr. Hawthorne invited him to come back. He thought Johnny had potential."

"To do what?" I say.

"Continue the institute's work. Ezra was always encouraging like-minded people from the next generation. In Johnny, he noticed a sensitivity most teenage boys lack. Unfortunately, those who are the most sensitive are sometimes also the most troubled. Which Johnny was. When he overdosed, it was a shock to all of us."

I turn to the Chens' house next door, the windows visible over the hedge all aglow. "No one at the institute knew he was using drugs?"

"Of course not."

"And no one there had anything to do with his death?"

Fritz takes one last drag before dropping the cigarette and stomping it out on the grass.

"Just so I can keep track, you're now accusing me of two murders?"

"Can you blame me for being suspicious? Two boys from this very cul-de-sac were at the Hawthorne Institute shortly before their deaths. One died of a drug overdose, and the other was abducted and murdered."

"And both were sad coincidences," Fritz says.

"Then why didn't the police search the grounds of the institute after Billy disappeared?"

"Because they never asked." Fritz makes a palms-out gesture of helplessness. "If they had, we certainly would have let them search the property. Especially if we had any inkling that Billy's body was there. He was found in the lake, you say?"

"Yes. The base of the falls."

"Could he have fallen in?"

I recall what Ragesh told me about Billy's injuries and the blanket he'd been wrapped in. It makes me wonder if Fritz's curiosity is genuine or if he's only pretending not to know the details.

"No," I say. "But his disappearance was all over the news. Why didn't you invite the police to take a look around?"

"I suggested it, but Ezra shot me down," Fritz says. "I disagreed, seeing how we had nothing to hide. But privacy was important to him."

"And that was the only reason?" I say. "Privacy?"

"He also knew the authorities would jump to the same conclusions you have if they knew Billy had been at the institute the afternoon before he disappeared."

"You knew about that?"

Fritz nods. "I spoke to him myself."

Yet he has the nerve to act offended that I'm suspicious of him,

Ezra Hawthorne, the entire institute. I shuffle on the grass, angry and impatient. Fritz notices and says, "I liked Billy. He and his family were good neighbors for several years. And think about it, son: If I did kill Billy—which I absolutely did not—would it make sense to dispose of his body at the place where I worked? The place I ran?"

I concede that it makes zero sense.

"The same thing applies to Ezra Hawthorne. Who, by the way, was ninety-four at the time. It would have been impossible for him to cut open a tent, kidnap a boy, kill him, and hide his body in the lake."

"Maybe he had help," I say.

"Would it lessen your suspicion if I told you Mr. Hawthorne was also deeply upset by the boy's disappearance?"

"No," I say. "Seeing how they didn't know each other."

"Oh, but they did. They had quite a lengthy conversation."

"About what?" I say, even though, considering Billy's interests, I have a pretty good idea.

"Communicating with the dead."

Fritz's cigarette smoke still hangs in the air, lingering. By now it's drifted all the way to woods—a gray cloud curling through the trees.

"That was Mr. Hawthorne's other main interest, by the way," Fritz says. "And another subject of much research at the institute. I never experienced any of it firsthand. But Mr. Hawthorne and a few others claimed to have made contact with spirits many times, through several different means."

I'm hit with a head-to-toe jolt.

It turns out Billy had been right.

At the Hawthorne Institute, they did indeed talk to ghosts.

Fritz Van de Veer isn't a believer in the things studied at the Hawthorne Institute. But he's not a disbeliever, either. In general, Fritz subscribes to the chaos theory, which, at its most basic level, can be boiled down to "Shit happens."

That, he thinks, makes him the ideal person to run a place like the institute. When things happen for seemingly no particular reason, he doesn't try to figure out the why of it all. He just rolls up his sleeves, takes care of the situation, and gets paid handsomely for his troubles.

For instance, when Joyce Marsh was surprised by a bunch of guys test-driving an ancient ritual with a pig's heart, he followed institute protocol, made sure she signed the necessary NDA, and sent her packing.

And when his ten-year-old neighbor is found stuck in the gates of the Hawthorne family mausoleum, he orders the boy brought inside to see if he's okay, do a little damage control, and, hopefully, avoid a potential lawsuit.

"So, Billy," he says. "I was told you were here with some other kids. Is that true?"

"No, sir," Billy says, a lie Fritz grudgingly respects. The ability to keep secrets is a trait he admires. Still, he'd prefer it if the boy gave at least some indication of how many there had been—and what they had been up to.

"What were you doing out there—all by yourself?"

"Just exploring."

"Exploring?" Fritz says. "That's all?"

"Yes, sir."

"And what about yesterday?"

Billy looks up, surprised Fritz knows about that. He shouldn't be. Of course Fritz was informed about it.

"There's no harm in exploration," he tells Billy. "That's the whole purpose of this place. Exploring the unknown. But next time, instead of sneaking onto the property, just ask me and I'll show you around."

The boy's eyes brighten, his fear replaced by eagerness. "Can you show me now?"

"I could," Fritz says. "But first I'm going to need something from you. A promise that you'll remain quiet about anything you see or hear. Don't tell your parents or your brother or your friends. They don't need to know what we do here."

"What *do* you do here, Fritz?"

Fritz Van de Veer smiles, pleased the boy remembered to use his first name. "We do many things, Billy."

"Do you talk to ghosts?"

Fritz contemplates the boy. Such a big, complicated question from someone so young. One he can't answer.

But he knows someone who can.

He takes him into what's known as the library, although it holds much more than books. It's the heart of the institute, where others gather to discuss, debate, debunk. Currently, only one man occupies the vast room.

Ezra Hawthorne.

He's looking at the photos that hang on the walls when they enter.

When he turns around to smile at Billy, Fritz sees the man as if through the boy's eyes. Tall, pale, and ancient, looking both dapper and ominous in his black suit.

"Hello, young sir," Ezra says, prompting tongue-tied consternation from Billy.

Fritz remembers being just as awestruck when he first met Ezra Hawthorne all those years ago. He was a grad student at Princeton, working on his master's in psychology, when he was invited to an informal gathering hosted by one of his professors. Also in attendance was a tall man in a black suit that made his pale features appear positively ghostly. After a few minutes of aimless chatting, Mr. Hawthorne introduced himself and invited Fritz to visit the institute.

"Let's see if you have any gifts," he said.

Fritz took part in a silly test in which he was asked to turn his back to a man holding a stack of flash cards with pictures of animals on them. All he had to do was guess which animal was on the card being held up. Even though Fritz failed the test in spectacular fashion, when the day was done, Mr. Hawthorne pulled him aside and said, "You're welcome to return anytime you'd like."

He had no intention of coming back. But then Alice suffered a miscarriage—her third—and Fritz found himself looking for something to believe in. He knew he wasn't going to find it in religion, especially the harsh fire-and-brimstone sermons his parents had dragged him to when he was a boy.

One night, for no particular reason he could think of, he found himself driving to the Hawthorne Institute. Ezra welcomed him like a long-lost friend. They talked for hours about why inexplicable things happen and how to make sense of a world that very often makes no sense at all. To Fritz's surprise, the conversation ended with a job offer.

Now he all but runs the place, which is how he knew to bring Billy here. It's an unspoken rule at the institute: If it involves ghosts, consult Mr. Hawthorne.

"Do you talk to ghosts?" Billy asks again.

"Not all the time," Ezra says. "But on occasion, I have communicated with spirits."

Fritz notices the boy's eyes light up. "So ghosts are real?"

"Oh, they're very real."

"Where are they?" Billy says, glancing around the room, as if one might be lurking in the corners.

"There are ghosts everywhere," Ezra Hawthorne tells him, "if you just know where to look."

For the next half hour, Fritz watches as Mr. Hawthorne regales Billy with tales of his exploits, showing him books about ghosts, photos of séances, the tools of the trade. The boy proves himself to be quite knowledgeable about the subject. Far more than Fritz, who doesn't know the difference between a specter and a shade. But Billy does, which Fritz can tell impresses Mr. Hawthorne.

"I see you're a mutual ghost admirer," he tells Billy. "I've never talked to one so young."

When the visit is over, Fritz starts to escort Billy out of the room, having already decided to drive the boy home himself. It's easier that way. Less conspicuous, too. But before they're completely out the door, Ezra Hawthorne has one more thing to say.

"It was a pleasure meeting you, Billy. You're welcome to return anytime you like."

TWENTY-TWO

stare up at the sky, suddenly dizzy. It's one of those perfectly clear nights when every star is visible, all of them seeming to pulse with extra energy. I'm buzzing, too, over what Fritz is telling me. I suppose I shouldn't be surprised that Billy, who so desperately wanted to believe in ghosts, eventually found his way to Ezra Hawthorne, a man who allegedly communicated with them. Yet it's a shock to hear, mostly because Billy never mentioned it in the tent later that night.

Then again, I didn't give him much of a chance.

"Do you think he was lying to Billy?" I say. "About making contact with spirits?"

"Mr. Hawthorne didn't lie about things like that," Fritz tells me. "If he said it happened, he believed it to be true."

"Which doesn't mean it is. Did *you* ever see it happen?"

"No," Fritz says. "Remember, I rarely took part in the institute's activities."

"But you're a believer?"

"I wouldn't say that, exactly." Fritz returns his hand to his pocket, removing another cigarette. Lighting up, he says, "You know that old saying 'Seeing is believing'? Well, I have yet to see anything that's made me believe. But I haven't outright dismissed it, either. Not after some of the things I've heard. Ezra regaled me with so many tales of communicating with the dead that I suppose I'm a bit of an expert on the subject."

Noise rises from the nearby woods, faint but distinct. A rustle in the underbrush. It might just be an animal.

Then again, it might not.

"What if I wanted to try it?" I say.

"Talking to the dead?" Fritz cocks his head, intrigued. "Why would you want to do that?"

I have my reasons, none of which I'm prepared to share with him.

"Just hypothetically," I say. "Can I talk to any spirit?"

"Only the ones who have something to say."

"What if I have something to say to them?"

"It's not that simple," Fritz says. "It's not like picking up a phone and calling someone. The majority of spirits can't be contacted."

"Why not?"

"Because they're at peace."

Fritz kneels and runs his index finger over the grass, drawing an invisible circle. "That's the land of the living," he says before drawing another circle that slightly overlaps it. "This is the spirit realm. Ezra believed that's where the souls of the deceased go. Most of them, any-way. A very few never quite make it because something is keeping them tied to the land of the living."

"Where do they go?"

Fritz taps the space where the two circles meet. "It's a kind of limbo between the two realms. If a spirit is there, you have at least a small chance of contacting them."

"But not if they're in the spirit realm," I say.

"Correct," Fritz says, pointing at me with his cigarette. "The spirit realm is the place you want your loved ones to be. It means nothing prevents them from moving on. No unfinished business."

"Like murder?"

Fritz stares at me. "This isn't hypothetical at all, is it?"

"The other day, you asked if I've seen something unusual on the cul-de-sac," I say. "I have."

"Billy?"

"Yes." There's no point in denying it. Fritz knows anyway. "He's been haunting the woods."

"Fascinating." Fritz moves to the edge of the yard and peers into the woods. "Is he here now?"

"I'm not sure," I say, thinking about the faint rustle I heard. "Maybe?"

Fritz takes one last, lingering look into the woods before turning back to me, puffing on his cigarette. "Do you know what he wants?"

"I don't. But I'm pretty sure he's been trying to tell me something. At first, I thought he was leading me to the Hawthorne Institute because that's where he was found."

"And because you thought we'd murdered him," Fritz says, his bluntness tinged with understanding. If he harbors any hard feelings toward me over that, he doesn't show it.

"Correct," I say. "But now I think I misunderstood him, and I'd like—"

"To flat out ask him what he wants."

I start to blush, for the idea continues to sound ridiculous. "Is that even possible?"

"If Ezra Hawthorne were here right now, I'm sure he'd suggest a dozen different ways in which you could attempt to contact Billy. Unfortunately, he isn't. And there's no way to reach him."

"He's firmly in the spirit realm?" I ask. "How do you know?"

Fritz gives me a sly smile. "Just because I don't yet believe doesn't mean I haven't tried."

"So I'm out of luck? My only option is to let Billy keep haunting me and try to figure out what he wants?"

"Maybe the haunting *is* what he wants," Fritz says. "Over the years, Ezra became convinced that some souls remain caught between the earthly and spirit realms by choice. His advice was always to leave them alone."

But I can't do that. God knows I tried. Running away as fast as I could, hoping the guilt and bad memories wouldn't catch up to me. But they did. They always do. Now they're always present, taking the form of insomnia, of The Dream, of Billy's shadowlike figure tossing baseballs into the backyard.

"Why?"

"Because there's something else that keeps a spirit bound to the earthly realm. Something stronger than unfinished business."

"What's that?" I say.

Fritz drops his second cigarette next to the first one. Extinguishing it with a mighty stomp, he says, "A grudge."

than doesn't stop running until both feet are firmly planted in the grass of his own backyard. He's never run that far in his life, and now he worries about the toll it's taking on his body. His legs feel like rubber bands, and his heart thumps so heavily in his chest he fears it's going to explode. He collapses onto the lawn, unconcerned that his mother might see him like this and ask what he's been up to. He'd gladly tell her. Because someone needs to know what happened to Billy.

Instead of his mother, the sight of Ethan splayed out on the grass draws Ashley, Russ, and Ragesh, who push through the hedge bordering Russ's lawn.

"Where's Billy?" Ashley says, peering into the woods as if he's simply lagging behind.

"He—" Still breathless, Ethan can barely get the necessary words out. "He got caught."

"Caught?" Ragesh says. "By that guy in the suit?"

Ethan nods, dizzy from the thought of it. He replays the image of the man in the black suit—so huge, so intimidating—reaching Billy, wondering what happened after that. Is Billy still trapped between the gate's bars? Or is he in the clutches of the suited man? The idea that, right now, Billy might be getting roughed up makes him want to puke.

Ashley kneels beside Ethan and helps him sit up. Rubbing his back, she says, "Okay, tell us what happened."

That's something Ethan can't do because it would mean admitting to the others not just that he left Billy behind, but his reasons for doing so. Instead, he gives them a hollow version of the truth.

"The guy got to him before Billy could get away."

Ragesh starts pacing in the grass. "Do you think he's going to tell on us?"

"*That's* what you're worried about?" Ashley says. "Billy could be in big trouble."

"And so could we," Ragesh says. "You saw that place. It's not somewhere we should have been trespassing."

"Which is why I didn't want you going through that goddamn wall."

Afraid the two of them are going to exchange blows, Ethan pipes up. "We need to tell someone. My mom. Or Billy's mom."

"No way," Ashley says. A surprise to Ethan. Until now, he'd assumed she was on his side. "I was the one in charge. If people find out about this, I'm never going to get a babysitting job again. And I need that money."

Suddenly, Ethan understands. Ashley has told him all about her plans for going to Woodstock and how the money she's earning from watching him will make that happen. Ethan, for his part, doesn't want another babysitter. Even though Ashley won't be with him every day, now that his mom lost her job, he at least likes knowing she'd still be his babysitter whenever she is needed.

"Then we can go back for him," Ethan says.

Ragesh scoffs. "And get caught ourselves? No thank you."

"But we have to do something. We can't just leave him there."

"Why not?" Russ says.

He stands at a slight remove from the rest of them, facing the woods. Whereas Ashley looks worried and Ragesh annoyed, to Ethan's eyes Russ appears contemplative.

"Because he might be in trouble," Ethan says.

"Maybe he should be. He's the one who led us there."

Ethan feels something snap inside him. Like there was an elastic band stretched across his heart, keeping his emotions in check. Now it's broken, and they come tumbling forth in an ungainly heap.

"You followed him there!" he yells, tears stinging his eyes. "You and Ragesh. I didn't even want to go."

"But you did," Ragesh says in a way that makes Ethan wish he were six years older, a foot taller, and a hundred pounds heavier. Then he'd be able to flatten Ragesh to the ground.

Instead, all he can do is cry more and say, "I didn't have a choice! Now Billy's in trouble."

"And we won't be," Ragesh says. "Not if we keep our mouths shut."

"Why are you worried about him anyway?"

This comes from Russ. A question Ethan can't quite comprehend. Not because it's hard, but because the answer is so obvious. Why wouldn't he be worried about Billy?

"Because he's my best friend."

"But why?" Russ says.

Ethan pauses, surprised he can't instantly give a response. Before this moment, he's never given it any thought. He and Billy are neighbors. They're the same age. They get along. Why wouldn't they be best friends?

"Because he lives next door."

"So do I," Russ says. "Does that mean I'm your best friend, too?"

Ethan doesn't answer with an immediate yes, which makes Russ react like he's just been shoved. A falter. A frown. A darkening of the eyes until they're all but black.

"We're friends," Ethan hastily adds.

"No, I get it," Russ says.

Ashley throws out her arms, grabbing their attention. "What's important right now is what to do about Billy. Let's vote. Those in favor of doing nothing, raise your hands."

Ethan watches as Ragesh's hand shoots immediately into the air. No surprise there. The same with Russ, who sullenly glares at Ethan as his hand is raised. The real shock is when Ashley's hand also goes up, albeit slowly and with noticeable uncertainty.

"I'm sorry, Ethan. It just seems like the best thing to do for all of us."

"But what if they hurt Billy?"

"That's not going to happen," Ashley says.

"Other than trespassing, we didn't do anything wrong," Ragesh adds. "We were just messing around."

"They're probably going to give him a lecture and call his mom to pick him up," Ashley says. "He might not even be in that much trouble. And he's definitely not in any danger. They wouldn't hurt a kid."

That seals the deal for Ethan. Although it doesn't fully erase his worry, Ashley's assurance is enough for him to cast his vote with the others. He even raises his hand so they can see it's unanimous.

They've chosen silence.

And Billy is on his own.

TWENTY-THREE

Scriiiiiiiitch.

I wake with a gasp, the sound of it a panicked hiss slicing through the remnants of The Dream. My eyes snap open to the soft light of dawn creeping across the ceiling. Under normal circumstances, the sight of daylight would bring at least a small amount of comfort.

Not now.

Not as my brain echoes with the noise of The Dream.

Which, alarmingly, was slightly different from every other time I've had it.

The Dream 2.0.

Rather than being hit with a brief glimpse of peaked tent ceiling above me and still-full sleeping bag beside me and long, dark gash running between us, this new, unimproved version gave me a longer look at all of it. Especially the sliced tent wall and the slash of darkness beyond it in which something is usually sensed but never glimpsed.

This time, though, I saw *something*.

What it was, I don't know. It was too quick, too hazy. A blur in the dark impossible to make out. But that mere glimpse is enough to unsettle me in ways I'm not used to. My heart continues to drum in my chest as I sit up, stretch, blink against the brightening sun still crawling over the ceiling.

I check the time. Quarter past seven. Too early to get up, too late to go back to sleep. Which makes it the perfect time to write about the new version of The Dream in my notebook. If, God forbid, I ever have it again, I'll have a record of when it started. Still unknown: *why* it started.

Still groggy, I reach across the nightstand, seeking out the notebook and my pen.

They're not there, even though I'm certain they were on the nightstand when I went to sleep. I distinctly remember writing in the notebook before turning off the light, summarizing the night's events in four succinct words.

Billy has a grudge.

But now both the pen and notebook are gone, making the nightstand seem vast and empty without them.

Panic hitches in my chest, making my still-thrumming heart beat even faster. I tell myself to stay calm. That there's a perfectly logical reason they aren't where I left them, even if that reason is something ridiculous, like sleepwalking. It certainly isn't burglary. Why would someone break in and only steal a notebook and a pen?

The answer, immediate and obvious, is that this possibly hypothetical burglar took more than my pen and my notebook. They also could have taken my wallet, my phone, anything else of value that's not nailed down. I picture the rest of the house, already sparsely furnished, now completely empty, one bare room leading into another.

The image is enough to propel me out of bed—and I instantly step on something on the floor next to it. Looking down, I see one bare foot atop a corner of the notebook. The big toe of my other foot brushes the pen.

I grab them both off the carpet, my panic evaporating. Replacing it is another emotion: embarrassment at my foolishness. Clearly, I knocked the notebook and pen off the nightstand at some point, probably in a fit of sleeplessness now forgotten.

There was no intruder.

I immediately overreacted. Again.

I open the notebook and flip through the pages, seeing similar overreactions scribbled down in the prior months. Stuff about being afraid to sleep, of being equally afraid that I won't sleep, of feeling lonely or sad or guilty. *It's my fault*, one entry reads, although I can't remember which transgression I was writing about. Maybe all of them.

I turn to the last entry in the notebook—and my fear comes roaring back. I think of the volume dial on a radio, ticking higher. If my earlier panic was at a seven, this renewed alarm is a nine, spinning perilously close to a ten.

Because on the page in front of me, scrawled in handwriting not my own, are three words as terrifying as they are familiar.

HAKUNA MATATA DUDE

TWENTY-FOUR

Five minutes later, I'm pounding on the front door of Russ's house, not caring that it's too early or that I'm wearing just a T-shirt and boxers and slipped-on sneakers, the laces still untied.

Jennifer answers the door while tugging on a robe, the fabric parting around her pregnant stomach. Her sleep-shrouded gaze tells me I woke her up. "Ethan? What's wrong?"

"Is Russ here?"

"No. He's at the store. They're getting deliveries this morning."

"You still have the spare key my parents gave you, right?" I say. "You didn't lose it?"

When I was ten, only the neighbors on each side of us had keys to our house—the Chens on the right and the Barringers on the left. They had them so Mrs. Chen could water the plants when we went on vacation and so Mrs. Barringer could enter if there was an emergency while we were away. Since I checked the whole house, finding no broken windows and every door locked, the only way someone could have come inside is with the sole spare key now in Russ's possession.

"I—I don't know," Jennifer says as she runs a hand through her tangled hair. "I think so. Why?"

"Because someone broke into my house," I say, barely scratching the surface of what I *think* is going on, even though I desperately hope I'm wrong about that.

"Really?" Jennifer's eyes go wide. Fully awake now, she pulls me inside and leads me to the kitchen. Along the way, we pass the family room, where Benji sits on the floor munching cereal and watching an episode of *Bluey*.

"I think it's in here somewhere," Jennifer says as she rummages through a junk drawer in the kitchen. "Did they take anything?"

"No," I say, which is why I don't think this was your average break-in. Even though half the furniture is with my parents in Florida, a burglar surely would have taken something. My laptop in the study. The TV in the living room. Hell, my wallet was on the same nightstand as the notebook and pen, the only things that were apparently touched.

"I can't find it," Jennifer says, closing the drawer with a nudge of her hip. She calls down the hallway, "Misty? Do you know where the spare key to Ethan's house is?"

Russ's mother appears in the doorway, looking like she's been awake for hours. Her clothes are crisp and her hair perfect. "The spare key?" she says. "It's here."

She guides me back to the foyer and a side table by the front door. Sitting on it are a lamp, a bin of mail, and a bowl of keys. Mrs. Chen plucks one from the bowl and hands it to me. I look at the white label attached to the key ring. There, in my mother's handwriting, is my last name.

"And everything here was locked last night?" I ask, desperate. "No signs of a break-in?"

"We have a security system," Jennifer says. "It was activated all night."

I hand the key back to Mrs. Chen, who says, "Maybe you should call the police."

"Thanks. I probably will."

It turns out there's no need. Because as I walk back to my house, my still-untied shoelaces flapping around my ankles, I spot Detective Cassandra Palmer on my doorstep. Her presence, unexpected and unannounced, sends my anxiety spiking again.

"Good morning, Ethan," she says as she takes in my ensemble of boxers, T-shirt, and untamed bedhead. "Is everything okay?"

I stop on the front walk, trying to think of the best way to answer that. I have the urge to tell her no, that everything isn't okay. That, in fact, someone was in my house. But I can't. Because it wasn't just anyone who broke in last night. The spare key still at Russ's house proves it. A regular burglar—a human one—would need some way to get inside.

But not Billy.

He's a shadow.

He didn't need a spare key or unlocked door to slip inside, creep up the stairs, stand inches from my sleeping form as he wrote in the notebook.

Hakuna matata, dude.

"Just had to run next door for a second," I finally say. From her unimpressed expression, it's clear Detective Palmer doesn't believe me. Still, she says nothing else as I open the front door and usher her inside.

"Make yourself at home in the kitchen," I say. "I'm going to run upstairs and put on some pants."

"Please do," Detective Palmer says.

At the top of the stairs, I pause in an attempt to sense Billy's presence the same way I did the night I first noticed the lights flicking on and off around Hemlock Circle. If he's still here, there's a chance I won't need to tell Detective Palmer anything at all. Maybe she'll detect his presence on her own. Billy, however, seems to be gone. Right now, all I feel is the heavy silence of a house with only one person living in it.

In my bedroom, the notebook sits face down on the carpet, where I'd thrown it after seeing what had been written inside. I avoid looking at it as I slide on the same jeans I wore last night. After splashing my face and armpits with cold water, I head back down to the kitchen and start brewing a pot of coffee. "You want some?" I ask Detective Palmer.

"No thanks. I won't be here long. I just wanted to have a quick chat."

That sounds ominous. I look to the coffee maker, where a thin stream of liquid has started trickling into the carafe.

"I heard you had a nice conversation with Detective Patel yesterday," she says. "After he picked you up for trespassing on the grounds of the Hawthorne Institute. I guess you're still convinced they had something to do with Billy's murder."

But I'm not. Not anymore. What Fritz told me last night makes sense. He's a smart man. Smart enough to know not to dispose of a boy's body on the property he oversaw. Since I also believe his assertion that Ezra Hawthorne was too old and unsteady to do it, the institute and everyone associated with it have been demoted to possible, yet unlikely, suspects.

"I've changed my mind about that," I say.

"Care to tell me why you were there?"

"Looking."

"Me and my team already did that," Detective Palmer says. "Technically, we still are. If I wanted to, I could charge you with disturbing a crime scene."

I turn away from the coffee maker, nervous. Just because Ragesh declined to arrest me doesn't mean Detective Palmer won't.

"I didn't disturb anything. I just want to know who killed Billy."

"You already do. You were right there when he was taken."

"But I was asleep."

Detective Palmer folds her arms across her chest. "Which I find very convenient."

"I'm not a liar," I say. "I didn't see anything."

"I have no doubt you really believe that. But sometimes people forget things for a reason. Especially little kids who witness something too confusing or traumatic for them to process."

"You think I saw who did it and blocked it out?"

"Don't you?" Detective Palmer says.

Of course I've considered that possibility, as has every mental health professional I've ever talked to. But nothing has ever backed up the idea. Not decades of therapy, hypnosis, and dream analysis, including a child psychologist who showed me endless drawings of tents just in case one of them sparked a memory.

"It's not as simple as that," I say as the coffee at last finishes brewing. I grab a mug and prepare to pour.

"Maybe you're right. Maybe this recurring dream you keep having is just that. A dream. Or maybe it's a repressed memory you have of seeing who took Billy. One that messed you up so much that your brain deleted it."

I stop mid-pour. "What could possibly be that traumatic?"

"You'd be surprised. Think about who could have taken and killed Billy. Remember what I said the other day about the culprit likely being someone from Hemlock Circle?"

I do. Vividly.

"You told me the reason Billy didn't make a sound when he was taken is because he could have known who it was," I say as I resume pouring the coffee, sloshing it into the mug with unsteady hands.

Detective Palmer nods. "If I'm right about this, and I think I am, whoever took and killed Billy not only knew about the falls, which was the most convenient place to dispose of his body, but also who he was, *where* he was. They knew him well enough that he didn't panic when he saw them, even after they sliced through the side of the tent. Not a whole lot of people fit that bill. And you knew every single one of them."

"It wasn't my parents, if that's what you're implying."

"No, not them," Detective Palmer says. "In my mind, there's only one person who could be responsible."

I throw my head back and rub my temples, already knowing where this is heading. Based on all the established facts—that the killer was aware Billy was camping in my yard, that Billy didn't scream or panic because he knew his abductor, that whoever it was had knowledge of the falls two miles from my backyard—there really is only one viable suspect left.

"Billy's mother," I say.

t's a mother's lot in life to worry.

No one told Mary Ellen this when she was pregnant with Billy, so it came as a surprise when she first held his wailing, wriggling body in her arms and was filled not with love or tenderness but worry. A worry so deep she felt it in her soul.

What would she do, she thought, if something bad happened to him?

She knows now—just as she knew then, after that first, fraught thought had passed—that worry is a by-product of love. What she still doesn't know is what to do with it. She thought it would pass with time, but it never did. Not even after Andy was born, though she'd been assured everything gets easier with your second child. Not in her experience. It just compounded her anxiety. Now she has two boys to worry about. And there's so much cause for worry nowadays.

"This world gets crazier every day," Trish Wallace said that very morning, and Mary Ellen has to agree. Everything outside of Hemlock Circle seems to be spiraling out of control, like the bus rigged with explosives in that movie she and Blake went to see last month. Mass slaughter in Rwanda. That pretty Nancy Kerrigan getting

whacked in the knees. O. J. Simpson killing his wife, which Mary Ellen knows with every bone in her body is the truth. An innocent man
doesn't try to flee the way he did a few weeks ago. Like everyone else,
she watched that white Ford Bronco driving on the freeway for hours.
The whole time, a lump of worry sat in the pit of her gut, fearing that
the chase would never end. That the Bronco would keep on driving.
All the way across the country. All the way to Hemlock Circle, where
no wife and mother would be safe.

That's what keeps her up at night. The idea that nowhere is safe.
Bad things can and do happen everywhere. Even here. Every time she
sees Misty Chen, she wants to grip her arms and shake the truth out
of her. Did she know her son was an addict? Did she do anything
about it? Does she blame herself? Mary Ellen needs to know so she can
keep it from happening to her boys.

Now Billy's upstairs, getting ready before heading next door to the
Marshes'. Mary Ellen told him he could still go, even though she
remains concerned about that stranger spotted roaming the woods
yesterday. The only reason she's allowing it is because Billy seems . . .
strange. Not quite upset, but not exactly happy. Muted. That's the best
word she can think of to describe him. Like something happened earlier today and Billy's not sure how to feel about it.

He's been hidden away in his room ever since slinking inside late
this afternoon, probably paging through that horrible ghost book he
thinks Mary Ellen doesn't know about. She almost threw it out when
she found it, but Blake stopped her.

"Let the boy have his book," he said. "It's harmless."

Mary Ellen scoffed at that. "Harmless? Have you looked at it? It's
morbid. All those pictures of ghosts and ghouls."

"Which is catnip to someone his age. Every boy goes through a
spooky phase. He'll outgrow it."

But it doesn't seem like a phase to Mary Ellen. Billy behaves like someone obsessed, talking about ghosts constantly. She was appalled when Blake helped him dress up as one for Halloween. She couldn't understand why a boy as sweet as Billy would admire something so scary.

It worries her, the way he's changing. She'd always thought of Andy as taking after her husband—smart, sly, even a little aloof and a bit of a loner. Until recently, she assumed that Billy took after her. Sensitive. So unlike the other boys in the neighborhood. So much like how she used to be. Well, how she still is. Over the years, she's learned how to tamp down her eccentricities, act like all the other moms, pretend to be normal.

As a little girl, she had been the school oddball. Not a total outcast. Her classmates seemed to like her well enough. But there was always something off about her. Something that kept her from being fully embraced by her peers.

Mary Ellen's mother told her, not unkindly, that she felt too much. That it ran in the family. "Our emotions run deep," she said when Mary Ellen was about Andy's age.

A perfect example is her porcelain doll, Stacy, which she received for Christmas when she was eight.

"Be very gentle with her," Mary Ellen's mother told her as she held Stacy for the first time. "She's fragile."

Mary Ellen didn't know what that word meant, and when she asked, the answer disturbed her.

"That she can break very easily," her mother said. "One wrong move and the whole doll will shatter and be lost forever."

Despite this very dire warning, Mary Ellen loved Stacy. She kept the doll on a shelf opposite her bed so Stacy was the first thing she saw in the morning and the last thing she saw at night. When Mary Ellen took Stacy down from the shelf, it was only to gently cradle her for a few minutes. She knew it was too risky to do more than that, just as she knew that, no matter how careful she was, there'd come a day when Stacy would break and be no more. In Mary Ellen's mind, it wasn't a matter of if but of when.

By high school, she'd learned to hide her constant fear enough to get by. She wasn't exactly popular, but she had a few friends, she dated a few boys, and, most important, she blended in. But just because she hid the worry didn't mean it had gone away. It was still there. A monster lurking in the dark, waiting to come out at the most unpredictable moments.

Tonight, for instance.

As Billy packs, Mary Ellen calls her husband, who's away at a conference in Boston. Another source of concern. Boston's so big and the drive difficult and the people, well, Mary Ellen feels bad stereotyping an entire city's population, but she's heard that they're rude.

"Do you really think I should let Billy camp over at Ethan's house?" she says.

Blake's answer—"I don't see why not"—doesn't surprise Mary Ellen in the least. He's always been more laid-back than her, a trait she finds both necessary and mystifying. Both of them can't be strung tighter than a tennis racket. Yet she also can't fathom how Blake manages to glide through life mostly worry-free.

"But there was a stranger roaming the neighborhood yesterday," she says. "Maybe he's still here, lurking."

"It's not like Billy's camping alone in the woods," Blake says. "He'll be with Ethan in Fred and Joyce's backyard. I'm sure they'll keep an eye on things."

When the call ends, Mary Ellen still hasn't decided what to do. But then Billy comes downstairs, a rolled-up sleeping bag under his arm and his mood still unreadable.

"Are you sure you feel up to it tonight?" she says. "There's always next Friday."

"I guess."

Mary Ellen sighs, wishing that he'd tell her what's wrong and that her husband were here instead of in Boston and that she could be like the other wives on Hemlock Circle and just fucking relax for an evening. Most of all, she wishes for the ability to control things that are wildly beyond her control. Because this worry—this bone-deep, exhausting, never-ending worry—is too much.

"Okay then," she says, choosing to no longer fight this particular battle. There'll be more in the future. More moods. More anxiety. More eagerness to grow up, which is a particular problem with Andy. It radiates off him like body heat. All of it makes Mary Ellen long to be able to preserve her sons as they are right now. That way they'd stay the same forever, and she could worry less instead of standing by helplessly as her sons get older, move out, move on.

"Have fun," she tells Billy, before adding the final two words she'll ever say to him. "Be careful."

As she watches Billy slip out into the twilight, Mary Ellen's thoughts return to Stacy, the porcelain doll she had adored so much as a child. By the time she was ten, the waiting for Stacy's inevitable destruction became more than she could bear. Rather than delay it— worrying and fretting and ultimately losing the doll before she was prepared to say goodbye—Mary Ellen decided it was best to take matters into her own hands.

One afternoon, she marched up to her room, picked Stacy up from the shelf, and cradled her for as long as she wanted. When it was over, Mary Ellen gave Stacy a kiss on her delicate cheek and smashed her porcelain head in.

After that, she worried no more.

TWENTY-FIVE

I take another sip of coffee as I again mull the possibility of Billy's mother being the killer. Detective Palmer is right that Mrs. Barringer fits all the characteristics of Billy's killer. It's the likelihood of it that continues to keep me from reaching that conclusion.

No, the Barringers weren't the best parents in the world. Blake Barringer was present but absent. One of those very smart men who could never quite get out of his head and engage with the rest of the world. I honestly can't think of a single time we spoke to each other one-on-one, despite having had ample opportunity.

I talked much more to Billy's mother, who was different in her own way. Even when I was a boy, Mary Ellen Barringer struck me as fragile. I once overhead my mother refer to her as "Nervous Nellie." Uncharitable, but accurate. She always looked slightly spooked, like at any moment she expected to see a ghost.

Detective Palmer wasn't there when Mary Ellen Barringer dragged Andy into the yard, begging me to remember anything more about that night. She didn't see Mrs. Barringer looking wraithlike in her nightgown and mismatched socks. Didn't feel her shockingly strong grip on my shoulders as she tried to shake the memories out of me.

That was a woman turned mad with grief, not guilt. It eventually got so bad that Mrs. Barringer had to be institutionalized not long after they left Hemlock Circle. A few years after that, Mr. Barringer died and teenage Andy was sent off to foster care.

Then again, maybe it was the opposite. Maybe guilt had driven Mrs. Barringer mad, and instead of trying to get me to remember, what she had really wanted was for me to reveal how much I knew.

Before she leaves, I ask Detective Palmer what the next steps are in Billy's case. It's not promising. With Mary Ellen Barringer's condition being what it is, there's not a whole lot they can do. Detective Palmer tells me she plans to visit Mrs. Barringer at the state hospital, even though doctors have warned her that she'll be unresponsive.

"So we might never know who killed Billy?" I say.

"Never say never," Detective Palmer says. "But at this point, it doesn't seem likely. Unless someone else emerges as a viable suspect, we might have to resign ourselves to never knowing what really happened."

Once the detective leaves, I go back upstairs and pick the notebook up off the floor. It's still open to the page Billy had written on.

HAKUNA MATATA DUDE

I know it was Billy because I never shared his last words to me with anyone. Not Russ, or my parents, or the police. Not even Claudia. It remained a secret because I wanted to keep something of Billy all to myself.

Just to be certain, I check the trail cam app on my phone, hoping it might have snapped a picture of the culprit as he emerged from the woods and crossed to the house. But most of the photos taken during the night are of me and Fritz Van de Veer talking in the yard. The ones in which we're absent show no shadow or specter or even a normal human being. Just a lone deer nibbling the grass at five in the morning.

Since the trail cam provided no guidance, I cross the hall to my old bedroom and open up Billy's copy of *The Giant Book of Ghosts, Spirits, and Other Spooks.* I find the page with Billy's handwriting in the margin and check it against what's in my notebook. It's not quite a match, but close enough that one could reasonably assume the words in the book and my notebook were written by the same person.

Now that I know Billy's not confined to the woods, I look for him everywhere on the way back to my new bedroom. In the shadow behind the door. In the darkness under the bed. After a thorough search that turns up nothing, I drop onto the edge of the bed and stare at the notebook. It makes me think about The Dream and how this last go-round had been the same as all the others except for that extra millisecond in which I saw a blur of motion just beyond the gash in the tent.

A blur that I assume is Billy's killer. That's the conclusion this new version of The Dream and Billy's message in my notebook, so much more invasive than a baseball in the yard, seem to be pointing to.

That I really did see Billy's killer.

Just a glimpse.

Was it Mrs. Barringer? Possibly. Detective Palmer certainly seems to believe it, even though it's a suspicion she'll likely never be able to prove. That might be fine for a state police detective with no personal connection to the crime, but for me it's unacceptable. I've spent thirty years aching for the truth, not sleeping, being startled awake by The Dream when I do. I refuse to exist that way for thirty more.

There's also Billy to think about. Is it possible for his spirit to find peace if his killer's identity is never revealed? My guess is no, hence the increased intensity of his messages.

Billy no longer needs me to play detective.

He needs me to remember.

As I continue to stare at Billy's message, with its series of triangular *A*'s, I can think of only one way to make that happen.

A half hour later, I'm showered, dressed, and parked outside Russ's store, which has been open for all of a minute. Russ spots me from the registers as soon as I enter and rushes over.

"Hey, Jen called me. You kind of freaked her out this morning. Is everything okay?"

"It's fine," I say as I keep walking deeper into the store.

Russ trails after me. "So there was no break-in?"

"It was all a big misunderstanding."

"Then what are you doing here?"

I stop at the campsite display in the center of the store. It's still so early that Russ hasn't had time to turn on the bells and whistles that made it so charming. No cricket sounds chirping from the fake rock. No fan blowing cellophane flames in the firepit.

"I want to buy that tent," I say.

TWENTY-SIX

According to the instructions, the tent can be assembled in fifteen minutes.

It ends up taking me two hours.

Even then, I know I did it wrong by the way the tent pitches slightly forward, as if it's on an incline and not the same flat patch of grass where a similar tent stood thirty years ago. Sure enough, one touch is all it takes to send it collapsing in a heap of orange.

I begin again, starting from scratch. I consider waiting for Russ to get home and enlisting his help. But his demeanor in the store earlier tells me he'd offer more questions than assistance.

"Why do you need this again?" he asked as he rang me up.

"It's for Henry Wallace," I said, making up the excuse on the spot based on my recollection of Henry being inside the tent when we visited the store days earlier. "I thought he might enjoy it."

While that seemed to appease Russ in the moment, I know he'll find it weird that I'm erecting the tent in my backyard with Henry nowhere to be seen. So I go it alone, taking a mere hour to assemble it a second time. Unlike the first, it stays upright, which causes no end of pride.

When I'm done, I go inside to the kitchen, where I'd left my phone, and see literally hundreds of alerts, all from the trail cam app. Of course. Since I'd forgotten to turn off the camera, my every move that morning has been captured and sent to my phone. I swipe through a few of them, cringing at the sight of sweaty, sweary me wrangling with the tent before deleting the whole batch.

The phone pings again, this time triggered by a blue jay streaking by, and I'm treated to the new view offered by the trail cam. Grass in the foreground, spreading to a backdrop of the forest at the edge of the yard, plus the addition of the tent. Well, part of it, at least. Only a portion of the tent's front half nudges into the frame, an orange triangle rising to a peak that's just out of view.

I don't set foot outside again until night falls and I return to the tent armed with a gross-smelling sleeping bag I found in the basement and a ratty throw pillow dug from the hall closet. Also with me: an LED lantern my father used whenever the power went out; my pen and notebook, in case Billy wants to try writing again; a bag of Scrabble tiles because I once saw a movie in which a ghost communicated with them; and a bottle of cheap bourbon because I'm pretty sure I'm being stupid.

No, it's more than that.

I'm insane.

Truly, utterly insane.

Yet my understanding of the situation—that I've lost it, fully and completely—doesn't force me out of the tent. I stay hunched inside, my shoulders scraping the sloped sides as I uncap the bourbon and take a swig directly from the bottle. Not the best idea, really. Especially since the goal is to get into a remembering mood by making things as similar to that night as possible, in which case I should be slurping Hi-C Ecto Cooler from a juice box.

After one more swig of bourbon, I wriggle into the sleeping bag, lie flat-backed on the ground, and wait. For what, I don't know.

Probably nothing. Five minutes in and already this feels like a colossal waste of time. I decide to give it an hour. Two at the most. It's not like I'd be sleeping if I were inside the house.

"Come on, Billy," I mutter. "You want me to remember? Then help me. Because only you know what happened. Only you were there. I didn't see a thing."

I stop talking, mainly because there's no one here to listen. Just me. Talking to myself like a psychopath. But I also stop because I'm not sure if what I'm saying is true. There's a very good chance I did see something in the tent that night.

That's why he's been haunting me.

Billy needs me to recall what he already knows, to tell the people who need to be told, to act as his voice now that he no longer has one.

"Fine," I say, ostensibly talking to myself but really addressing Billy. "I'll try my best."

I shift, uncomfortable. Despite the cushion of the sleeping bag, the ground is harder than expected, not to mention slightly uneven. I wiggle to the left, trying to even myself out, and stare up at the tent's vaulted ceiling.

It is, I realize, the exact view I had when I was ten. I remember watching the shadows gathered there, as they are right now. A vaguely threatening darkness looming over the interior of the tent. And while it summons a dozen memories—my mother bringing out the oven-made s'mores, the way the tent's zipped flap trapped the July heat— none of them strike me as vital. They certainly don't shed light on the hazy half memories depicted in The Dream.

The *scriiiiiiiitch*.

The moment Billy was pulled from the tent.

Definitely not a hint of the person responsible for both.

I shift again, try to start over. It dawns on me that staring at the tent ceiling could be a distraction and that I should instead focus on how the space affects my other senses. How does the inside of the tent sound and smell? How does it *feel*? Thinking the key to unlocking my memories lies in the aura of the tent and not in visual clues, I close my eyes and take a few deep, cleansing breaths.

Then I concentrate.

At first, I notice nothing but the new-tent smell that surrounds me. A cross between a plastic bag and a latex glove, it's powerful enough to make my nose twitch. Once I get used to it, though, other things emerge.

The chirp of a single cricket, louder than the others, suggesting it's right outside.

The hint of grass that can still be felt underneath both the sleeping bag and the tent's floor.

The trapped air itself, motionless and hot as it covers me like a second sleeping bag. Beads of sweat form at my temples, and I get my first true flashback to the night I'm so desperately trying to remember.

Me zipped inside the tent, waiting for Billy to arrive, wondering if that will happen after the events of earlier in the day. Guilt churned in my stomach—a sensation I would become intimately familiar with over the next thirty years. But then it was still something foreign, something unsettling. I remember worrying that something bad had happened to Billy. That he was still trapped in that gate and that I'd never see him again.

Little did I know that would soon come to pass.

Outside the tent, there's a noise. A soft whisper of movement so faint I can't tell if it's real or a memory. Then I hear it again, closer this time, and I tense inside the sleeping bag.

Something has entered the yard.

It sounds again. Less a whisper than a rush across the grass.

Deep in my pocket, a noise bursts from my phone.

Ping!

My entire body clenches, for I know what it means.

Billy has arrived.

E than huddles in the tent alone, quaking with nerves after the most agonizing few hours of his young existence.

It began when he returned to the house after agreeing with the others not to tell anyone about Billy being caught at the Hawthorne Institute. His arrival startled his mother, who was still in the kitchen, staring at the wall. Ethan expected her to immediately ask him about the argument with Russ, Ashley, and Ragesh that she surely had witnessed from the kitchen window, but there was nothing. Nor did she mention how he'd seen her crying in the kitchen—an incident Ethan thought would definitely be acknowledged.

Instead, his mother simply stood and went about her day, cleaning the kitchen and prepping dinner. She did it all with an unspoken yet palpable sadness, her bad mood evident in every heavy footfall, every slam of a drawer. Even Barkley felt it, retreating to a corner of the living room and softly whining.

Ethan tried to escape it by going upstairs to his room while his father hauled his orange tent from the basement and set it up in the backyard. Ethan watched from his bedroom window, surprised by the reminder that he was supposed to camp out with Billy tonight. He'd forgotten all about it. He wondered if Billy had, too. That is, if Billy was even around. Ethan had had no contact from him since they were at the Hawthorne Institute, a fact that allowed all sorts of bad thoughts to march through his brain. That Billy was in trouble. Or still stuck in the gate of that horrible mausoleum. Maybe he was even dead. If so, it would be all Ethan's fault because he had left Billy instead of facing punishment together.

At dinner, Ethan barely ate, picking at his single slice of cheese pizza while staving off nausea.

"Aren't you hungry?" his mother asked, and not in a concerned way. It was annoyance Ethan heard in her voice, which made his stomach clench even tighter.

"Not really," he said, barely able to push out those two very simple words. Caught between the urge to confess everything and the fear of getting in trouble, he found it hard to speak at all.

"You're not sick, are you?" his father said, making it sound like an accusation.

"No."

"Because if you are, you should have told me and spared me from having to put up that stupid tent."

Now, as Ethan sits alone in said stupid tent, he realizes that would have been a perfect time to admit what happened. Because his parents will clearly know something is wrong when Billy fails to show up. And then Ethan, despite telling the others he'd remain silent, will have to admit what happened.

Maybe he should just do it now and get it over with.

Part of him wants to, if only to relieve some of the guilt he's feeling, while another part of him wants to because he knows it'll get Billy into trouble, too. If he isn't already. And Billy deserves it, Ethan thinks with a surprise flash of anger. Russ was right when he said it was all Billy's fault. None of this would have happened if he hadn't led them to the Hawthorne Institute.

Where he had gone yesterday.

Which he had failed to tell Ethan.

Because he was too busy buddying up with Russ.

Ethan starts trembling again, a by-product of all these clashing emotions. He feels sorry and guilty and scared and mad all at once. Humming through it all is a sense of wanting.

He wants to remain best friends with Billy, just as he wants Billy to be, well, different. When the Barringers first moved in next door, Ethan had been intrigued by Billy's eccentricities. It was refreshing to meet someone his age so utterly himself. Now Ethan worries what will happen if Billy remains quintessentially Billy.

Not that he'll ever find out. After today, he'll be shocked if Billy ever speaks to him again. Which is all the more reason to suck it up and tell his parents what happened.

Mind made up, Ethan starts to crawl out of the tent, only to be stopped when he notices something completely unexpected.

There, standing stock-still in the yard, is Billy.

TWENTY-SEVEN

I hold the phone in my trembling hand, too nervous to check the trail cam's app but too curious to ignore it entirely. A feeling of dread, thick and clammy, spreads in my chest as I keep my index finger hovered over the app's icon.

Billy might be right outside the tent.

The only way to find out is to look.

Which I'm still not sure I want to do. It's not that I'm afraid of Billy. Despite what Fritz said about ghosts holding a grudge, I suspect that if Billy's intention was to hurt me, he would have done it days ago. But I'm not unafraid, either. Understandable, considering it's a ghost I'm dealing with.

Billy or not, whatever's outside remains there. I continue to hear it between the chirping of crickets. And I won't know how to deal with whatever it is until I see it.

With a jab of the screen, the trail cam's app springs to life. I avert my eyes, focusing on everything but my phone. The pads of my fingers gripping its edge. The battery level in the top right corner. Finally, with nothing left to look at, I peek at the screen through half-closed eyes and see the now-familiar view of the backyard at night and . . .

A deer.

Two feet from the tent.

Grazing on the lawn.

My entire body, tensed to a breaking point, suddenly relaxes. A sigh of relief slides out of me. I even let out a chuckle, for the whole situation is absurd.

The deer outside the tent suddenly sprints away. I hear the startled thump of its hooves just before the phone, still clenched in my palm, erupts once more into sound.

Ping!

This time, there's no hesitation. My gaze zooms directly to the screen and the latest picture taken by the trail cam.

The deer is gone, but nothing else has taken its place. The image on my phone shows unoccupied lawn, trees behind it, half of the tent I currently sit in filling the left side of the frame.

So what set off the trail cam?

Ping!

A new picture arrives while I'm still looking at the previous one. An image switch that would be jarring if the two photos weren't exactly alike. I even toggle between them, making sure they're not one and the same.

They aren't.

Because there's something in the most recent one not found in its predecessor.

A bit of shadow in the woods.

Darker than other nearby shadows.

And shaped differently, too.

I lean in closer, squinting at the screen, trying to get a better look.

Ping!

The image changes again, and this time it *is* jarring. Because instead of empty lawn, the trail cam has captured something else.

A face.

Inches from the camera.

Staring directly into it.

The sight of it makes me jump so hard it jolts the entire tent as I let loose with a string of obscenities. "Jesus fucking Christ, fuck!"

Outside the tent, a familiar voice says, "Wow, Mr. Marsh, that was a lot of swears."

I take another look at the phone and collapse with relief. It's not Billy, but another ten-year-old—Henry. The calm is short-lived because the tent's front flaps suddenly burst open, prompting another startled "Fuck!"

"Another swear," Henry says as he pokes his head inside the tent, the lenses of his glasses reflecting orange. "I see you bought the tent."

"Yeah," I say, pressing a hand to my chest in an attempt to calm my pounding heart. "Saw it in the store and couldn't resist."

Henry looks around the tent's interior and, in that adorable way of his, says, "May I enter?"

"Sure." I scooch over so he can join me, making sure to hide the bourbon bottle under the sleeping bag. "Make yourself at home."

Henry crawls inside and lies down, hands behind his head. "Does this mean I'm camping right now?"

"I guess," I say. "You've never gone camping?"

"No. Mom says bad things happen to people who camp."

While that's certainly true on Hemlock Circle, I know it's not the case elsewhere. Still, I admire Ashley's attempt to make Henry want to avoid camping at all costs. It's safer that way.

"I camped out here a lot when I was a kid," I say, stretching out beside Henry, awed by how much taller I am, awed even more by the realization that I had once been as small as he is.

"Mr. Marsh, isn't it weird to be camping in your own backyard?"

"I don't know, Mr. Wallace," I say as I nudge him in the side with my elbow. "Do you think it's weird?"

"I think it's neat."

I gaze up at the shadows gathered in the peaked space where the tent's sides meet, now questioning the wisdom of the purchase. I was so hopeful that being in the tent would somehow conjure memories of the night Billy was taken. But the longer I stay here, the more I doubt it will happen. It's not that easy remembering something your mind insists on blocking out. Decades of failed therapy sessions have taught me that.

"You can come here anytime you want," I tell Henry, figuring I might as well make the excuse I gave Russ for buying it a reality. Then the purchase won't be a total waste after my strange experiment inevitably fails. "Think of it as a quiet place to read. Or hide from your mom."

As if summoned by the mention of her, I hear footsteps in the grass, followed by Ashley's voice as she says, "Henry? Where did you go?"

"We're in here," Henry calls.

Ten seconds and a rustle of tent flaps later and Ashley is on her hands and knees, peering at us with a questioning look. "What's all this?"

"We're camping," Henry says.

Ashley flicks her gaze my way. "I can see that."

"Henry, chill here for a minute while I talk to your mom." I start to crawl out of the tent, making sure to snag the bourbon on my way out. Ashley's eyes widen when she sees it.

"We won't be long," she adds.

We cross the yard and head into the kitchen. As soon as the patio door is shut, Ashley says, "What the hell is going on, Ethan? I sent Henry over to ask if you wanted to have dinner with us. Instead, I find the two of you hanging out in a tent. Since when do you have a tent?"

"Since this morning," I say. "I thought it would help me remember."

"Remember what?"

"Who killed Billy."

Ashley pulls a chair away from the kitchen table and slumps into it. "Do you really think that will happen?"

"I don't know. Probably not."

"Then why are you doing it?"

"Because Billy told me to."

Ashley gives me a slack-jawed look, her eyes shining with concern. "By Billy, you mean—"

"His spirit," I say.

"Right," Ashley says with a nod. "That's what I was afraid you meant. Why would Billy's spirit—"

"Or ghost," I interject. "I guess."

"Sure. Why would his ghost—which isn't a thing, by the way—Why would he tell you to do this? Wait, here's a better question: *How* did he tell you?"

I proceed to tell her everything I omitted the other night when I first mentioned the idea of Billy's presence on the cul-de-sac. The garage lights flicking on around the neighborhood and the baseballs in the yard. I even tell her about what Billy wrote in my notebook, knowing it sounds preposterous at best, clinically insane at worst. But I'm compelled to forge ahead anyway, in the long-shot hope that speaking it out loud will make it sound less crazy. I end by saying, "What if Billy wanted to be found? What if he made it happen?"

"But why now?" Ashley says. "Why, after all these years, would he let himself be found? Why now and not decades ago?"

I'm losing her. Obviously. I start talking faster.

"Because he knew I was here. Back on Hemlock Circle full-time for the first time since he disappeared. And now he wants me to find out what really happened to him."

Ashley stays silent a moment, letting it all sink in. Her concerned look has shifted somewhat, edging closer to fear. What's unclear is if she's afraid *for* me or *of* me.

"You really think Billy's ghost is asking you to solve his murder?"

"Yes."

"You know that only happens in the movies, right?" she says. "That in real life, ghost kids don't urge people to solve their murders? But let's say you're right. You're not. This is batshit insane. But for now, let's say Billy's ghost is haunting your yard and throwing baseballs into it. Where would a ghost even get a baseball?"

An excellent question. One I haven't considered and have no logical answer for.

"I don't know," I say. "But it's been happening. And I'm not the only person who's noticed it. You heard your dad the other night. He said he saw Billy."

"I told you not to listen to him. My dad doesn't know what year it is half the time," Ashley says, the words catching in the back of her throat. "Today, he asked me what my mother was making for dinner. She's been dead for years, Ethan. And it was like he didn't even know."

"I'm sorry," I say.

"You don't know the half of it." Ashley says it without anger or accusation or even seeking pity. It's simply a statement, hinting at untold depths of misery. "And all I wanted to do—the reason I came over—was to invite an old friend for dinner in the hope I could forget about everything for a few minutes."

"Instead, you encountered a crackpot talking about ghosts."

"You're not a crackpot." Ashley exhales a long, exasperated sigh. "Honestly, this all would be easier to deal with if you were. But I can tell you honestly believe it."

"I do," I say, with a quickness that's startling. We're talking about Billy's ghost, for God's sake. The very idea should give me at least some pause. Yet it doesn't. Not anymore. "Even though it's crazy, I believe it. Because who else could have done it? Who else could have entered this house even though every door and window is locked, and written in my notebook something that only me and Billy knew he said?"

Ashley responds with a sad shake of her head. "I don't know."

"And who's been tossing baseballs into my yard? Something Billy—and only Billy—used to do?"

"Somebody playing a cruel trick," Ashley says. "Or maybe it's you, Ethan. Have you ever thought of that? Maybe you're doing it and you don't remember. Maybe it's always been you."

I give her a look, shocked by the implication of her words. *"Always?* Do you think I had something to do with what happened to Billy? Do you think I killed him?"

"Of course not." She reaches across the table, seeking my hand. Clasping it with both of hers, she says, "I know you didn't hurt Billy. Everyone does. But I also know that what happened to him hit you harder than anyone but his family. And I just think that, maybe, all the things that have been happening aren't really happening at all."

I snatch my hand away from hers. "You think I'm making it up?"

"No," Ashley says. "I think it's possible you're doing it without knowing what's going on. Kind of like sleepwalking. *You* might have written in that notebook. And *you* might have put those baseballs in your yard. Then you forgot all about it."

"Why would I do that?"

"Because you want to believe it's real. You want to believe that people can come back from the dead and communicate with you. Just like you want to believe this is just about Billy, when I have a feeling there's more to it than that."

"What do you mean?" I say. "Of course it's about Billy."

"And nothing to do with your wife?"

My body goes numb. When Ashley takes my hand again, I can barely feel it.

"I know what happened to Claudia, Ethan," she says. "I know she died."

TWENTY-EIGHT

At first, I say nothing. No words can adequately sum up what it feels like to lose your spouse. Especially when it's so unexpected, when you incorrectly thought you still had decades left together. Yes, Claudia and I were going through a rough time when she died, arguing over not wanting to have kids, wondering if, after fifteen years of marriage, we weren't the people we thought we were.

But I knew.

Claudia, although she'd changed in many ways, was still the person I met at that party in college, and I had zero doubts that we'd work it out. And when she left after our last fight about parenthood, I assumed she'd return. Because our last words to each other weren't angry. They were resigned.

"I'm sorry."

"I know."

But Claudia didn't come back.

And unlike with Billy's disappearance, I remember all of it.

The phone call as it neared midnight. The somber voice of the patrolman who told me he found an unresponsive woman inside a car registered in my name. The frantic, gnawing anxiety of the drive to the hospital, the body on the table, the white sheet being lifted, the face of my dead wife.

The car had been parked at a cute little lake where Claudia liked to go to think. There was no drama to her death. No foul play. She died of an aortic aneurysm that had gone undetected.

And I was left alone.

That was a year ago.

I remained in the Chicago area for as long as I could, reluctant to leave the house I'd shared with Claudia and the place where she was buried. But it all got to be too much. The pain. The grief. The stress of trying to keep it together when every fiber of my being wanted to fall apart. So when my parents told me they were moving and suggested I come back home and take over the house, I said yes, even though I knew bad memories of Billy were waiting for me.

That's the irony of this whole situation. Billy wasn't the most devastating loss in my life. It was Claudia. And when forced to decide which memories were easier to face, I chose Billy.

Had I known Billy himself was still waiting here, well, that would have changed my mind.

Unfortunately, I'm not able to change Ashley's.

"You think this is about Claudia," I say, using my fist to swipe the tears threatening to leak from my eyes. Christ, I feel so stupid. So weak. And that's without Ashley knowing how I never canceled Claudia's cell phone plan. How I still dial her number just to hear the sound of her voice and pretend she's not gone. How I continue to text her as if she's still around to read them.

"And Billy, too," Ashley says. "Grief is weird that way. It can make you think things you shouldn't be thinking. Or believe things that, deep down, you know are impossible. And I suspect you desperately want to think Billy is back because it means—"

"That Claudia can come back, too."

I'd be lying if I said it hasn't crossed my mind. That this experience with Billy is a sign that I'm—I don't know—*touched* somehow. That if he can leave me messages from beyond, then so can Claudia.

Now, though, the idea has been muddied somewhat by the things Fritz Van de Veer told me last night. What if Ezra Hawthorne was right about the different realms—earthly, spirit, and in between? If I was somehow able to communicate with Claudia, does it mean she, like Billy, isn't at peace? In many ways, that's a worse thought than knowing I'll never talk with her again.

"I know it's hard to deal with when someone you love dies," Ashley says. "I was devastated when my mom died. And I miss her every day. But I've also learned to let her go."

"What if I can't?" I say.

"You can at least try." Ashley stands and gives me a hug so warm and tender that it breaks my heart a little when it ends. "Maybe that's the point of all this. Instead of Billy trying to make you solve his murder, maybe it's your subconscious telling you it's time to say goodbye to both of them."

She leaves after that, going back into the yard and gathering Henry from the tent. He gives me a wave through the patio window. I wave back, thinking about what Ashley said. Maybe she's right and this is all my doing. I don't know how I'd forget throwing baseballs in the yard on a regular basis, but it wouldn't be the first time my memory has failed me.

As for saying goodbye, I'm willing to give it a try. Not for my sake, but for Claudia's. I know she'd hate seeing me like this. I know she'd want me to be happy.

In my new bedroom, I go to the closet and a cardboard box hidden away in a back corner. Inside is the purse Claudia had with her when she died. A kindly ER nurse gave it to me, pressing it into my numb hands as she said, "You might want to look through this at some point. Not now. But someday."

Which turns out to be today.

I open the purse, finding Claudia's sunglasses, a pack of gum, her favorite lipstick. I pull out her wallet and sort through it, my heart aching at the sight of her driver's license and the photo she hated but which I adored because it showed off her smile.

When she died, my wife had twenty-six dollars on her, plus two credit cards—one she never touched and one she used often, buying books and fresh flowers and that expensive cheese she loved to eat alongside equally expensive wine.

I put the wallet inside and dig out what I'm really looking for.

Her cell phone.

Although the battery died long ago, I use my phone's charger to bring it back to life. Then I scroll through the texts, reading the most recent ones first.

walking in the woods and thinking of you

can't sleep. of course

i miss you, Claude

I keep scrolling, skimming over a year of texts I sent even though I knew my wife wasn't going to see them. Some—such as watched jaws again. still holds up—are insipid. Others read like open wounds.

i miss you so much right now i can't breathe

I scan the dates and times, looking for a pattern in the moments when I couldn't resist firing off a text. Holidays, for instance. Or Claudia's birthday. Or late nights when sleep was impossible. But no such pattern exists. I missed her all the time. I still do.

I stop reading the texts when I come to the first one I sent knowing she was dead. Two weeks after her funeral, 3:46 in the afternoon.

i don't know how to do this

After the texts come the phone messages, made with less frequency but with the same randomness. The most recent is from a few nights ago. I listen to it from the chagrined start—"Hey. It's me again"—to its desperately honest end. "I think Billy might be haunting me, Claude. I know, it's ridiculous. But weird things are happening that I can't—"

The last voice message is the earliest, sent minutes after Claudia had died, when I didn't know it yet. When I press play, the sound of my voice—so naive, so hopeful—brings an ache to my chest that's so intense I fear my rib cage is about to crack open.

"Hi. Listen, I don't know where you are or where you intend to go, but I think wherever it is, you should turn around and come home. Because I love you, Claude. I've loved you since the moment I met you. And your happiness means the world to me. Much more than any stupid hang-ups I have because of something horrible that happened when I was a kid. In a lot of ways, I think what happened with Billy just gave me an excuse to avoid facing things that scare me. And being a father scares the shit out of me. But you're braver than me. You always have been. So if having a baby will make you happy, then I think we should do it. Let's have a baby."

Astonishingly, I make it most of the way through without crying. It's not until I hear those last four words—*Let's have a baby*—that I lose it entirely. As the tears flow, I picture an existence in which everything in that message happens. Claudia comes home. We make love. A child is conceived. We prep and plan and babyproof the house and buy too much furniture and finally bring home an infant boy who will grow into someone not unlike Henry Wallace. Smart and kind and a little weird. Someone exactly like me and Claudia.

Then the fantasy ends, and I'm shuttled back to a reality in which I'm alone and clutching my deceased wife's phone. Fitting, for that's basically been my go-to mode for the past year. I envision a future spent frozen in this position, the years speeding by and me staying exactly the same.

That's when I realize the time to say goodbye is now.

I reach for my phone and call Claudia's number. In my other hand, her phone rings and my name appears on the screen. When the call goes to voicemail, I have to force myself to speak.

"Hey, Claude." Sadness clutches at my heart when I realize I might never address her this way again. "I, um, need to tell you a few things."

And I do, telling Claudia how much I love her, how she meant the world to me, how happy she made me even though I sometimes didn't show it. When I run out of time and the message cuts off, I keep talking.

Minutes pass.

Then an hour.

Then I'm done.

I've said my final goodbye.

Claudia's phone goes back into her purse, which goes back into the cardboard box, which I return to the closet. Then I take my own phone and delete Claudia's contact information, an act that sucks all the air from my chest.

It feels like a betrayal.

It also feels like liberation.

Even though it's well past midnight, I decide not to sleep in the bedroom. It seems too lonely here, too packed with the still-fresh sting of letting go. So I return to the tent, with its lumpy pillow and mildewed sleeping bag. While they're no match for my bed, I'm more comfortable out here knowing that Billy might be nearby, just a silent shadow in the woods, and that Claudia might also be here, somewhere. A wisp of cloud in the night sky. A pulsing star that I could see if I only knew where to look.

I close my eyes and imagine both of them, so near and yet so far, watching over me as I fall asleep.

TWENTY-NINE

Scriiiiiiitch.

The ending of The Dream is so loud I wake convinced it's happening in real time. I'm in a tent, after all, its walls sloping to the ground beside me. I sit up and whip my head back and forth, checking each side of the tent, certain I'll see a slash running from tip to grass.

Both are unblemished. Just two rectangles of orange fabric brightened by the predawn light.

Next to me, my phone springs to life with a familiar sound.

Ping!

Opening the trail cam app, I'm greeted by the sight of a loose sheet of paper caught on the breeze and skating across the lawn. The trail cam captured it mid-flight, the page hovering half an inch above the grass.

Odd.

I search for my pen and notebook, both of which had been in the tent with me when I went to sleep. I can't find them, even after looking through everything else in the tent. Under the pillow. Inside the sleeping bag. An anxious knot forms in my chest when, instead of the pen or notebook, I spot another single sheet of paper.

It sits near the foot of the sleeping bag, right next to the tent's flaps. When I pick it up, I notice how one edge of the page is ragged, like it's been torn from the notebook. When I turn it over, I see three scribbled words that send fear streaking through me.

HAKUNA MATATA DUDE

I find another torn page just outside the tent.

And still more pages farther into the yard.

Dozens of them.

Scattered across the patio.

Covering the grass.

All of them bearing the same phrase that seems like it's both mocking me and crying out for help.

HAKUNA MATATA DUDE

I stumble around the yard, gathering the pages, clutching them to my chest. One has somehow gotten snagged in the low-hanging branches of a tree on the edge of the woods. As I grab it and stuff it with the others, I spot the notebook itself sitting nearby on the forest floor. All but a few pages have been torn out. I pick it up, my gut churning.

These were some of my deepest, darkest thoughts, written down in the middle of the night. Now they've been defaced, scribbled over, tossed across the lawn. If this is Billy's doing, it's crueler than I ever expected of him.

And if it's my doing, as Ashley suspects, then I'm seriously fucked in the head. Because I have no memory of doing this. Nor can I think of any reason *why* I would do it.

But if it wasn't me, and it wasn't Billy, then who the hell was it? The only way to find out is to, as sportscasters used to say when I was a kid watching Jets games with my dad, go to the videotape. Or, in my case, the trail cam.

I return to the tent and my phone, which now shows several new photos taken by the trail cam, all of them depicting me gathering up the loose pages torn from my notebook. I swipe past them to the photo I saw this morning—the single page gliding over the grass. The one before that, taken several hours earlier, shows a raccoon crossing the lawn on the edge of the woods. After that comes another picture of me, an unflattering ass pic as I crawled into the tent late last night.

Between those three images is . . . nothing.

Either the trail cam malfunctioned, conveniently fritzing out for a few hours, or someone—Billy? me?—snuck up behind the camera and turned it off while the notebook was stolen and destroyed.

The more I think about it, the more I suspect it was Billy, because the time stamp on the most recent photo displays a very important date.

July 15.

Thirty years to the day that Billy was taken.

No wonder he resorted to such extreme tactics. He wasn't being cruel. He was being urgent. All in an attempt to emphasize the importance of this day. And those three words on every page? His *final* words? I suspect they're to remind me of everything that happened on this night thirty years ago.

Not that I need reminding.

I remember everything.

Everything but one vital, missing detail.

I'm still looking at the time stamp on the phone when it hits me—the solution I've been circling around ever since that first baseball landed in the backyard. In fact, it's been right there for decades, visiting me at night on a regular basis.

It's not enough to simply keep having The Dream.

If I'm going to remember—truly, irrefutably *know*—what happened that night, I'm going to need more than that.

Instead of having The Dream, I need to relive it.

U no," Ethan says for the third round in a row. A rarity. Usually, it's him losing again and again as Billy, a far better strategist, racks up the points. Tonight, though, Billy's playing is lazy and distracted. Twice now, Ethan caught him forgetting to say "Uno" when he had one card left, which has never happened before. As he tallies their scores and sees he's won his first game ever against Billy, Ethan feels not victory but disappointment. He knows he would have lost if Billy had been playing like his usual self.

"Rematch?" he says.

"Nah," Billy replies, disappointing Ethan further. He'd hoped the answer would be yes, because playing a one-sided game of Uno means they wouldn't be talking about what happened that afternoon, a topic they've expertly avoided so far.

Ethan had assumed it would be the first thing Billy mentioned when he entered the yard with his sleeping bag and pillow. He'd even braced himself for it, the apology already formed in his mind. Yet Billy didn't bring it up when he crawled into the tent and unfurled his sleeping bag. So Ethan didn't bring it up, either, even though it was totally weird not to.

The avoidance continued the rest of the night. When they ate the s'mores Ethan's mother had made. When they roamed the edge of the woods trying to catch fireflies. During the entire game of Uno, in which Ethan constantly snuck looks at Billy, searching for signs he was mad at him. And while Billy looked no different, Ethan knew something had changed. He was quieter, slower, less animated. It was as if the old Billy Barringer remained stuck in that mausoleum and had been replaced with a newer model. One missing all the quirks that made Billy special.

Ethan reminds himself that's what he wished for when he was huddled alone in the tent before Billy arrived. A different version of his friend. But now that a more subdued Billy is in his midst, Ethan has changed his mind. He longs for the old Billy, and if hashing out the events of that day will make it happen, he's willing to do it.

Still, he waits.

Until after his dad raps on the side of the tent and says, "Time to get ready for bed, boys."

Until after he and Billy go inside to brush their teeth and wash their faces.

Until after his mother comes out, wine on her breath as she pokes her head into the tent and asks if they need anything before they turn in.

Ethan waits until he turns the lantern out and it's just him and Billy stuffed into their sleeping bags, the silence as thick and stultifying as the July night. Finally, when it gets so unnervingly quiet that Ethan thinks he might scream if it continues for one second longer, he says, in a voice that's little more than a whisper, "Did you get in trouble for today?"

"What do you mean?" Billy says, when he knows exactly what Ethan means.

Ethan sits up. "For getting caught. What happened? What did they do?"

"Nothing." Billy says it with such boredom. As if he can't believe Ethan's bringing it up now.

"That guy in the suit wasn't mad?" Ethan says. "He *looked* mad."

"He wasn't," Billy says, again leaving Ethan wanting more.

"What did he say, though? What *happened*?"

"Nothing," Billy says, stretching out the word for emphasis. *Naah-thing*. "They told me I shouldn't be there and let me go home."

Although the answer doesn't satisfy Ethan, he knows it should at least relieve him. If nothing happened, there's no need for him to feel guilty. No harm, no foul. Yet Billy's demeanor suggests there was harm. Or at least something that changed him dramatically.

"So your mom doesn't know what happened?"

"No."

"And they didn't call the police?"

"No."

This leaves Ethan with only one question left, regarding not earlier that day but the one before it.

"Why didn't you tell me you went there yesterday?"

"Why do you care?" Billy says, finally sitting up so he and Ethan are eye to eye.

Ethan flicks on the lantern, not caring that his parents might see the tent glowing from the house. From the weird way they've been acting, they probably won't care even if they do.

"Because we're supposed to tell each other stuff like that." *And it hurt my feelings that you didn't* is what he wants to say, but pride, youth, and a refusal to be vulnerable even in front of his best friend keep him from doing so. Instead, he says, "So why'd you go?"

"You won't believe me," Billy says.

Ethan's heart sinks. Because he knows what Billy's talking about. The thing that everyone but him understands isn't real.

"You think there are ghosts there."

"I know there are," Billy says.

"Ghosts don't—" Ethan stops himself, frustrated. He wonders if maybe he really did mean it when he wished Billy would change. All day, he's felt their bond slowly unraveling. Like rope that's been worn down to the snapping point.

"Why did you leave me there?" Billy says, whispering the question Ethan's been expecting.

"I didn't mean to."

"You *ran away*."

Billy's chest hitches as he says it. A hiccup of pain that even Ethan can hear. He thinks he hears something else, too. Not inside the tent, but just outside. A vague rustle in the yard that might be an animal, although he assumes they'd be scared off by the tent and its lantern glow and the voices rising from inside.

"We all ran away," Ethan says quietly, a weak defense.

"Without me!"

Spikes of annoyance run down Ethan's spine. "Because you'd been there before!" he replies, shouting now himself. "You went there without telling me and got caught and now you're blaming me for it. Even though we shouldn't have gone there in the first place. And you knew that!"

"I told you, they talk to—"

"Ghosts? There's no such thing! They're not real, Billy. It's all bullshit."

Ethan stops then, stunned that he's spoken a curse word out loud for the very first time.

"It's not . . ." Billy's voice trails off, making Ethan feel cruelly triumphant. Unlike him, Billy can't even swear.

"Why can't you be normal?" he says. "Why do you have to be such a weirdo? Why do you always have to be such a freak? If you like ghosts so much, why don't you just die and become one?"

Billy looks for all the world like he's just been slapped. His face takes on a dazed expression, his mouth agape and his eyes suddenly vacant. Ethan thinks he sees tears forming in them. A tiny glisten in the lantern light that makes him feel so vicious and petty and small.

"I'm sorry," he says. "I didn't mean it, Billy. Honest, I didn't."

But it's too late. The words have been spoken, and Ethan knows they will now always be there, a faint ghost haunting their friendship. If there is one after tonight. He wouldn't blame Billy for never speaking to him again.

But Billy does speak, letting out a half-murmured "It's okay."

"It's not," Ethan says. "I shouldn't have said it."

"I know."

"So you forgive me?"

On the other side of the tent, Billy fakes a smile. "Hakuna matata, dude."

THIRTY

"A re you really sure you want me to stab this tent?" Cassandra Palmer says as she stands in the backyard holding the sharpest knife I could find in the kitchen.

"Yes," I say.

Detective Palmer eyes the orange triangle in front of her. "But it's a nice tent. Looks expensive. Not gonna lie, I feel weird about ruining it."

"I won't hold it against you," I say. "I swear."

"I'm just giving you the option of finding someone else."

"You're the best person for the job."

In truth, Detective Palmer is the only person I could think of. After our talk last night, I knew Ashley was out. I briefly considered Russ but was afraid he'd balk at the weirdness of it all. Ditto for Ragesh. That leaves Detective Palmer, who I called as she was leaving the state hospital where she had tried to interview Mary Ellen Barringer. It resulted in nothing. Mrs. Barringer was, in Detective Palmer's words, "as silent as a clam with its shell taped shut."

Now that she's here, I see the value in having a nonbiased third party help me. Detective Palmer's presence eliminates the risk of familiarity possibly clouding the memories I hope will arrive.

That's not the only precaution I've taken to achieve the desired outcome. Rather than do it the moment I got the idea, I insisted on waiting until darkness arrived. I didn't want the presence of daylight to ruin the experiment. I also arranged the inside of the tent so it's as close to that long-ago night as possible. Two sleeping bags, laid out side by side. The lantern placed between pillows. I even tried to dress the same way—shorts, T-shirt, and a pair of Nikes.

If this doesn't work, it won't be for lack of trying.

As Detective Palmer gets into position next to the tent, I pass her a picture of the original one I printed off the internet earlier today. It's the famous picture. The one that ran in every newspaper in the country showing the tent with a dark gash marring its side. Detective Palmer takes one look and her brows rise questioningly.

"For verisimilitude," I say. "Try to make the cut look as close to the one in the picture as possible."

"What if I'm off?"

Then all of this might be for nothing. Something I don't tell Detective Palmer. She's uncertain enough as it is.

"Let's go over it one more time," I say. "You wait—"

"Until you're inside the tent," Detective Palmer says with a nod. "And I'm not allowed to tell you when I'm going to do it. I just—"

"Slice." I've dropped to my hands and knees in front of the tent, preparing to enter, when I'm struck by an idea. "It might be better to wait until I'm asleep."

Detective Palmer waves the knife, confused. "You want to sleep through all this?"

The irony isn't lost on this insomniac. But it strikes me as the best course of action. To summon memories of the night Billy was taken, I need to replicate it as much as possible. And since I was asleep when the event that would later become The Dream occurred, it stands to reason that I should sleep now.

"How will I know you're asleep?"

That beats the hell out of me.

"You'll need to wing it," I say. "Listen to my breathing. That should be a good indicator."

"I probably shouldn't be telling you this, but I've got some confiscated Ambien in my purse," Detective Palmer says, deadly serious. "Pop one, wash it down with some whiskey, and you'll be out like a light. It usually does the trick for me."

While I'm tempted—and increasingly intrigued by her personal life—I decline the offer. The goal here is to wake up as the tent is being sliced open, not drop into a coma.

"All ready?" I ask.

The detective gives me a look. "Can anyone truly be ready for something like this, Ethan?"

The answer is no, especially with so much uncertainty. I have no idea if I'll remember anything when she slashes the tent. I don't even know if I'll be able to fall asleep. But I have to at least try. Tonight, the thirtieth anniversary of when Billy was taken, seems the most likely time for my memory to produce something tangible.

"Well, I'm going in," I announce before crawling into the tent and zipping it shut behind me. I then move to the sleeping bag on the left, the same side I was on when Billy was taken. I wriggle into it and tap the side of the tent. A signal for Detective Palmer to recite the words I instructed her to say once I was ready to go.

She does, reluctantly. "Hakuna matata, dude."

I slide deeper into the sleeping bag and shut off the lantern, plunging the tent into darkness. I lie still for a moment, basking in the deep blackness. There's a heaviness to it, thick and slightly oppressive. That also describes the air inside the tent, which has quickly increased in warmth thanks to the closed tent flaps. Due to the darkness, the heat, and the sounds of summertime in July just outside the tent, familiarity begins to creep in. It may not be an exact reenactment, but it *feels* like that night.

Now it's time to sleep.

I close my eyes and try to rid my mind of all thoughts. I focus instead on everything I remember sensing that night. The tickle of sweat on the back of my neck. The cricket closest to the tent, sounding extra loud. The smell—a sickly sweet combination of earth and stale air and two boys after a long summer day.

Shockingly, it seems to be working. I find myself drifting closer to sleep as, one by one, my surroundings seem to fall away. First the tent walls, followed quickly by the sleeping bag around me and the ground beneath me. My pillow is the last thing to slip into nothingness, and when it does, I feel like a man floating in space.

Then I hear it.

Scriiiiiiiitch.

My eyes snap open, adjusting to a darkness different from what was there when I closed them. It's lighter. A gray haze. Like I'm trapped inside a black-and-white movie.

Only it's not a movie.

It's The Dream.

And I'm not reenacting it.

I'm *inside* it.

My surroundings grow clearer as my eyes adjust to the darkness. I'm still inside the tent, only it's not the one currently in my backyard. This is my old tent. The one the police took when I was ten.

I even feel like I'm ten. Lighter, younger, carefree. Gone is the weight of thirty additional years and all the stress, guilt, and heartache that came with them. I literally feel like my old self again, a fact that would fill me with joy if I didn't know what was coming next.

But I do.

The *scriiiiiiiitch* made sure of that.

I look to my left and the sleeping bag that's a Billy-shaped lump beside me. Next to him, a long gash runs the length of the tent's side. It looks so much like a wound that I half expect to see blood gushing from it at any moment.

The freshly split tent walls ripple slightly, and the dark gash widens. Just a tad. I peer through it, even though I know I'm not going to see who's on the other side. I've never been able to see.

This time, though, something's different.

Someone is *there*.

I see their face.

I recognize it.

For a slice of a sliver of a second, our eyes meet.

No.

If the word is spoken or merely thought, I can't tell. It sounds the same to me. A loud, emphatic noise echoing through me.

No.

It can't be him.

I blink in shock, and it's all gone. Then is replaced by now. And through the new slash in this new tent, I glimpse a sliver of Detective Palmer eyeing me from the other side like a Peeping Tom.

"Did it work?" she says.

Rather than answer, I shimmy out of the sleeping bag, unzip the tent, and push out into the yard. Detective Palmer follows me as I keep going, marching to the driveway at the side of the house.

When I pass the garage, the security light above it snaps on, bathing me in brightness, my shadow stretching all the way to the curb. It shrinks as I hit the sidewalk, then stretches again as I run to another house on the cul-de-sac.

Over the lawn.

Up the porch steps.

Pounding on the door until it opens a crack and Russ Chen peers out of it, looking nervous. Looking, in fact, like an older version of the person I glimpsed through the tent slash thirty years ago. Those dual views—one remembered, one happening right now—tell me I'm right.

"It was you," I say. "It was all you."

*O*ne.
    Five.
Ten.

Russ Chen collapses onto the floor, his chest tight, his arms pulsing. A feeling he's grown to enjoy after his umpteenth set of push-ups for the day. He especially likes the way it clears his head. There's no anger when he does them. No sense of inferiority. Just the strain of forcing his body past a point of resistance.

Only after he's done do the bad thoughts trickle back in. Of Johnny. Of Russ's likely futile plan to become just like him. Of the way Ethan chooses Billy over him every time, even though Billy isn't worth it.

He now regrets the way he followed Billy around earlier in the day, pretending to like him because he thought it would make Ethan see him in a different light and decide that the three of them could become best friends.

Because it's still just Ethan and Billy, camping out in Ethan's backyard. Russ knows because they've been doing it every Friday that summer. Not once have they mentioned it to him, though. Not once has Ethan asked Russ if he'd also like to camp in the backyard.

Still lying on his bedroom floor, Russ realizes the angry thoughts are back in his head. No longer a trickle. A full-on wave. He does another set of push-ups (*One . . . Five . . . Ten*), but it's no use. Rather than calm him, the thump of his heart makes him antsy and irritable. He wonders if Ethan and Billy are still awake. If they're talking about him right now. Making fun of him.

Without quite thinking what he's doing, Russ leaves his bedroom. He creeps down the hallway, careful not to wake his parents, who sleep in separate rooms on opposite sides of the hall. An abnormality he'd be humiliated by if anyone found out. He pads down the stairs and out into the backyard, where he can see the top of Ethan's tent peeking above the hedge.

It's all so unfair that he wants nothing more than to march into that yard and rip apart the tent so that Ethan and Billy can never camp out without him again.

Which, he realizes, isn't such a bad idea.

A plan forms, unspooling in his brain like film through a reel. If he ruined Ethan's tent and convinced his parents to buy him one instead, then he could invite Ethan to camp out for the rest of the summer.

Russ knows that the more he thinks about it, the sooner his plan will fall apart. Already, doubts tiptoe in. Would he really be able to convince his parents to buy him a tent? Would his mother really let him sleep outside?

So he doesn't think any more.

He simply acts, marching back inside and pulling a knife from a kitchen drawer filled with them. Russ grabs what he thinks is the sharpest one. A knife with a black handle and a thin blade. Once it's in his hand, there's no stopping him. Those earlier doubts are a distant memory, replaced by the very real feeling of his fingers curled around the knife.

He returns to the yard and pushes through the hedge onto the

Marsh property, which looks silvery in the moonlight, almost like it's Christmas and not the middle of July. In that wintry glow is the tent, now dark and silent.

Russ approaches it, cautiously circling it, checking for signs Ethan and Billy are still awake. He doesn't hear anything, so he creeps closer, now on the other side of it.

Doubt returns the moment Russ presses the knife tip to the side of the tent. A voice in his head—his mother's, of course—whispers things he already knows.

This is wrong.

You're a good boy, Russell. Not like your brother, who's bad, who failed, who let down the family in every way.

Russ tries to block it out as the knife's tip scratches against the tent. He's surprised by how flimsy it is. He'd expected something thicker, sturdier. Canvas. But this is as thin as that kite his auntie gave him for his birthday a few years back. The one his mother later threw in the trash because she said it was too cheap to take flight.

He thinks about that kite and how it was never used because his mother decided on a whim it was worthless, and wonders if she feels the same about him. Maybe the moment Russ was born, she had looked at him, compared him to his brother, and deemed him inadequate. And maybe Russ has known this his entire life and has lashed out whenever he's reminded that it's true.

He is inadequate.

In every possible way.

And will be for the rest of his life.

Russ closes his eyes and forces his mother's voice out of his head. He pushes away all of it. Every thought, every emotion, every memory. All of them banished until it's just him and the knife in his hand and the tent fabric straining at the blade's tip.

Then he gives the knife a shove and the blade pierces the fabric.

THIRTY-ONE

Russ confirms I'm right without saying a word.

It's all there in his expression—a guilty slackening of his features. When he does try to speak, rage flashes through me and I find myself slamming against the door. The motion rocks Russ onto his heels and I barrel inside, throwing myself at him.

"Ethan, what the fuck?"

I smash against him in the middle of the entrance foyer, not caring that he's twenty pounds heavier than me, all of it muscle. I shove and grunt and curse, managing to push Russ across the foyer only because he's too stunned to fight back.

He responds once I back him against a sideboard next to the stairs, the framed family photos on display there toppling like dominoes. The clatter wakes something in him and he starts pushing me backward.

First with one mighty shove.

Then another.

I try to fight him off by swinging a fist at his face. Russ easily blocks it with his left arm and slams the forearm of his right into my nose. I let out a strangled huff as my vision goes fuzzy like TV static.

In the haze, I'm aware of Russ charging me again.

Of Detective Palmer thrusting herself between us.

Of me knocking into the wall and sliding down it until I'm on the floor. I touch my nose and realize it's bleeding. Even though Russ clocked me in the face, I hurt everywhere. Yet none of it stings as much as the betrayal I feel.

For thirty years, Russ not only pretended to be innocent; he pretended to be my friend. He could beat me to a pulp multiple times, and it still wouldn't cause as much pain as knowing it was all a lie.

Ping!

The sound erupts from the phone shoved deep inside my pocket. I ignore it, too dazed and angry and pained.

My vision's cleared enough for me to sort of see Detective Palmer in the center of the foyer, arms outstretched like a ref in the ring. "Everyone needs to calm down!" she shouts, the boom of her voice bringing Russ's wife out of their bedroom to the top of the stairs. Not missing a beat, Detective Palmer flashes her badge and says, "State police. Please stay where you are."

"Russ?" Jennifer says as she leans over the banister to peer into the foyer. "What's going on?"

Detective Palmer looks between me and Russ. "I'm trying to figure that out myself."

"I'm okay, Jen," Russ says, keeping his gaze fixed on me. "Ethan's just confused."

Down the hall, Russ's son, Benji, starts calling for his mother. Detective Palmer hears him, too, and addresses Jennifer. "Go to your son, and don't come out until I say it's okay."

Jennifer hurries off to do just that, while Detective Palmer turns back to me and Russ. "Can one of you please tell me what the fuck is happening here?"

"It was him!" It hurts to speak. All my teeth ache. I run my tongue along them and taste copper. More blood. "He did it!"

"The tent thing worked?" Detective Palmer says.

This time I merely nod. It hurts less.

"You remembered?"

Another nod.

"And he's who you saw?"

"It was Russ," I say, wincing through the jaw pain. "I'm certain of it. He slashed the tent."

On the other side of the foyer, Russ leans against the sideboard I'd backed him into, unsteady now all on his own. I hope at least some of that is my doing.

"You have to understand," he says. "I wasn't in my right mind back then."

"So you admit it?" Detective Palmer says.

"Yes."

Ping!

My phone again, barely noticed as I shout across the foyer. "Why?"

"Because you were always with Billy! You never wanted anything to do with me."

"He was my best friend," I say.

"Yeah, you made that clear."

The phone sounds yet again—*Ping!*—the sound drowned out by Russ's voice saying, "You have no idea how much I've struggled since that night."

"You? How do you think I feel?"

Anger pushes me to my feet as I think about all the ways in which I've suffered. The guilt. The insomnia. The Dream.

"I know it's hurt you, too," Russ says. "And I know you've had a hard time since Claudia died."

I stalk across the foyer, intercepted by Detective Palmer. Caught in her surprisingly strong grip, I glare at Russ. "Don't you bring Claudia into this. Don't you fucking dare. You still have a wife. You have a child. I don't. Also, I didn't kill Billy. You did."

Russ sways at the accusation. "Wait. That's what you think? I didn't lay a hand on Billy."

"Bullshit," I say, sounding like I'm ten again and trying to convince Billy there's no such thing as ghosts. "You killed him!"

Detective Palmer raises a hand to silence me. Turning to Russ, she says, "So you're telling me that you slashed the tent and just . . . walked away?"

"Yes," Russ says. "That's exactly what I did."

"I have trouble believing that," Detective Palmer says.

As do I. "If you didn't kill Billy, then why didn't you tell anyone you cut the tent open? You had thirty years to do it, yet you said nothing."

"Because you're right," Russ says. "What happened to Billy is my fault. If I hadn't slashed your stupid tent, whoever it was that snuck into your yard might have kept walking. But they didn't. Instead, they saw that gash in the side and realized it was easy access to whoever was inside."

"That's going to be hard to prove," Detective Palmer says.

"Well, it's the truth."

"Do you have any proof? What happened to the knife you used to cut the tent?"

Russ's broad shoulders rise and fall. "I don't know."

"Now that's *really* hard to prove."

"I swear," Russ says. "I brought it inside with me after leaving Ethan's yard. I set it on the kitchen counter and went back upstairs to bed. In the morning, it wasn't there."

"And you never saw it again?" Detective Palmer says.

"No. I looked for it after the news that someone took Billy got out. I wanted to—"

"Hide it?" I say, unable to help myself.

"Yes," Russ snaps. "I was going to hide it. Because I was afraid I'd get in trouble if anyone found out what I'd done. But I couldn't find it. It was gone."

"Knives don't hide themselves, Russ," Detective Palmer says. "If you didn't do it, who did?"

"It was me."

The voice floats down from above, making all three of us crane our necks to look at the top of the stairs, where Misty Chen stands in a silk robe cinched tightly over a set of white pajamas. She looks so old and frail as she starts to descend the steps. Like she's aged twenty years since I saw her this morning.

"I hid the knife," she says. "Because, in my heart of hearts, I know Russ is a good boy."

Saturday, July 16, 1994
12:46 a.m.

Misty Chen hears her son return, just as she heard when he left. Nothing gets past her in this house. Not anymore. Gone are the days when Johnny would sneak out unnoticed, scurrying off into the night to poison himself. By the time she realized what he'd been doing, it was too late, and Johnny was gone.

Now she's become the eyes and ears of the house, seeing everything, hearing everything. It's why she moved across the hall not long after Johnny died, leaving the bed she'd shared with her husband. In her grief, she could no longer be distracted by his tossing, turning, and snoring.

She needs quiet.

To pay attention.

To listen for the small changes that occur when someone in the house is doing something they shouldn't. Which Russ is doing right now. Creeping through the kitchen and tiptoeing up the stairs.

Misty charts his progress based on the sound of his footfalls. The creak means he's reached the third step. The groan indicates he's now at the sixth. She hears a swoosh—Russ turning at the landing—before two more creaks, the second an octave higher than the first. The last two steps.

She doesn't leave her bed until she hears the groan of the floorboard right outside Russ's room. As he closes his bedroom door, Misty opens hers, intent on learning what her son has been up to. When he left his room, the sound woke her from a dead sleep, so loud in her mind it was like cannon fire and not a boy stepping on a faulty floorboard. She sat up in bed, ears alert for every telltale noise, as Russ went downstairs, then outside, then in and out again.

Misty knows most mothers would have immediately followed. Russ is ten. He has no reason to leave the house in the middle of the night. But Misty learned her lesson with Johnny. The more she openly pried, the sneakier he became, until his actions were all but invisible to her. She won't repeat that mistake with Russ. It's best to let him think she's not paying attention, when in fact she sees everything.

She knows, for instance, that he was out in the woods today with his friends and returned upset about something. That he was moody all night. She's certain it involves the Marsh boy.

As she creeps downstairs, Misty knows to avoid all the things that alerted her to Russ's movements. Groaning floorboards skipped, creaking stairs averted. In the kitchen, nothing is amiss except for a knife incongruously sitting on the counter.

The sight of it sends alarm bells clanging through her thoughts. What on earth had Russ been up to?

Misty examines the knife, relieved to find it clean of food and— her main concern—blood. The very idea that her Russell could stab someone fills her with shame for thinking it. He's a good boy, but she's had enough parent-teacher conferences about Russ's anger issues to know they're a problem. They even started sending him to therapy once a week, not that it seems to be doing much good. The knife in her hand is proof of that. The reason her son felt compelled to grab it—and what he intended to do with it—are less clear. Rather than ask Russ about it, she decides to monitor the situation for the next few days. Maybe whatever was going through his head has passed. Maybe it was nothing to begin with.

Satisfied with her plan, Misty washes the knife, dries it with a paper towel, and hides it under her bed. She goes to sleep blissfully unaware of what's to come.

How, in just a few hours, she'll hear about the slashed tent next door and the missing Barringer boy.

How she'll instantly know Russ had something to do with it, that he used her best knife to slice through the tent, that he might have used it to do even worse.

How she'll never mention her suspicions to anyone, including her husband and her son, preferring ignorance to knowledge for the first time in her life.

How she'll vow to do whatever is necessary to help Russ get better, whether it be more therapy or additional attention or just taking it easier on him than she did his brother.

How, once word gets out that the police will be searching every house on Hemlock Circle for a potential weapon, she'll remove the knife from its hiding place and bury it deep in her garden. Deep enough that no one will ever find it. So deep that she will eventually forget it's there.

But on the night she covers the knife with dirt, Misty will think of Johnny and how, having already lost one of her sons, she refuses to lose another.

THIRTY-TWO

The lights of the patrol car carrying Russ cast a multicolored glow over Hemlock Circle. I stand in the front yard, watching the exterior of the Chens' house shift from red to blue to searing white and back again. The light begins to fade as the car slowly pulls away from the curb, a uniformed officer behind the wheel. In the passenger seat next to her is Ragesh. Russ occupies the backseat, gaze fixed on the back of Ragesh's head, his expression dazed.

I imagine I look the same way standing here on the lawn. Shell-shocked and spent, with blood still drying on my hands and shirt. I always assumed that, if I were to ever learn what really happened to Billy, I'd feel relieved. That the burden of ignorance would be lifted. That with closure would ultimately come healing. Instead, I only feel sadness. Rather than one lost friend, I now have two.

Because I don't believe what Russ said about simply slashing the tent and walking away. It's too convenient, too dependent on the idea that someone else entered the lawn and saw a golden opportunity to take Billy. The odds of that being the truth are a billion to one.

Ahead of the cruiser is Detective Palmer's vehicle, leading the way for what's sure to be another long night. Following those two vehicles is a CR-V carrying the two Mrs. Chens—Jennifer and Misty. Neither woman looks at me as the car leaves the driveway. The only person in the car who acknowledges my presence is Benji, relegated to the back-seat like his father. Unlike Russ, Benji is turned around, staring out the back window, offering a single wave before the car exits Hemlock Circle.

Watching it go, I can't help but think that I've just ruined Benji's life. Ironic, seeing how his father has ruined mine—twice. First, by coming into the tent and taking Billy. Second, by pretending for thirty years that he didn't.

With both cars gone, I turn my attention to the rest of Hemlock Circle. Others have come outside to watch the unfolding drama. Ragesh's parents, Mitesh and Deepika, stand at the end of their drive-way. Two doors away, Fritz and Alice Van de Veer linger on their front stoop. All of them look my way, their stares accusatory.

This is my fault.

I couldn't stop digging, and now life on Hemlock Circle has been disrupted once again.

I am no longer welcome here.

Once the Patels and the Van de Veers have returned indoors, some-one emerges from the house that sits between them.

Ashley.

She leaves the front door wide open as she sprints across the cul-de-sac. There's a frantic edge to her voice as she calls my name. "Ethan, have you seen Henry?"

"No," I say, caught off guard by the question. One, has Ashley not noticed what was happening at Russ's house? Two, why would she think Henry is with me? "He's not at your house?"

"I thought he was," Ashley says. "I thought he was in his room, reading or something. But when I went up to check on him, he wasn't there."

"And you have no idea where he could be?"

Ashley shakes her head. "I searched the entire house. My dad hasn't seen him, either. I thought maybe he came out here to see what was happening with the police. Are you sure you haven't seen him?"

I'm sure, which doesn't mean he's not out here somewhere. I'd been too focused on watching Russ be led out of his house by police to pay attention to much else. There's a good chance I missed Henry as he roamed the cul-de-sac.

"He's got to be around here somewhere," I say, suddenly remembering the pings that came from my phone as I confronted Russ. There were three of them, each one alerting me to activity in the backyard. Likely all were the work of Henry.

"I think I know where he is," I say as I pull out my phone and check the trail cam's app. Sure enough, there are three new photos. I tap the first to be taken—an image of Henry making his way to the tent. Caught mid-step, a Goosebumps book in hand, he eyes the camera with a look of worried guilt. A kid who knows he's just been caught doing something he shouldn't, even if that something is as innocent as sneaking away to read by lantern light in a backyard tent. The only thing he should feel guilty about is worrying his mother.

I show Ashley the image and she lets out a huff of relief. "Thank God," she says. "I'm sorry for freaking out like that."

"Completely understandable," I say.

We make our way to the backyard, rounding the side of the house via the driveway. At the garage, our movement triggers the security light, which flicks on with a startling glow. It's not lost on me that this whole long, strange week started with similar lights turning on around Hemlock Circle. Now that it's come to an end, it all feels hazy. A dream, if not The Dream.

"The police at Russ's," Ashley says quietly. "Does that have something to do with Billy?"

"Yes," I say, knowing that single word doesn't come close to telling the full story.

The backyard is pitch black, save for a light on inside the tent. The LED lantern, which makes the orange tent glow like a campfire. I picture Henry inside, stretched out on a sleeping bag, holding his book near the lantern so he can see better. It's only when Ashley approaches the tent that I realize something's not right about the scene.

"Ashley, wait."

But it's too late. She's mere feet from the tent now, passing in front of the trail cam. The phone in my hand pings as I receive a still picture of the action unfolding right in front of me.

Ashley at the tent.

Parting the front flaps.

Peering inside as she says, "Come on, Henry. Let's—"

She stops talking, processing what I already know. If Henry were inside the tent, we would have seen his silhouette from outside. But there is no silhouette, no shadow. Just the unobstructed glow of an interior that's completely empty except for a slim paperback sitting spine-up.

"He's not here," Ashley says with renewed panic. She scans the yard, her head jerking like a startled bird's. Even her movements are birdlike. A hopeless, helpless flapping of the arms.

"Henry!" she yells into the night.

"Let's not panic," I tell her, even though I can feel it rising in me as well. I'm hit with a strange sense of déjà vu, like I've been hurtled back in time to thirty years ago. In my chest is the same dread I felt the morning I woke to find Billy gone. With it comes confusion, uncertainty, and a bubbling panic that I know will soon reach full boil if I don't do something about it.

I rush to Ashley, also setting off the trail cam. I hear the slightest of clicks as it takes my picture, followed by the near-instantaneous alert to my phone.

Ping!

The sound reminds me of the two additional alerts I received while confronting Russ. Since one of them pictured Henry entering the tent, the others might show him leaving and the direction he went after that.

I raise my phone and check the app, swiping through the most recent pictures. When I get to the one I'm looking for, my legs almost give out.

"What is it?" Ashley says. "What do you see?"

I hold out the phone so she can see what was captured by the trail cam—a dark figure wearing a hoodie, presumably a man, parting the gash in the side of the tent so he can push his way inside.

Ashley emits a strangled choke, making me terrified to check the next image from the trail cam. My index finger shakes uncontrollably as I swipe to it. In the photo, Henry and the dark figure both stand outside the tent. The man has a tight grip on Henry's hand, which the boy seems to be fighting. Henry's face is set in a defiant scowl as he looks at the trail cam, knowing it will immediately send the image to my phone.

A solid plan on his part. It would have worked, too, if not for two things that went wrong. The first is that I didn't check my phone until it was too late. The second was that Henry's gaze at the camera made the man with him aware of it, too.

He joins Henry in looking at the trail cam, his face slightly blurred by the quick turn of his head.

"Oh God!" Ashley shrieks when I show it to her. "Who *is* that?"

I study the man's face, shocked to realize it's similar to a photo I've looked at a hundred times. And while the age-progressed picture on the NamUs site didn't get it completely right, the family resemblance is close enough that I can recognize with certainty the person who minutes ago stood in this very yard.

But it's not an image of Billy I'm looking at.

It's his brother.

THIRTY-THREE

I continue to stare at the screen, caught in a state of suspended animation as everything clicks into place. Of course it wasn't Billy's ghost haunting the edge of the woods. It wasn't his spirit putting baseballs into the yard and scribbling in my notebook. It wasn't Billy who Vance Wallace saw rushing through his backyard. Something I should have realized from the start, for Vance never uttered Billy's name. He always referred to "the Barringer boy."

Andy Barringer.

Flesh and bone.

Pretending to be his dead brother for reasons I can't begin to understand.

That I was duped so thoroughly would consume my thoughts if not for several more pressing ones.

First, Andy is *here*.

Not off the grid but on Hemlock Circle.

And he's been here for days. At least since the day Billy's remains were found at the falls. I know because the next morning was when the first baseball was left on the lawn, setting off this whole chain of events.

Now he has Henry, a fact that snaps me back to action. I start across the yard, heading to the woods. "I think I know where he is."

I'd tell Ashley more, but it's too complex to explain. In this moment, I simply need her to trust that I know what I'm doing. Apparently, she does, because she's now right behind me as we crash through the trees. Darkness closes in around us the moment we're inside the woods. I point the flashlight on my phone at the ground ahead of us. Ashley does the same, the forest floor a blur in the harsh light.

"He's at the falls, isn't he?" Ashley says.

"Yeah," I say, for it's the only place I can think of where Andy would go. It's where I suspect he's been staying all this time. I think back to my trek there. The open barn door, the footprints in the dirt, even the can of tuna. All signs that someone was squatting on the grounds of the Hawthorne Institute.

Then, of course, there's the fact that it's where Billy was found. His resting place for thirty long, lonely years. It feels right that it all leads to that cursed place. So right that it almost seems inevitable.

Ashley and I don't talk as we push on through the woods. It's too loud, the insects here not singing but screaming. The frantic screeching sounds like a thousand sirens as we keep our lights on the ground ahead, watching our step, focused only on getting to the falls as fast as we can. When we reach the road at the halfway point, neither of us pauses to look for oncoming cars. That's precious seconds we can't afford to waste. We simply burst from the forest like swimmers emerging from water to catch their breath before plunging back in on the other side.

Not long after that, the lights latch onto something ahead of us.

The wall, looking extra forbidding at night.

We make a right until we reach the gap in the stone. I push through it first, followed by Ashley right behind me, breathing as heavily as I am, the puffs hot on the back of my neck.

On the other side of the wall, the night noise of the forest is joined by the distant roar of water, which gets louder each step we take. Once it drowns out all other sounds, I know we're there.

Pushing through the thinning trees, I point the phone's light straight ahead to the outcropping. Caught in the glare are two people.

The first is Andy Barringer.

He's bigger than the photos from the trail cam suggest. Not only taller, but thicker. A frame built by hard labor and not the gym. His eyes are big and round and attentive. Like an owl's. They make him look otherworldly. Almost spooky.

Andy steps to the side, revealing Henry at the edge of the precipice, looking so small, so helpless. His hands have been bound together at the wrists with rope, giving the awful impression of someone being forced to walk the plank.

Ashley cries out when she sees him. "Henry!"

He jerks to life. "Mom?"

"I'm here, baby," Ashley says as she starts to rush toward him. I pull her back and whisper in her ear.

"Wait. We don't know what he plans to do."

Up on the ledge, Andy wraps an arm around Henry's shoulders that could be there to keep him from falling or to keep him from escaping. In the dark, it's hard to tell. One thing I do know is that Andy's not interested in Henry.

I'm who he really wants.

Henry was just a way to get me here.

"Let him go, Andy," I say, trying to keep my voice calm. Still, panic underscores every word. A thin treble I can't get rid of. "I'm here now. That's what you wanted, isn't it? You and me at the place where Billy was found?"

"On the thirtieth anniversary of his death," Andy says. "Which wasn't the plan, but it does feel appropriate."

I risk a step toward the outcropping. When Andy doesn't react, I take another.

"What *is* the plan? I know it's not to hurt Henry. He has nothing to do with this."

"I had to get you here somehow, didn't I?" Andy says.

My gut tightens even as I'm flooded with pity for Andy Barringer. He's endured unimaginable pain. His brother vanishing into thin air, his father's death, his mother's slow sinking into madness. It's all too much for one person to bear. Yet none of it excuses what he's doing now.

"I know what you're going through," I tell Andy. "What happened to Billy messed me up in ways I can't even articulate."

"Then imagine how much worse it's been for me." A light breeze picks up, curling a tuft of his hair into a cowlick. Finally, he resembles the seven-year-old boy always begging me and Billy to let him tag along. "Billy was your friend, but he wasn't your brother. You don't know what it's like to have someone you love, someone you look up to, someone who was a constant presence in your life suddenly be gone."

He's wrong there. I do know. Her name was Claudia.

"But I know what it's like to miss someone," I say. "To miss them so much it sometimes feels impossible to keep going, yet somehow we do. And I know how that pain makes us do things we know we shouldn't."

I take a step closer, my hands raised so Andy can see them. When he doesn't try to stop me, I continue to edge forward.

Slowly.

So very slowly.

Like Henry's life depends on it.

Which it might.

Once I'm on the outcropping, I hang back, keeping enough distance between us so that Andy won't do anything rash. Now that I'm closer to Henry, I can see how brave he's being. With his glasses sitting crooked on his nose and swallowing back tears, he looks scared but calm. And blessedly unhurt, other than some redness caused by the rope around his wrists.

"Everything's going to be okay, Henry," I tell him. "I won't let anything happen to you."

Henry nods, and I hope he really believes me. Because I'm not sure I do. I'm concerned about how close Andy is keeping him to the outcropping's edge. I sneak a glance at the falls below, the water at its base frothing in the moonlight.

"Come on," I say to Andy. "Let him go."

"Please," Ashley says behind me. "He's a good boy, Andy."

"I won't hurt him," Andy says. "Enough boys his age have been hurt here."

"I assume this is because you want to talk about the night Billy died," I say. "So leave Henry with his mother and we'll talk."

Andy tightens his arm around Henry's shoulders. "Or we can talk with him here."

"Fine," I say, not having any other choice. "When did you know they found Billy's body here?"

"Not long after it happened. An ex told me. One of my mom's nurses."

I remember Ragesh mentioning how the police, assuming the remains found at the falls belonged to Billy, immediately tried to tell his family. He said the nurse had attempted to contact Andy but didn't know if she had reached him. Obviously, she did.

"As soon as she heard about it, she left me a message," Andy says. "She didn't know where I was or what I was doing. Turns out I was just across the state line in Pennsylvania, doing day labor on a farm. I quit and came here. To my surprise, you were here, too. So ever since, I've been . . . lurking."

An apt description of his actions. For Andy's spent most of this week hiding in the woods, watching. I now know he was the shadow person captured by the trail cam, likely crouched on the edge of the forest. What I can't understand is why. If he wanted to talk, he could have revealed himself. Instead, he continued to creep between the

Hawthorne Institute and my backyard, usually with a baseball in hand.

"Why the baseballs?" I say.

Andy smiles. "The third one belonged to Billy. I kept it all these years. The others were bought at your friend Russell's store. He rang them up himself and didn't even recognize me."

"If you put them in the yard to get my attention, it worked."

"I wanted more than that," Andy says. "Just like right now, you need to do more than just talk. You need to *remember*."

At least I was right about that. I might have been off base about who was behind it all, but the goal of everything was to get me to remember that night. I even know why. I think about the morning Mrs. Barringer came into my yard, dragging Andy behind her, begging me to remember. I never stopped to wonder how much that affected him at such a young age. How it seared itself into his memory. How it poisoned his brain.

"We don't need Henry for that," I say.

"Apparently, we do. Since throwing baseballs into your yard like Billy used to do didn't work, and since breaking into your goddamn house using my mom's spare key didn't work, it became clear I needed to do something more drastic."

Andy pulls Henry against him, like they're old friends. But the gleam in his eyes is anything but friendly.

"I did remember," I say. "I'm surprised you don't know already, seeing how you've been keeping tabs on me."

Just like that, Andy releases Henry, who bobbles at the sudden movement. He sways toward the falls before straightening again and taking a shuffling step away from the edge of the outcropping. Andy acts quickly, grabbing Henry by the collar and dragging the boy back to his side.

"Tell me," Andy says.

"I will." I nod toward Henry. "Once I know he's safe."

Andy returns his arm to Henry's shoulders, this time even tighter. "No. Now."

"It was Russ Chen," I blurt out. "He slashed my tent. And then he hurt Billy."

Behind me, Ashley gasps, and I realize she didn't know, either. I'm sure the police presence at Russ's house made her suspect it, but that's different from hearing it confirmed out loud.

Billy's brother, though, doesn't appear surprised in the least. Instead, he looks doubtful.

"No, he didn't," Andy says. "Russ Chen might have slashed the tent. But I think someone else killed Billy."

I take a tentative step toward him, pulled closer by curiosity. "Why?"

"Because I was there, outside that tent." Andy gives me a look, daring me to doubt him. "And I heard what you said to my brother."

Andy wakes from a fitful, restless slumber feeling like he hasn't slept at all. The events of earlier in the night keep marching through his mind, as potent a reminder as the blades of grass still stuck to the soles of his feet.

That grass had felt cool between his toes as he walked toward the hedge rising between his family's yard and the one belonging to the Marshes.

A yard he'd started watching after his mother sent him up to bed.

And a yard he visited once she herself had retired for the night.

Andy was allowed to stay up past his bedtime because his mother knows how left out he's been feeling all summer. There are no kids his age on Hemlock Circle, forcing Andy to spend these endless school-free days playing by himself as Billy gets to roam anywhere he wants with Ethan.

But an hour of extra television isn't enough for Andy. He wants to be in the thick of things like his brother. That Billy never lets him tag along—or even tells him about what he's been doing—feels unfair to Andy. He wants to experience things, too, even if it's just vicariously. So if he couldn't go camping, he could at least enjoy watching Billy do it.

Thanks to the location of his bedroom—on a corner of the second floor, with one window facing the woods and the other offering a side-long view of the Marshes' yard—he could see Ethan's orange tent and the way it glowed like a single flame when the lantern inside it was lit. He could even see the silhouettes of the two boys inside, blurry and indistinct.

Watching them, Andy imagined what they were doing, what they were talking about, what it was like to be older and have a best friend. He thought about these things long after the tent went dark. And when it began to glow again—an unexpected triangle of light in the July night—his curiosity was too piqued to resist.

So he snuck outside and crossed through the hedge from one lawn to another. Andy didn't plan to be there long. Even though his father was away and his mother asleep, he knew he could get in big trouble if he were caught outside this late. He simply wanted a glimpse of Billy's life. Ethan's, too. The life of any boy older than him felt both huge and limitless.

But as he tiptoed closer to the tent, Andy started to suspect he was wrong about that. Because Billy and Ethan were arguing, and their voices sounded small and scared. Especially Ethan's, as he said things that shocked Andy.

Bullshit.

Weirdo.

Freak.

It wasn't the words themselves that were shocking. Even at age seven, Andy's heard plenty of curse words. It was the way Ethan said them that rattled him. There was a meanness to them that Andy had never associated with Ethan before. And he didn't like it one bit. Especially the last part.

"If you like ghosts so much, why don't you just die and become one?"

As he turned away from the tent and began to run toward home,

Andy heard his brother's voice, not knowing it would be for the last time.

"Hakuna matata, dude," Billy said.

No worries.

But Andy can't help but worry as he tosses and turns in his bed. Is this what being older is like? Is this how best friends talk to each other? Above all, did Ethan really mean what he said?

That last question lingers in his mind as he falls asleep, and will remain with him for a very long time. It will be there in the morning, when his parents sit him down and tell him that Billy has been taken. It will be there when detectives with interchangeable names and faces and badges ask him if he saw anything suspicious that night, anything at all.

Andy will remain silent about what he heard Ethan say because he's been told by everyone that Billy had been taken, most likely by a stranger who grabbed him after slashing the tent.

It will be years before Andy begins to doubt this theory, and years more until he forms one of his own. By then his father will be dead, his mother will be institutionalized, and Andy Barringer, long past the age his brother got to reach, will have no one left to tell it to.

THIRTY-FOUR

stagger backward as Andy's words hit me like a haymaker. Harder than Russ's blow to my face. That I remain standing is a minor miracle. When I speak, my shell-shocked voice sounds foreign to me.

"You heard what I said?"

"Every word," Andy says. "And I've spent most of my life wondering if you meant it. I think you did. I think you meant it so much that you tried to make it come true, even if you can't remember doing it."

I reach out, grasping at the air, wishing it were something tangible with which I could steady myself. Because now I understand everything. Andy wants me to remember, yes. But there's something else he's after.

He wants me to confess.

"You think I'm the one who killed Billy?"

"You're the only person it could have been," Andy says.

"I never would have hurt Billy. I loved him."

"But I *heard* you!" Andy yells, spittle flying from his lips. "I was in your yard that night. Right outside that tent. I heard the things you said. How he was a freak. How you told him to die. That didn't sound like love, Ethan. It was hatred, pure and simple."

"No, it was—"

Frustration. Immaturity. Cruelty.

That's what I want to say. But there's no point. Because the things I told Billy that night were horrible. Even worse, they were unforgivable. Knowing that someone else heard them causes guilt to press against my chest, so heavy I think my rib cage is going to collapse from the strain.

"I shouldn't have said those things. I know that. And I've spent thirty years wishing I could take it all back." I step closer to Andy, hand outstretched, hoping he'll take it, hoping even more that he'll believe me. "But I didn't mean any of it. And I absolutely didn't kill Billy."

Andy thinks it over, the mental wheels turning inside those big, spooky eyes. Then he nods and says, "Maybe this will get you to tell the truth."

He wraps an arm around Henry's waist and, in one smooth, shockingly fast motion, hoists him off his feet and holds him off the outcropping's edge.

"No!" Ashley yells as she scrambles toward them. I spin around and grip her shoulders, forcing her to look away from the sight of Henry dangling helplessly in Andy's arms.

His glasses slip from his nose and vanish into the darkness below.

"Mom!" he screams. "Help me!"

I take two more steps toward Andy, pleading, "Let him go. *Please.* If you want me to confess, I will."

"It was me!" Ashley shouts, the words reverberating through the pitch-black woods.

Andy freezes.

Henry does, too.

Only I move, turning slowly to face her. "Ashley, no. You don't need to lie to get Henry back."

"It's not a lie, Ethan." Ashley looks into my eyes, her face splintering into a thousand warring emotions. "It's all true. It was me. I killed Billy."

t took all the strength Billy possessed not to cry himself to sleep. Even though he managed it, he wept on the inside. A waterfall of tears pouring from his broken heart and trickling down his ribs.

All because of what Ethan had said.

It didn't matter that his best friend had apologized immediately. Or that Billy accepted it with a casual "Hakuna matata, dude." They both knew a horrible thing had been uttered in the tent that night, and that no amount of apologies could reverse it. It didn't mean that he and Ethan weren't still best friends. But something had irrevocably changed, a fact that made Billy feel as sad and lonely as he's ever felt in his life.

Still, he slept. For a little bit at least. During the night, he'd wake every so often and look across the tent to Ethan's sleeping form, consumed by a desperate urge to shake him awake and make him again swear that he hadn't meant the things he'd said. Just like the tears, Billy fought the urge and went back to sleep, only to wake again a few minutes later, burning with the same pleading desire.

The last time he woke, his eyes remained closed. In the sleeping bag next to him, Ethan stirred, making Billy think he was also awake. He considered saying his name, the two syllables forming on his lips, on the verge of being made real.

Then he heard something.

A rustling in the grass right outside the tent.

It was followed by a sound Billy didn't recognize. Something so strange that it kept him frozen in terror, his eyes clenched tight.

Scriiiiiiitch.

Beside him, Ethan stirred again. Had he heard it, too? Billy wanted to check to see if Ethan was awake, but he remained too scared to open his eyes.

Minutes later, they're still closed, even though Billy now feels air on his face. A sliver of freshness cutting through the stuffiness of the tent. The sensation overrides his fear, making him curious enough to finally open his eyes.

That's when he sees it: a long gash in the side of the tent.

Billy stares at it, feeling astounded and confused and about a thousand other emotions. The one that stands out the most, though, is awe.

In his mind, only one thing could have caused it.

A ghost.

One previously unknown to him. One not mentioned in his giant book. It's no surprise to Billy that a mysterious and rare spirit is roaming these woods. Of course there would be. He remembers what Mr. Hawthorne told him.

There are ghosts everywhere, if you just know where to look.

Billy knows. They're right here.

As he peers through the slash in the tent, searching for signs of the spirit that created it, it dawns on him that he's not afraid. Nor should he be. If the ghost—whatever it is—intended to hurt him, surely it would have done so by now. Instead, Billy suspects there's another purpose to the visit, and it makes him curious to learn more.

He slides out of the sleeping bag and just as quickly pushes through the slice in the tent. Moving through it feels special somehow. Monumental. Like he's being reborn.

Billy takes a few steps toward the forest before pausing. He feels no sadness. Already he's forgotten most of what Ethan said to him. He only remembers a few key words.

Weirdo. Freak.

He doesn't blame Ethan for calling him those things. They're the truth, after all. He is a weirdo. He is a freak. Which is why he thinks the ghost came for him. It sensed that Billy is a kindred spirit and came all this way to announce that he isn't alone. That there are others just like him.

And Billy knows exactly where to look for them.

The Hawthorne Institute.

A place he can return to anytime he wants.

Which is why Billy quietly continues to the forest's edge. He didn't think to put on shoes when he left the tent. Now it's too late to go back and fetch them. It might wake Ethan, and then Billy will have to explain what's happened and where he's going. Not a good idea. Although it's not a short walk to the falls and the Hawthorne Institute, it's manageable, even in bare feet.

Before entering the woods farther, Billy allows himself a brief backward glance toward Ethan's tent and then his own house. He's not sure when he'll return to either, or if he'll be back at all. He has no idea what the ghosts have in store for him.

When Billy finally turns away from his house and his best friend, it's not with fear, sadness, or regret but with fondness. He's grateful for every moment he's spent with his family and friends because it's led him to this.

Billy starts to push through the woods, eager to find out what awaits him on the other side. He's so eager that when he reaches the road bisecting the forest, he's unaware of the headlights popping over the horizon in the distance.

Or the car careening through the darkness.

Or the teenager behind the wheel, nervous because it's late and she shouldn't be driving at all. Not without a license. Not with several drinks making her brain fuzzy.

As the car gets closer, Billy steps into the road, his eyes focused only on his destination, and how when he reaches it, he'll be accepted at last.

THIRTY-FIVE

I t was an accident."

A puzzled look crosses Ashley's face. Like she didn't mean to say it. Like it's not her speaking but some other person forcing the words out. A ventriloquist. A demon. But now that she's talking—and now that Andy has set Henry back on the outcropping's solid ground—she keeps going, even though I don't want to hear any of it.

"I need you to believe me," she says, looking at me but addressing all of us. "I never would have hurt Billy on purpose. It just happened, and I'm sorry. I'm so, so sorry."

The words come faster now, riding the rush of confession.

How she went to a party with her friend Tara, driving them there in her mother's car despite not yet having a driver's license.

How Tara had hooked up with some guy named Steve Ebberts and Ashley got angry and left without her.

How she was buzzed, not drunk, because a drunk person wouldn't have had the foresight to avoid the cops by taking only backroads home.

How one of those roads was the one that cut through the forest.

How she was speeding down it, worried about getting caught by her parents, paying more attention to the dashboard clock than the road itself.

How maybe she *was* drunk and that's the reason she didn't see a deer in the middle of the road and careened right into it.

How afterward she pounded the brakes and screeched to a stop and looked in the rearview mirror, the road behind her glowing crimson from the car's taillights.

How she unhooked her seat belt. Slowly. And got out of the car. Slowly. And crept around it. Slowly. And saw that it wasn't a deer she'd hit.

"It was Billy," she says, her voice melting into a sob.

The more Ashley talks, the worse the story gets. Every word brings a spike of pain to my chest. Like nails being hammered into my heart.

She tells us about seeing Billy in some brush on the side of the road and knowing immediately he was dead. She tells us about screaming, then crying, then crawling to his side and cradling him and telling him she was sorry, so deeply sorry.

"I stayed like that for an hour," Ashley says, crying now, the tears flowing unabated. "The whole time, I kept waiting for another car to come by and stop and see what I'd done. I wished for it. I *prayed* for it. But no one did. It was just me and Billy."

She continues. More waiting. Fetching a blanket from the trunk. Wrapping him in it. Even more waiting. Thinking through her options, all of which were bad.

"I was fifteen, drunk, driving without a license, and I had just killed someone," she says, her bitter tone making it clear she hates herself for every single one of these sins. "I knew my life would be over. And Billy's already was. And while I couldn't save him, I knew there was a chance I could still save myself."

Ashley's story ends with her sobered up and carrying Billy to the falls. It wasn't easy, but she was strong and Billy's body seemed so light. Dawn was spreading over the forest by the time she got to the falls, where she weighed the blanket down with some rocks and pushed Billy into the water from the spot where all of us currently stand.

"Then I went home and told my parents that I borrowed the car and hit a deer," Ashley says. "They yelled at me and grounded me, and I didn't care because I knew the police would find Billy and then come and arrest me. It was just a matter of time before everyone knew what I'd done and how awful a person I was. But Billy was never found and the police never came. And that was the worst part. Knowing I was getting away with killing that sweet, innocent boy. Because getting caught is easy. It's living alone with your guilt that's hard. That's worse than any prison. You have no idea how many times I almost confessed. How much I just wanted to rid myself of the guilt. But then Henry came along, and I knew I had to live with it. For his sake."

Andy lets go of Henry completely now, the boy all but forgotten. Rather than run to his mother, Henry remains fixed in place, eyes aimed toward his shoes. Andy leaves his side and approaches Ashley as if he intends to hit her—or worse. Ashley readies herself for whatever's to come, closing her eyes and steeling her body.

"Do whatever you want to me," she says. "But please don't hurt my son. He's the only good thing I've ever done."

Andy places a hand on her shoulder, the touch startling her into a gasp.

"Thank you," he says.

Then he collapses onto the ground and begins to weep.

I go to his side, put my arms around his shoulders, and weep with him, both of us crying over what we have lost while simultaneously shedding ourselves of the heavy load we've been carrying a long, long time.

"I'm sorry," Ashley says again. "I've caused you all so much pain."

Unlike Andy, I'm not able to acknowledge her, let alone thank her. Because scores of people have been hurt by her actions. All of Hemlock Circle, starting with Billy and ending with her son.

Henry finally lifts his head, and I immediately see that no matter how much Ashley's confession has gutted me, it's twice as terrible for him. He's got a dazed look in his eyes. Like he's just been punched. I'd think he was in shock if not for the sorrow etched into the rest of his features.

Seeing it bruises my soul.

No child, I think, should have to endure what's happening to him right now.

"Henry," Ashley whispers, her arms outstretched.

Henry doesn't respond.

Ashley draws closer. "Baby, please."

Henry shakes his head, takes a backward step, loses his balance.

I experience a moment in which everything slows down, gets louder, snaps into focus. The clatter of stones giving way beneath Henry's feet. The bobble of his arms as he tries to stay upright. The sound Ashley begins to make next to me. Part gasp, part scream. The way my heart, already thrumming, starts to thunder in my chest. Then my body, frozen along with everything else, springs into action. Muscles flex. Limbs stretch. I find myself sprinting.

Across the outcropping.

Toward Henry.

Reaching out to him as he reaches back.

But it's too late.

He flounders some more before slipping, tilting away from me, falling backward over the edge and disappearing from view.

I follow Henry over the edge, ignoring any sense of hesitation, of second thoughts, of self-preservation. All I'm aware of as I dive forward are my feet leaving land and Ashley screaming behind me and a faint splash below, all but drowned out by the roar of the falls.

Henry hitting the water.

Then everything fades to nothing as I plummet into the darkness after him.

THIRTY-SIX

I hit the water hard.

A body-rattling slap, followed by a spinning, dizzying drop beneath the surface. As if I'm being dragged to the bottom by an unseen hand.

The water is darker than death. An all-encompassing blackness that leaves me disoriented in seconds. I flail in the murk, unsure which direction to swim, searching for light, for air, for safety. It isn't until I touch bottom—a surreally gentle sink into silt and mud—that I know which way to go.

Straight up.

I push off and rocket upward, kicking furiously, my chest tightening from exertion and lack of oxygen. I break the surface, mouth wide open, simultaneously gasping for air and screaming Henry's name. It echoes through the night air, like a stone skipping across the water.

Henry. Henry. Henry.

As the echo fades, I hear something else—a water-choked croak that quickly vanishes with a light splash.

I dive toward the sound, immediately getting lost in the dark water again. I can't see anything beyond my hands reaching blindly into the depths. Even then, they're distorted, murky, the dark water slipping like silk between my fingers.

I remain that way—frantically spinning and groping—for another minute.

Then another more.

When the tightness in my chest returns, so sudden and fierce I think my lungs are about to burst, I resurface.

I gulp down some more air and drop back under.

Tumbling so fast and so far that suddenly I can't tell which direction is up and which one is down. I swim toward what I think is the surface, surprised when I hit the mucky bottom of the lake. I reverse course, springing to the surface, only to find myself bumping again into the mud and the silt.

All I can think about is Henry doing the same thing. Disoriented and terrified and trapped underwater as his chest tightens as much as mine is doing right now, the pressure so agonizing I fear my lungs might burst.

I know what that sensation means.

I'm running out of air. Which means Henry is, too. If he hasn't already. The thought of him drifting in the depths, his wrists still lashed together, on the verge of death, sends me blindly kicking and thrashing through the black water.

Suddenly, something clasps my hand.

The touch is feather-light, almost soothing. The grasp immediately calms me, and I find myself being tugged forward. I let myself be led through the water, thinking that it must be Henry. That he's found me instead of the other way around.

But when I stretch out my free arm, reaching through the murky water in front of me, I feel nothing. There's literally nothing there.

Yet that gently insistent grip remains. A stranger's hand holding mine.

A boy's hand, I realize.

And not a stranger.

Billy.

I know it's him because his presence is everywhere. It feels exactly like it did when he was alive. Calm and happy and kind.

This isn't Andy.

Nor is it a hallucination.

It's Billy Barringer, my old friend, reuniting with me at last.

I let him continue to guide me, not knowing which direction we're heading but trusting it's the right one. Maybe he's here to lead me upward to safety. Maybe he's here to take me down to the afterlife.

Whatever it is, I accept it.

Billy keeps pulling me. Faster now. Our destination just ahead. Then I break the surface, the night air slapping me into alertness. Paddling in place, I gasp for air while clutching at the invisible hand that led me here.

Only it's no longer there.

I yank my hand out of the water and stare at it, flexing my fingers in the pale light.

Billy is gone.

But suddenly Henry is there, alert to my presence, struggling to stay afloat. I sweep him into my arms, checking for signs of injury.

"Are you hurt?"

Henry, too shocked to speak, can only shake his head.

"You're fine," I reassure him. "We're both fine."

I duck under the water again, this time to maneuver myself through the space between his bound arms. When I emerge again, he's on my back, his arms secured around my neck. Once we're in that safe but awkward position, I swim to the water's edge, not stopping until I've dragged both of us onto dry land.

As I go about untying Henry's wrists, I look to shadowy nooks around the falls, hoping for a glimpse of Billy.

I don't see him, of course, because I couldn't see him when I was being rescued. I simply felt his hand in mine and knew it was him. It's only now, waiting for further rescue, that doubt creeps in.

I thought I'd seen Billy's ghost before and was proven wrong. Now might not be any different. It's more likely that it had simply been a way of coping with what I assumed would be my death. That kind of thing happens, I know. People claiming to see relatives long passed welcoming them to the afterlife right before they're yanked back to the land of the living.

Just as I'm starting to lean toward hallucination, Henry says, "Mr. Marsh, did that boy help you, too?"

My heart hiccups in my chest. "What boy?"

"The one who pulled me out of the water."

While it's possible that both of us experienced similar near-death hallucinations, it's also doubtful. Especially when there's still no explanation for how I was able to find Henry in the vast, dark water of the lake.

Because of that, I choose to believe there was another force at work. A benevolent hand that guided me out of the depths and to Henry's side.

"Yes," I say. "He did. But he's not just any boy. He's my friend. His name is Billy."

Fat, wet snowflakes hit the windows as Ethan waits for midnight. He stretches out half asleep on the couch, barely watching the hordes of revelers whooping it up in Times Square. On the coffee table in front of him is a half-finished beer, a half-drunk root beer, and a half-eaten pizza.

I sure know how to party, he thinks with a lazy smile.

In his defense, it's been a busy day. Ethan's parents came up from Florida for Christmas, heading back only that morning. That afternoon, he visited Vance Wallace, finding him blessedly lucid, which isn't always the case. Then that evening, Ragesh and his husband came over for dinner, leaving early when the snow started to fall.

If the forecast is correct, there'll be almost a foot on the ground by morning. Ethan makes a mental note to brew extra coffee tomorrow so he can pass it out as everyone on Hemlock Circle gathers to clear their driveways. The cul-de-sac always seems to take on a party atmosphere when it snows. A far cry from the somberness that descended over the neighborhood once the truth about Billy's death was revealed.

It was chaos there for a little bit, as reporters swarmed the cul-de-sac like wasps. Ethan had so many people sneaking into his yard that he had to take down the trail cam because it kept pinging from dawn to dusk.

The attention, thankfully, didn't last long once people realized there was nothing sensational about what had really happened. In unsavory areas of the internet that Ethan no longer bothers to venture, people even expressed disappointment that the truth was so mundane, so boringly human.

There were no villains in this story.

Nor were there heroes.

Just a neighborhood of flawed people, some more than others.

So the media moved on. Hemlock Circle did, too. It's amazing to Ethan how much the neighborhood has changed in eighteen months, with new faces moving in now that most of the old ones have departed. Vance Wallace was the first to go. With Ethan's help, he put his house on the market and used the proceeds to pay for an assisted-living facility. Thanks to the skyrocketing housing market, he'll be taken care of for the rest of his life.

Fritz and Alice Van de Veer were next, followed, dishearteningly, by the Chens. Russ claimed it was because they needed more space after his second child was born. A girl. He and Jennifer named her Hannah. That may be true, but Ethan suspects he had something to do with the move. Once it became clear Ethan wasn't going anywhere, Russ decided to do it instead.

Ethan and Russ are no longer friends. Nor are they enemies. They exist in that strange space where too much has been done and said to each other for the rift to ever truly heal. Still, Ethan wishes him well, and hopes Russ does the same for him.

As for Andy Barringer, Ethan has seen him exactly twice since that night at the falls. Once when Billy was at long last buried next to his father, and six months later when Mary Ellen Barringer joined them. Having narrowly escaped a kidnapping charge, thanks to some pleading from Ashley, and Detective Palmer for once looking the other way, Andy is again off the grid.

But his old house finally sold, making it the fourth home on Hemlock Circle to have changed hands. Soon it will be five, because at dinner earlier, Ragesh told Ethan that his parents would be listing theirs in the spring. When that happens, Ethan Marsh will become the last original resident of Hemlock Circle—a development he never, ever expected.

But it's been nice seeing new families move in and breathe life into the place. All of them have children, ranging in age from six to sixteen. There's even a boy next door who's Henry's age and, wonder of wonders, just as intellectually curious. They spent most of the summer together collecting insects, identifying plants, and plowing through a mind-boggling number of Goosebumps books.

To Ethan, seeing Henry blossom is the best change of all. He attends the same private school where Ethan teaches. He has friends there, too, plus the adoration of the school librarian, Miss Quinn, who might also have a little bit of a crush on Ethan. Before the holiday break, she asked if he wanted to go out for coffee sometime. Ethan said yes, even after Henry informed him that "going out for coffee" is secret code for a date. Ethan's not sure where Henry heard this, just as he's not sure he wants to know.

"How is he?" Ashley asks every time she phones Ethan like clockwork each Thursday evening. A collect call from the Edna Mahan Correctional Facility for Women.

"He's doing great," Ethan always tells her, and he always means it.

It took Ethan awhile to come to terms with what Ashley did. Some days, he still grapples with it, and a flare of anger will hit him so hard it takes his breath away. He found it surprisingly easy to forgive her for killing Billy. It was an accident, Ashley didn't intend to hurt him, and she's made her remorse clear ever since. It's the cover-up that Ethan still can't quite move past. It would have spared everyone so much pain if Ashley had simply confessed then, instead of waiting thirty years.

Then again, if she had, there would be no Henry. And Ethan can't imagine his life without the boy.

On the couch, watching the hour tick ever closer to midnight, Ethan thinks about that night at the falls. He often does. How he and Henry remained slumped by the water as cops and rescue workers stormed the area, Detective Cassandra Palmer and Ragesh Patel among them.

Ashley was still there, too, already in police custody, although Ragesh had delayed putting her in handcuffs until she got a chance to wrap her arms around Henry. He returned the hug hesitantly, as if unsure she was still his mother and not a stranger.

"I'm going away for a little bit," she told him. "I just need you to know that I love you more than anything in this world."

Then Ashley grabbed Ethan, pulling him into a desperate, clutching embrace so she could whisper in his ear.

"I want you to take care of Henry," she said. "I know I'm asking so much of you. But my dad can't do it on his own. Henry needs you. *I* need you. Promise me you'll take care of my son."

Ethan did.

And he has.

And he wants to continue to do so for as long as possible.

After pleading guilty, Ashley was sentenced twice, ten years for the vehicular manslaughter of Billy Barringer and ten years for disposing of his body. Because she was a minor at the time and showed remorse, the judge is allowing her to serve them concurrently, with a chance for parole after eight years.

"Henry will be at least eighteen when I get out," Ashley told Ethan a few months into her sentence. "He deserves to have a family until then."

"You're his family," Ethan said.

"A legal family. A *real* family. Right now, all he has is a convicted killer for a mother, and that's going to hang over him for the rest of his life." Ashley paused then, and even in her silence Ethan could tell she was crying. "That's why I think you should adopt him."

Ethan didn't resist, and with Ashley's official consent, he legally became Henry's father. A decision Ethan knows was the right one when, at midnight, he goes upstairs to what was once his childhood bedroom. It's Henry's now, reflecting the boy's interests and tastes. Animals and planets and dinosaurs. Peering inside, Ethan can barely remember what it looked like when it was his.

Henry's in bed, reading in the soft glow cast by his bedside lamp. Not a surprise. He often stays up past his bedtime to read.

For a time, Ethan had worried that the events at the falls would dim Henry's special light. That he would harden his heart so it would never be wounded again. So far, that hasn't happened. Ethan's trying his best to make it stay that way.

After watching Henry unnoticed a moment, he says, "Happy New Year, sport."

Ethan stopped calling him Mr. Wallace long ago, just as Henry stopped addressing him as Mr. Marsh two nights after his mother was arrested. He's called him Ethan ever since. But on this night, Henry looks up from his book and says, "Happy New Year, Dad."

It takes Ethan a minute to collect himself after that. He never expected to be called that word. He never wanted it, either. But now that it's been spoken, he never wants to hear Henry refer to him as anything else.

"What are you reading?" he says, trying to keep his emotions in check.

Henry pushes his glasses higher onto his nose. "An old book. I found it on the top shelf."

He lifts the book to reveal a familiar title: *The Giant Book of Ghosts, Spirits, and Other Spooks.*

It provides Ethan with a pleasant zip of surprise. Although he'd forgotten the book was still there, it makes him happy to see that Henry discovered it.

"Have you looked at it before?"

"No," Henry says. "But I'm intrigued. It looks like Goosebumps."

Ethan sits on the edge of the bed. "It's like a thousand Goosebumps. It used to belong to a friend of mine. Someone very special."

He doesn't tell Henry it once was Billy's for the same reason they don't talk about that fateful night at the falls. Considering all that's happened, Ethan's not sure how Henry would react. He suspects Henry knows anyway, for he handles the book with a gentleness not used on his battered paperbacks.

"Then you should have it," he says.

"No," Ethan says. "I've looked at it enough. It's yours now. Although you should get some sleep. It's late."

"Five more minutes?"

Ethan smiles before indulging him. He knows that five will be at least thirty. "Sure. But only five."

Henry touches the book, as if he can sense how valuable it is to both Ethan and the boy who once owned it. Ethan then puts his hand on top of Henry's, and together, they turn the page.

ACKNOWLEDGMENTS

Thanks are due to everyone at Dutton and Penguin Random House, but especially my amazing editor, Maya Ziv, and the publicity and marketing dream team of Emily Canders, Lauren Morrow, Stephanie Cooper, and Caroline Payne. Additional thanks goes to Christopher Lin for the stellar cover design and to Alberto Ortega for allowing us to use one of his amazing paintings as the cover art. You all rock!

The same is true for my agent, Michelle Brower, and everyone at Trellis Literary Management.

Thanks also to Hilary Zaitz Michael, Carolina Beltran, and everyone at WME for keeping things humming on the film and TV side.

I owe a huge debt to Michael Livio, who walked hand in hand with me through the joy, frustration, and self-doubt that occurred while writing this book. He gets bonus thanks for keeping the backyard filled with animals and for buying a trail cam years ago that eventually inspired so many fun scenes in the book.

ABOUT THE AUTHOR

Riley Sager is the *New York Times* bestselling author of eight novels, most recently *The House Across the Lake* and *The Only One Left*. A native of Pennsylvania, he now lives in Princeton, New Jersey.